The author was born in Blaenavon, Monmouthshire, but now resides in Atherton, Greater Manchester, with his wife Jean. Most of his working life was spent as a college lecturer whereas in his spare time he spent 25 years in uniformed service, firstly with the TAVR (REME) followed by the RAFVR (T) and finally with the RNR (SCC). Nowadays when not caring for his wife he writes, reads books and builds model aircraft. He also has a craving for Brass Bands and is notorious for having his head in the clouds.

I dedicate this book to my long-suffering wife, Jean, who has been forced to live with my obsessive imagination. Throughout my self-enforced sessions of scribing, she has supported me with an endless supply of cups of tea.

Thank you, dear (any chance of another brew?)

Tony Smith

THEY LEFT IT TOO LATE

AUSTIN MACAULEY PUBLISHERS™
LONDON • CAMBRIDGE • NEW YORK • SHARJAH

Copyright © Tony Smith 2024

The right of Tony Smith to be identified as author of this work has been asserted by the author in accordance with sections 77 and 78 of the Copyright, Designs and Patents Act 1988.

All rights reserved. No part of this publication may be reproduced, stored in a retrieval system, or transmitted in any form or by any means, electronic, mechanical, photocopying, recording, or otherwise, without the prior permission of the publishers.

Any person who commits any unauthorized act in relation to this publication may be liable to criminal prosecution and civil claims for damages.

This is a work of fiction. Names, characters, businesses, places, events, locales, and incidents are either the products of the author's imagination or used in a fictitious manner. Any resemblance to actual persons, living or dead, or actual events is purely coincidental.

A CIP catalogue record for this title is available from the British Library.

ISBN 9781035840328 (Paperback)
ISBN 9781035840335 (ePub e-book)

www.austimacauley.com

First Published 2024
Austin Macauley Publishers Ltd®
1 Canada Square
Canary Wharf
London
E14 5AA

20240201

I would like to acknowledge the help that my daughter Hayley gave me in seeking out an image of Roa Island to use on the front cover of this book. The location of image generators was achieved via the Facebook page of 'The Bosun's Locker', a 'Phoenix Catering' establishment on Roa Island and via Elanor Findlay of 'Piel Ferries' who lives in the islands old school house. Both of these establishments are to be found on the island.

I received generous offers of high-quality images from David Faratian a hypnotherapist who has a Hypnosis Mindfulness Clinic on Roa along with John Prince, Lee Heseltine, and David White.

Table of Contents

It's New Year	11
It Can't Be True	33
Marital Aftermath	52
An Uncertain Future	72
Willpower or Passion	91
A Return to the 'Roa Boat'	110
Revealing Truths	130
A Month of Routine	151
Moving on	171
Is This the End of the Beginning?	192
Final Preparations	211
The Final Coming Together	231

It's New Year

It was New Year's Eve, December 1958, and at number 11, Marine Terrace, 26-year-old Justin Ebberson was busy getting ready for the New Year's Eve Ball that he had two tickets for. His heart was pounding inside his chest as he anticipated his date with Jean Baxter. This was a feeling foreign to him as he had never experienced anything as intense as this in his life before.

Looking in the bathroom mirror as he shaved, Justin couldn't help to try and work out in a rationale way what had happened to him but the sheer joy of feeling this way simply accelerated the speed at which he stroked his chin with the razor.

There was no-one else at number 11 to share his excitement with since he lived alone in this terraced house which had been left to him earlier in the year by his late uncle Dick and auntie Annie. He was so fortunate to have inherited this property on Roa Island where he had spent so many happy times during school holidays in years gone by and here he was again, feeling very happy.

A touch of aftershave ended the bathroom session and all that remained was to get his best shirt and tie on and then comb his hair which he would then hold in place with a touch of Brylcreem.

'This is crazy' thought Justin to himself. 'How can a 26-year-old grown-up feel this way? Surely, it's only kids that get this kind of feeling, it really isn't rationale'.

No matter how Justin tried to come to terms with how he felt, he could not come up with any sensible reason. What was true was that the first time he had come into contact with Jean, he had begun to feel this way. Maybe this was the chemistry of life that his late father had talked to him about and he had never believed in. With a university degree under his belt and two years of National Service in which he had gained the Queen's commission, it wasn't reasonable not to be able to say why he had these glorious feelings but it was certainly good.

'Stop day-dreaming' Justin told himself, it's time to get going. He had arranged to meet Jean at the entrance to the car park on Theatre Street in

Ulverston at 8:00pm and he was going to be late if he didn't get a move on. It was pretty cold outside and he donned his scarf and overcoat to keep himself warm. He grabbed the two tickets that he had bought for the ball at Ulverston's Coronation Hall and headed for the back door which opened onto his back yard where his Ford Popular car was parked.

"Damn! Where are the car keys?" Justin shouted to himself and a voice from number 12 piped out over the yard wall, "Happy New Year, Justin, hope you enjoy the dance with that lovely young lady of yours."

"Thanks, Nellie and a happy new year to you and Arthur. I will enjoy the dance if I find my car keys."

'Nellie and Arthur, both in their early sixties were a grand couple,' thought Justin as he dived back into the house to find his keys. He was just about to step outside again when he suddenly thought 'Blast, I have forgotten the gift I bought' and he dashed back in again. He really wasn't his normal self-controlled self.

How could he possibly forget that beautiful necklace with a ruby to focus one's eyes on? He had purchased it at Samuels in Barrow-in-Furness and it cost him a bomb but he was thrilled at the prospect of seeing Jean's face when he gave it to her. He had got her something for Christmas but the necklace was bought on an impulse and he didn't regret it.

Fortunately, Justin's car started first time and he backed it out of his yard and on to Piel Street and then across the causeway that connected Roa Island to the mainland. Roa had been an island until 1847 and could only be accessed by boat or on foot across the sands when the tide was out. The causeway had changed all that and this small island, a part of the Furness group of islands, was now far more accessible.

The half mile long causeway led to the village of Rampside and from there it was a ten mile drive to Ulverston along an attractive coast road looking out over Morecambe Bay although not much would be seen of it on a dark December night.

As the journey to Ulverston progressed, Justin looked back on how he had reached this point in his life. At the time of his uncle and aunt's death, he had been working for English Electric at Samlesbury Airfield and had digs with the Brierley family in nearby Mellor. He remembered how Mrs Brierley had been a bit disappointed when he hadn't taken up with her daughter Pauline. She was a pretty girl and most pleasant but Justin simply wasn't interested in her, at least not in terms of starting a relationship.

Mrs Brierley had remarked to him how good-looking she thought he was and what a good partner she thought he would make for Pauline. She never laboured the point and he never felt uncomfortable. Feeling Pauline's firm breasts could have been a problem but she had enjoyed him doing so. It was not an issue! It wasn't just a physical thing, Justin did like Pauline but felt no passion toward her.

Isherwood and Son—'Etching Specialists' had a small manufacturing business on Roa Island and were in need of a 'Plant Inspector' and when Justin saw the advert in the local press he was immediately drawn to it. With the knowledge that number 11, Marine Terrace had been left to him Justin applied for the post at Isherwood and Son and got it. He moved into number 11 in June 1958 and took up his new appointment in July.

There were only 31 people employed by the Etching Specialist firm on Roa and they were a close knit and friendly group. It was shortly after Justin had started work at Isherwood's that he first noticed Jean and he experienced the so-called 'chemistry of life' for the first time. Jean was tall and slim with a figure that had all its feminist curves in the right place.

The clothes she wore were inexpensive but were well-chosen to bring out the best in her appearance. She was good-looking and had lovely teeth. She wore light lipstick and make-up which amplified the striking qualities of her face. A brunette with brown eyes she was a bit of a show-stopper but she was in no way vain or flamboyant, indeed she appeared to be a little shy which was another thing about her that had attracted Justin.

It was a couple of months before Justin plucked up the courage to ask Jean for a date and a month later, she left Isherwood's to take up a post with 'Johnson's Pharmaceuticals' in Ulverston. Up to this point, Jean had been living with two work colleagues, Sheila Dobson and Nadine Dorris, at number one Marina Terrace and seeing Jean was free of any logistical problems.

This all changed when Jean moved into a small apartment in Ulverston to be nearer work. From October onward, Justin and Jean had met once or twice a week and their relationship had blossomed. Dancing, going to the pictures, walking and the occasional drink or a meal all featured in their dates.

As time passed, Justin became more and more aware of feelings he had never experienced before and they were becoming more powerful. Looking into Justin's face it would be impossible not to tell that he had fallen for this girl and was 'head-over-heels' in love with her.

He hadn't verbalised these feelings to Jean largely because he was too embarrassed to do so but he didn't understand why. It appeared to be much the same for Jean and if Justin had read her face as she had him she was just as much in love with him. How much more lucky could a chap be?

Justin had just reached Ulverston and he had to concentrate a little more to find the Theatre Street car park where he had arranged to meet Jean. His heart stepped up a beat as he anticipated seeing her again.

There were quite a lot of people around in Ulverston on New Year's Eve and Justin didn't see Jean as he drove into the car park. There were not many places available but he spotted one out of the corner of his eye and drove into it. He took a final look in the car interior mirror to check that his tie was straight and he looked OK.

Then he checked that he had the tickets for the ball in his inside coat pocket before finally opening the car glove compartment and took out the necklace he had bought in its decorative case which he had carefully wrapped in some purple wrapping paper.

Now, it was time to go and he stepped out of the car and locked it before walking to the Theatre Street car park entrance.

Jean was standing where she had agreed to meet Justin and she was wearing a very smart brown coat but it was not until Justin reached her that he could make out the colour in the relatively dim street lighting. When he had got up close, she looked stunning and his heart beat started to race.

He greeted her cheerily but could tell from her facial expression that something was not quite right. Before he had the chance to start a conversation with her, Jean looked at him in a serious way and he wondered what was coming next but when she did speak, he was completely unprepared for what she said.

"Justin, I have had a long think this week and I think I must tell you that I am not ready to have a serious relationship with you."

Justin was stunned. He had no idea how he should respond, in fact he couldn't get any words out. It was if he had been shot and wounded. He was in shock. He just looked at Jean's face, that face that had captivated him since the first time he had seen her at Isherwood's factory. A deafeningly silent minute passed and before he could say anything, Jean walked away from him in the direction of Coronation Hall.

Not knowing exactly what he should do next, he saw a wooden seat close to the small green patch to the left of the car park entrance and decided to sit down a moment and try to take in what had just happened and to compose himself as the hurt was beginning to set in, it was all so confusing.

As he sat in a dejected fashion, a lady across the road in Theatre Street who was stood outside the front door of her house and had witnessed the event, couldn't help but feel for the young chap, especially as it was New Year's Eve and after contemplating for a moment or two, she decided to cross the street and see if she could offer him some comfort.

"Are you OK dear?" she asked.

Justin looked up and could see the kindness in the lady's eyes but could only nod to her in response to tell her yes.

That was obviously not true and the lady took a seat at the side of Justin before speaking to him in a comforting voice.

"Was she your date for tonight?"

"Yes, we were going to the New Year's Eve Ball," said Justin looking up at the lady's face.

"This is not a nice experience for you, dear. Would you like to come across the road and I will make you a cup of tea?"

A cup of tea, that seems to be the British cure for all things thought Justin before he kindly declined the offer.

Justin fumbled in his pocket and took out the necklace in its wrapping paper. As the lady looked on, he took the paper off and opened the decorative case to show the lady what he had intended to give to Jean. The lady gasped as she saw how beautiful it was.

'This young chap must have been in love with this girl,' she thought.

"Well dear, there are many more fish in the sea."

That's a platitude that must have been used a thousand times over thought Justin as he recalled hearing it in a number of cinema films.

"What are you going to do next, dear?"

"I think I will go back home," replied Justin.

"Have you got far to go?"

"I live on Roa Island."

"You will find it difficult getting a bus there so late at night dear."

"I have a car," replied Justin.

"Well, be sure you drive careful, you're in a bit of state, dear."

"Thank you for being so kind to me."

With that, Justin stood up and made his way to his car leaving the kind lady with a tear in her eye thinking what an awful experience to have on New Year's Eve and wishing him all the best under her breath.

It seemed like a long journey back to Roa on this dark and cold December night and Justin had to fight hard to retain his concentration.

'What have I done wrong, was I coming on too fast, have I misread things?' he thought but he had no answers to any of these questions.

After what seemed like an eternity, he found himself driving across the causeway and he suddenly considered whether he should bring in the New Year in the islands only pub, the 'Roa Boat' but he wouldn't be good company and there were to many things on his mind and so he settled for going home.

Justin parked up the car in his back yard and closed the gates before going in to the house through his back door.

Next door at number 12, Arthur heard Justin's car and said to his wife Nellie, "Justin's back early, I thought he was going to the New Year's Eve Ball in Ulverston?"

"That he was," replied Nellie who went on to say, "perhaps, he's brought that young lass to his home for a more intimate beginning to the New Year."

Arthur looked at Nellie with raised eyebrows but declined from commenting.

Taking the tickets for the ball and the necklace case out of his pockets, Justin removed his coat and sat in his favourite living room chair, totally bewildered and feeling sombre. He thought he would try and think things through with the hope of understanding what had happened and what to do next but everything was just a blur.

Realising that there was nothing to be gained trying to chew things over tonight, he decided to go to bed. He lay for quite a while as uncontrollable thoughts drifted through his mind and much to his chagrin, he felt the tears emerging from his tired eyes running down his cheeks before he finally drifted off to sleep. There were no church bells chiming for Justin at midnight on this News Year's Eve!

The following morning, Justin looked out from his front room window. Number 11, Marine Terrace was in a row of twelve terraced houses, all facing south. The view was splendid looking out over Piel Channel toward Piel Island and its castle. To the left was Morecambe Bay and to the right, Barrow-in Furness. Immediately in front of the terraced row was a green on which the locals had been allowed to establish some plots.

It was only a short distance to the water's edge and a small pier from which a seasonal ferry sailed to Piel Island. On the other side of the pier was an elevated walkway to Barrow Lifeboat house. When the lifeboat was launched, it would slide down a steep ramp before splashing into the estuary and then sailing on into Piel Channel.

Although his mind was in turmoil, Justin instinctively knew that the only way he was going to get through the next couple of days until work started again was to keep busy and in spite of the cold, he decided to do some work on his plot. After some breakfast, he headed outside and viewed the plot that his uncle Dick had taken so much pride in. There was clearly a lot of work that he had to do to get it looking good and to grow things even though growing things was not something he had any knowledge of.

However, first things first, it was the fence around his plot and the shed that contained all his inherited gardening implements that needed his attention. As Justin began his toil, he rapidly realised how exposed this place was. With no windbreak whatsoever in front of his house, the chill was acute but being well-wrapped up and doing physical work allowed him to cope.

After an hour or so, a voice was heard calling from an adjacent plot.

"Good morning Justin and a happy New Year to you!"

It was Arthur from next door and Justin politely replied.

"Good morning Arthur and a happy New Year to you and Nellie."

Arthur could see that Justin was a little downbeat which was pretty unusual for this young chap.

"How did the ball go last night?" asked Arthur.

Justin squirmed a little before replying. This was something he was trying to hide away from, for the moment, but manners dictated that he give an answer and as he did so he caught a view of Nellie coming out of her house.

"I didn't get to the ball, Arthur."

Nellie butted in in a surprised sounding voice.

"Whyever not, Justin, you were so looking forward to it?"

There was no way of being subtle about it and Justin replied in a shaky voice, "She dumped me!"

Nellie was shocked by this response and looked at Arthur who was also shocked.

"Well, I'm sorry to hear that lad. It must have been upsetting, and on New Year's Eve."

Nellie could see that if this conversation was continued, it was only going to make things worse and she signalled to Arthur for the two of them to go back indoors but before they did so, they left Justin with a few parting words.

"If you need a chat, Justin or a cup of tea, you know we are only next door. You are welcome to call any time," and they both walked away.

It was a relief to get back into work after the New Year break. As Plant Inspector at Isherwood & Son, he was always kept busy ensuring that the production line continued without any undue interruption. They didn't produce vast quantities of stuff at Isherwoods but it was all top quality.

Currently, they manufactured electronic circuit boards destined to be fitted into radio and radar equipment on Royal Navy ships. Isherwoods were subcontracted to the firms Plessey and Ferranti to produce the boards and both did all the research and design of them to meet the Navy's specification.

Isherwood and Son had been established in 1946 by Captain RN (Rtd) William John Isherwood who had had the foresight to realise that there was an opportunity for this kind of enterprise and with his vast range of contacts took the plunge on his retirement from the Navy.

William Isherwood was a down to earth individual and preferred to be referred to as Mr Isherwood although he would use his naval rank on letter headings and any meetings that he had with the Navy along with Plessey and Ferranti. He knew how to play his cards right!

Mr Isherwood was now 68 years of age and beginning to feel it. He was preparing his son Rupert, another ex-Royal Navy man, to take the business over and had got to a stage where he only felt the need to be in his Roa Island-based factory on three days of each week. Rupert was currently Joint Managing Director of the firm and although he was stand-offish in comparison with his father, he was always polite and approachable to those who had the courage to try and converse with him.

It was during the first day back at work that Rupert approached Justin regarding a new development. Currently, the electronic circuit boards that the firm produced had no components fitted to them such as valve bases, resistors and capacitors but this could change if the firm prepared itself, appropriately. Rupert felt that Justin had the knowledge and skills needed to make the necessary changes in the factory but it would have to be done outside the firms normal working hours.

None of the existing production line must be affected during this preparation. A detailed discussion took place between the two men and in the end it boiled down to Justin being prepared to work on the new development two evenings each week plus every Saturday. Rupert indicated that this was important for the whole workforce and he would pay Justin well for his input which was scheduled to take twelve months.

Time was something Justin didn't want to have on his hands right now. At times when he had nothing to do, his thoughts would turn to that beautiful girl he had grown to love and his emotional pain would return and it became difficult to switch it off.

It didn't take Justin long to make a decision about the extra work and Rupert was very pleased that Justin was coming onboard. The development work would start that very evening and every Tuesday and Thursday night thereafter.

On the first Saturday night after work, Justin joined five working colleagues in the only pub on the island, the 'Roa Boat'. This was a tradition started way back and Justin had been welcomed into the group six months ago when he had first arrived. It seemed peculiar at first to have five young women as his drinking friends but in reality, they were some of the few people on the island in the same age group and four of them had come from other places, only one was a Roa native. The group had been six until Jean had left three months ago to live in Ulverston and had only visited infrequently since.

Sheila Dobson worked in Isherwood's as the 'Final Inspector'. Sheila was 27 years of age and the eldest of the group. She was the most-worldly person of them all, fiercely independent, and good at reading situations and was the first to spot the change in Justin. As the four other girls chatted rather loudly whilst enjoying their drinks, Sheila discretely enquired as to the change in his demeanour and she was taken aback by Justin's story.

"What are you going to do about it?" Sheila enquired.

"There isn't anything to do about it. Jean has made a decision and that's that. I must live with it." replied Justin.

"That may be so but don't you feel she owes you an explanation as to why she dumped you and more importantly why she chose to do it on New Year's Eve. That was pretty insensitive."

"I don't think she owes me any explanations. She has a life of her own and a right to choose how she wants to live it."

"But how are you going to cope Justin? You look cut up by it."

"I can't answer that Sheila but cope with it I must. Keeping busy helps and having you lot around me for company, will, I am sure be a great help, thanks Sheila," and the other four girls looked round at him.

Sheila placed an arm around him and said, "We are all your friends, Justin and you can always count on our support," and the words were accompanied by a unanimous 'course you can' and then they all got on with some serious drinking and talking whilst Justin ruminated with the fact that it had been quite a week.

The following day, Justin embarked on another renovation session on his plot. There was a lot of fencing to repair and a lot of work was needed on the shed as well, enough to last him a couple of months at this time of the year. Arthur was also busying himself on his plot and a short conversation over the garden fence inevitably occurred.

"Good morning, Justin. How are you doing, lad?" asked Arthur.

"Ok, thanks Arthur. How's Nellie?"

"She's fine, just a few niggling pains in her hips but when you get to our age, that's something you have to expect. Have you got over that lass of yours?"

That was a question that Justin could have done without. He couldn't help dwelling on things from time to time but it didn't help. He was still a prisoner of his own emotions and only time and work could act as a form of remedy.

"Not exactly, Arthur but you have to carry on, don't you?"

"I, you do lad, but I'm sure it will get easier."

With those last few words, the two men went on with their work putting their plots to right but in Justin's case, it was a poor substitute to being with Jean.

It was a busy week at Isherwood's, dealing with the normal production run and then the two extra evenings not to mention Saturday working as well. The extra work had started by preparing a room adjacent to the drilling section in the existing setup. This, eventually, would become the room where components would be soldered onto the boards the firm made. This would be the sixth manufacturing stage in the process.

Before that could happen, all the extra materials required would have to be acquired including single and double sided copper plated boards and these would all go into the stores until required. One of Justin's drinking partners, Lyn Gore, looked after the stores. When boards were required, they went first to a cutting section and cut to the appropriate sizes.

From there, the cut boards went to the tracing section and here the laborious job of tracing the circuit required took place. This was followed by a process that involved painting over the traced circuit with a preservative varnish. Then it was off to the etching section in which Nadine Dorris, another of Justin's drinking group, emersed the boards into an acid bath which ate away the copper around the varnished circuit.

This was the most dangerous part of the process and at the end of a day's production run the acid baths had to be emptied and made devoid of any debris. The bath contents were emptied into a special vat which was collected each week by a specialist contractor. Next came the drilling section where holes were drilled in the circuit board to allow various components to be soldered in place.

"Amy Fisher, another member of the regular 'Roa Boat' Saturday drinking group, worked in the drilling section along with one other individual. The final section before eventually reaching the one that Justin was preparing was the edge connector section which did exactly that—fitted edge connectors!"

On Tuesday morning, Justin drove his car the 100yards from his back yard to work which was situated opposite the gable end of number one Marine Terrace. The security man at the factory entrance, Albert Clitheroe, couldn't help joking with Justin.

"Got bad legs have you this morning, Mr Ebberson? Touch of heavy drinking perhaps?"

Justin laughed, "No, the car exhaust is blowing and I have to take it to Barrow mid-morning to get it fixed."

"I'll believe you but thousands wouldn't," replied Albert as he tipped his hat to Mr Ebberson.

Albert had served in the Royal Navy with the firm's founder at some point in time and Justin made a mental note to find out more about that but not just now, there was a lot to take care of before he could drive to Barrow.

By the time Saturday tea time had arrived, Justin realised that his food stocks were getting fairly depleted as were his supplies of other domestic necessities and he needed to do something about it. He nipped next door to number 12 to have a word with Nellie.

"Why don't you have a word with Flora Campbell at number five? She might be able to help," was the advice Nellie gave him.

Flora was married to Angus Campbell and they were both in their thirties. They had two daughters, Peggy aged seven and Jill aged five. Angus, originally from Glasgow, worked as a plumber for a firm based in Rampside on the Ulverston Road. Flora, a Barrow-in-Furness girl had been a nurse before the children were born but now had a part-time job as a doctor's receptionist in Barrow which fitted in well with the children's school arrangements.

Flora answered the door and asked Justin to step inside. Her two young daughters wasted no time being in on the act, they didn't want to miss anything. Justin outlined his shopping needs and mentioned that Nellie thought Flora may be able to help, with a payment of course. There was no real need for any discussion as Flora didn't think it would be a problem.

"I drop the children off at school on my way to the doctor's surgery every morning and collect them again later in the day when school finishes. There's plenty of time to do my shopping in Barrow and fitting in some for you would be no trouble at all," said Flora.

A greatly relieved Justin agreed to drop a list off on Sunday, Tuesday and Thursday evening for Flora to use and gave her a sum of money to purchase things with and a promise to top it up every Saturday. Finally, he gave Flora a key to number 11 so that she could drop things off for him. A payment was agreed and Justin left number five with a cheery wave from Flora and her two daughters.

Justin's five drinking partners arrived in the Roa Boat before he did and within minutes, they were drinking and catching up on everything they already knew. Not much really happened in a place as small as Roa but it was worth checking up. There was a rumour doing the rounds that Jean had left Isherwood's because Rupert Isherwood the Joint Managing Director kept pestering her for a date. A few mouths were wide open at this stage. This was very much a surprise topic that Amy had brought to the groups attention.

"But he's already married," said Nadine.

"He is and he has two children. His wife is called Nicola and they met in Plymouth when he was serving in the Navy," replied Amy who it appeared was now the expert on Rupert's private life.

"What are the children's names?" asked Joanne.

"Well Nicola married Rupert in 1950 and their first child, Simone, was born in 1952 and their second, Ian, in 1954."

"Just seven and five then," remarked Lyn.

"How long was he in the Navy?" asked Nadine.

Amy replied, "He joined in 1944 when he was just 18 and got demobbed in 1956 to join his father here on Roa. He was a Naval Commander when he got demobbed."

"That makes him 32 then," remarked Joanne.

"I never took him for a wayward lad," said Lyn.

Amy, the font of knowledge in this matter filled everyone in with a bit more information.

"Rupert was born in 1926 in Rosyth where his father was serving in the Royal Navy and as his parents moved around the world it was inevitable that he would attend a boarding school and that is where wayward boys are created." Amy continued, "It was a family tradition to serve in the Navy."

As everyone sat back to digest all this information Amy came back with one more titbit that shocked them all!

"Rumour has it that Rupert has put Jean up in an apartment in Ulverston."

At this point, Justin came in to the pub and Sheila immediately instructed everyone that not a murmur of this was to get back to Justin, he was already hurt enough.

An awkward silence descended on the group who now wrestled with what topic of conversation they ought to carry on with.

The stress of the moment was interrupted by Joanne, "Justin, did you know that there is a Brass Band concert on at the Roxy tomorrow night?"

"Yes, I did and I will be going," replied Justin.

Sheila turned to look at him and smiled, thinking to herself that this just may be Justin moving on and she couldn't help feeling relieved.

The following night, Justin drove to Ulverston and the journey evoked some painful memories of the events that had unfolded two weeks ago. Jean's image kept creeping to the forefront of his mind and more than once he had to remind himself that he was driving. The fact that it was a dark winter night didn't help but he got to Theatre Street car park safely and got out to walk the short distance to the Roxy Cinema.

The Roxy Cinema had a huge stage that was put to good use on a number of occasions during the year thus breaking its usual routine of showing films. The top Brass Bands in the UK played here on the third Sunday night of each month with the exception of July and August. These concerts were hugely popular and were very profitable for the place. Tonight's concert was being given by the Yorkshire Band 'Brighouse and Rastrick'. The band had been formed in 1882 and had won many accolades over the years. Justin was looking forward to listening to them play.

Justin walked out of the car park and into New Market Street and on past Coronation Hall to County Road where he would turn left for the Roxy which was just behind it. As he approached County Road he spotted the unmistakable image of Jean.

She stood across the road wearing the same coat she had worn two weeks previously. The sight of her brought a surge of emotional feelings back and he had to wrestle with them as she walked away without seeing him. This was something Justin could have done without at that moment but he forced himself to continue on to the Roxy.

Brighouse and Rastrick sounded fabulous but Justin found his mind wandering and many of the band's numbers escaped his attention. He did however get caught up with one or two particularly enjoyable pieces such as *Nessun Dorma* composed by Puccini and a piece by Tyran and Roberton called *All in the April Evening*.

The drive back to Roa had to be endured with a range of mixed feelings but Justin did his best to be positive and try and view things for what they were.

Monday and the start of another busy week, just what the doctor ordered. The business of making electronic circuit boards for Navy equipment had to go on and it had to be top quality. There might only be thirty-one people on the firms payroll but they all depended on the income they got and that was good reason for Justin to push the gremlins out of his mind and get on with the job.

One thing he hadn't got round to sorting out was arranging for himself some canteen food for tea on Tuesdays and Thursdays and also for Saturday dinner. As soon as Justin got the chance he nipped in to the canteen to have a word with either Brenda or Gladys the works wonder girls!

What they did with the meagre supplies they had was really something. The two jolly, plump canteen ladies espied Justin approaching and they both had a good look at this handsome chap whilst wiping their hands on their aprons at the same time as if they were preparing to make the best of him.

"Now then, Justin, what can we do for you?" enquired Brenda.

Sheepishly, Justin told the two of them what he hoped they could do for him before he started preparing the new work section. He always had a tendency to be wary of these two ladies for they could be quite forthright but their hearts were in the right place and they both responded in a positive fashion.

"You leave that with us. We can prepare you something and leave it on the side for you," said Brenda.

"What do you like and what do you not like?" enquired Gladys? With raised eyebrows and a cheeky look on her face.

Justin found himself blushing when faced with the suggestive looking Gladys but he took it in good part and gave her the answers to her questions.

Just as he was about to leave, he remembered something else.

"Ladies, I have to come in and work on Saturdays. Is there anything you could do for me then?"

He wished he hadn't phrased the question in that way since it left himself wide open to some ribbing and he got it. When the laughter died down the ladies agreed between themselves to take turns on alternative Saturdays to pop in to the factory mid-morning and make something for him and Justin gave them a promise that he would call in to the firm's Treasurer's Office and see if they could be compensated for their trouble.

'Failing that,' he thought, *'I will pay them myself and there things were left.'* It was fortunate that both these ladies lived on Roa and hence lived within walking distance to the place.

By Wednesday, it was obvious that Justin was running out of clean clothes and he didn't seem to have much spare time to sort the problem out. For a second time, he nipped round to number twelve to have a word with Nellie and see what advice she could offer him.

"No problem at all," was the response Justin got from Nellie.

"Mrs Quinn at number three takes washing in and does ironing. She does it for the lifeboat station and the Roa Boat. Nip round and ask her if she can take a bit more on."

"Thanks Nellie, you are a real treasure," said Justin.

Marion Quinn was in her late fifties and so was her husband Roger. Both came from Ulverston originally and Roger worked for Barrow Council Parks Department. He was a tree specialist which was odd in a sense since there were no trees on Roa.

The pay for a tree specialist was not so great and that was the reason that Marion had created her own side line business taking in washing and ironing. They had a son but he was killed in the war serving with the Royal Air Force. They were a nice couple and Justin was pleased that he could bring a bit more business Marion's way when she agreed to his request. Justin was gradually getting adjusted to his new set of circumstances.

Getting nice and comfortable in his favourite fireside chair, Justin looked around his living room and felt comfortable although the view into his back yard was nothing to write home about. A knock on the front door suddenly interrupted his chain of thoughts and he jumped up to walk through his front room to open the door.

"Hello, Justin, I just thought it would be nice to come and have a chat with you," said Sheila standing there, shivering, in the cold January air.

"Don't stand there, come in, Sheila. You look as if you are freezing. I'll put the kettle on."

"That sounds like a good idea," and Sheila walked into number 11 pulling the top of her coat around her neck.

The two of them sat cosily in front of the fire drinking tea as Sheila began the conversation.

"I think it was good that you made the effort to get back to your old self by going to the concert in Ulverston. Did you enjoy it?"

"I did, Sheila but I couldn't concentrate on all the pieces the band played."

"And why was that?" asked Sheila who thought she already knew the answer to the question.

"I saw Jean as I was walking to the Roxy and it kept bringing things back to me," replied Justin.

"Did you speak to her?"

"No. I don't think she saw me. You know, it may sound childish, but when the band played certain numbers, I had to choke back the odd tear to stop myself looking foolish."

"Justin you must have loved that girl very much and you are still raw from the experience. You must give yourself time to get over her."

At this point, Sheila thought it would be best to change the subject.

"I didn't know you were interested in Brass Bands."

"My father was a keen Brass Band follower and that's where I got it from."

"Tell me a bit about your background, Justin. I really don't know much about you."

"There's not much to tell, really. I was brought up in Bolton by my mother and father, John and Glenda Ebberson. I have no brothers or sisters. My dad followed the world-famous Wingate's Band and often took me to concerts at Victoria Hall in Bolton which was regarded as the band's spiritual home."

Sheila interrupted, "Why's that then?"

Wingate's Band was formed by Wingate's Methodist Church members in 1873 and was a temperance band and Victoria Hall was a Methodist Hall.

"Ah, I see."

"My mother and father were a hard working class couple and they supported me well through my school years and onwards to university."

"I heard that you had been to university, Justin, and that's a feather in your cap."

"Yes I am lucky and in order to allow me to complete my university studies, my National Service call-up was deferred."

"What was the degree you got, Justin?"

"I got a Bachelor of Science in Electronics."

"And did you do your National Service?"

"Oh yes. Just like all my age group, I had to do my two years' service."

"What service did you go into?"

"I went into the Royal Air Force."

"Did you enjoy it, Justin, and what rank did you reach?"

"I did enjoy it but it was boring at times and I missed being free to do what I wanted. When I first joined up, I went to Cardington to pick up my uniform and then it was off to RAF Henlow to train to be an engineering officer. I passed out as a Pilot Officer but I got made up to a Flying Officer before I was demobbed."

"What did you do after your National Service? I'm being a bit nosey, Justin, you don't have to tell me if you don't want to."

"I don't mind, Sheila. In fact, it's nice to talk like this. When I was demobbed, I got a job with English Electric at Samlesbury Airfield near Blackburn. That's when I got the little car you can see in my back yard. I drove from Bolton to Samlesbury every day but when my mother and father had both passed away, I found digs with a family in Mellor and from there I came here."

"How did you know about this house?"

"This was the house that my uncle Dick and auntie Annie owned. I used to come here in the school holidays and I loved it. They left the house to me when they both passed away in early 1957. When I got to know about the job I have at Isherwood's, it was ideal since I could move in here straight away and here I am."

Sheila enjoyed listening to Justin's story and felt that she knew him much better now.

Now, it was Justin's turn to ask Sheila a few questions although he already knew some things. For example, he knew that Sheila jointly rented number one Marine Terrace with Nadine Dorris and they jointly owned a car. Justin also knew that Sheila, a slim brunette, 5'8" tall with blue eyes was the eldest of the Roa Boat drinking group at 27.

She could be explosive if the occasion demanded it but to her friends, she was cheerful, considerate and understanding. She was fiercely independent and good at reading situations. Sheila was more than capable of looking after herself.

"Do you come from Roa Sheila?" asked Justin.

"No, I'm from Barrow-in-Furness but when the job at Isherwood's cropped up, I jumped at it. I really wanted to be independent and get away from my parents. The rented house I live in has given me a good start and I like it."

"How long have you lived and worked on Roa?"

"I came here in 1955 and since arrival, I have worked on a few sections at Isherwood's before my current role on final inspection."

Sheila rose from her chair realising that she better get back to her place and finish off whatever she had started before calling at Justin's.

"I better go now, Justin but before I do, are you in the Roa Boat on Saturday?"

"No, I'm going to watch a play in Ulverston."

"Well, you are getting around, good on yer! Will you be coming to the dance in Rampside Village Hall a week this Saturday?"

"I'm not sure," replied Justin.

"You have to go. There are at least five partners for you on the night and don't forget there's a dearth of young men in the area as a result of the war. We need you there, Justin, to bring us all a little happiness," and with that Sheila grabbed her coat and dashed out through the front door.

The rest of the week at Isherwood's was fairly routine and Brenda and Gladys made sure that Justin was fed which pleased him no end. Preparing the new room that was to accommodate a new process section was not going to be just a question of cleaning and painting, an extensive amount of electrical work was also required and doing all this part-time meant it would be the end of March before new equipment could be installed in it. At least, Justin had until the end of the following December to get it all done.

Driving down to Ulverston to see the play being performed at the Roxy was not totally free from anxiety but it was not as bad as Justin may have anticipated and there was no new sightings of Jean on this Saturday night. The local Drama Club staged four play's each year at the Roxy and each one was performed on five consecutive nights—Tuesday through to Saturday. They all got good bookings and this kind of diversity along with Brass Band concerts kept the Roxy in the green!

'Tonight's play was called The Girl On The Train and it told the story of a young woman longing for a different life, a bit like Jean,' thought Justin. The young woman commuted daily by train and she looked through her carriage window and observed a couple who looked so happy and in love and then the woman she was secretly following disappears and for some mystical reason, the girl on the train finds herself a suspect in a strange mystery. *'It was a bit hard to follow the story line but Justin couldn't help applying it to his own situation with Jean but it was stretching things,'* he thought.

"Where's Justin tonight?" asked Amy as she sipped her drink in the Roa Boat.

Sheila answered saying, "He's gone to see a play at the Roxy."

"Who has he gone with?" asked Lyn.

"He's gone on his own," replied Sheila.

"He could take any of us at any time," interjected Joanne and after a little tittering Sheila responded.

"Let's leave that young fellow be. If he wants to take any of us anywhere, he'll do so when he's ready."

That's not where the conversation regarding Justin ended, but the dating side of it did.

Sunday afternoon was freezing as Justin tried to saw to length some sections of fence he was making to replace those that were in tatters around his plot. He was almost relieved when Arthur shouted across to him.

"Perishing cold today, Justin!"

"Not half, Arthur. I don't think I'll be doing much more out here."

"I don't blame you, lad."

And that was the end of the conversation as both men downed tools and headed for the warmth of their homes.

Mid-Monday morning, Justin went to see the Company Treasurer Ronald Bright. He knocked on the treasurer's door and waited to be asked in. He didn't have to wait long and found himself standing in front of Mr Bright's desk. Ronald, Ron to his management team and close friends was in his late fifties. He wore thick rimmed glasses and smoked a horrible smelling pipe. An empty 'Black Twist' tobacco packet lay on his desk next to his tobacco pouch.

Ron was from Workington but now resided on the outskirts of Barrow with his good lady. Justin had been told in the past by the office typists that Mr Bright, as he was known to them, had been a bad-tempered bugger before the war, but they emphasised that this was what they had been told. He had been in the Army serving in Burma and came back as a Major. He was a changed man since then and all the staff at Isherwood's liked and respected him.

"Good morning, Justin. Do sit down. Can I arrange a cup of tea for you?"

"Good morning, Ron. No tea, thanks. I'm a bit pushed for time."

"What can I do for you then?"

Justin explained about the extra time he was having to work to get the factory organised in time to produce the new component mounted circuit boards and he went on to tell Ron about the extra time and work the two canteen ladies had agreed to do to keep him nourished.

"I wonder if you might consider rewarding these two ladies with a little extra pay?"

"Well that's rather irregular Justin," was the reply given.

"That may be so but they are helping to make my life a bit simpler and they eradicate the need for me to nip home and make myself something, and that saves time."

"You have a point there. I'll instruct the wages clerk to pay them both an extra two hours pay every fortnight and a little extra for the inconvenience. I know Brenda and Gladys are helpful souls and very reliable."

"Will you have to run that by the Managing Director's?"

"No. They leave these kind of matters to me and anyway William and Rupert would only agree. Leave it with me and I'll pop into the canteen later and let the ladies know."

With that, the meeting ended, and as Justin left, he looked at Ron's office door on which it said 'Company Treasurer's Office'. Presumably that would have read 'Finance Department' anywhere else but given that Ron was the only financier in the firm he was entitled to use whatever title he wanted on his office door. With a smile on his face, Justin headed back to where he was needed.

'This place of mine is beginning to look grubby,' thought Justin. It was just one more of those domestic chores that he no longer seemed able to get around

to doing since he took on all that extra work at Isherwood's. This time he knew who exactly to approach to do some cleaning for him.

Arthur heard the knock on his front door and got up out of his fireside chair to go and see who it was.

"Evening, Justin. Come to see the missus again, have you?" It was almost as if Arthur could read Justin's mind.

"Yes, please. I wondered if she would consider doing my house cleaning for me?"

Nellie overheard the conversation and almost before Justin had entered her living room, she said in her usual way, "That's not a problem Justin. I can fit it in around my other cleaning jobs."

At this point, Arthur interjected informing Justin that Nellie already cleaned for half the households on Roa as well as the Roa Boat pub.

Well that's something else sorted out thought Justin as he made his way back next door.

It was just approaching finishing time on Friday afternoon and Justin was completing the week's production record as Sheila approached him.

"Justin, I do hope that you will join your friends at the dance tomorrow night. We'll all miss you if you don't."

After a few moments of thought, Justin replied, "I will be going, Sheila. I treasure the friendship of all of you."

"Good. It's nice that you are moving on."

"I may not be the best company but I hope you will put up with me."

Sheila hugged him and waltzed off with a 'cheerio, see you tomorrow'.

When Saturday evening arrived, Justin felt hesitant once more. *'Rampside Village Hall dances had been one of the highlight's for Jean and himself, or so'* he thought. But it was time to get a grip, grow up and move on. There were more fish in the sea and he needed to hook one. These damned feelings seemed outside his control but he was going to try and overcome them.

It was just over half a mile to Rampside driving over the causeway and within ten minutes he pulled into the village hall car park. Inside the hall tables and chairs were arranged down two sides whilst at one end there was a small stage upon which a five-piece band played headed by Mrs Pringle on piano.

She was an accomplished pianist and taught music in Barrow girls grammar school. At the opposite end was a few trestle tables on which a range of drinks, alcoholic and non-alcoholic, and some food could be purchased. There was a nice atmosphere about the place and everyone attending the dance had a tendency to greet each other.

Justin's five female friends were already sat around a large table and there were two empty seats, one for him and the other would have been for Jean but it was to remain empty tonight. The five girls all had several requests to dance and they did so happily before swapping notes about their partners and not always very complimentary.

Both Amy and Joanne danced with Justin in the first half and he found it nice to feel the close proximity of their bodies but not in the way he had enjoyed Jean's.

In the second half of the dance, the girls were in just as much demand by the young men present but they were a bit of a scarcity. Both Nadine and Joanne danced with Justin and he loved the way they smelled. They wore nice perfume.

All of the girls were chatty but none of them made any effort to bring up Jean, if anything they all made cloaked suggestions about making a date but Justin whilst immensely flattered had no inclination to pursue any veiled invitations. It was left to Sheila, the most-worldliest of the group, to have the last dance with Justin and she tantalisingly danced, much closer than the other's.

"I'm glad you came, Justin. All the girls have had a great night and part of that is down to you."

It didn't get much further than that as a scuffle broke out near the Hall entrance and everyone's attention turned to it. The noise soon died down and the dance came to an end. The National Anthem was played and everyone departed. It was a month now since New Year's Eve.

It Can't Be True

It was becoming a bit of a ritual on Sundays to do some work on the plot but at this time of the year, it was cold on the exposed bit of land in front of Marine Terrace and the amount achieved never amounted to much. Justin paused from the repairs he was carrying out on the fencing around his plot and looked out toward Piel Island and further south to Fleetwood on the other side of the entrance to Morecambe Bay. He couldn't help day-dreaming a little. He started to picture in his mind the ferry that would have sailed from here in years gone by and the railway that would have brought its passengers from Barrow and further afield.

There was no evidence of either the ferry pier or the railway terminal left on Roa and he promised himself that he would visit the library in Barrow some time and see what he could find out about them. His mind then jumped from one era to another and he tried to visualise an aircraft carrier sailing toward him up the Piel Estuary before following the estuary as its direction went from north to west to head into the docks in Barrow. That must have been quite a sight from this position.

Justin remembered an old school pal that he had when he lived in Bolton. Most of his pals got called up at eighteen for their two years National Service. Most of them went into the Army, the rest into the Royal Air Force but Wilfred was the odd one out. He went into the Royal Navy and after his first six months he did an eighteen month cruise on the aircraft carrier HMS Illustrious.

'Jammy fellow,' thought Justin, who had been deferred until he was twenty-two so that he could complete his studies at Manchester University. He and his old school chums never really got back together again after National Service, they all went their own independent ways and it didn't help that when they were serving he wasn't and when he was serving they were not.

It started to rain and Justin withdrew indoors to think about what he wanted to do with his plot once the fence and shed were fixed. He was going to have to consult one of the gardening books his uncle Dick had left him and which were now gathering dust on a front room shelf. For now though a cup of tea would not go amiss and he ambled into his kitchen to make one.

On Tuesday evening, Justin was taking a breather in the room he was preparing at Isherwoods to house the new process that the firm wanted to carry out on its circuit boards. The work so far had been pretty menial dealing with things like the floorboards, wall plastering, window frames, decorating and the electrics. It was a boring and laborious job to be doing but it was important and that kept him going.

On the subject of electrics, he would have to pause at some point to work out where the electrical sockets would be needed and if any special power and lighting requirements would also be needed to enable the machines being installed to work. Fitting electrical components to a circuit board would require a solder bath for the boards to roll over and this required a lot of power.

A noise behind Justin disturbed him and he turned around to find that Mrs Isherwood the wife of the managing director had just stepped into the room.

"Hello, Justin. How are you?"

Annie Isherwood was always a very polite lady with a professional dress sense and an elegant posture. She was very well spoken and renowned for being able to converse on a wide range of issues which made her very popular in social circles that would befit a Naval Captain's wife.

"I'm very well. Thank you, Mrs Isherwood and how are you?"

"I'm very well indeed. I was just about to pick William up when I saw the light on in here and thought I would take a look at how things were progressing."

"There's not a lot to see at the moment. I don't expect that we will be installing any equipment in here before the end of June. As you can see it's all about getting the room looking ship-shape first."

"Well, I can see you have been getting on with all that. You know William took a huge risk when he set this place up and I must admit that I was very dubious that he could make anything out of his endeavour but it really has come a long way since he bought this place in 1946."

"Would you mind telling me, Mrs Isherwood, how your husband developed his idea to start this place?"

Annie Isherwood then related the following background story to Justin: William John Isherwood came from a long line of seafaring Barrow-in-Furness families. He joined the Royal Navy in 1906 at the age of 18 and reached the distinguished high rank of Captain before retiring in 1946 after 40 years' service. During his service in the Navy, he had taken a great deal of interest in the way electronics was making an impact especially in terms of radio communications and radar.

On retirement, the Captain took a great risk when he purchased premises on Roa Island that had been used during the war years by the Army. The premises were relatively small in which to develop work in the electronics field not to mention its isolated location that might turn out to be a deterrent to a skilled workforce but nevertheless he went ahead and purchased it. For the work he had in mind, large premises would not be required and its location could turn out to be good from a security point of view.

The factory was kitted out to manufacture, on a small scale, circuit boards to go inside electronic equipment cabinets onboard RN ships. Thermionic valve bases and wiring looms were the order of the day in 1946 but as time went on thermionic valves and wiring looms were replaced by transistors and more complex circuit boards that only required plug-in edge connectors as opposed to wiring looms.

The construction of these circuit boards became more automated as time went by and only a small workforce was needed. Most of the unskilled workers came from Roa although some were recruited in Ulverston and Barrow and found accommodation on the island. The skilled staff largely came from Barrow and commuted to the factory daily.

In 1956, William Isherwood, as he preferred to be known, decided, at the age of 68, to step back a little and work part-time, allowing his only son, Rupert, to take over the managing of the business.

William Isherwood was a good employer and treated his work force well. He knew the names of all his employees and always took the time to take an interest in both their families and their well-being. He was respected as a Managing Director and as a family man. William's contacts in industry and the Royal Navy, coupled with the high quality products that were manufactured, largely photo-etched circuit boards, almost guaranteed the future of Isherwood and Son and the stability that it engendered led to a contented workforce.

Justin already knew quite a bit about Mrs Isherwood via Jean who had worked in the firm's admin office and had met her on a number of occasions. Jean had told him that Annie Isherwood came from the well to do Taylor family who had a retailing business in Barrow-in-Furness.

She had known William Isherwood since he was 18 and had followed his naval career with great interest. She spent many happy hours with him when he was on leave and they married in 1914 at the outset of the Great War. Once the war had ended Annie travelled around the world with her naval husband and acquired the grace and charm that were needed to support him within all grades of society.

Annie was a little saddened by the fact that she had had only one child, Rupert, and that, for his own benefit, he spent a great deal of his time away in boarding school. Like many women of her time she had a degree of stoicism that enabled her to march through life come what may.

It was a massive change in life when her husband left the Navy in 1946 to set up a business on Roa.

They moved into a large house on the outskirts of Rampside overlooking Morecambe Bay and Annie took to village life like a duck takes to water. She also enjoyed time spent in their extensive garden. Whilst William had taken a huge risk setting up his business on Roa, Annie knew that her role was to give him as much support as possible and often she visited him at work to show an interest.

The Isherwood workers took a strong liking to Annie. She was very personable and homely and although well-versed in the graces of high society she was as equally at home with those from less privileged backgrounds. She seemed to know everyone by name and chatted with them when the opportunity arose. The residents of Rampside also embraced Annie and her ability to join in and help with village activities.

She was certainly held in high esteem. Having her son Rupert and his wife Nicola living nearby together with her grandchildren was making up for lost times and it was doubly pleasing to see Rupert taking over the business set up by her husband, William.

"Thank you, Mrs Isherwood. That really is an inspirational story," remarked Justin who was genuinely impressed.

"I believe you are quite an individual too," expressed Annie who went on to say, "you are a well-educated man and have served in the Royal Air Force. You are regarded by my husband as a good asset to the firm. A Manchester University Degree in Electronics is quite an achievement. Where did you serve in the Royal Air Force?"

"I only did National Service, I was not a career service man."

"Even so you served, so tell me where you served?"

"I spent my first six months at RAF Henlow in Bedfordshire training to be an engineering officer specialising in communications. Following that, I was posted to RAF Sealand, near Chester, for eighteen months, overviewing work on communications equipment," replied Justin.

"And what rank did you have?"

"I only reached the rank of Flying Officer, I'm afraid."

"Well, you got a commission, didn't you! That's something to be proud of. Well done, Justin."

Mrs Isherwood turned to retrace her steps and collect her husband and then she paused and turned to face Justin before saying to him, "I was sorry to hear what happened to you on New Year's Eve."

Justin was a little taken aback by this and wondered to himself how Mrs Isherwood knew about this.

Annie could see Justin blushing and realised from his demeanour that she had just opened up a relatively new injury and decided that it was best to take her leave of him but as she turned to go again she said, "That young lady doesn't know what a mistake she's made."

Amy in the drilling section was very friendly with Janice Jones, a typist in the admin office and Janice was the source of all the information Amy got about Jean and the rumour regarding an ongoing relationship between her and the joint managing director, Rupert Isherwood. Whilst Amy took a lot of what she was told with a pinch of salt she couldn't believe what she was hearing this time over a cup of tea in the corner of the firm's canteen.

"Did I tell you, Amy, about the row I overheard in the bosses office the other day?"

Amy was all ears and couldn't wait to hear what Janice was about to tell her.

"Well, apparently, Rupert has been having an affair with the Office Manager, Eileen Atherton."

"Get away. Eileen's married and has two children," exclaimed Amy in an unbelieving way.

"I tell you she has. She was complaining to Rupert that she wasn't seeing as much of him since he started knocking about with Jean."

Amy's jaw dropped as she heard this since it tied in with what she had already heard about Jean leaving the firm to avoid Justin's amorous advances.

Janice continued, "And what's more, Eileen blasted him for setting Jean up in a flat in Ulverston so that she could become his private whore."

"What was Rupert's response to that?" asked Amy.

"He didn't deny it and he tried to placate Eileen by telling her that there would always be a place in his heart for her."

"It's what he has in his trousers for her, more like," replied Amy and both girls had a giggle.

"What happened next?" enquired Amy.

"Nothing happened next. The big boss, Mr Isherwood dropped in and the conversation ended."

Amy was staggered about what she had just heard. Jean Baxter had never come across as a two timing bitch, she had always given the impression of being shy, a bit naive perhaps but certainly not someone who would be inclined to knock about with a married man. Amy was flabbergasted that Jean could have been involved in this masquerade whilst courting with Justin.

She had always come across as being in love with him. Janice and Amy got up from their chairs and headed back to their respective places of work and Amy thought to herself that what she had just heard was probably best kept to herself with one exception and that would be Sheila who was close to Justin.

Sheila was equally staggered when she heard the story from Amy but very sternly told Amy to keep it to herself, at least for the time being. There was no point in stirring up a potential wasps nest without being absolutely sure of the facts and that's where it was left for the moment.

Justin was relieved that Saturday evening had arrived and he could wind down in the Roa Boat with his five female colleagues. Many a man might envy me he thought as he looked around at his female friends. He looked across momentarily at the empty chair that Jean used to occupy in better times but he forced himself back to the present and noted that Sheila wasn't here.

"Is Sheila not coming tonight?" Justin asked.

It was Nadine, Sheila's house-mate that answered, "She's got a date with that big brute of a farmers lad she met last Saturday at the dance."

'That's a pity,' thought Justin, for Sheila was the one he tended to share more intimate matters with.

"Will we not do for you then, Justin?" asked Joanne in a cheeky kind of way.

Justin smiled, sat back and took a drink from his pint glass.

It poured down on Sunday and working on the plot was out of the question. Listening to the radio or reading a book seemed like the only options open to Justin but before he could make a decision as to which it would be there was a loud rat-a-tat-tat on his back door. On opening it, Justin found Nellie Elwell standing outside getting very wet as she held something under a tea towel in front of her.

"Come in Nellie, come on in out of the rain. It's a bit warmer indoors as well."

"Right you are, lad, I will. I'm fair soaked and I've only come from next door. Make a bit of space for me on the table, will you?"

With that, Nellie unveiled a large potato pie in a cooking pot and a Jam Roly Poly from under the tea towel and it all smelled very good.

"Nellie, this looks really good but you shouldn't have gone to so much trouble."

"It's no trouble lad, I was cooking for Arthur and me anyway and it brightens your day when it's like this outside."

"Have you time to put your feet up and have a cup of tea whilst you are here?" asked Justin.

"I have and I will," replied Nellie as she plonked herself down in one of the two easy chairs that Justin had in his living room. Once Nellie was settled and had a cup of tea in her hand Justin thought he would take the opportunity of finding out a little about the Elwell family and she told him that she and Arthur were both in their early sixties.

They were originally from Ulverston and moved to Roa when they got married in 1922. Arthur worked for the 'Roa Island Boating Club' and had done for most of his working life doing boat building and repairs. It was not the best paid job in the world but it was just enough to meet the needs of her and Arthur. She tried to bring in a little extra by doing a bit of house cleaning and the occasional baby-sitting.

The Elwells had a son and daughter but they had moved on when they got married in the mid-forties. Their son had moved to Workington and their daughter to Maryport and they both visited now and again.

When Nellie had finished talking about her family, she turned to Justin and asked him, "What about that pretty lass you were courting with, are you going to see her again?"

This was something Justin could have done without. As he struggled to come to terms with being dumped, his friends kept reminding him of her as if he didn't have enough reminders as it was but he responded politely.

"I don't think so, Nellie. She had decided that she wanted to move on and so that's that."

"These things don't always go that way, lad. She might find herself changing her mind. She lost a good chap when she walked away from you, Justin. Any road, I better get back to Arthur," and with those last words, she got up from the armchair she was sitting in and headed for the back door adding as she left, "Now enjoy your tea tonight lad."

'What a good hearted lady,' thought Justin as he eyed the golden crust on top of the potato pie.

On Tuesday, Justin had cause to call in to the stores section at the factory to talk to Lyn who was in charge of it. There was going to be a lot more stuff coming into the store room when the new section got going in January 1960 and Lyn needed to make sure where she could put the extra stuff and also to expand her store inventory.

Lyn was the most serious and sensitive of all the girls working at Isherwoods. 24 years of age, brown eyes, 5'6" tall and slightly on the tubby side, Lyn, who had a gorgeous smile, moved to Roa Island to get away from an abusive boyfriend in her home town—Ulverston. It was an experience that had made her nervous about young men but not totally averse.

She had moved into a rented house on Roa Island with working colleague, Amy, in 1957 and they got on well. She enjoyed reading and meeting up with friends in the pub. She enjoyed music and tolerated dances to stay part of her female companion group in which her shyness and serious demeanour were accepted and ignored. At Isherwoods, working in the stores suited her temperament.

"Hi Lyn, I thought I better come and have a chat with you about the changes we might have to make in the stores section in readiness for next January when the new section starts up."

Lyn listened carefully to what Justin was telling her and made copious notes. There was little general chit chat between them. When Justin left Lyn, he was confident that she would have everything ready in her department on time and be ready to go. Lyn was someone you could rely on.

On Thursday, it was the turn of the circuit tracers section to receive a visit from Justin. Bob Burns and John Smith performed the task of marking out the circuits on the copper covered circuit boards which would arrive, cut to size, from the cutting section. This was a fairly intricate job and there was no room for error. Once the circuits had been traced out on the boards they were painted over with a purple coloured solution that would prevent them from being etched away in the acid bath.

Both Bob and John would have to become acquainted with the blueprints for the boards they would work on next year and that was the purpose of Justin's visit. Both Bob and John were trained as draughtsmen by Vickers and they had completed their apprenticeships in the Barrow factory before being called up. William Isherwood had been looking for a couple of individuals to do the tracing work and he had found these two guys via an inside contact. It didn't take much to persuade the two men to join Isherwood and Son and the commute to Roa from their places of residence in Barrow was not a trying one.

The extra remuneration they got was very helpful for two newly wed young men and the pace of the work was comfortable. They fitted in well with everyone else at the firm in which William Isherwood, with help from his good lady, Annie, had cultivated a warm family atmosphere. Justin left the section feeling confident once more that he could rely on these two guys when it came to the new work that was going to be carried out in the not too distant future.

It was a lot warmer in the Roa Boat than outside and the heavy rain on the pub windows made the place even more cosy. Justin looked toward the corner in which his group of female friends usually sat and their presence assured him of a pleasant hour or two.

The pub landlady, Emma Barton, called over to him and asked, "Same as usual, Justin?"

His usual was a pint of bitter and he knew that when Emma pulled it, it would have a nice frothy top to drink through and that enhanced its taste. Pint in hand, Justin walked over to the girls and as he did so, he thought he detected a sudden change in the topic of conversation but he was too polite to ask what he was missing out on but he took comfort from Sheila being there.

"Hi Sheila, what happened to you last week?"

"She was busy snogging a farmer's lad," shouted Joanne, much to everyone's amusement including Sheila's.

"Well, that's exactly what I was doing," said Sheila.

"Well, come on then, are you going to go farming again?" asked Amy.

"Not likely. With hands the size he had and the amount of roving they did, he can go and date a cow," replied Sheila.

"More, more, more," was the collective cry but Sheila was not going to go into every detail about what this farming lad had tried with his extra-large hands.

Sheila then turned her attention away from the other girls and focussed on Justin.

"What's your week been like?" she asked.

"Fine, Sheila, fine. Just routine really. Getting a bit more organised with the new future project at work and generally plodding on."

"There should be a concert on around about this time at the Roxy. Will you be going?"

"Yes, there is. I'm going tomorrow night," replied Justin.

"And which band will you have the pleasure of listening to tomorrow?"

"*Leyland Motors* Band."

"Are they any good?" enquired Sheila.

"One of the best. They only get the best at the Roxy."

From this point on, several conversations could be heard going on simultaneously and Justin just sat back happily drinking his pint and letting everything go over his head. He found this scenario very comforting but he was not aware of the warning the girls had had from Sheila in advance of him arriving, to stay away from any talk about Jean Baxter, the firms Deputy Managing Director or the Office Manager. They were all strictly off-limits and the warning was adhered to.

Driving to Ulverston, Justin's mind turned to the concert he was about to attend. Leyland Band, unlike the majority of Championship Section Bands in the UK was not formed in the nineteenth century. The band was established in 1946 in the heart of industrial Lancashire as the Leyland Motors Band, taking its name from the world famous truck and bus maker. The band's first Musical Director was Harold Moss, a prolific composer and arranger.

Many of his original manuscripts are held in the band's library. In the late forties and early fifties, music from the classical repertoire provided the source for many of his transcriptions. Popular overtures were a particular feature of the arrangements done by him. One march composed by Harold Moss became the band's signature tune, *Royal Tiger,* Named after one of Leyland Motors' most famous coach products.

'*This concert as all the makings of a good one,*' thought Justin as he parked his trusty Ford Popular car in what was becoming its usual parking place. Walking out of the car park toward the Ulverston Roxy Cinema, he momentarily stopped as he saw the young lady that had stolen his heart last year. It can't possibly be true, he said to himself! He looked again and he was shocked that he was seeing Jean arm-in-arm with someone well-known to him.

Jean turned her head and saw Justin looking at her but didn't acknowledge him in any way. That was a disappointment but nowhere near as big a disappointment as seeing her arm-in-arm with Isherwood's joint managing director, Rupert Isherwood. But he's married and has two children, what is she doing going out with him? Justin turned away from looking at the couple who were walking away from where he stood. '*This would take the shine off the concert he was about to attend,*' he thought.

When the band started playing, they began with their signature tune, *Royal Tiger* and, much to his surprise, Justin enjoyed it in spite of what he had just seen. However, his mind kept drifting in and out of the music being played and the concert lost some of its musical attraction. There were one or two exceptions.

Three very lively pieces roused him from his thoughts. The first piece was called *Galop* and the second was called *A Spin Through Moscow* both of which were arrangements of compositions by Dmitri Shostakovich. The third was rather apt thought Justin, a piece by Peter Tchaikovsky called *Dance of the Buffoons* and he couldn't help thinking that he had witnessed a 'pair of Buffoons' as he had arrived.

The drive back to Roa was a little sobering as Justin once more tried to digest what he had seen. He couldn't come to grips with the idea that Jean could go out with a married man, her ex-boss of all people! One side of him told him he was well rid of Jean but the other side simply couldn't accept that what he had witnessed was really what it may seem to have been. There must be a story to tell, facts to learn. But this was Justin's emotions at work for he clearly hadn't let her go in his heart.

On Monday morning, Isherwood's was alive with gossip. Evidently, Justin was not the only person that had seen Rupert Isherwood and Jean Baxter arm-in-arm together in Ulverston the previous night. This was not a healthy topic to be talking about in a small place like Isherwood's and some of the staff were waiting to see what kind of reaction they would get from Justin.

As was her usual habit on a Monday morning, Annie Isherwood arrived at her husband's Roa factory and within minutes, she detected the gossip involving her son circulating amongst the staff and she didn't like it.

Raised voices could be heard coming from Rupert's office and Annie couldn't help hearing Rupert being harangued by the Office Manager, Eileen Atherton. This had to be stopped and Annie marched into her husband's office to find out what he was doing about it. William had been engrossed in a letter that was on his desk and was completely unaware of the fracas developing on the shop floor, so to speak.

"William you have to sort this out and fast," said Annie.

"Annie, what on earth are you talking about?"

Annie began to appraise her husband of the situation unfolding as she understood it.

"As I understand it, our son, Rupert was spotted last night in Ulverston with Jean Baxter, that pretty young woman that was courting with Justin Ebberson until the New Year. He had also been seeing our Office Manager, Eileen Atherton and right now, she is having a loud row with him in his office."

William sat back in his chair, astounded by what he had just been told.

"Annie, are you sure about all this?"

"I have just heard this with my own ears, it's the talk of the factory and everyone seems to be waiting to see what Justin does about it. William, you must take action and fast."

William Isherwood had not been a Captain in the Royal Navy for nothing and he was no stranger to the need for decisive and urgent action. He got out of his chair and walked out of his office telling Annie to stay where she was. He went straight into Rupert's office where Eileen was still confronting his son and told her to leave the office with a promise that he would speak to her later.

"Rupert, what the hell do you think you are doing?"

There was no reply from Rupert. He had got himself, and others into a bit of a mess.

William continued, "Have you been having an affair with Eileen?"

After a rather long pause, Rupert replied, "Yes, I have."

"You're a bloody fool, Rupert. You are married and have two beautiful children and Eileen is married and has two children. Where do you think this was going?"

Before Rupert could respond, his father continued.

"Just to make matters worse, you two-timed the woman you are having an affair with and the other young woman just happened to be the girlfriend of our plant inspector who right now is probably waiting to 'stick one on you'. What a bloody mess."

"I'm sorry, Dad. I've screwed up pretty badly."

"I also understand that you were providing an apartment in Ulverston for this young lass you were spotted with."

"That's not the case. I did intend finding her a place but she was having none of it."

"Well, at least she had some scruples," replied William.

"The point now is what am I going to do about it all. I want you to go home, Rupert and stay there until further notice. That is of course providing your wife hasn't got wind of what you have been up to. You will stay at home until the dust settles and I can work out what to do after that."

William left Rupert's office and went back to Annie. Rupert left the factory shortly after and his departure was watched by several pairs of eyes.

Annie couldn't wait to find out what action her husband had taken but she also knew that whatever it was that he had decided to do, she must give him her support. This crises was not of his making and he could do without it at his time of life.

William gave his wife the run down on what he had done and Annie responded by saying, "I hope he learns a lesson from this and I hope that Nicola will forgive him since she's bound to find out what he's been up to. What are you going to do about Eileen?"

William looked at Annie and in a despondent manner told her that he felt he had no other option but to get rid of her. She had no credibility amongst the workforce now and she would be a barrier to Rupert coming back, if in the future, he thought that that was a possibility. Annie looked at her husband and in a pleading style of voice she drew his attention to the fact that Eileen was married and had two children to bring up.

"She's got a lot to face up to when her husband finds out what she has been up to."

"Annie, I know that but she must have known what she was doing, it takes two to tango. Affairs never end nicely. I will give her some severance pay to help her until she can find some other work."

"What are you going to do about, Justin. He may not want to remain here any longer especially if Rupert comes back?"

"I know, Annie. I will have a chat with him and see how the land lies."

Later during the same day, William asked Justin to meet him in his office and they had a lengthy talk. The upshot of this was that for the moment Justin would continue in the role that he had with Isherwood's and when or if the time came that Rupert was being considered for a return to the firm Justin would be consulted well in advance in order that he could consider what he wished to do.

Before Justin left William's office, Annie, who had been absent during their discussion, stepped in and in her wordly-way, advised him not to draw too many conclusions about Jean. There was more to the story, in her view, and he must allow time for the truth to emerge. It was evident to Justin that Annie felt that he and Jean would eventually find each other again. It was also evident that Annie did not accept that Jean was the kind of hussy some were making her out to be.

"You know, Justin, it's too easy to make a judgement about someone on the basis of here-say, it's best to wait until the truth emerges." Before Justin left, she gave him a hug.

Doing his tour of all the production sections in order to start the preparation for next year's changes, Justin visited the cutting section on Thursday morning. This is where Bert Farrington worked. Bert was in his late fifties and lived on Roa. He was a bit of a father figure to Lyn in the stores section and was well aware that she had come to Roa to get away from a very abusive boyfriend and he gave her reassurance by keeping an eye out for her.

This was perhaps just as well since Lyn rented number two Marine Terrace with the very scatterbrained Amy Fisher but it was working well. Bert spent his time in the cutting section marking copper sided boards to the size they were required to be, before cutting them to size and sending them to the circuit tracers. There were a range of different sized copper sided boards required and Bert kept a stock of each one. When the new products come on line in the New Year, it would only be a question of new copper board sizes as far as Bert was concerned and Justin left him with some blueprints that gave the details.

Unfortunately, Saturday night in the Roa Boat was a bit frustrating for Justin since the only conversation the girls wanted to have was about Rupert Isherwood and Eileen Atherton, and fortunately from Justin's point of view not Jean Baxter. The topic swung from the possible break-up of Rupert Isherwood's marriage to the possible break-up of Eileen Atherton's and the potential impact on their children.

Theories abounded but no conclusions were reached. Following on from this was the question of who the next Office Manager may be and more importantly, will Rupert still take over the firm from his father. Sheila kept her flock in check and there was no debate about what would Justin do if Rupert did come back. Whilst there was some talk about Jean Baxter, it didn't seem to occupy too much time although they all claimed to be surprised at what she may appear to have been involved in.

No-one would have guessed that she was that way inclined much to the relief of Justin who didn't want to see his world torn to shreds. It was Sheila that broke the conversation trend by asking Justin if he was going to the village dance next week and he confirmed that he would.

After a week of turmoil at Isherwood's, it was good to do something on the plot thought Justin and by the end of this month the fence around it and the shed should be finished. He decided to take a break and he was joined by Arthur who had been doing similar restoration work on his plot. They got talking and for a change it was not about all the goings on at Isherwood's.

Arthur seemed to know a lot about the development of Roa Island and he told Justin something about the characters and firms tied up with the place in the past. A London banker by the name of John Able Smith bought the island in the early 1840s with the idea of developing a harbour company but local ship operators objected and it wasn't until a Parliamentary Act was passed that he could start on his plans for Roa Island.

In 1843, he built the causeway and pier. The Furness Railway Company was created in 1844 and they laid a track to Roa Island in 1846. A ferry service from the pier to Fleetwood made a faltering start using a vessel called the *Ayrshire Lassie* but it kept going aground and the service was suspended until the following year. The Railway Company found it difficult to negotiate terms with John Able Smith and it was not a happy relationship. By 1848, however the Furness Railway had the steamer *Helvellyn* on the Fleetwood service and the *Zephyr* sailing to Liverpool from the pier on Roa Island.

Arthur went on; A severe storm in 1852 damaged the pier and the causeway and John Smith could not afford to repair them and the Furness Railway bought him out for £15,000. The service to Fleetwood moved to Barrow in 1867 when the first docks were created there. In the same year, the pier was found to be unsafe and was rebuilt, being finished the following year. Services were inaugurated from the rebuilt pier to Belfast and the Isle-of-Man by the Barrow Steam Navigation Company but were terminated in 1881 and the services moved to Barrow. The pier was dismantled in 1894.

"Arthur, you are a font of knowledge when it comes to this place," remarked Justin before they both departed for home and some tea.

By Wednesday, Justin was getting a little tired of the constant comments he was overhearing at Isherwood's not specifically about Jean but certainly by innuendo and there was only so much a chap could take. Most unlike him he decided that a drink at the Roa Boat with the landlady Emma Barton for comfort would be far better than drooling at number eleven Marine Terrace and off he went to seek solace.

Emma Barton was the landlady of the Roa Boat pub, the only pub on the island. She was helped by her 'Jack the Lad' son George who she had to keep a close eye on were girls were concerned. The pub had a steady flow of drinkers during the week but Saturday was its busiest night although it was never full. 50 year old Emma had run the pub on her own after the death of her husband Fred who was killed in action serving in the Army in 1944. They had jointly taken on the lease for the pub in 1938, just five years before Fred was called up. They had married in 1928 when they were both 20.

No-one seemed to know where they came from but it wasn't local. George was born in 1933 and started helping his mother in the pub when he was 18 in 1951. Emma could be firm with her clientele when needed but could also lend a sympathetic ear when anyone wanted it. In her position, she knew most of the comings and goings on Roa and it was unlikely that any rumours going around the island wouldn't reach her ears. Emma was of a rather buxom build but she had the warmest of faces that drew the punters and that got the pints pulled.

"Well this a surprise," remarked Emma as Justin strolled into the Roa Boat.

"What brings you in on a Wednesday night?" she asked Justin.

"I just wanted a bit of company to take my mind off things," he replied.

"And what things might they be Mr Ebberson?"

"Come on Emma, nothing that goes on here on Roa ever escapes your notice."

"Oh those things! I see! Getting at you a bit is it?" Emma asked although looking at Justin's face it was all too obvious that it was.

"Justin your just a bystander in all that's going on in Isherwood's. Don't you be bothered about it."

"How do you work that out then?"

"Look, Justin. You had nothing to do with Rupert Isherwood having an affair with Eileen Atherton. That was entirely of their own making. The same goes for his goings on with Jean. It wasn't of your making so why get worked up about it.?"

Justin pondered for a moment trying to work out what he really thought about everything.

"I just can't see Jean having an affair with a married man and especially, Rupert. I can accept, or I'm trying to accept that she doesn't want to see me anymore. These things happen and I'm mature enough to know this and accept it. What I can't accept and what everyone is implying is that she was seeing Rupert at the same time as me and didn't care how it would affect me. I know Jean could be a little insensitive but she never came across as two faced or was malicious or duplicitous, it just didn't seem to be in her nature."

At this point, Emma had to leave Justin to his own thoughts as she moved up the bar to serve a couple of flashy gents from the sailing club. She put up with this clientele group, they spent a lot, but she didn't have much time for them, a snobby lot generally she thought but she kept it to herself. What was more important was Justin, a charming young chap who had taken his breaking up with Jean very hard and still was some eight weeks after it all happened.

"Justin, are you still in love with Jean?" asked Emma when she returned. she really knew the answer to that already.

Justin looked a bit startled by Emma's question.

"Yes, I suppose I still am. I just don't seem able to file her image away in the back of my mind. I keep getting prompts that bring her back to the forefront of it."

"Well, I know what all the prompts are, Justin but they will get less and less as time goes by."

Emma placed both of her elbows on the bar in front of Justin and leant into him so that her face was intimately close to his and then looked around to see that no-one else was stood close by, especially those 'toffs' from the sailing club.

She spoke to Justin in a quiet voice, "There may be a lot more to what's been going on Justin but you will have to wait and let the true story emerge. Don't worry about all the gossip going around and stay optimistic about what you think. In my view, this will get sorted."

The landlady had to leave Justin at this point to serve the darts players that had come into the pub. They had a match on tonight and this would be a good earner and she wasn't going to allow Justin Ebberson's love life stop her from pulling pints, money is money and the Roa Boat needed it.

With the thoughts that Emma had planted in Justin's head rummaging around inside him, he decided to get back home but dwelling on Emma's final words he wondered what she knew that he didn't. The reality of life came back fast however as he opened the pub door and was greeted by a freezing cold wind that cut through him in spite of wearing his big coat.

"Shut that bloody door! It's bleeding freezing in here!" shouted one of the more vociferous darts players.

Rampside Village Hall was pretty full for the February monthly dance and everybody seemed to be enjoying themselves. All five girls in the Justin circle, Amy, Lyn, Nadine, Joanne and Sheila were in good spirits and none were short of partners on this Saturday night although a certain farmers lad with big hands was given a miss.

They all spared a dance for Justin who was beginning to feel that his private harem was gaining a certain notoriety amongst the villagers but more prominently by the local young men and Justin's reluctance to ask any of the local girls present for a dance only enhanced that notoriety.

Everybody enjoyed the hot pot during the interval. Perhaps the cold outside added to its tasty appeal. This was a good occasion to hold a conversation and the focus tonight was the good-looking saxophone player that was accompanying Mrs Pringle on piano.

The saxophone players musical ability seemed of no consequence, it was the vision of a potential wrestling match on a settee with him that gained most interest, at least it did with the five girls whilst Justin was left wondering what was in the hot pot the girls had eaten that wasn't in his. The only factual content involved with all this chit chat was the saxophone players name which disappointingly turned out to be Ivor Ball which induced a number of unfair loud giggles.

During the second half of the evening Lyn was asked to dance by the Roa Boat Landladies son George, a bit of a 'Jack the Lad' by reputation and everyone was surprised when she accepted. Lyn's friends were immediately on their guard when she walked out onto the dance floor with him. They had Lyn's welfare at heart.

It wasn't that long since she was in a very abusive relationship with a man who had beaten her several times leaving her shaken and heavily bruised. She was too frightened at the time to go to the police, instead she left the brute in Ulverston and settled on Roa with Amy.

George was definitely a ladies man. From what the girls knew of him, mostly from his mother, he had no desire to settle down with anyone. According to his mother Emma, 'Any girl daft enough to accept a date from her son better watch out for his wandering hands'. In her blunt assessment, he was an arses and tits man but not cruel, just lustful.

George and Lyn waltzed their way around the dance floor a couple of times before separating and returning to their own respective circle of friends upon which Lyn announced, "We are going on a date." Alarm bells rang but what should they say to her at this moment, she was clearly very happy and no-one wanted to spoil it. Perhaps, a word of advice could wait a day or two and that's where it was left.

Marital Aftermath

Justin had a late start on Sunday morning. The dance last night was enjoyable and he had drunk more than he usually did which was not such a good thing since he had to drive home when it ended. Sure, it was less than a mile from Rampside to Roa via the causeway but nevertheless it was not wise to drink and drive but here he was resting in his Marine Terrace home with a cup of tea in one hand and a plate of toast in the other.

His mind wandered from one topic to another including the girl he couldn't get out of his head but his wandering did eventually come to a halt and he began focussing on the subject of his garden plot. Not the sexiest destination but it would have its attractions if he worked at it.

From his living room window at the back of his house, he could see that it wasn't raining, there was little cloud about and the blue sky was making an appearance for once. Justin could sense that it was cold out but if he wrapped up well he could get some work done on his plot. He had fixed the fence and the shed so what comes next he asked himself?

Being devoid of gardening skills he decided to consult one of Uncle Dick's books and he went into his front room to find it on one of the shelves that adorned one whole wall. It took a few minutes to locate what he was looking for. There were a lot of books on the shelves, maybe two hundred or more and they were not arranged in any orderly way.

Uncle Dick had been an avid reader and not just on the subject of gardening. There were copies of books by both George Orwell and Aldous Huxley which for no special reason, surprised Justin. He had no explicable reason why he thought that Uncle Dick wouldn't be interested in the serious stuff. Orwell who wrote *Nineteen Eighty-four* and Huxley's *Brave New World* were the last things he thought he would be interested in.

At the other end of the literary scale was *Fanny Hill* by John Cleland. This was turning out to be something of an eye opening exercise! In the end, however,

Justin found what he was looking for and took from one of the shelves a copy of a book called *Practical Gardening and Food Production* by Richard Sudell F.I.L.A. This was going to be his guide to successful growing on his plot or at least that's what he hoped.

After a period of reading, Justin went out to his plot and began making a plan to implement during the month of March. He began working by breaking down the hardened top soil so that it would be ready for seed sowing and planting and then he hoed and raked the top soil thoroughly and added some fertiliser. When he had finished, there was two or three inches of fine crumbly soil on the surface.

By the time he had done all this, it was time to call it a day and get something to eat. He admired what he had achieved and looked forward to getting some crops planted in the coming weeks, weather permitting.

As the week progressed, the time arrived for Justin to take a look at another section of Isherwood's factory to review and consider the implications of the addition of a new process. He had already taken a look in three sections, stores, the cutting section and the circuit tracing section. This week would be the turn of the photo-etching section in which Nadine worked.

Nadine Dorris was another good looker with hazel eyes a slim figure and 5'7" tall. A chirpy, cheerful lass with an eye for the boys when she got the chance. Aged 24, Nadine shared a rented house with Sheila and looked up to her friend and house-mate as her fairy-godmother. She was honest and reliable.

Nadine could gain the trust of anyone, sometimes too easily, but having Sheila by her side generally kept her out of trouble. She was a brunette who had flirted more than dated but with a little more maturity that would all change to her advantage.

Originally from Barrow-in-Furness, Nadine had been introduced to Isherwoods by Sheila and she joined the firm in 1956. Like her friend, she enjoyed music and dancing and nights in the pub with friends.

Nadine received the copper boards from the tracing section and carefully emersed them into an acid bath which etched away all the copper not covered by a marker's ink. She then timed the etching process allowing ample time for the solution of ferric chloride to do its job. The boards had then to be carefully removed from the acid bath, washed down and, finally, inspected.

This was, potentially, the most dangerous job in the factory and Nadine had to wear a raft of protective clothing. The room in which the process was carried out had windows on all four sides in order that other workers could see what was happening inside and if anything untoward happened they could step in to help. Safety posters together with emergency protective clothing were mounted on the walls outside the etching room and staff underwent periodical training on how to cope with an accident involving acid.

Probably, the most dangerous job that needed performing in this section was the emptying of the acid bath when it was finished with. The contents were emptied into special drums and there was always the possibility of an acid splash, hence the need for wearing a protective face mask whilst doing this. The drums were collected from Isherwood's on a monthly basis for disposal by a specialist company. The etched boards would then be passed on to the drilling section.

When the planned new section was up and running, it would make little difference to what Nadine did. The boards she would receive may be physically different in size and the circuits marked on them might be different but in the end they would be etched in the same way as any other and Justin simply gave Nadine some blueprints showing what was to come her way in 1960.

It occurred to Justin that the job Nadine did was a key job and if she was off-work for any reason, not just anyone could step in and do it, training would be required. He made a note to make some contingency plans to cover this possible scenario and to have a word with the firms Personnel Officer who was responsible for organising employee training.

Having satisfied himself that everything was functioning correctly as it should be, Justin sat down in his office to muse over what he needed to do next when there was a knock on his door.

"Come in."

It was Annie Isherwood making a call on Justin to see how he was coping.

"I'm OK, Mrs Isherwood. I always have things to do to keep me occupied but what about Mr Isherwood? He seems to be in the factory every day now?"

"That's a sore point Justin as you may know. He had been so looking forward to reducing his time here to be in the garden at home and with the grandchildren."

Justin didn't know how he should proceed at this point, this was a delicate family matter, but Annie continued before he had formulated any ideas.

"Rupert will not be here for some time. William is not happy with him but he hasn't made any concrete decision yet. After Rupert was suspended from work, he had some explaining to do to his wife, Nicola, but instead of coming clean he tried to convince her that he had a row with his father over the new contract with Plessey and Ferranti and they nearly came to blows. Nicola seemed to buy that at first but only until Eileen Atherton's husband came round to their house."

Justin took in a deep breath and waited for what was to come next.

"Eileen's husband Frank, was evidently very irate and demanded to know what was going on between him and his wife. Poor Nicola was taken aback and had no idea what had been going on and when Eileen's husband went on to call Rupert a bastard and gross womaniser, quoting his wife's account about the apartment Rupert was renting for another woman he was knocking off at the same time, she broke down."

Annie stopped for a moment just realising what she had said and the wound it may re-open for Justin.

"Oh Justin, forgive me. I got a bit carried away and wasn't thinking about how this may hurt you."

"It is what it is, Mrs Isherwood. Please carry on."

"There isn't a lot to say after that except that the two men broke into a fight which frightened the grandchildren to death and Nicola had to hide them away. From what I can make out, Eileen's husband came off worse and left but Rupert had taken some punishment and had cuts and bruises to prove it. Nicola rang William and we went round and brought her and the grandchildren to our place and they stayed with us for a few days until Nicola decided what she wanted to do."

"I'm very sorry to hear all this, Mrs Isherwood. Have they got together again now or are they still separated?" asked Justin.

"Nicola has taken the children with her back to her family in Plymouth and at present, we have no idea what will happen next. By the way, I might add that Rupert is adamant that he never rented an apartment in Ulverston or anywhere else for Jean, she wouldn't have anything to do with any arrangement like that and I hope that will be of some consolation for you, Justin."

Annie prepared to leave Justin's office and as she did so, she mentioned, almost in passing, that Paul Edwards, the firm's Personnel Officer hoped to be doing some interviews next week for a new Office Manager. She then left, leaving Justin to come to grips with what he had just heard.

Finally, Saturday came around again and the Isherwood's drinking group gathered once more for their weekly session in the Roa Boat. It was always a relief to leave behind the daily grind of the factory. The mystery for Justin was why these five girls who shared their Saturday nights with him didn't want to be somewhere else rather than here but his expectations were shaped by what young men and women did on Saturday nights in his home town of Bolton.

He had to remind himself that Bolton had a lot to offer young people with a desire for fun on Saturday nights, the pictures, dance halls, a skating rink not to mention the plethora of pubs. Roa was very different with one pub and limited public transport to either Ulverston or Barrow and young folks resident here had to make do with what they had and Justin had to admit that he liked it this way. Justin, having his own harem might be a joke to some but to Justin it was grand.

The conversation tonight kicked off with the week at work and the absence of Rupert Isherwood but Justin did not add anything that he had been told by Annie. Things moved on then to Eileen Atherton and the current lack of an Office Manager. On this subject, Justin could offer some news and let it be known that interviews for the job were being held sometime next week. From this point, things moved on to more girly things such as lipstick, hair shampoo, dresses and shoes, very much shoes.

All this provided respite for Justin who simply sat back, pint in hand, and let it all go over his head, the conversation that is, not the pint. Later, enquiries surfaced as to the success Lyn had with George, the landlady's son. Unashamedly, Lyn blushed and displayed a reluctance to give much away but that only drew more attention from her female friends.

"Come on Lyn, tell us, where did you both go?"

"Yeh, and what was he like?"

"Where did his hands get too?"

A barrage of personal questions were ignored by Lyn, at least until she had drunk a bit more, but even then her answers were a bit vague and her friends moved on to other points of conversation when they realised that they were not going to illicit anything worthwhile.

Justin hoped that all the effort he was putting in to grow things would pay off as he made the walk from his front door to his plot. *'It was a miserable looking Sunday morning and the rain might not hold off'* he thought. There was a bit of a mist hanging around and he could only just make out the castle on Piel Island.

The guys in the sailing club would be spending the day either in their club house or the Roa Boat but at least that would bring a smile to Emma Barton's face, she liked nothing better than taking money off sailing club members. This weather would not be good for planting any seeds but maybe, he could prepare some rows, which true gardeners called drills, and then wait for a better day for seeding.

Justin began in his plot by marking out rows with taut string held in position at each end by wooden pegs. He planned on seeding a considerable number of rows and it took quite a bit of time doing this and he was glad of a brake when lunchtime occurred. Lunch time over it was back to work and using his hoe Justin drew each row in the fine crumbly soil alongside the staked out lines of string which meant that they were straight and parallel to each other.

Once this was done, it was time to pack in. Maybe, next Sunday the weather would be more suitable for sowing the seeds. Just as he was about to get back into his house Nellie from next door shouted to him and asked him to pop into number twelve for a cup of tea and some cake that she had made and Justin was only too happy to do that.

Arthur wanted to talk about the weather or gardening or Barrow-in-Furness Rugby League Club but Nellie had other ideas, she wanted to know about Justin's love life and the gossip coming from Isherwood's.

"I don't have a love life Nellie, not now, anyway."

"Well a young man like you should have a girl on his arm. Now what about that Jean lassie, you really fancied her didn't you?"

"You know already, Nellie, that she didn't fancy me and that's that."

"Well, what about them girls you have a drink and a dance with; you know, that harem of yours?"

Blimey thought Justin this old girl doesn't miss a trick but it all sounded funny when she said it and he began to laugh.

"Nellie, I don't have a harem as you call it. First, I work with those girls, second, they live here on Roa but don't have family here like me, the only exception being Joanne and thirdly, there are no other people of our age and single that live here."

"What about Emma's son, George?"

"George chooses not to join us and anyway, he helps his mother out in the Roa Boat."

"Well, you need a girl, Justin, to brighten your day up. What about Sheila from number one or is it number two? She has an eye on you."

Arthur butted in at this stage to end the conversation.

"Now, just you stop trying to get this young chap married off, Nellie and anyway, I want to put the radio on now. You know I don't like missing my favourite programme on a Sunday."

"Oh aye, that'll be the Navy Lark," remarked Nellie and Justin took his cue and left.

Back to the routine in Isherwood's, Justin carried on with his supervisory role as Plant Inspector ensuring that normal production continued to the time scale laid down. The circuit boards had to be top quality and he couldn't afford to take his eye off the ball although in this case it was less of a ball and more of a board.

When time allowed, Justin would visit each section in the factory with a view to the changes that would be implemented next year and the next on his list was the drilling section. The circuit boards arrived here from the etching section. Currently two people did the drilling, Amy Fisher and local man Stuart Naylor. Amy was of course well-known to Justin being a member of his drinking harem.

Amy was a scatterbrained and giddy 25-year-old, loved by everyone, which could be a disadvantage at times. 5'9" tall and slightly thin, Amy was no calendar girl but her personality more than made up for it. With blue eyes, dark hair, and a not very prominent bust, Amy found it difficult to attract many possible suitors but she was never going to give up.

Music and dancing were in her DNA but she enjoyed the nights in the pub with friends especially if the conversation focussed on men. She shared a rented house on Roa with Lyn and being as different as chalk and cheese they got on exceedingly well and being from Ulverston gave them something in common.

Amy had worked at Isherwood's since 1956.

Stuart, the other driller was in his late fifties and lived on Roa with his wife. He was a good solid worker and was a steadying influence on Amy which made the section tick over harmoniously. He was a very patient man and tolerated Amy's giddy approach to life without fuss, in fact he was generally amused by her and had a soft spot for her in a fatherly way.

Drilling the holes was done by high precision drilling machines and Amy along with Stuart simply had to make sure that the drilled holes were in exactly the correct position and of the correct diameter. Boards of different sizes and configurations necessitated the resetting of the drilling machines and hence a lot of concentration was required.

One hole in the wrong place would result in the rejection of the whole board. Their job when the new section was added would not really change much they would simply get some circuit boards with slightly different positions for them to drill holes in. From here, the completed boards would be passed on to the edge connector section. After a short conversation with the pair of them, he handed them some blueprints illustrating the new boards for future reference.

At tea break, Justin sat next to Janice Jones, one of the typists in the admin office who used to work with Jean before she left the firm. Justin wanted to enquire about any progress being made in terms of a replacement for Eileen Atherton but Janice was more interested in how he was coping after his break-up with Jean.

"I do miss her Janice but if a girl decides you're not for her then you have to move on and that's what I'm doing."

What Janice really had in mind is what Justin felt about being two-timed by a girl who had swapped him for an older man and she was persistent.

"How do you feel about Jean now that you know what she was up to?"

Justin began to feel annoyed and frustrated. *'This line of questioning was occurring to often and not only that,'* he thought, *'so much of this is irrelevant, Jean dumped him and that was that.'* For some reason, he couldn't help being annoyed that everyone seemed to be concluding that Jean was not a very nice person and all based on what?

As far as he could make out it was all rumour, no-one knew the true story as to what had been going on and in his experience Jean was not the kind of person they were making her out to be. He ignored Janice's question and asked his own.

"What's been happening about a new Office Manager?"

Janice quickly realised that she had touched a raw nerve and dropped her inquisitive enquiry, at least for the time being.

"I think there have been some interviews but you would have to speak to the Personnel Officer. I don't know if any shortlist has been drawn up but I will be glad when it's all sorted out."

"Did your typist colleague apply for the job?"

Janice, looking at her finger nails, replied, "No. Neither of us wanted the responsibility. We would have had to have had a lot more direct contact with the senior management and if that included Rupert Isherwood then we didn't want to know. It was him that made Jean leave."

Those last few words were a bit of a sting in the tail of the conversation and Justin realised that this was the moment to make a getaway and he did, leaving Janice slightly stunned.

Later in the day, Justin had reason to pop into the Personnel Officers office and hand over the details of the training that the drill operatives would require when the firm's new section came on line.

"Well then Justin, you are creating a comprehensive list of training that our employees will need."

"You're doing my job for me and well in advance of the new project. Looking at what you have given me so far, I think we would be best to devote a whole week in December to training. What do you think?"

Justin had an admiration for Paul Edwards, he was a good Personnel Officer. Paul was in his fifties now, married with a grown-up family and a loving wife. He lived in a nice house just on the approach to Barrow-in-Furness.

He was a keen rugby fan which was something that Justin had initially been surprised about tending to think of him as more of a tennis and or cricket person. The topic now turned to Office Manager's and saving Justin the trouble of asking, Paul told him how things were progressing.

"We had five applications for the job but one dropped out before being interviewed and with one exception three of them were of good calibre."

Is he going to tell me who the odd one out was thought Justin.

"That silly girl in the admin office, Janice, made an application but she couldn't match the talent of the other three. I thought it prudent however to give her an interview and let her down gently. We have had enough problems in this place recently."

Justin couldn't possibly let Paul know that Janice had told him that she had not applied. The lady's integrity was dubious, he thought and he kept it to himself.

"Have you made any decision Paul?"

"Oh yes. I am giving the job to a Mrs Martha Appleton. She is very experienced and mature. She will present herself and the firm in good stead in any high level meetings she may have to attend. She's well-spoken and has a pleasant manner. She's business-like and has excellent short hand skills."

"Is she local?" asked Justin.

"Yes. She lives in Barrow with her husband and transport isn't a problem, she has her own car."

"When does she start?"

"The first week in April, and that's a relief because I'm not keen on leaving those two typists in admin to fend for themselves. Don't get me wrong, they are both good workers, but they can attract the attention of our young men distracting them in the process."

On Wednesday evening, Justin was just finishing washing the dishes after his evening meal when Amy from number two came knocking on his back door and she did not look as if she was in the best of moods.

"Can I come in Justin, I'm fed up?"

"Of course. Come in. Let me get you a cup of tea and whilst I'm making it perhaps you can tell me what it is that's upset you."

Amy was pleased to have been received in the way she was but she knew that was Justin's way. What a good-looking bloke he is she thought and felt an impulse to grab him close and snog him but she resisted, at least for the moment.

"Oh it's nothing really. I just had an argument about nothing with Lyn. We both get bored some times. Let's face it, there is bugger all here on Roa except the pub."

Justin had to agree with her and then added, "There are the village dances once a month."

"That's so but we girls are not spoiled for choices with the boys there are we," she answered.

"Well, why don't you get off to Barrow or Ulverston? There's a bit more life there you know."

"Maybe so. I need a good kicking that's what I need," replied Amy who went on to add, "What about an orgy, you me and Lyn? That could be fun," and she leapt out of her chair and came up behind Justin as he was drying dishes, closed her arms around him, squeezed herself tightly up against him and kissed him on his cheek.

Justin found himself aroused but he didn't lose control, he was wise enough to realise that this could be dynamite if he wasn't careful.

"Amy Fisher, you are a sexy Jezebel but I'll forgive you if you finish these dishes for me."

Suddenly, the heat and passion of the moment lost its momentum and Amy declined Justin's offer and returned to the chair she had leapt from muttering something unintelligible at the same time.

"Justin, did you hear what happened to Eileen Atherton?"

"I didn't know anything had happened to her apart from getting the sack. Go on, tell me."

"When she stopped going in to work, her husband wanted to know why and it all came out about her and Rupert. Her husband was none too pleased and they had a stormy row which upset their kids. Then he stormed off to Rupert's place and had a fight with him."

"What happened after that?" enquired Justin.

"Eileen's husband was concerned about the impact this would have on their children and, more to the point, the drop in income in the house. You see, they had a joint mortgage and his income wouldn't cover it alone. Frank, her husband doesn't have a high wage paying job and unless Eileen gets another, they could default on payments and lose the roof over their heads."

"That's a lousy position to be in," commented Justin.

"She's looking for another job now and regrets what happened with all her heart."

"How has Frank taken it?"

"Apparently, he is prepared to forgive her but it will take time to build trust again. Frank was silent when Eileen told him how Rupert had mithered her for ages to go out with him and when she did, it turned out he only wanted to take her back to a flat he had in Ulverston and bed her. Once he had his way with her, Rupert turned his eye on Jean but kept it going with Eileen until he could replace her with the new love of his life."

'So that's where the flat in Ulverston came in to play,' thought Justin.

"I suppose, I better get back to number two, Justin," and as Amy said this, she leapt on him again and kissed him before he could do much about it.

Then she beat a retreat for the door shouting at the same time, "Think about that orgy with me and Lyn!" and he did, with a smile on his face.

Saturday night at the Roa Boat came around once again and the chit chat between the six regular drinkers was much the same as any other Saturday night with one or two minor variations. Justin took the opportunity to look across at Amy and silently phrase the word 'orgy' and she giggled at the slightly less than discrete secret message.

"It's your Brass Band night tomorrow, isn't it?" asked Sheila.

"Yes, it is."

"Who's playing this time?"

"Grimethorpe Colliery Band from Yorkshire," answered Justin.

"Are they any good?"

"They certainly are. They only get the best bands at the Roxy."

Attention now focussed on Lyn and the success or otherwise of her date with the landlady's son, George.

"He was very nice to me," said Lyn.

"How nice?" blurted out Amy.

"Never you mind."

"I know George Barton," said Joanne in a loud voice. "I had a date with him and my father made me a pair of metal knickers. And do you know what, George turned up with a tin opener."

Needless to say, there was a roar of laughter after this but it remained to be seen as to whether Lyn had got the message.

Just before leaving, Justin mentioned to Sheila that he would be missing next Saturday. He was going to see another play at the Roxy. He detected a note of disappointment on her face and thought for a moment that Nellie was right in what she had said about Sheila the other week.

Another Sunday and another opportunity to get something done on the plot thought Justin. For a change, it was a relatively warm March day and there was going to be a chance that he could plant some seeds. He strolled out of his terrace house toward the plot and felt the warmth of the sun which was something of a novelty. The winter just gone had been fairly grim from a weather point of view but the first signs of spring made everything feel a little better.

Justin had a few different seeds to sow which included broad beans, carrots, radish, parsnips, peas and turnips. He was feeling adventurous and was edging his bets, thinking that at least one of this lot will grow. Having put the seeds in the rows he had previously prepared he thinned them out to prevent crowding and then covered them with loose soil.

When the sowing was done, he removed the lines that he had put in place to ensure each row was straight and parallel with each other. There were some rows left unused but he thought he would get round to them next week or the following week. When finished, he stood back to admire his work praying at the same time that something would grow.

Later that day, Justin made his monthly journey, as it was now turning out to be, to the Roxy in Ulverston. Brass Band popularity was strong in the country at this time and every concert held in the Roxy was pretty much a sellout. This evenings concert would be by another great band from Yorkshire—Grimethorpe

Colliery Band under the baton of its Musical Director George Thompson who had held this position since 1950.

Grimethorpe Colliery Band was formed in 1917, during the years of the First World War by members of the disbanded Cudworth Colliery Band. From these early days in the face of adversity came a story of drama and success unmatched by any other Brass Band in the world. The band's history is littered with contest success and has also been prolific in the recording studio, and made their first radio broadcast in 1932. It went on to feature on national radio between 1941 and 1951.

Justin had always thought that music was a great source of both stimulation and escape. Music provided relief from a myriad of thoughts and feelings. He regretted that he couldn't play an instrument and had often thought about buying a piano and taking lessons but somehow something always seemed to get in the way and hence attending concerts had become his musical forte. Tonight he was not to be disappointed.

The concert programme was excellent and the band sounded superb. He warmed to Elgar's *Nimrod* and Coates smooth sounding *By The Sleepy Lagoon*. The whole evening reverberated to the rich sound of brass and other pieces of music struck a chord with him including *Largo from The New World Symphony* by Dvorak and Sullivan's *The Lost Chord* both truly sounded splendid. Unlike the last two visits to the Roxy, Justin had arrived ready to enjoy what was on offer and there was nothing on his mind to distract him. Perhaps, he was getting back to his old self.

This was the golden era for Brass Band music and Justin was sharing it with the rest of the audience but he was inclined to think how much nicer it would be to have someone to accompany him to these concerts, someone like minded in music, someone like Jean.

This week in the factory, Justin was moving his plans on. Getting the factory prepared for the new boards that the Admiralty required next year had to be carefully thought out. The new contract would keep Isherwood's going for quite some time and that was good for all who worked here. Last week he had taken a look at the section that was responsible for drilling holes in the circuit boards, this week he would be leap frogging the section that didn't currently exist, that is to say, the new section that would eventually mount components on boards.

He was simply going to move to the section that currently received boards from the drilling section and fitted edge connectors to them. Edge connectors, as the name implies, fit on the edge of circuit boards and connect to the copper circuits thereon. The boards can then be placed in equipment cabinets and be plugged in via the edge connectors. This avoids the need for wiring looms and also makes it easy to replace a board when a fault develops.

Sandy Fredericks and Johnny Davies, both middle aged married men from Roa, fitted edge connectors to the boards currently being produced and would continue to do so when the new ones came on line. As far as these two were concerned their work wouldn't change. They would continue as before but they would require blueprints for the new boards and Justin supplied them.

Everyone in the factory would need preparing for the new products that would come on line and it would be necessary to include some training sessions before Christmas. '*I better make sure that the Training Officer sorts this and recruits a couple of extra workers for the new section,*' thought Justin who could now put another tick in his planning box.

The play being performed at the Roxy in Ulverston this week was called *Glorious* and Justin fully expected to have an hilarious Saturday evening after reading about it in the local press. Once again, the Roxy was almost full and the audience seemed to have an air of expectancy about it and they were not disappointed. The cast did a brilliant job telling the story of an American socialite and amateur soprano Florence Foster Jenkins who became known and mocked for her flamboyant costumes and poor singing ability.

She was described as 'the world's worst opera singer' and listening to the play staged tonight, enabled the audience to be tortured by her voice in the worst possible but laughable way. Florence was excruciating to listen to but it was all highly enjoyable and it was hard to believe that she once sang in New York's Carnegie Hall to a sellout concert audience.

The voice of Florence singing in the Roxy was certainly a contrast with the music that Justin had enjoyed the previous Sunday. '*What a great way to end the week,*' thought Justin as he drove back home to Roa Island.

Justin's gardening prowess seemed to be coming along fine. Sundays could be guaranteed to find him on his plot and up to a point he enjoyed it but there was no getting away from the fact that gardening, as with his extra work schedule, were really just ways of keeping busy so that he couldn't dwell on what had happened to him on New Year's Eve. If circumstances were different, he would, more than likely, be pursuing different things.

Justin's strategy was working up to a point. He was getting through each day without feeling much in the way of emotional pain and he was successful in preventing himself from chasing after the girl that had dumped him. What was not helping was the frequency of his colleagues updates on matters which Jean seemed to be tied up in one way or another.

If it wasn't for these bits of tittle tattle, perhaps he would have moved on much quicker, when all said and done, he had only seen his ex twice since she gave him the push. Part of Justin was telling him that he was being a bit of a wimp and he should get a grip as well as another woman. On the matter of the latter, Sheila and the orgy girls swam around in the more lecherous parts of his brain.

Having been stood still on his plot for more than ten minutes, Justin suddenly woke up to why he was here. He went into his shed and picked up the potato seedlings that he was going to plant in the rows he had previously made but not yet used. As he had done with his other seedlings, he placed them in the empty rows making sure that he didn't crowd them together before covering them with loose soil.

Then it was time to remove the taut lines that marked the rows out. A final bit of tidying up completed the day's work and he returned to his house—his blasted empty house, which he sometimes hated, just for its emptiness. Never mind, at least there's work tomorrow.

On Wednesday morning, Annie Isherwood called into to Justin's office and he made her welcome. Mrs Isherwood looked strained and Justin got one of the shop floor workers to nip to the canteen and bring her back a cup of tea.

"Are you not well, Mrs Isherwood?" asked Justin.

"I'm rather upset," began Annie who then went on to tell Justin what was going on in her family and how it may affect the factory.

"William is so upset. I have never seen him like this before including the war when he was serving in the Navy. He's upset at losing his grandchildren. They are in Plymouth at present and we don't think Nicola will have Rupert back again."

Justin mulled over what he had just been told but didn't respond, there was more to come.

"William is infuriated with Rupert. He discovered through a close friend of his that Rupert had bought a flat in Ulverston and had been taking various women friends of his there for overnight stays. We don't know how long this has been going on but we do know that he has been using the flat for this purpose for at least two years. Rupert has bragged to his drinking friends how many conquests he has made. The whole of Ulverston is talking about him. His father realises that Rupert doesn't have the integrity to run this firm and he knows that if this gets out, then the MOD will regard him as a security risk and Isherwood & Son would collapse."

"Good God, Annie! Beg your pardon, ma'am, I mean Mrs Isherwood. This is a terrible story, I really am sorry to hear all this. Has Mr Isherwood decided what he will do about it?"

"He intends to have a meeting with his senior management team during the second week in April and I'm sure that you will find out more then. In the meantime, Rupert has been put on half pay and given two months to find himself another job. After two months, his pay will stop and he will have nothing to do with the firm."

"What about his wife, Nicola, and your grandchildren?"

"Rupert will have to sell that lovely family house that he owns in Newbiggin and use the money to provide a roof over his family's head."

"That reminds me Justin, William wants to speak to you next week to get an update on the preparations you are making," Annie continued, "William doesn't know what he wants to do at the moment but I know he wants both of us to be as near as possible to our grandchildren and that will mean us moving to Plymouth. William has friends there from his Navy days."

"But what about this place?" Asked Justin.

"He could simply close it all down but he has too much money invested in it for that to happen. He could try and sell the firm and either Plessey or Ferranti may be interested or, and which I think the more likely, he may try to find someone to run the business for him. He hasn't made his mind up yet but he does want to get everything resolved as soon as possible."

There was a lot to digest and both Annie and Justin agreed that it would be best if the firm's employees were kept out of things until a clear way forward had been determined.

As Annie got up out of her chair she turned to Justin and said, "That pretty young girl of yours had nothing to do with Rupert, when he tried to lure her to his flat, he never bedded her. That young lady eventually stood up to him. Don't believe the rumours that are going around," and she left.

It had been Justin's intention to review the firm's inspection section this week but after the visit by Mrs Isherwood and the information that she had confided in him, he decided to delay it until next week. His decision was partly made by the fact that he had, of late, been looking at his inspector, Sheila, in a rather amorous way even though he didn't feel it was like he had with Jean. She was attractive though and had a figure that he couldn't ignore.

It was what Annie Isherwood had said to him that was holding him back. For some reason, he could just not bring himself to do anything that may burn his boats, as if he hadn't already burnt them, with the girl that he still loved. *'Sheila's inspection could wait another day,'* he thought, chuckling at the same time at the thoughts that he conjured up in his mind.

The monthly dance in Rampside Village Hall should bring some light hearted relief thought Justin after a fairly traumatic week. The important thing to remember though was to keep his mouth shut regarding the possible future of Isherwood's. All five female drinking partners had taken their chairs by the time that Justin arrived but they had, as they always did, saved a chair for him. The conversation was pleasant and all the girls were in good spirits.

Justin looked discretely at Sheila and for a moment he contemplated asking her out at some point during the evening but didn't want to rush into anything. At this point, the Band Leader, Alison Pringle, standing on stage, welcomed everyone present and was about to announce the first dance when Justin spotted Jean sitting across the other side of the Hall with some other young women and momentarily he couldn't take his eyes off her.

The band began to play and almost all of his friends were approached by potential partners and they all rushed off onto the dance floor obscuring his view. The first half of the dance went pretty much as it usually did. The girls were never short of partners but they found time to drag Justin up even though he seemed a bit reluctant.

As he danced with Sheila he could see Jean dancing and Sheila remarked to him, "Are you going to ask her for a dance?"

Justin knew that he would love to do that but he was scared of rejection and he was too embarrassed to admit it. Inside of him, he was of the conviction that if Jean had changed her mind about him, then she would let him know.

"I don't think so, Sheila."

"Well, I'm going to have a chat with her at the interval. It's three months since I last laid eyes on her."

Justin simply let the conversation to come to an end and continued with the dance which had now become less enjoyable.

At the interval, Justin remained sat with his five colleagues and they all enjoyed some refreshments. His eye's kept drifting to where Jean was sat and occasionally they looked at each other. Jean acknowledged that she had seen Justin but not with a full blown smile. *'Damn, she looked beautiful,'* he thought.

Sheila went across to speak to Jean and was away for some time, leaving Justin feeling a bit awkward for some reason he couldn't fathom. The band began to play again and there was a rush for partners all over again, an activity that Justin refrained from, the exception being Lyn who wanted to enquire about his thoughts on a possible orgy and got him up to do so. This rather broke the ice and he laughed.

At one point, when they were all sat down Joanne asked everyone if they recognised the band drummer. This drew a blank response and since Joanne already knew, she filled them in.

"That's Dave Clitheroe. He's Albert Clitheroe's son. You know Albert. He's one of our security people. They live on Roa."

The group applauded Joanne for enriching them with this gem of information and she took it in good part.

Inevitably, the dance came to an end and Justin could see Jean leaving with her friends. A short smile was shared between them and she was gone.

The day after the dance, it poured down and that put paid to any work on the plot. Consequently, Justin was at a bit of a loose end and he desperately wanted to occupy himself so that he wouldn't dwell on things. Reading might help, he thought but in the end he decided to get some letters written that were long overdue.

Having put off reviewing the inspection section at Isherwood's for a week, Justin decided to crack on with it. Sheila was the firm's inspector and it was her responsibility to ensure that the finished circuit boards that came to her from the edge connector section were perfect before she allowed them to be moved to the packing department. This was a job that demanded a lot of concentration.

What was evident at this early stage was that when the new circuit boards eventually arrived here, there would be a lot more to inspect. Unlike the current boards which were devoid of any components, the new one's would have many, such as capacitors, resistors, transistors and valve bases. It was obvious that there was going to be too much to inspect for one person to handle and after a little discussion with Sheila, she agreed. Much to Justin's relief, there was no reference to what Sheila had talked about with Jean at the Village dance.

Justin knocked on his bosses door and he was asked to come in. Sat behind his desk William John Isherwood was an imposing figure and he came to the point immediately.

"Justin, I trust that my wife as brought you up to speed regarding developments?"

"Yes, she has."

"Well, what I want you to do now is bring me up to speed on the preparations being made for the production of the new boards that we will be manufacturing next year."

Justin began by describing the work that had been carried out in the room that would accommodate the new section, "The room has been cleaned up. New floor boards have been laid and new window frames fitted. The walls have been plastered and the electricity supply and lighting done. The next two months will be occupied doing the plumbing and decorating."

"Good. Now what about the changes that the shop floor workers will have to undergo?"

"I have been visiting and reviewing each section to determine just that. All that remains to take a look at are the packing and dispatch sections plus the maintenance people. Training for the staff will be pretty minimal and I have talked with the Personnel Officer to set aside some time to carry that training out. We will need three extra staff however."

"What do we need them for?"

"We need two staff in the new section to handle the fitting of components to the new boards and an additional inspector because of the additional detail to inspect."

"Thank you, Justin. It looks good to me and I want you to carry on with the preparation work. We can meet again at the end of April to see how things are progressing again."

"Are you sure that this is still going ahead, Mr Isherwood?"

"I will give you an affirmative on that at the senior management meeting next month."

With that, Justin got up from his chair and left the office.

The landlady, Emma, greeted Justin as he arrived for his usual Saturday night drinking session with his five work colleagues.

"Come to visit your harem have you, Justin?"

"I most certainly have, Emma and how are you?"

"I could be better. I've just had to give George a good telling off."

"What's he been up to then?" enquired Justin.

"It's that young lass Lyn, that's what he's been up to. She's a young lass that can't tell a decent lad from a lecherous bugger like George and she's still fragile after her encounter with that brute she knocked about with before. When our George starts getting his hands up her knickers, she freaked out. Fortunately, George panicked and left her."

"Where did all this happen then, Emma?"

"He took her to the pictures in Ulverston, that's where, the randy bugger. He takes after his late father, he does."

Joining the girls in their usual place in the pub, Justin could see that Lyn was being tenderly cared for by her close companions.

'Blow goes my orgy,' thought Justin.

The evening passed pleasantly and Sheila took the opportunity of letting Justin know what had passed between herself and Jean on the previous Saturday night. Apparently, Jean liked her new job but doesn't like living on her own.

'I know the feeling,' thought Justin.

"She doesn't have a boyfriend," went on Sheila. "She also told me that she had left Isherwood's to get away from Rupert but he still kept trying to see her when she had left. She had two dates with him to try and shake him off but it was the row he had with Eileen, the Office Manager, that brought it to an end."

"That's kind of you to tell me, Sheila."

Justin didn't love Sheila but his respect for her was growing.

An Uncertain Future

The sun was shining but there was not much warmth to feel, indeed it felt quite cold but there was no evidence of any frost on this Sunday, April morning. There was a strong smell to the sea air which was blowing in from the south and it was a good day for sailing judging by the yachts bobbing up and down in the Piel Estuary. The view out to Piel Island was good in the clear air and the islands castle stood out prominently. For once, it felt good to be here thought Justin. It beats Bolton any day! He was very clear on that score.

"Morning Justin."

It was Arthur from next door calling from the adjacent plot.

"Did you get woken by the lifeboat siren last night?"

"No, I didn't Arthur but I wondered why the lifeboat is tied up this morning at the bottom of the jetty."

"Blimey, you must sleep well. A cargo boat sailing from the Isle-of-Man to Glasson Dock ran aground last night in Morecambe Bay and was in need of help. It was in danger of capsizing. The lifeboat was launched at about 2:00am."

"Did anyone get hurt?"

"I don't think so. From what I was told, the lifeboat was on station, close to the vessel in case anything went wrong. The coastguard called a tug out from Heysham and they managed to refloat the vessel."

"An exciting night then, Arthur."

"Oh aye. We get em now and again," and he went on, "How's the seedlings coming along?"

"They're beginning to show through now."

"Good, man. You'll be selling stuff down the market next."

Justin laughed at Arthur's last remark. Now, however it was time to get a bit of work done on the plot. His seedlings were beginning to show through the top soil and it was time to run his hoe through the soil that divides the rows and to pull out any weeds. He would also take the opportunity of thinning out the seedlings to prevent any crowding if it was necessary.

There were a lot of rows to tend to and the job took quite a bit of time but that was of no consequence and Justin carried on until he was satisfied that he had done all that he could do and then it was time to go and make something to eat and that was not a chore that he warmed to.

The new Office Manager started work at Isherwood's on Monday morning and amongst the four young women she would be managing there was an air of apprehension. It hadn't been easy working for Eileen Atherton, the previous Office Manager, but a lot of that was down to her having an affair with the Joint Managing Director, Rupert Isherwood. Eileen could easily fly into a temper or alternatively she would get depressed and no-one could get through to her. The last month had not been easy to get through with no-one being in charge but at least the atmosphere was less stressful and all four hoped it would stay that way.

Martha Appleton, the new Office Manager was smart in her appearance and quite good-looking. She was quite tall and slim and had brown eyes. There was no pretence about her and she came across as being down to earth and began by treating the four girls on an equal footing which they greatly appreciated. She wanted each of them to introduce themselves so that she could get to know them. Janice Jones began the introductions.

Janice was twenty-two years of age, single and lived in Ulverston. She had been to night school to learn how to be a shorthand typist. Janice had worked at Isherwood's for eighteen months. Marion Holmes was also a trained shorthand typist but she lived in Barrow. Marion was twenty-three years of age, single but had a regular boyfriend. She had joined Isherwood's six months ago when Jean Baxter had left the firm. Both typist's were good-looking and drew the attention of the young male employees in Isherwood's particularly when they all met up in the works canteen.

It was not unusual for some of the male employees to make all kinds of excuses to call on the 'admin girls' has they were known, but that would probably change now under new management. Eunice Critchley was older than Janice and Marion, she was twenty-eight years of age, married and had a two year old daughter who was cared for by her mother when she was working. She and her husband were buying a house in Barrow and they needed the money to pay for the mortgage.

Eunice was another attractive young woman and didn't mind flirting with the young men but that was as far as it went. She worked largely for Mr Bright the Company Treasurer but was under the supervision of Martha. That left the wages clerk Joyce Turnbull a lady from nearby Rampside to introduce herself. Joyce was qualified in accountancy and was also well suited to do work for the firm's treasurer.

Joyce was the eldest of the four being thirty-two years of age. She was a widow. Her late husband had been killed in early 1953 serving in the Army in Korea. They had a little girl called Susan who died in 1956 from Diphtheria. She now lived on her own which was a surprise to many since she had a lovely personality and was extremely good-looking. It was Joyce that had held the admin office together in the absence of an Office Manager and the other three girls were surprised that she hadn't applied for the post.

Martha Appleton introduced herself to the girls by telling them that she hoped they would all get on well together. Everything would be fine if work was done on time and correctly. She would insist on a level of professionalism when dealing with senior managers at all times. Providing these simple rules were adhered to they would all get on fine.

Martha introduced herself to her team, as she would now call them. She told them that she was thirty-two years of age, married and lived in Barrow. She had not long been out of the Women's Royal Naval Service in which she had been a writer by trade and a Petty Officer by rank. The team rapidly realised that their new manager was not going to be a pushover in any sense of the word.

Over a cup of tea in the works canteen Justin asked Janice what she thought about her new Office Manager but she was a bit reluctant to say anything at first but her reluctance softened as she saw Martha leave.

"She seems nice but we all think she could be a bit of a stickler."

Justin responded by telling Janice that she and the other office girls would have to give her some time to settle in before making any judgement and Janice agreed. Talk now turned to Eileen Atherton, the previous Office Manager.

"Have you not heard Justin?"

"Not heard what?"

"She's gone and got herself in the family way and just as she was settling in to a new job."

"She already has children, doesn't she, Janice?"

"Yes, a boy and a girl."

"Will she and her husband be able to cope? I understood that she and her husband Fred were dependant on two wages coming in to pay the mortgage they had…"

"Well, that's true and Eileen had just got a new job, but not one as an Office Manager."

"Whyever not?"

"Don't be daft! When employers found out that she got the sack from Isherwood's for having an affair with a senior member of staff, they wouldn't touch her with a barge pole."

'That's a bit harsh,' thought Justin. Eileen was paying a high price for her indiscretion.

"What kind of a job did she manage to get then?" asked Justin.

"Woolworth's took her on as a sales counter person. The money isn't as good as she got here but it was keeping the wolves from the door and that's what matters," replied Janice.

"How far gone is she?"

"Four months."

"How long can she go on working?"

"She says she will carry on for as long as possible and that might take her through to September. After that, she has no idea how they will cope and she's worried sick."

"How has all this gone down with Fred?"

"That's another part of the story," replied Janice but before she could go into it her colleague Marion came bursting into the canteen shouting that the Office Manager wants her back in the office right now, and that's were things had to be left for now.

This week, Justin was going to take a look at Isherwood's packing section in order to establish whether any alterations would be required to meet the needs of the new production run in the New Year. As with most of the sections in Isherwood's there was only one person in packing and in this case it was Alan Tinker a middle aged man born and bred on Roa. All the inspected circuit boards came to him for packing before going on to the dispatch section.

Alan had a myriad collection of cardboard boxes and a pile of straw that he used to ensure that the boards wouldn't move when they had been placed in one of the boxes. It was also Alan's job to print off address labels to stick on each box. He received a list of addresses from the admin office. Alan ran a fairly proficient dispatch section although looking around the place it would be hard to tell so.

Boxes here and there, packing straw in odd places etc gave a false impression as to how the place really functioned. Little change would be required here in the future except, maybe, a few different sized boxes to handle and some new addresses for the labels to be attached to them. All these things could be covered in the future training sessions that were to be organised.

Alan Tinker was one of Justin's neighbours. He lived at number nine Marine Terrace with his wife Mabel. They were a happy couple with one son who was doing his National Service in the Army. Mabel did a bit of cleaning for Isherwood's now and again, in fact cleaning was something that needed sorting out at Isherwood's.

At present, it was down to each section to clean up its own territory at the end of a working day which was not really satisfactory. It would be much better thought Justin if the firm used a cleaning firm. There were several in Barrow that did contract cleaning. Alan enjoyed fishing and reading and he benefited greatly from the library service in Barrow who sent a mobile library to Roa once a month.

A second opportunity occurred to speak to Janice later in the week over another cup of tea.

"How did you go on Janice when you got back to the office the other day?"

"I got told off proper and it was my own fault, I just lost track of time. Martha's OK with me now but I mustn't be late back."

"You were going to tell me more about Eileen. I remember you said she was pregnant."

"She's pregnant alright but it's not Fred's child she's having."

Justin could guess what was coming next but he waited to be told.

"It's that bugger Rupert's baby."

It didn't stop Justin from gasping. That bloke has caused no end of trouble as he sought to satisfy his carnal lust.

"What has been the reaction from Fred?"

"He's not happy about it but he hasn't kicked Eileen out. He puts their two children first. He thinks that Rupert should help with the finance given that he is responsible for this situation but he doesn't know what he can do about it."

"What a lousy situation to be in," remarked Justin just as tea break came to an end.

'What a relief to be able to relax,' thought Justin as he took his regular Saturday night seat in the 'Roa Boat' pub with his five female companions. Will I ever be able to enjoy an all-male group of drinking partners again thought Justin to himself. Tonight's conversation was largely to do with the new Office Manager, Martha Appleton, and the plight of Eileen Atherton.

Most of all, this went over Justin's head, he had heard it all before, but he had not heard the expletives directed against Rupert Isherwood spoken in the way these ladies were using them and he couldn't help being amused by it. There was also some conjecture about the special management meeting being held next week but he gave nothing away about that. It had been quite a start to April but it was going down better with the aid of a good pint of bitter and five nice young women to look at.

Looking around his plot, Justin was pleased to see so many seedlings showing through the top soil and just like the week before he methodically began to hoe through the soil that divided the rows and took out any weeds that were appearing. There was still some thinning to do to prevent the seedlings from overcrowding. Arthur was also busy in the adjacent plot and it was inevitable that he would chat with Justin at some point and when he did he began by commenting on the Managing Director of Isherwood's and his son in particular.

"That lad Rupert at your place, Justin. He's let his old man down badly."

It would not be a good idea to talk indiscriminately about what was going on in Isherwood's thought Justin. These things have a nasty habit of getting back to the wrong person but it looked, right now, that word had already got out and it certainly wouldn't be a bad idea to listen to Arthur and find out what the folk on the island already knew.

Arthur went on, "The old man was hoping to step down from the business by the end of this year and let Rupert run the place, I can't see that happening now, can you, Justin?"

That was a leading question and best circumvented at this stage and like a true politician he answered by saying, "I don't know what's going to happen but I do know that the firm is preparing for some new work in a year's time and is probably going to have to recruit some extra staff."

Arthur seemed a bit put out by this reply, he had been thinking that he was well in the know about Isherwood's. Nellie appeared on the scene at this juncture and spoke to Justin.

"That lovely lass of yours was trying to save you when she dumped you. Did you know that?"

"Nellie, I really don't know what you are talking about."

"I have it on good authority that that lass of yours realised that as long as she worked at Isherwood' and that bugger Rupert was after her and she kept turning him down, then he would make life rotten for you. He knew that you and her were knocking about with each other and he was jealous."

Justin was stunned by this. He had never thought that this could be a possibility. He was totally flummoxed when it came to understanding why Jean had told him that she didn't want to see him again but this would put a totally different light on things. On the other hand, if what Nellie had told him was correct then why had Jean not made some kind of approach to him in the last three months? He was bewildered.

When Nellie had gone back indoors, Justin got back to work on his plot but with less enthusiasm.

There were still some rows of seedlings that needed thinning out and weeding to do and so he continued until every row had been given his attention and then it was back to home cooking and another dratted thinking session.

Another working week began and apart from ensuring that everything was ticking over as it should be Justin pressed on with his review of each section. This week he would take a look at the dispatch section in which Joanne Cooper, one of his drinking friends, worked. Jo to her friends and the youngest of the six Isherwood's shop floor female employees at 23. She was a genuine Roa Island girl and still lived on the island with her parents. 5'6" tall, slim with brown eyes and rather plain looking, Jo was an extremely pleasant young woman.

Practical and sensible by nature, she was one that the other's would turn to for advice on matters not related to men. She had little experience in that direction, a situation not helped by the fact that almost no eligible and desirable young men lived on Roa. Nevertheless, there lurked below the surface a desire to find a male partner.

Jo enjoyed meeting in the pub, and dancing when she got the chance. She got on well with her parents and did not find it a handicap living with them, in fact it was often a talking point with her friends who often pulled her leg about it but she took all the banter in good stead. Joanne received the packed items from the packing section and ensured that they were dispatched to wherever they were required and this involved liaising with a number of goods carriers including the GPO.

In some cases, individual firms would send their own vehicles to Roa to collect. Accurate records had to be kept to show where each item leaving the factory was dispatched to and signatures obtained. All in all, this was a simple but responsible job and little would change when the new products came on line. There might be some fresh places to send completed goods to but that would only entail additions to the current dispatch list.

The big event of the week was scheduled for Wednesday and Isherwood's senior management team gathered together in the Managing Director's office at precisely 2:00pm. At the head of the large table which in larger firm's would be called the boardroom table, sat William John Isherwood looking rather strained.

Gathered around the table were the following; Joshua Turner, Company Secretary, Ronald Bright, Company Treasurer, Paul Edwards, Personnel Officer, Justin Ebberson in his role as Plant Inspector and Martha Appleton, Office Manager. William's wife Annie was seated away from the rest and close to his office window which overlooked the Piel Estuary. Refreshments had been prepared by the two canteen ladies and was placed on a small table on the other side of the room.

William began the proceedings by announcing that he would remain seated. He looked both tired and dejected.

He began, "Ladies and gentlemen, no doubt you are aware of why I have called this meeting today. It had been my strong desire to hand over the running of this company to my son Rupert this year. I was hoping that by the end of this December, I could enjoy full time retirement at home with my good lady, Annie, and like all grandfather's, enjoy watching my grandchildren grow up. Unfortunately, as a result of the actions of my son, those plans have had to be squashed."

This generated a great degree of expectancy amongst those around the table and in addition to expectancy there was anxiety. What was the boss going to do and more importantly, how would it affect each of them.

William went on, "I won't go into all the details but, as you all probably know already, my son had an affair with our previous Office Manager, Eileen Atherton, who I had to remove from the firm. My son's wife, Nicola, subsequently left him and went to her parent's home with our two grandchildren and they live in Plymouth. Nicola will not be taking our son back and will not be coming back up north to live. In addition to this, Eileen is pregnant with Rupert's child."

This was all getting a bit uncomfortable to listen to but there was considerable empathy felt for both William and his wife, Annie.

"Now, let me come to the point in terms of how this all affects you and all my employees here on Roa. Rupert is currently suspended from coming into the factory and is on half pay. This can't continue. If Rupert had returned, he would have been considered a security risk in the eyes of the MOD and we would have lost all our business. After consultation with the Company Secretary, Josh, my son will have his contract terminated at the end of May. I can't continue here indefinitely and Annie and I have decided to sell our house in Rampside and move to Plymouth at the end of this year."

All those present looked at each other in anticipation of what would come next.

"After a long and arduous period of analysis, I came to the conclusion that I had three possible options. One, I could just close the factory and sell its assets but I would lose a lot of money going down this route and all thirty-one of our employees, including yourselves, would be out of work. I don't consider this as a suitable option. Two; I could try and sell the firm. The problem with this option is that the firm may not be an attractive buy on the market. We don't have a marketing department or one to do research. We have avoided the need for these by doing contract work for firms like Plessey and Ferranti and left it to them to perform these functions and so I have ruled this option out. So gentlemen, we come to my option three; I have decided that the best thing for me to do for everyone concerned is to employ a Managing Director to run the factory on my behalf."

Everyone gave a sigh of relief and began clapping.

The rest of the meeting dealt with a ream of details concerning what would happen next and a diary of events was compiled. Essentially, advertising for the post would begin at the end of May when Rupert disappeared off the payroll. A shortlist of candidates would be drawn up at the end of July and interviews conducted in August. An appointment would be made in September and the new appointee would take up the post in January 1960. William would stay in post until then.

At this point, everyone relaxed and headed for the refreshments and as they did so Annie caught Justin's attention and the two of them exchanged pleasantries. Annie did take the opportunity of suggesting to Justin that he really should consider getting in touch with that pretty girl he was fond of and which Annie was too.

The major talking point in the Roa Boat, amongst the girls at least, was the impending departure of Mr Isherwood. Who would take over from him was the next point for debate and it seemed that these five were pretty convinced that it would be one of the firm's senior managers.

"Justin, we might be sitting down in the future having a drink with our new MD." When everyone laughed, it took away any compliment that may have been intended and the subject of conversation changed.

"Are you Brass Banding tomorrow night, Justin?"

"Yes, I am and before you ask it's the *Fairey Engineering Band* playing tomorrow and they are one of the top bands."

Justin went on to mention to Sheila how Nellie seemed to know so much about what was going on in Isherwood's.

"I don't know why you should be surprised Justin. When all said and done, half the factory employees live in Marine Terrace."

And on that note, Justin thought it best just to drink and listen and drink and listen.

Sunday morning was rather damp and misty and Justin was not likely to spend too much time on his plot. Judging by the ship's horn he could hear, there was a vessel moving either into the estuary or out of it but either way he couldn't see it.

Potatoes and other vegetables were coming through the soil in several of the rows that Justin had planted and since the time for frosty weather was not yet passed, he threw a little soil over or against the young stems to protect them before scattering slug killer pellets around each one. It took a little time to do this since there were so many rows.

"Good morning, Justin," Arthur was in his plot as usual.

"I hear you're going to have a new man at the top in Isherwood's?"

'How does all this information get out into the world,' thought Justin but of course he knew, but it was in a sense frustrating. It didn't seem right that folks outside the factory knew as much about what was going on inside it as those that worked inside it. This was a blatant case of loose tongues.

"The old man was going to retire and that's all that's going to happen this year, Arthur."

"I well! How do you feel about having a new boss?"

"It happens in every company. We will all have to get used it."

Arthur had a habit of sneaking off when he realised that he was not going to illicit any inside information and that's what he did whilst wearing his old gardening shoes as he did so.

"Arthur Elwood! Don't you think you can come in this house with them muddy shoes on."

Nellie's voice cascaded down Marine Terrace and into Piel Street and probably half way down the causeway toward Rampside.

Shortly after Nellie's world address, two muddy shoes came flying through the air and ducking his head, Justin allowed them to continue on their flight path before they landed heavily on one of Arthur's rows of fledgling potatoes breaking one or two stems in the process.

'It's getting dangerous out here,' thought Justin and he hung up his gardening shoes for another week and went back indoors.

Sunday night at the Roxy was here again and Justin was looking forward to another evening of music provided this time by the *Fairey Engineering Band*. The band is based in Heaton Chapel in Stockport, Manchester and its name comes from Sir Richard Fairey and the Fairey Aviation Company. The band was formed in 1937 by workers at the aircraft factory and is one of the most successful contesting Brass Bands in the world.

The band achieved many successes under the brilliant direction of Harry Mortimer, their Musical Director for many years. The band's appearance in Ulverston was taking place just two months after winning the North-West Area Championship and qualifying for the National Championship later in the year. Fairey's had already won the National Championship four times: 1945, 1952, 1954 and 1956 in addition to victory in the British Open Championship on seven occasions: 1941, 1942, 1945, 1947, 1949, 1950 and 1956. This was a band with a pedigree.

Once again, the music was splendid and the audience had a treat. The pieces which particularly stuck out in Justin's mind included *Winter* by Antonio Vivaldi, *Freikugeln Polka* by Johann Strauss and *Ave Maria* by Giacomo Puccini. It was a pity that the concert had to come to an end but an end, it came to and Justin made his way back to Roa with Flugel horns, trombones and euphoniums still ringing in his ears.

The last section that Justin wanted to review in Isherwood's was not really a section at all but it was referred to as the maintenance section. True, it had a room which incorporated a number of special tools, manuals and spares for all the different pieces of equipment used throughout the factory. Two men used this room as their headquarters and there job was to ensure that all the equipment used in Isherwood's was working OK and presented no safety issues.

It was a source of irritating humour to the two men, both brother's, working in maintenance that every time they approached a job they would be greeted by the same words; 'Hello, it's Bill and Ben the maintenance men' but as time had gone by they had learned to accept it. Bill and Ben Stone were brothers and came from Barrow were they still lived with their wives and children. Both had been in engineering for many years but didn't always work for the same company.

Maintenance work often involved shift work. In most large engineering production plants, machinery could only be serviced when production came to a stop and that usually meant evenings, sometimes nights and frequently weekends. This kind of routine played havoc with family life and both brothers had been looking for something more family friendly. It was a great relief to both of them when they heard about the posts going at Isherwood's.

Initial reaction when the brothers came for interview on Roa Island was that it was a bit out of the way but given that both of them had cars they could drive here and if they shared cars they could save money. There was also a bus service that they could use from Barrow if needed. It was the lack of any need to work late or at weekends that swung the deal for them and they gladly accepted the posts.

The two maintenance men had married two sisters which was a bit unusual and there was a rumour that they shared them now and again but it was only a rumour, no-one dared asking them if it was true, they were both big fellows.

The Roa Boat 'Team Five' as Emma was now calling her regular Saturday night drinkers from Isherwood's was down to four, not including Justin of course.

"Where is Lyn tonight?" asked Joanne.

Emma watched the gathering from a distance but for the moment kept quiet.

It was Amy, Lyn's house-mate that responded, "She's gone on a date. It was all last minute."

"Who has she got a date with?" asked Nadine.

Amy blushed and looked away from everyone.

"Don't tell me she's gone out with George again?" asked Sheila.

Amy felt that she ought to face everyone and tell them the answer.

"Yes."

It was as much as she could say.

Sheila now took the floor, "Amy, did you not warn her of the risk she would be taking, going out with George again?"

"Of course but she makes up her own mind about things, doesn't she?"

Emma coughed loudly and everyone turned in the direction of the bar.

"What's Emma waving about in her hands?" asked Nadine.

On closer inspection, it was a pair of ladies frilly knickers.

"I warned you girls!"

Justin had sat through this conversation and listened intently thinking to himself that girls were just as bad as boys when it came to matters of sex but it was so enjoyable, not the real thing but still enjoyable.

"That girl needs to be careful," remarked Joanne and it brought that bit of the evenings conversation to an end.

Sheila turned to Justin and asked him if he enjoyed the concert at the Roxy and he confirmed that he had. There was something a little unsettling about the way Sheila progressively moved nearer to him and looked at him but he wasn't stopping it either.

The thought crossed his mind that if he wasn't going to see Jean again then he could try dating Sheila. Justin was annoyed with himself that he should be thinking this way. It was the comment made by Mrs Isherwood last week that had got his mind in a muddle. He really needed to get Jean out of his mind for good, or should he?

Sunday morning looked rather nice thought Justin as he looked out of his front room window. Unlike the Sunday before the view was excellent and he could make out Blackpool Tower in the distance. Whilst the view from his front room window was picturesque, in all kinds of weather, Justin didn't spend much of his time in here. The room was furnished with a settee and two easy chairs plus a coffee table. He also had a radiogram which he rarely listened to but he didn't know why.

Book shelves adorned two walls along with a built in writing desk for which there was a suitable chair. The room was really for entertaining visitors but few had ever been here since Justin had moved in. The back room of the house was the one that Justin tended to live in and that's why it was called the living room.

At one end of the living room, there was a coal fire and a television to the left hand side of it.

To the left of the TV set was a door that led to a built on kitchen. At the opposite end of the room was a sideboard in front of which was a dining table and four chairs. Two easy chairs faced the coal fire and tv and it was here that Justin would relax. Rather than use his front room writing desk, he would write either on his lap whilst sitting in front of the fire in one of his easy chairs or he sat at the dining table and wrote.

Justin was well into the habit now of gravitating to his plot on Sundays to look over his gardening handy work which he had confined to growing vegetables. He wasn't sure what his parents would have made of him working on a plot, they never had one, or a garden, just a few flower pots on window-sills. The rows of seedlings he had planted looked quite good. Row after row of different green shoots was something to marvel at.

Blokes from back to back terraced houses like the one he used to live in in Bolton didn't get to see this kind of thing very often and it gave Justin a feeling of satisfaction. Doing his rounds of the rows he spotted a couple of Caterpillars and decided that some remedial action was needed before they devoured his cherished shoots and from his shed he took some Derris Dust to sprinkle on each row.

Derris Dust is an organic insecticide derived from the South American Barbasco plant. It controls most chewing and sucking insects, including white Butterfly and Diamond Caterpillars on vegetables and flowers. It didn't take long to sprinkle the dust and he was just about to go back indoors when his next door neighbour shouted across.

"Morning Justin."

"Good morning, Arthur."

Nothing else was said and both men just carried on with whatever they were doing which in Justin's case was going back indoors.

It was Wednesday evening and Justin was sat in his favourite living room chair making notes for his upcoming progress report for the Managing Director in relation to preparations for the new circuit board production section. A knock on his back door broke his concentration but when he saw who was standing at the door he rapidly forgot about what he had been doing. Sheila looked alluring in her loosely fitting cotton dress and she was immediately asked in.

"What brings you here, Sheila?"

Sheila was tempted to come straight out with it and say 'you', you dope, but she refrained from doing so and in a refined manner told Justin, "My house companion, Nadine, has gone on a date and I just wanted to chat to somebody. I hope you don't mind?"

"Not at all, come in. I'll put the kettle on."

The two of them sat on the living room easy chairs in front of the fire. The heat from the fire was welcome since there was a chill on this late April evening. They talked about a few mundane things such as work and life on Roa Island and whilst doing so Justin couldn't help looking at Sheila and the way she was sat on her chair. She had sat crossed legged revealing much of her shapely legs and the fact that Justin was looking over her did not escape her notice and she rather enjoyed it.

Viewing female flesh close up could spark feelings, usually lust, in any man and Justin was no different than any other. Before being driven to make a lustful move, Justin refrained from doing so and he was motivated by something that had been said to him some time back and it ran like this—*Lust at your Peril—Love first, Sex lasts—Sex first, Love loses.* He couldn't remember who had said this to him and for reasons he couldn't fathom, he ascribed to the view and now here he was thinking about putting the idea into his pending tray.

Sheila broke the short silence that had stepped in as Justin was admiring her.

"What are you going to do about Jean?" she asked.

That was the last thing Justin had thought that Sheila would wish to talk about. She must be completely aware of the way he was desiring what he was looking at and he stammered as he tried to reply.

"I saw the way you both looked at each other at the last dance in Rampside. You know, there is another one coming up this Saturday. One of you needs to break the ice."

'This is so confusing,' Justin thought. He was sure that Sheila had a thing for him so why would she be encouraging him to try and get back with Jean. He was beginning to think that he would never understand women.

"I must be truthful, Sheila. I had been planning to ask her for a dance if I got the chance come this Saturday."

"I think you should, Justin. You will never be able to move on until you get her out of your head. There are plenty of girls that would like to have you as a partner," she went on.

And there's one just looking at me thought Justin but it would not be fair to take advantage of her when she is being so upfront and kind with him. He also thought that if things continued as they had done since the New Year then he may very well look elsewhere and that elsewhere might just be right here.

Mr Isherwood looked imposing behind his oak panelled desk. He was a distinguished looking man and well-respected. Politeness and good manners were is hallmark. Today would be an opportunity for him to get an update by his Plant Manager, Justin, on how preparations were coming along.

Apart from the fact that he looked tired it was hard to tell how he was coping with the strain that his son had created and the consequent change that was going to make to his family life. The support of his wife, Annie, was a Godsend but she had been that way all the time he had known her and he loved her for it.

"Come in, Justin. Sit down. How are you coping with everything?"

What does he mean by everything, wondered Justin, was he referring to work or my private life?

William realised that he ought to have clarified his question a little.

"My wife keeps me in the picture about a lot of things and I know you were seeing one of the typists before my son came onto the scene and messed things up. Roa is a fairly isolated spot and living on your own in the house you have on Marine Terrace could be lonely for a young chap like you. I assume that the young lady was brightening your life up and that perhaps you thought the two of you would become permanent?"

Justin couldn't remember his boss being so personal before but he wasn't put off by it.

"Well, Mr Isherwood, I fell for the girl but it wasn't to be. I suppose, in the back of my mind, I had thought about what it would be like if we got married and settled in my house but I never got as far as talking about that with Jean."

"Ah, Jean. Forgive me, I couldn't remember her name for a moment."

Justin continued, "Life goes on and I have found it helpful doing the extra work that you gave me preparing for the new section in the factory. And, I might add, I have been lucky with female friends who have supported me when I have felt down."

"I believe they are called 'Team Five'," butted in William.

'How the hell does the boss know that,' thought Justin who also wondered if his boss thought he was some kind of a womaniser.

"Right, down to business, Justin. Tell me how things are coming along in the factory?"

"As you know, the room in which the new machinery will be installed is quite a large one and it was in a poor state. Working on it part-time means that progress may look slow but I have been concentrating on getting the room ship-shape before preparing to fit any equipment in. At present, I am about half way through the necessary plumbing and decorating and I am on course to complete that by the end of May."

"What about the staff in the existing sections?"

"I have reviewed all the shop floor sections. The Personnel Officer and myself are preparing a training programme to take them all through and a date will be set for us to carry that out."

"Good. Now, I understand we will need some extra employees. Where are we with that?"

"We need three and the posts will be advertised in September."

"Have you spoken to the Company Treasurer about that?"

"No. Not yet. I wanted to be sure that I knew exactly how many extra people we needed first."

"That's fine but when you do know, please, discuss it with him."

"I will, Mr Isherwood."

"Now, I understand that you have mooted the idea of us bringing in contract cleaners. Is that so?"

"Yes, it is. You see, it's essential for the factory to meet the hygiene standards laid down so that the circuit boards can be manufactured to the high standards demanded by the MOD. Doing things as we do now will not be acceptable."

"In that case, raise the point with both the Personnel Officer and Company Treasurer, we will need to pass these costs on."

With that, the meeting was concluded and an agreement was made to look at this again at the end of May.

Driving to Rampside, Justin had the same feeling that he had when he drove to Ulverston on New Year's Eve. He was excited at the prospect of dancing with the girl he had fallen so deeply in love with. No matter what, he couldn't get her out of his head. He was also profoundly aware that she may not be going to the dance or that she may not want to dance with him but for the time being he put that to the back of his mind.

Was he really being wise doing what he was planning to do, he didn't know, but it had to be put to the test. What confidence he had had been instilled in him by a combination of Mrs Isherwood, Sheila and Nellie from next door. Surely they can't all be wrong and that's how he came to be doing what he had planned. *'Damn it,'* he thought, *'I'm only asking someone for a dance when all said and done, but thinking like this did not reduce the enormity of the action.'*

Team Five were in place and Justin took his place amongst them. Most of the conversation that his arrival interrupted involved Lyn and the date she had had with George. Where was George now was the question on everybody's lips.

"He has to work in the pub tonight," replied Lyn.

"What was he like on your last date?"

"Did he try it on?"

These were just part of a collection of questions made by Lyn's friends but they didn't achieve much, she was keeping everything close to her chest.

"How did your date go, Nadine?" asked Joanne.

"Alright, he was a nice chap."

"Will you be seeing him again?"

"I might do, if he asks me."

That was a rather pointed answer thought Sheila and best left, not followed up.

'Anyone listening to this lot would think it was a dating agency,' thought Justin.

Sheila was the first to notice Jean and when she did, she thought about Justin and decided to let him spot her before saying anything to him. Justin had been distracted by the conversations going on around him but feeling his heart bumping, he began scanning the village hall to see if he could pick Jean out. His eyes scrolled past her, stopped and retraced to the table she was sat down at.

No! It couldn't be true. His heart dropped to the floor. She was with another man.

Having descended into a form of depression in full view of his friends who themselves were now temporarily stunned, the band struck up and there was the usual race for a partner. Four of Justin's colleagues were snapped up by a pack of hungry potential male suitor's, leaving Sheila, who made several refusal's to remain back with Justin. They watched together as Jean got up to dance with this new man in her life.

The evening was a real strain and Justin was ashamed for being such a sore loser and spoiling the night for his friends who continued to give him some moral support.

"I know that bloke she's dancing with," remarked Amy who went on, "he's a boring fart that I went out with. He works at the Library in Ulverston. Loads of girls have been out with him."

Whatever kind of bore he was, he was dancing with Jean right now and that was enough for Justin, it just wasn't his night. This was not something he had contemplated and it had unseated both his plan and his thoughts about her. It would be better if he left and he got up to do just that. Sheila pulled his hand and her face told him how she thought.

"Do you want to come back with me, Sheila?"

"We might do something we both regret at a later date if I do, Justin. You go if you must but drive carefully."

With that, Justin left.

Jean saw Justin as he was leaving but he didn't see her. She was suddenly saddened and slightly overcome with a feeling of apprehension which was not helped when she looked in the direction of his friends who looked back at her in a scornful way.

Before the dance ended, Jean and her new partner left separately and it didn't go unnoticed.

Willpower or Passion

The morning after the dance in Rampside did not find Justin in a mood to do anything but he realised that the world was not going to stop for him and unless he was going to make a move, he had better crack on and make the best of it. It took some determination to go to his plot and concentrate on whatever needed doing. He paced up and down the rows of seedlings he had planted and carefully inspected them. The crops were now liable to be attacked by pests.

Onion and carrot flies tend to arrive this month to lay their eggs. From what he had read in his uncle's gardening book if he dusted along the rows with soot and lime, it would keep the flies away. Justin had some lime in his shed but no soot. Arthur, next door, had a coal fire and more than likely would have some. A call over the fence brought Arthur to the shared fence and when asked about soot he sauntered off to his shed and brought a bucketful back.

Justin was then able to dust all of his vegetable rows, plus himself at the same time, before retiring to the handy bench seat on the seaward side of his shed. Shortly after sitting down, he could hear footsteps approaching and as he turned round he was greeted by Nellie and Arthur and Nellie was carrying some drinks and Arthur some cake. The three of them could just squeeze onto the bench seat but none of them seemed to mind.

"There you are Justin a nice cup of tea and some of my home-made cake to brighten your day," said Nellie.

"Thanks, Nellie."

There was a short pause for eating and drinking before Nellie remarked, "I was sorry to hear what happened last night, Justin."

"Nellie, I really don't want to take my mind back to last night. I made a mistake thinking that all might not be lost but I was mistaken and, as I have said several times before, it's time to move on."

"I well, perhaps, you're right pet."

Looking south from the plot, Justin had a grand panoramic view today with Piel Island in the forefront of it.

"Arthur, I have never got round to studying anything about the group of islands that Roa is a part of. Do you know much about them?"?

"I do, lad. Roa is part of the 'Islands of Furness'. Within England, they are the third biggest collection of islands."

"Are they all as small as Roa?"

"No. Walney Island is the eighth biggest in England."

"Are they all lived on?"

"Only four are lived on, Walney Island, Barrow Island, Roa Island and Piel Island."

"How many islands are in the group, Arthur?"

"Seven altogether. Apart from the four, I have told you about there's also Sheep Island, Foulney Island and Chapel Island. There are also two small islets. One is called Dova Haw which is also known as Crab Island and the other is called Headin Haw. Together they are the largest group of islands between Anglesey in Wales and the Firth of Clyde in Scotland."

"Can you get to any of these islands?"

"When the tide is out, it is possible to reach Foulney, Piel and Sheep Islands plus Chapel Island which is nearer to Ulverston but it can be dangerous and anyone wishing to do it should seek advice before setting out."

"That was interesting, Arthur. Thanks for telling me."

"No trouble, lad."

Justin rarely had anything to do with Joshua Turner, Isherwood's Company Secretary who handled all the firm's legal matters which included contracts of employment and it was completely out of the blue to be asked to join him one lunch time in the Roa Boat.

'Come to think of it,' thought Justin, hardly anyone in the firm had much to do with Joshua, Josh to his friends, he was something of a secret 'Legal Beagle'. The two men stepped inside the island pub and were greeted enthusiastically by the landlady.

"Hello, Josh. Your usual is it, and what about you Justin?"

It was pretty obvious that Josh and Emma were acquainted.

"What will you have to eat, Justin?" asked Emma.

Justin looked at the menu and settled for steak pie and chips to go with his pint. He was not a dinner time drinker as a rule but *'what the hell,'* he thought.

The conversation between the two men was constantly interrupted by mouthfuls of pie and chips or beer and chips and it was debatable as to whether it was totally comprehensible but talk and eat, they continued to do. The problem with their conversation was that, in general, it was all to do about nothing, it was just a time filler, but what for?

The lunch time break was being extended well beyond Isherwood's agreed lunch time but when you are sat with the firm's top legal man why bother! Josh was having two drinks to Justin's every one and both men were getting slightly worse for wear and Justin, for once, didn't give a dam and neither did Emma whose till takings were getting higher by every half hour. Josh kept remarking as time went on how much nicer Emma was looking, it never seemed to occur to him that it was the till that was putting a smile on her face.

When there was a slight pause in drinking, the two slightly inebriated men swapped some personal details. Josh, it turned out had had a slight drinking problem since his wife had left him ten years ago. He lived on his own in Barrow but he was working on it. He did not elaborate on this last statement. He had a daughter but she had taken her hook with her mother, was the way Josh put it.

Justin couldn't help feeling sad for this legal man who was obviously lonely, or was he? Justin had been so wrong lately about so many things and if he was not careful, the alcohol he was consuming might just add to that conviction.

"Have you always been a legal man, Josh?"

"I suppose, I have. I spent twenty years in the Royal Air Force, you know. I hardly saw any aircraft. I did my time in the Provost Marshall's Office. Bloody boring job that was but there were some cracking females in there. That was where I met the old bat that married me. Worse thing I ever bloody did."

Clearly the tone of the conversation was lowering and Justin just kept enough self-control to prevent him talking about his latest entanglement or lack of it with the opposite sex.

Emma came over minus more drinks and suggested to Josh that he ought to go and have a lie down.

"Usual bed, is it, Emma?" he asked whilst grabbing one of the cheeks of her backside.

"You're going to give the game away," replied Emma who did not seem displeased and the two of them walked over to the stairwell before disappearing up them.

Justin was left in awe at what had just happened and had to pinch himself to check that he hadn't just dreamt it.

"What are you doing in here at this time?" shouted Sheila as she came bounding through the door.

"Just dreaming, I think."

"Everybody at work have been wondering what happened to you."

"So have I."

"Anyway, let's get you back home. It's gone finishing time."

Sheila got Justin to his shaky feet and with one arm around him, she took him home via Piel Street to the front door of number eleven Marine Terrace, past several twitching curtains on the way. Once the front door key had been retrieved from Justin's pocket, she got him inside and plonked him on the settee.

Her closeness and his drunken state combined to give him some false courage which he used to grab her left breast and kiss her at the same time. Unfortunately his joy was not matched by Sheila's and he was exposed to a side of her that he had never witnessed before. She left without all her dignity intact and he was left with a rather bruised ego plus a black eye which would be an excellent souvenir to take to work tomorrow.

'Work oh work, do I have to go tomorrow?'

They may have been the last thoughts that Justin had this day for he now slunk off into something between a stupor and a sleep which he would be reminded of tomorrow.

She couldn't call in his office at a worst time but she did.

"Good morning, Justin!" proclaimed Mrs Annie Isherwood as she dropped into Justin's office.

"My, what a black eye that is," she exclaimed whilst almost laughing at the same time. She went on, "I see you met Josh yesterday."

A very tired looking Justin Ebberson with a real shiner that had escaped no-one at Isherwood's would rather be on his own right now but he could hardly ask the boss's wife to leave. Before replying, he poured himself some water that Brenda in the canteen had given him along with a couple of Aspirins and took them but there was no instantaneous relief, worse luck!

"A hangover as well!"

"You have caught me at a bad moment, Mrs Isherwood."

"I can see that. Was it all self-inflicted or was the black eye an optional extra?"

"If you must know I got a bit drunk and did something, I should not have done."

"Well, come on, spill the beans! I must confess, I haven't enjoyed myself so much for a long time."

"Sheila got me home from the pub and I got a bit frisky and she rewarded me with this black eye. I don't suppose she will speak to me again."

"I doubt that very much, Justin. Sheila is a very level-headed woman but you could make amends."

"And how do you propose I do that? On second thoughts, don't tell me how to make amends, I was about to follow your advice last Saturday and that didn't get me very far."

"That's not fair, Justin but let me leave that for a moment. You could make amends with Sheila by taking her with you to the next band concert you are going to or the next play at the Roxy."

"I can't think about that at the moment. She might think I'm ready for dating her on a regular basis."

"And are you not?"

"I don't know what I want to do right now. At this moment in time, women are not at the top of my priorities list."

"I can see that you are rather delicate in more ways than one, Justin, but I will say one thing about last Saturday before I move onto something else. I don't think Jean went to the dance with any intention of hurting you. Like you, she thought she had burnt her bridges with you and she had a date because her friends were going somewhere else and she was lonely. She doesn't like living in that flat of hers in Ulverston on her own and as long as Rupert lives in the same town, she feels vulnerable. She realises that it was insensitive to go to the dance in Rampside knowing that you probably would be there. Don't be too hard on the girl or yourself."

"Mrs Isherwood, you are a kind person and I hope you will understand when I tell you that for the foreseeable future, I just want to get on with my work here and make my life as uncomplicated as possible."

Annie understood and arranged for a couple of cups of tea to be brought in before she returned to the conversation she had been having with Justin when she first arrived.

"Josh is something of a character, you know. He has won many legal battles in court but he can't win his battle with alcohol. Since his wife left him, he has never been the same. She was his bedrock."

"Why did she leave him?"

"When he was in the RAF, she was knocking about with an Army Major and when he found out, she did a runner. She left him with an enormous debt that he only recently paid off. I suspect that's what he was celebrating when he asked you to have dinner with him. He has had lady friends but none that stood the test of time or his drinking. I don't suppose his friendship with the landlady at the Roa Boat will last but we shall see."

"How are things going for you, Mrs Isherwood?"

"Rupert has moved into his flat in Ulverston and intends to put his family house on the market at the end of this month. He swears that he will not part with that maroon-coloured Alvis car of his. His wife Nicola will bring the children up north in the July school holidays and take from the house what she regards as hers and they will stay with William and I. The children are very upset about what is happening and that really is sad."

"Has Rupert got another job yet?"

"I don't know about that but I believe he is looking for one. His funds must be getting a bit depleted by now."

Annie got up to go and looked at bleary eyed Justin and she patted him on one of his shoulders and left saying that she hoped that he would recover soon but in the meantime, don't go grabbing ladies breasts without an invitation and she left smiling.

When Justin arrived for his weekly drink with the so-called Team Five, he was clearly embarrassed and his female drinking companions were determined to take advantage of it. He was embarrassed both by the black eye he had, which, fortunately, was beginning to fade and also because he didn't know what kind of reception he would get from Sheila. The nearer he got to where his friends were seated, the more anxious he got and he started to blush.

"Come on, Justin, come and sit down and relax. We're not going to eat you but we might interrogate you," commented Nadine.

Sheila looked at him and could see that he wasn't sure that he should take his usual place next to her.

"Sit down, Justin. I'm not going to bite you or hit you."

Justin was relieved by Sheila's command and took his usual seat. With a bit of luck, he would disappear into the background but for a while that didn't happen and his booze-up with the Company Secretary became the main talking point for some time.

There was also a temptation to establish the more intimate details of his sexual encounter with Sheila but she was having none of it, spoil sport. The conversation did move on but not very far and the landlady Emma became the new focus of attention.

"Emma and Mr Turner, who would have thought it?" remarked Amy.

"I shouldn't think it would be much fun having sex with a drunk," said Lyn and everyone looked at her but no-one would admit to trying it.

As the evening moved on, Justin plucked up the courage to apologise to Sheila and went on to ask her if she would like to come to the next Brass Band concert with him or the next play at the Roxy or both.

"Don't overdo it, Justin. You know, I don't insist on compensation when my breasts are felt, just be gentler." Justin nearly fell off his chair laughing and narrowly avoided getting his other eye blacked.

"I wasn't asking you for that kind of reason, Sheila."

"Perhaps not but I don't want to get a man on the re-bound and anyway, I have a date when the concerts are on but thank you for asking."

Justin didn't know whether he was relieved or disappointed and before he could make his mind up, he had received four requests to accompany him and he blushed once more.

'Sundays seemed to come around more quickly every week,' thought Justin who then realised what a stupid thought to have. Under the circumstances, that couldn't be such a bad thing. There was still a bit of a nip in the air and he put a coat on before heading out to his plot for his weekly spell of agricultural work. Black fly on beans are likely to arrive in May and he knew, again from his uncle's gardening book, that he needed to spray his crop to prevent its appearance.

He used Derris powder in liquid form as an insecticide which was most useful in keeping flies away from his peas and other crops. The job didn't take long but he wasn't too bothered about doing anything today. He had to admit that working on gardens or plots was not something that he was madly interested in.

It was Justin's good fortune when Nellie shouted for him to join her and Arthur for tea and cake and he had no hesitation accepting her offer, Nellie made exceedingly good cake. The three of them sat gazing out toward Piel Island enjoying what they saw in the process.

"Arthur, do you know much about Piel Island?"

"I do indeed. The Duke of Buccleuch gave it to Barrow-in-Furness in 1922 and one of its duties includes selecting the 'King of Piel'."

"A King on that small island! Surely, there can't be many people living on it," replied Justin.

"That's true. The 'King' is the landlord of the island's pub and he and his family are the only permanent residents. There are eight old fishermen's cottages on the island but they are either used by sailors or used as second homes."

"What about the history of the place, Arthur, does it have much of an history?"

"It does so. It goes back a long time. In the 12th century, Cistercian Monks from Furness Abbey used Piel to store grain, wine and wool and in 1327 they started building the castle you can see. When it was built, they reckoned it was the largest of its kind in north-west England. A lot of smuggling went on around here and Piel Island was at the centre of a lot of it."

"I think, I have heard something about that," remarked Justin who was enjoying this history lesson by his next door neighbour.

"There's a story or two to tell about that small island. On June 4th, 1487, a man called Lambert Simnel had been crowned as Edward VI in Ireland and he arrived on Piel Island from Dublin with his supporters. He was accompanied by 2000 German mercenaries and he was intent on gaining the throne of England but on the 16th of June in the same year he was defeated in a battle near Newark-on-Trent."

"He gets all this stuff off his fag cards," remarked Nellie.

"That's not true," said Arthur but it started to rain and they all went indoors avoiding a family war in the process.

Richard Smith was on duty as Security Officer today and Justin took the opportunity of saying hello. There were four Security Officers employed by Isherwood's to cover 24 hours a day, 365 days a year and that was a lot for four to be covering but somehow they did. Richard, like his three other colleagues, lived on Roa. They were all ex-Army guys bar, Albert Clitheroe who was ex-Navy, and all three were keen followers of Barrow-in-Furness Rugby League Club. Because of the shift patterns these three worked there was rarely an opportunity to watch a live match but it didn't seem to dent their enthusiasm.

The four of them shared a radio in their office at the entrance to the factory and not one single rugby match went unheard. The match results were generally the focus of the following weeks conversation and the inquests they held were extremely analytical and biased but it kept them happy. Richard lived at number six Marine Terrace with his wife and young boy but their paths rarely seemed to cross.

"Morning, Richard. How are you today?"

"Fine, Mr Ebberson. How are you?"

"Same, thanks."

The short curt exchange lasted all of a few seconds and Justin left Richard standing at the works gate in his smart uniform to head off to his own office to begin another day's work.

The Security Officers checked everyone in to the factory and out again which was a most important thing to do in case of fire. Outside normal working hours they checked that all doors and windows were closed as well as the factory gates. The Personnel Officer ensured that the security team had a weekly staff rota in order that they knew who would be coming and going each day. They would be notified of any other visitors by members of the senior management team.

A meeting was arranged between the Company Secretary Joshua Turner, the Company Treasurer Ronald Bright and the Plant Inspector Justin Ebberson and it was to be held in the Company Secretary's office. They were also joined by the Personnel Officer Paul Edwards. At the agreed time, the four men assembled together and after polite greetings they got down to business and Justin kicked matters in to play.

"As you all know, I have been tasked with getting the firm set up to produce circuit boards in the New Year that will have components mounted on them and that will involve the addition of a new section on the shop floor to perform the extra task involved. I have concluded that we will need to acquire two extra staff to run this new section. In addition, the finished boards will require a final inspection more rigorous and of greater complexity than we carry out at present and I recommend that we take on an additional inspector."

Ronald turned to Josh and Paul and they conferred with each other for a moment before Ronald announced that they would advertise the new posts in September and interview candidates in early November. The extra salaries plus the cost of setting up the new section had been budgeted for when the firm had submitted to do the work.

Matters now turned to training and Justin suggested that the week before Christmas be given over to training and all current production terminated to allow that to happen.

"Do we need a full week of training to get the shop floor staff ready?" asked Josh.

Paul answered this one, "No, we don't. I will be putting a training programme together with Justin but there are a couple of other things we could fit in during that week."

"What are they?" asked Ronald.

"The boss likes the firm to hold a Christmas party for all its employees and we could hold it during or at the end of the training week," remarked Justin.

This was followed by a vote which unanimously decided that the end of the week would be advisable. The question then arose as to the venue. It could be held in the factory, the Roa Boat or Rampside Village Hall but it didn't take much debate to make a decision and the vote was five for the Roa Boat, Josh casting two.

"Right, now, what's the final bit of business for us to deal with?" asked Paul.

The answer fell to Justin once more.

"It's going to be the last day at work for William and I, for one, think the whole factory should give him a good send off."

"Here, here!"

With all the business concluded, Josh opened his wine and spirit's cupboard and invited everyone to take a glass of port or sherry, and he had port to match the colour of his nose.

Justin met up with Amy in the works canteen and over a cup of tea, they chatted and sorted out the world's problems before turning to more serious issues.

"Have you heard anything about Eileen recently, Amy?"

"I have a cup of coffee with her in Ulverston now and again when I'm doing a bit of shopping. She told me that Mrs Isherwood has a coffee with her in Ulverston occasionally, too."

I wonder if she also has a catch up with Jean now and again. '*She always seems to know a lot about her,*' thought Justin.

"She's soldiering on. She's keeping her job going and the pregnancy is fine. Her and Fred still have a strained relationship and it isn't helped by the fact that Rupert is living closer now that he has moved into his Ulverston flat. They are struggling financially and they may have to sell their house and ask the council to find them something."

"Is Rupert not helping?"

"No, he's not and Fred is getting pretty fired up about it. If something doesn't give, there's going to be trouble, big trouble!"

Amy changed the subject at this point and began talking to Justin on a more delicate matter.

"Justin, I wonder if you would consider taking Lyn with you to your next Brass Band concert?"

"Why are you asking me that?" replied Justin who was slightly worried as to where this was going.

"I don't want to give you the wrong impression, it's not that she fancies you in a serious way or that she especially likes Brass Bands, it's just that we, that is her close friends, are worried that she might be getting too close to that sex maniac George."

That's a bit of a let-down thought Justin but he waited for what might be coming next.

"If you take her out, it will be one Sunday night that she won't be available for George."

"Amy there are 365 days in a year, unless I marry her, there's no chance I could keep her out of George's clutches."

"Will you marry her?"

"Certainly not."

"Look, Justin. If you take her out for a night, she will, at least see what a decent bloke is like and that might influence her bit when George makes his next move."

It was pretty obvious that Lyn had some caring friends and, in the end, he agreed that he would ask her when they all met up next in the Roa Boat.

Team Five met up, as they usually did on a Saturday evening, in the Roa Boat and with a little help from alcohol, conversation flowed back and forth on a multitude of trivial but interesting issues. Amy kept looking at Justin in anticipation of his impending invitation.

Up to this point, Justin had kept himself largely to himself, as he usually did with 'Team Five', a name which seemed to be sticking rather than the old 'harem'. The comfort he enjoyed from being sat with five good-looking girls and a pint to boot vastly exceeded any that he derived from being sat at home in front of a black and white television with a 14" screen.

Justin became aware of a pause in the conversation taking place and he startled everyone by looking straight at Lyn and blurting out that he would like her to come to Ulverston with him tomorrow night to listen to the great Black Dyke Mills Band. The pause in conversation then became more permanent and a great air of expectation swept over everyone.

Lyn looked at Justin and then looked at everyone else almost as if she was looking for advice as to what answer she should give. George didn't seem to be in the picture either physically or metaphorically and this must have influenced Lyn who stood up and shouted 'yes please' and everyone cheered including several other people in the pub who didn't know why but thought it was fun.

Sheila nudged Justin and whispered to him, "I thought you wanted to take me to the concert?"

"You said you had a date and anyway, I thought you were in on the plan for me to take Lyn."

She had to admit that was true but a touch of jealousy may have been at work.

The rest of the drinking session was fairly mundane and when Justin had dealt with the arrangements for the following evening, Lyn kissed him on the cheek and they all left. No-one noticed George behind the bar, drying glasses with a frown.

The crops planted by Justin on his plot should be showing more growth by now, at least that's what he thought. A quick acting fertiliser like 'Nitrate of Soda' should help to bring them on and following the instructions in his gardening book he used a teaspoonful for every yard of row dissolved in water to create a suitable solution. The plan would be to apply this to each row once every two weeks and review the progress it was making as he went along.

Arthur was busy on his own plot but when Nellie made her appearance with a tray of tea and cake he could indulge Justin once more with historical anecdotes about Piel Island.

"Well, Justin, where did I get to, last Sunday?"

"You got as far as 1487."

"Ah, you were listening then, Justin. In 1537, Piel Island and its castle became the property of the King after the dissolution of the Monasteries. The castle was strengthened in time for the Spanish Armada in 1588. The area around here was a Parliamentarian stronghold during the Civil War which ran from 1642 until 1651 and the Parliamentarian fleet retreated here when the Royalists captured Liverpool. Charles II was restored to power in 1662 and Piel Island and its castle was given to the Duke of Albemarle."

Nellie broke up the history lesson telling Arthur that she needed him to help her with something in the house.

Later in the day Justin called at number two Marine Terrace to collect Lyn. She was ready and had been for some time. Justin wasn't late it was Lyn who couldn't wait. She looked very nice in the rose coloured cotton dress she had chosen and the smile on her face lit up when she saw who had arrived.

The two of them walked the short distance to the end of the Terrace where Justin's car was waiting. The drive to Ulverston was very pleasant on this Sunday spring evening and Lyn gave the impression of wanting to know as much as she could about the band she was about to listen to. Justin was only too happy to tell what he knew about the *Black Dyke Mills Band'*.

"The band formed in 1855 in a place called Queensberry in Yorkshire and Mill owner John Foster provided financial help and a room for them to rehearse in."

"So, that's where 'Mills' comes into the band's title."

"Yes, that's right," Justin continued, "Black Dyke Band is famous for all the contest victories it has accumulated including the National Championship and the British Open Championship."

'On arrival in Ulverston, the two of them strolled along to the Roxy, arm-in-arm and it was quite nice,' thought Justin. They took their seats and the concert got underway. Lyn appeared to enjoy the music and that was a relief. Anyone attending the concert with a general disdain for what they were hearing would not have enhanced Justin's enjoyment but with Lyn, the performance had been excellent. One of the real joys, however, was the lovely smile on Lyn's face as she looked at Justin after each piece of music had been played.

The journey back to Roa was no less pleasant than the journey to Ulverston and when they both stood on the doorstep of number two, Lyn thanked Justin for taking her and hoped he might consider taking her to the next one. With the thank youse over, she stood on her toes and kissed him on his lips before rushing indoors.

Sat down in the Personnel Officer's room, Justin had spent the last couple of hours putting a training programme together with Paul Edwards. With the main work out of the way, the two men got chatting and Paul posed a question about the upcoming weeks holiday in July. Isherwood's could not function if staff took their holidays at different times and all had agreed to take time off at the same time. Annual holidays fell during the first week in July and the second week in September.

"Got any plans for July, Justin?"

"Not really. I can't find the motivation to think about holidays and anyway, I was thinking of getting as much money as I can in the bank this year," replied Justin.

Paul who was twice as old as Justin and a lot more experienced about life took a serious look at the young man sat in front of him.

"You know, Justin, you do need to get away from here, not just Isherwood's but Roa as well, now and again. You need time to refresh yourself and come back rejuvenated."

"Maybe you're right but I can't seem to turn my mind to it."

"Look! I tell you what, I have a place on the Isle-of-Man and me and my good lady will be there during the July holidays. We have a little chalet at the bottom of our garden, you could have it for the week. It won't cost you anything. What do you say?"

Paul was pretty well off. His family had left him a lovely house in Barrow and a lot of money when they died and his wife also came from a well to do family and had inherited considerable funds.

"How would I get there?"

Justin realised that having just been offered the free use of a chalet it was rather inappropriate to be asking how he could get there but Paul took it all in his stride.

"You're lucky. On the Monday of that first week, I will be flying over from the Isle-of-Man to Walney Airfield to pick my daughter up. I could pick you up at the same time. I will also be flying her back to Walney the following Sunday, so you could join her on the flight back."

"I didn't know you were a pilot, Paul."

"Like a lot of chaps, I was in the RAF during the war and did a lot of flying then."

"What did you fly?"

"Mostly, Sunderland flying boats. I spent a few years flying from Castle Archdale in Northern Ireland, Pembroke Dock in South Wales and from Wig Bay near Stranraer. When I left the service, I carried on flying as a hobby."

On the spur of the moment, Justin decided to accept the offer and his July holiday was a done deal.

He left Paul's office in good spirits.

Saturday came around and Justin headed into Ulverston in his Ford Popular car. The journey was far less enjoyable than the one he had made almost a week before and he missed having company. He had thought about asking Lyn to come and see tonight's play with him. Sharing the Brass Band concert with her had gone much better than he expected. Nevertheless he was determined not to lead her on. He knew from experience how that could feel and he did not want to inflict that on her.

The Roxy was almost full once again for this last of the season drama. The next would be in October. Tonight's play was called *A Last Tango in Little Grimley* and was hugely funny. The play told the story of the Local Amateur Dramatic Society in Little Grimley which was in financial trouble.

Its membership had dwindled and dramatic action was needed to ensure its long term survival. There was a reluctant acceptance of the fact that these days only sex will sell tickets but how will the locals react to a promise of a sizzling sex comedy? All was revealed, in more ways than one and if the Roxy audience was anything to go by Grimley ADC had a long life to look forward to.

'Although it was the last Sunday in May, there was still a chance that late frosts could occur and it would be prudent,' thought Justin, 'to cover up his potato tubes and other shoots in his plot with soil and he proceeded to do that.' He then turned his attention to his pea seedlings which now looked as if they could do with some support and he provided this by placing some small sticks amongst them. The whole plot looked as if it was coming on just fine.

"Hello, Justin. Nellie has brought the usual, do you want to join us?"

That was convenient thought Justin, his back was beginning to feel sore after all the bending down he had just been doing.

Tea and cake were soon followed by a bit more background to the history of Piel Island and Arthur began by saying, "Piel Island was an important trading post in the 18th century and customs men were stationed there. A lot of smuggling went on at this time. The place became an outstation for the port of Lancaster and a lot of ships called here. The ownership of the island was passed on to the Duke of Buccleuch and the 5th Duke who developed industry around Furness and built the fishermen's cottages in 1875. It was the 7th Duke that donated the island to the people of Barrow-in-Furness."

Nellie butted in at this point to say it was time for Arthur to stop boring Justin and then added a little gem of her own, "I'll tell you something about that island that George doesn't know. Sir George Beaumont did a painting of it in 1805 and I'll tell you something else, that painting inspired William Wordsworth's *Elegiac Stanzas* based on the time he lived in Rampside."

"What is *Elegiac Stanzas?*"

"It's one of Wordsworth's poems and it's about his Piel neighbours that he observed during the four weeks he spent living in Rampside."

Arthur looked on at Nellie in amazement but avoided complimenting her since it might usurp his position as the island historian. He followed her departure from the plot feeling slightly dazed by her oratorical prowess.

Justin was called in to his bosses office to provide him with his monthly update on the progress being made to set up the new section in the factory.

"Sit down, Justin and give me an update."

"The room that's going to accommodate the new machinery is ready now. I have finished all the plumbing work and I have decorated it. It has taken a long time to get the room ready but it was in a sad state."

"That room has not been used since the Army left in 1946 so I'm not surprised," commented William.

Justin invited William to take a walk in the factory and have a look for himself. Once in the room, William could appreciate the work that had gone into it.

"Well done, Justin, this looks fine now. What are you going to do next?"

"The new machinery gets delivered at the end of July so I have two months to decide exactly where everything should go."

"How are you going to do that?"

"First, I will make a scale model of the room which will include the positions of all the power supplies. Then, I will make scale models of all the machinery and furniture that are going in it. Finally, I will experiment with different layouts of the equipment until I hit on the best."

"That sounds interesting but when you have created a finished model of the room, what comes after that?"

"Well, I'll be in a position to mark out the room so that when everything arrives I know exactly where to put it."

"You seem to have everything under control. Is all the equipment we ordered going to arrive on time?"

"At the moment, all the different manufacturers tell me that we will be getting everything on the date we requested it for, so I don't expect any delays."

"Justin, I'm pleased with the progress. Give me another update at the end of June, please."

"That's already in my diary."

"Hello, Justin."

Mrs Isherwood arrived in Justin's office and caught him by surprise.

"Is this a bad time to be calling in to see you?"

"No, not at all. It's always nice to see you."

The two of them sat down and Brenda brought in two cups of tea. Evidently, Annie had planned to see Justin and was going to spend a little time with him.

"I believe you had a partner at the Brass Band concert last Saturday."

'How the devil does she get to know about these things,' thought Justin.

"Yes, I did. It was Lyn."

"Did the two of you enjoy it?"

"Yes we did and before you ask, I am not seriously dating Lyn."

"Oh! What's wrong with the girl then?"

"If you must know, I was asked by her friends to take her out. They wanted to create a blank in George's diary."

"What George?"

"The one from the Roa Boat."

"Oh that one. Anyway, how does he fit in with all this?"

"Lyn's friends are anxious to wean her off George. They don't like him."

"So, they want to wean her onto you."

"Not exactly. I'm just a distraction."

"You hope! You better be careful with that young lass. She's a sweet girl and very trusting and she's already gone through an abusive relationship, it would be a shame for her to have her heart broken again."

"I won't do that Mrs Isherwood, I have too much respect for her to do that."

"I understand you will be going to the Isle-of-Man for a holiday in July?"

There she goes again, is she psychic? wondered Justin.

"I wasn't planning to go anywhere but Paul offered me his chalet for the week and he's going to fly me there and back."

"I'm pleased to hear it. Paul is a very good pilot. He's flown William up and down the country for meetings. He flew a lot during the war. Is his daughter going to be in the Isle-of-Man at the same time?"

"Yes. Paul is picking us both up from Walney Airfield and flying us both back at the end of the week."

"Don't let her spoil your holiday."

"Why are you saying that to me?"

"Unlike her mother and father, she's a stuck up young woman, good-looking but an absolute snob. She's been that way ever since she started at university. Stay out of her way, Justin."

"How are things with your family, Mrs Isherwood?"

"I do wish you would stop calling me Mrs Isherwood, it makes feel so ancient. Rupert is off the firm's payroll now and next week, his house in Newbiggin goes on the market."

"Is there no chance he will get back with his wife?"

"No, not at all. She's made her mind up. Apparently, he's been something of a philanderer for some time and she's not going to put up with it anymore."

"I can't say I blame her. Are you and Mr Isherwood still planning to move?"

"Yes, we are and Nicola keeps sending us property brochures to look at but we haven't made any decisions yet."

"As Rupert got another job yet?"

"I know that he has been looking for something but I don't know where he's got to with that."

For some reason, Annie felt the need to try and maintain a link between Justin and Jean no matter how tenuous that may be.

"I think Jean could do with a holiday. She's down in the dumps at present. She hates living in that flat of hers and she's not that keen on Ulverston. I think it's because Rupert lives in the same town and she's anxious not to bump into him."

"She had a partner at the last dance, what's happened to him?"

"She wanted to go to the dance but none of her friends were available to go with her and she was too shy to go on her own. When that dozy librarian asked her out, she thought he would be a good excuse to take to the dance but it all backfired didn't it? She knows it was a silly idea."

Justin made no comment but it was obvious that Annie's coffee mornings with Jean were keeping the 'pot on the boil' in her eyes.

The village hall monthly dance was graced with a happy throng of locals, young, not so young and old and all got on very well. The music was not that good but it made little difference to those in the mood for dancing and there was no shortage of those. All the 'Team Five' members were in great demand and the table they sat round was more often than not vacated each time the band struck up.

The girls did however ensure that Justin got to dance and he enjoyed it. Lyn was attentive to Justin but she didn't overdo it and her four female friends were most impressed by her mature approach to partnering him, they doubted they could demonstrate the same degree of restraint. Sheila in particular was keeping her eye on the way things were progressing or not.

Alison Pringle, the Band Leader announced at one point that her daughter Patty would be the star player on trumpet for the next piece but the microphone coughed and spluttered as she made the announcement and no-one got to hear her but they all got up to dance when she played and gave a round of applause at the end. Alison was pleased no end by the applause but Patty wasn't to fussed knowing that the applause was somewhat obligatory anyway.

"Do you know that Patty lives with her mother in Rampside?" asked Joanne, for no particular reason.

"Does she! Could her mother not have given her a better name, don't you think? I mean 'Patty Pringle', that's not a name, it's a punishment," said Amy and there was a distinct titter amongst the girls.

It was an enjoyable evening for Justin in spite of the fact that his eyes had drifted more than once in the direction of the place Jean had sat in at the last dance.

A Return to the 'Roa Boat'

Another Sunday and another couple of hours working on the plot, this was getting bloody boring thought Justin. He didn't mind his time at work although on Tuesday and Thursday evenings along with Saturday he was the only person there apart from the security chap on the front gate. Back at home he had four evenings to kill, sometimes only three when there was a play to watch or a Brass Band to listen to at the Roxy. Those evenings were getting incredibly tedious.

There was only so much reading or tv watching or radio listening a chap could put up with and Justin was just reaching his too much point. Finances played a part and he only had a certain amount of money to play about with. He needed a hobby but couldn't decide what he wanted to do. He had a number of chores to perform every day like making meals, washing and drying dishes, making the bed and a bit of tidying up but they didn't take up that much time and they certainly didn't leave him feeling any sense of fulfilment.

He recognised that he needed a holiday for once and he would have to continue his boring routine for a few more weeks yet before he would have one in the Isle-of-Man. In the meantime, he vowed to make some changes. For a start, he could wash and dry his own clothes and do his own ironing and that would save him some money.

Maybe, he could see a bit more of the girls that made up his 'Team Five' and see what they did to fill their time. Justin was at a bit of a loss. The thing was, it hadn't been like this when he was seeing Jean but there was no point dwelling on that. Or was there! Maybe he should give some consideration to getting himself a new female companion. But for now he was going to get some more work done on his plot and off he went.

The important thing to do at this time of the year was to feed his crops regularly along with hoeing. Hoeing keeps down weeds and aerates the soil and this is precisely what Justin spent the next couple of hours doing half hoping at the same time that Arthur would soon appear on the scene and is hopes were soon fulfilled.

"By the heck, Justin, you're looking a bit down."

"I'm ready for a break, Arthur."

"I can see that, lad. Nellie tells me you are off to the Isle-of-Man the first week in July."

"Yep, I am lucky in that respect, it's all happened suddenly but I'm looking forward to it now."

"They have some decent pubs on the island that are worth seeking out and having a drink in. Are you taking anybody with you?"

"No but Paul Edward's daughter, Irene, will be travelling across with me but not as a partner."

"You wouldn't enjoy yourself with her Justin, believe me. She was a lovely young woman until she went to university but now she's grown up into a real snob."

"You're the second person to say that to me. Anyway, talking about pubs, I believe that there is a pub on Piel Island."

Arthur was pleased to have been given an opportunity to demonstrate, once more, his local historical knowledge and lost no time in getting started on his captive audience.

"You're right, there is a public house on the island and it's called 'The Ship Inn'. Its origins are a bit obscure but some think it's 300 years old. The landlord is known as 'The King of Piel'. Local fishermen created a tradition known as the 'Knighthood of Piel'. This is a ceremonial knighting and is carried out by the King of Piel or a fellow knight and anyone who wants to become a knight has to buy a round of drinks for all those present."

"Once someone is knighted, they are given the privilege of demanding food and lodging if they should be shipwrecked on Piel. The first person who can confidently be identified as a landlord of the Ship Inn is James Hool who was listed in the 1841 census as a publican. The longest recorded serving landlords were Thomas and Elizabeth Ashburner who were there between 1894 and 1922."

Right on cue, Nellie appeared on the scene, bearing cake and tea and a cheery smile.

"Is our Arthur boring you again with all his history stuff?"

"Not at all. He's been telling me about the Ship Inn over on Piel Island."

"You two want to get across there on the ferry and have a pint. It's a nice trip."

Paul Edwards was scratching his head as Justin entered his office.

"Hi Justin, just hold on a moment, will you? I'm just trying to put some finishing touches to an advertisement I'm putting together, but do sit down."

Justin sat down and looked around the Personnel Officer's office. Books, books, books, all around the room. Mr Edwards must be a pretty well-read person.

A couple of framed photographs were of particular notice, one was of a Sunderland flying boat and there was a caption below it but it was too far away to read, the other was probably a fairly recent family photograph with Paul, his wife and Irene, their daughter. Justin gave this latter photograph some scrutiny because if that young lady stood at the side of her mother was Irene then certainly she was a stunning looker.

"I'll have to come back to this again later," said Paul as he put down the pad he was holding and turned to face Justin.

"You seem to have a big job on your hands," said Justin.

"I'm trying to create an advert to find a replacement for William. He's going to be a hard act to follow."

"Can I be of any help?"

"Not really, Justin. A place like this requires someone with the knowledge of what we do and how we do it, but not just that. A small family business like this needs someone with good social skills, someone with empathy, someone who is approachable and considerate and that's a tall order."

"William had a lot of contacts, will you expect the same from your candidates?"

"I'm sure we won't find anyone identical to William but there must be others out there who have the experience of doing sub-contract work for the likes of Plessey and Ferranti. It may help also to have a Royal Navy background like William had both from the point of view of knowing what the Navy wanted and also from a contacts perspective. It is a bit of a tall order but we will see."

"Will Isherwood's be able to offer an attractive package?"

"It can't be as good as some of the bigger companies but the salary won't be bad compared to what our competitors can offer and there is a good pension to go with it and holiday periods in line with the general trend."

"Do you think our location will make much difference?"

"That's a good question. I'm not sure. At least, we are only a few miles from Barrow and not that far from Ulverston so any candidates coming from these places can commute daily without any problem. If on the other hand a candidate has to relocate to the area than we can offer a relocation package."

"There's a lot to think about isn't there," remarked Justin.

"Yes there is but we will get there in the end."

"When do you expect to carry out interviews?"

"August hopefully. Sometime next month, I want to be in a position to draw up a shortlist of candidates for interview."

"Do you really expect a lot of applicants? We are a bit isolated here, you know."

"That's so but William knows a lot of places to place adverts that I don't know about and which will appeal to a lot of individuals that know him."

The conversation now turned to photographs.

"Paul, I was looking at that photograph over there of a Sunderland flying boat. I wonder if you can tell me where it was taken?"

"I think it was taken at the RAF Maintenance Base at Wig Bay near Stranraer. Why, do you have an interest in flying boats?"

"Not particularly. When I did my National Service, Sunderlands were still being flown by the RAF."

"What year was that then?"

"1956. They were last flown from RAF Pembroke Dock and withdrawn from service the following year."

"You will have to come round to my place sometime and have a look at my photo album."

That was an invitation that Justin would certainly take up in the near future.

The two men then got on with the development of a staff training programme which was the reason Justin was here in the first place.

The subject of works cleaning staff had to be discussed at some point and Justin got together with the Personnel Officer and the Company Treasurer to thrash out what would be the most practical solution. They looked first at the total number of rooms that needed cleaning at the end of each working day and that amounted to twenty.

They then went on to determine how much time should be allowed for cleaning each room and they concluded that this should be thirty minutes. This meant that there was ten hours of cleaning required in the factory each evening. All agreed that this should be revised with practical experience.

Once the cleaning requirements had been specified, the matter of who should do it came under the microscope. Using a contract cleaning agency seemed initially to be the easiest solution and a list of potential firms in the area was drawn up.

"Would there be any legal considerations we ought to be aware of?" asked Paul Edwards the Personnel Officer.

"That's a good point because we are doing work which is high security," replied Ronald Bright the Company Treasurer.

There was reason to call in the Company Secretary and check this out and Josh came into the meeting at this point to provide a legal answer.

"If you engage a contract cleaning agency, you will have a problem because all the people they send to the factory would have to have security clearance and that may amount to quite a lot of different people and you would be faced with the problem of keeping check and you would be faced with paying for each one to be security cleared," was the advice he offered.

"In that case, it would be easier to employ our own cleaning staff," suggested Justin and his colleagues agreed.

Further debate led to the notion that giving two hours a night to five cleaners would be the best way forward and Paul was left with the job of advertising the roles and arranging interviews and the meeting then came to an end.

Justin strolled into the Roa Boat to join 'Team Five' for their weekly get together and chinwag. He immediately saw Jean sitting just where she had always sat when she had been part of the drinking group. Whether he wanted to or not he was delighted to see her and paused before walking over to join everyone. She looked as beautiful as she always did.

She wore a light blue suit that complimented her slim figure and her light touch of lipstick and make-up made her face sparkle. The shape of her legs had always entranced him. She smiled at him but it wasn't a full blown smile, more of a nervous smile but it was well-received and Justin smiled back, too. None of this escaped the notice of the rest of the group.

Sitting with six young women instead of five was something of a novelty and conversation easily flowed from one to another as the evening progressed. Justin rarely contributed much, it was their presence that made him feel comfortable and in that respect, this evening was no different than any other.

Jean joined in joyously with all the female talk and her animated face lit up a burning fire inside him and he had to force himself not to look at her for too long at a time. God, she had aroused that great desire he had long felt for her.

It was Justin's turn to go to the bar and get some drinks for everyone. Emma had been watching the scene with great interest and when Justin strolled over, she seized the opportunity.

"Are you and Jean back together?"

"No. I didn't know she was coming tonight."

"You're still in love with that girl, aren't you?"

Justin blushed and there was no need for an answer and Jean strolled over to the bar to join them.

Her close proximity altered Justin's composure and he felt himself feeling that his self-control was evaporating as his heartbeat increased.

"Hello, Justin. How are you," she asked?

"I'm OK, thanks. How are you?"

"I'm fine, too."

For some inexplicable reason, neither knew how to take this fumbling conversation any further and that's where it stopped.

Drinks purchased, they both went back to join the others but just before they reached them, Justin managed to force himself to say, "It's lovely to see you here, Jean," and this time, she blushed.

As the evening went on, Justin looked at Jean frequently and although they didn't converse, there was something in the way she looked at him that made him feel that she still had feelings for him. The evening was drawing to a close and Sheila almost kicked Justin's ankles to get his attention.

"What the devil are you playing at, Justin?" she whispered in his direction.

"I'm not playing at anything."

"Then why don't you ask the girl out? She's crazy about you!"

"I can't. She told me she didn't want to be involved with me and I don't want to get that feeling of rejection again. If Jean would like to see me again, she only needs to ask."

"You two are both dumb, you will both end up leaving it too late."

Everyone started to prepare to go home and Justin left with a final look and a final smile at Jean as he did so.

A knock came on Justin's back door before he had set out for his plot. It was Arthur from next door who had come to see if Justin would like to join him on a visit to Piel Island and a pint in *The Ship Inn*. That would be an excellent distraction thought Justin after a night wrestling with the images of Jean in the Roa Boat.

"Thanks Arthur, that's a brilliant idea. What time are you setting out?"

"The first ferry is at 11.00am so I reckon, we should walk to the pier at 10–45am."

"That's fine, Arthur. I'll join you at 10–45am."

The jetty from which the ferry to Piel Island sailed was almost just outside the front door of every house on Marine Terrace and it operated on a seasonal basis for tourists. It was a small boat that sailed when the weather was fair and could accommodate twelve persons.

Arthur and himself stepped aboard the 11:00am boat along with four or five others for the ten minute sail to Piel. The weather was fine and the crossing was smooth. Justin closed his eyes and felt the sea breeze on his face and it induced an image of Jean in his mind. He felt the slight wind in his hair and it could have been her hand rustling through the strands and massaging his scalp.

"Come on, Justin lad. We're here!" shouted Arthur who was shaking him back to life at the same time.

The ferry pulled up alongside the pier on Piel Island that led directly to the Ship Inn and the two men stepped out of the boat and walked ashore. Arthur dictated that they took a look at the castle first and then the fishermen's cottages before heading on to the pub to meet the King of Piel. The weather was being kind to them and the island exploration was enjoyable but a pint and a pie beckoned.

The Ship Inn was quaint inside with lots of models, pictures and general maritime bric a brac. It was certainly special being served by a King ably supported by his Queen alias the Landlord and landlady. The fresh air and exercise had given both men a strong appetite and pie and chips plus a pint went down well.

It was not the only pint that went down well as several more followed and the day began to get hazy but it was an alcohol haze they were both enjoying. A point was reached mid-afternoon when they both had to admit that if they didn't get down to the boat soon they might not get back at all and the King was blamed for getting them into this state of oblivion.

The walk down the jetty was a little perilous and both men had a strong feeling that it wasn't wide enough by a half. They stepped or stumbled into the boat and tried to sit as far away from everyone else as possible to minimise the possibility of giving anyone a dose of alcoholic poisoning. It didn't stop the kids on the ferry commenting on their breath and Arthur and Justin had to stifle a laugh but in Justin's case it made him want to pee and he became worried that if he laughed out loud he would probably piss himself.

'How can a ten minute voyage feel like ten hours,' thought Justin as is bladder made great demands on his will power. The rest of Sunday was something of a blur which under the circumstances was not such a bad thing thought Justin.

On Tuesday evening, Justin was busy at work preparing for the arrival and installation of new machinery in the room he had prepared. All the room dimensions had to be taken and noted on a scale drawing as well as showing accurately where every mains socket and room lights where located. Following this was the complicated process of producing identical drawings in $1/48^{th}$ scale and he would then build a model of the room too that scale out of cardboard.

When all this was done, he would do exactly the same for every piece of machinery and furniture that would be going into the room. It was going to be a long and laborious job but this had to be done so that eventually he could find the best location for everything. At least, he had allowed himself a couple of months to complete it.

It was whilst doing this that Albert Clitheroe, Security Officer dropped by on his rounds, Albert took a keen interest in what went on in the factory and Justin described to him what he was doing. Albert had a fairly lengthy service in the Royal Navy and that's where he had met William Isherwood.

"I served under Captain Isherwood onboard HMS Implacable which was part ot the British Pacific Fleet in 1945 and a fine Captain he was."

"Did you stay on in the Navy after the war Albert?"

"I did and I had some interesting experiences."

"Would you mind telling me about a couple of them?" enquired Justin.

Albert was not the bragging type and rarely talked about his Navy days unless specifically asked but when he was, he was happy to re-iterate exploits in years gone by and sometimes, he forgot to drop anchor.

"I served on the frigate HMS Amethyst and in 1949 during the Chinese Civil War, we got stuck in the Yangtze River for a while and that was pretty scary but we eventually got out but we lost a few of the crew. Then during the Korean War I served aboard the aircraft carrier HMS Ocean patrolling on the west side of

Korea. The US Navy patrolled the east side. Our piston-engined Sea Fury fighters were up against the North Korean MIG 15 jet fighters in those days."

"When was that?" asked Justin.

"The Korean War lasted from 1950 until 1953 but I wasn't there for all that time."

Whilst the conversation with Albert had been fascinating it had to end, Albert was doing his rounds and had to get on with it.

One evening at home, during the week, Justin was reading a copy of the North-Western Evening Mail and scanning the pages for anything that might catch his eye. He spotted an article about the Territorial Army which was trying to recruit volunteers. He read it with great interest.

Maybe, this is something I could consider doing.

Reading on, the article described the level of commitment that the TA were expecting volunteers to accept; two evenings each week, one weekend every month and two weeks annual camp. The first two would not be a problem thought Justin but the annual camp was a bit more contentious, he would have to take that up with Isherwood's. On the training front, all volunteers would be expected to attend a basic training course (square bashing) and a trade training course.

Volunteers would receive the same pay as their regular counterparts and would receive an annual bounty. That sounded pretty good but what would the volunteers be doing? There were vacancies for a number of different trades and managerial roles and there was a good chance that Justin's background and service experience would fit in somewhere. The nearest TA unit was based in Holker Street in Barrow which was not far away.

If he decided to do something like this, he would have to discuss it with the managing director before doing anything else. One good thing about joining the TA would be that he wouldn't need to start washing, drying and ironing his own clothes again and the money he would earn as a volunteer could pay for it to continue to be done in the future. He cut out the article and saved it to be reviewed after his holiday in the Isle-of-Man.

'Saturday night had soon come round again,' thought Justin as he walked to the Roa Boat with a degree of anticipation but he was disappointed when he discovered a certain empty chair. The rest of the girls were present and he joined them for what would turn out to be for him a long night filled with conversation that had for once little interest for him. Eventually, it was his turn to go to the bar and face Emma has he had on numerous occasions before.

"Not here, is she then?" asked Emma.

"I'm afraid not," replied Justin.

"Well, it's your own fault Justin, you should have asked her out last week."

"We didn't really talk."

"And whose fault was that then?"

Justin felt a little stupid and wished Emma would spend more time pulling pints than grilling him but he also realised that in her own way, she was watching out for him.

"Maybe, it was mine, I don't know."

"Next time, if there is a next time, talk to her. That can't do any harm."

And with a promise that he would, he walked back to his friends with a tray of drinks. Sheila gave him a nudge and enquired if he was going to the Brass Band concert at the Roxy tomorrow night.

"Yes, I am and before you ask, it's *Wingate*'s *Band* that's playing."

"Will you be taking Lyn? I know she would love to go. She enjoyed the last concert you know."

"I do know that but I haven't asked her."

"Well, ask her before we all go home."

Justin didn't like being pushed into anything but he also knew that her company had made the last concert enjoyable. What bothered him was that he didn't want to give Lyn the wrong idea. He need not have worried. Lyn sidled over to him later in the evening and came out with the question outright.

"Justin, I know you haven't got over Jean but if you aren't taking her out tomorrow night, I wondered if you would take me? I mean, to the concert at the Roxy. I enjoyed it last month and I know there is nothing between us and never will be. I just want to go and listen to a good band."

Justin looked at Lyn and smiled at her. She really was a nice girl and good company and sitting with her in the Roxy was much better than sitting on your own and so he said he would take her and he got a kiss on the cheek as a thank you, much to everyone's delight but which left Emma wondering what the real score was.

Jean didn't make an appearance and Justin had to admit to himself that it had robbed the evening of something special and personal and how much of that was down to him he just did not know and he was tormented by that thought.

What these crops could do with is feeding thought Justin and from what he had read grass cuttings would be just the thing but where would he get grass cuttings, he didn't have a lawn. The answer was staring him in the face. The land in front of Marine Terrace was a large area of grass with two, not overly large plots on it, and Arthur mowed it quite regularly.

"Arthur, do you keep the grass cuttings after you have mowed around the plots?"

"I do, lad, I do. Do you want some?"

"Yes, if you don't mind."

"Come and help yourself. Take what you need. There's more than enough for two plots."

Grass cuttings are a good mulch for dry soil and Justin set about scattering them onto each row he had sown and especially between his turnips which would greatly benefit from them. When the crops were eventually taken out of each row, the mulch could be mixed in and it would decay and enrich the soil for future growing.

Soon, it was time to go indoors, organise some tea and then get spruced up for the evenings Brass Band concert at the Roxy.

Lyn was ready when Justin called for her at number two and they made the journey to Ulverston to enjoy an evening of music. Lyn was cheerful and threw several smiles at Justin that made the drive most pleasant.

"Are you seeing anything of George these days Lyn?" asked Justin.

He could perhaps have chosen something else to talk about but Justin couldn't think of anything.

"No, I kicked him and his roving hands into the long grass."

"Really!"

"All that George wants is a woman's body. He could charm the knickers off a brass monkey! Well, he's not having mine."

"Lyn, I think you made the right decision."

"I hope you are right because I would like a regular boyfriend. Just listen to me, I'm talking to you just like I would talk to my girlfriends."

"Team Five, you mean."

Lyn laughed at this comment and then remembered she had something she had been meaning to mention to Justin.

"I was in Ulverston last weekend and I saw Rupert in his maroon-coloured car."

"And?"

"He had a young woman with him."

Justin just hoped that the name Jean Baxter was not going to crop up in this conversation.

"I'm not sure but I think it was Mr Edward's daughter."

Justin hadn't seen that one coming but strangely, he was relieved.

"Were you not mistaken?"

"I could be, but I have met her in the past, and I would say that if she hasn't got a double, it must have been her."

Before the conversation got any further, they had arrived in Ulverston and it was time to park the car and head for the Roxy.

The Roxy Cinema come Theatre was once again almost full for tonight's concert being given by a band from the north-west—Wingate's Band and Lyn wanted to know as much about it as Justin could tell her and hence he went on to tell the band's story.

"Wingate's Band was formed in a place called Wingate's which is near Westhoughton. The band formed in 1873. Originally, it was known as Wingate's Temperance Band because of its Methodist connection and it regarded the prestigious Victoria Hall in Bolton as its traditional spiritual home. The band has performed every year since its formation including through two world wars. The band had a major setback in 1910 when there was a major explosion in a local pit called the Pretoria Pit. It was a disaster of major proportions in which some 344 miners were killed including some who were players in Wingate's band."

"That was a sad day," commented Lyn.

"That's so but over the years since its formation, the band had lots of successes, one of its most highly acclaimed being the so-called 'double, double'. This refers to the band winning both the British National Championship and the Open Championship two years on the trot in 1906 and 1907 under the baton of William Rimmer. They were third in the North-West Area Championship earlier this year."

Before Justin could go on any further, the band walked onto the stage and was greeted with the traditional round of clapping before being seated and striking up the first piece of music.

The evenings music was a journey through time and each decade of the band's existence was represented by a piece of music from that period. Lyn particularly enjoyed William Rimmers *The Australasian* from 1915, John Irelands *Elegy From a Downland Suite* from 1932 and the *William Tell Overture* by Rossini, arranged by Grant in 1958.

It didn't seem like five minutes since the concert had started and now it was coming to an end and the band under its Conductor, Hugh Parry, were taking their final bow in front of a very appreciative audience.

The journey back to Roa passed fairly quickly as the two occupants conversed about the evening's entertainment and soon they were on the causeway that joins Rampside to Roa and in a way it was all concluding too fast. Once they had got out of the car, Justin walked the short distance to number two and wished Lyn goodnight but before she disappeared indoors, she flung her arms around him and kissed him. Once recovered, he strolled on to number eleven in a rather good mood.

Mrs Isherwood, Annie, as she preferred to be addressed by Justin, had developed, a habit of calling in to his office, generally on Wednesday afternoons at about 3:00pm. She knew that he would be there then catching up on paperwork and she now had an arrangement with the girls in the canteen to bring in some tea or coffee and cake.

A knock on the door announced Mrs Isherwood's entry and Justin looked up from his paperwork. He could have been annoyed by this distraction but he wasn't. He found Mrs Isherwood a relaxing interlude from the routine daily chores of running the factory production line.

There was little new to be reflected on this week the exception being the fact that Rupert had now put his family house on the housing market.

"It's a lovely place in a grand position overlooking Morcambe Bay. He shouldn't have much trouble selling it and he should get a good price for it," commented Annie.

Things then moved on to Paul's daughter, Irene.

"I hope that girl knows what she is doing if she's seeing Rupert. I don't think Paul will be too impressed and you better watch out for yourself when you get to the Isle-of-Man."

Irene seemed to be developing a lot of baggage thought Justin who was somewhat intrigued by all the innuendo being sent her way.

"Before I leave you today, Justin, I just want to say that if you have any desire to embrace that girl of yours, and you know who I mean, don't be seen with other young ladies, it gives the wrong impression."

Justin turned and twisted in his chair before responding.

"This is getting out of proportion. I have taken Lyn to two Brass Band concerts simply because she likes to listen to Brass Bands. There is nothing between us."

"That may be so and I'm not suggesting you shouldn't see other girls but take my advice and be discrete. Remember, what the eye can't see the heart can't grieve over and you know what that's like."

Looking around the table at his drinking friends Justin couldn't help wondering how long his good fortune would continue to last. Team Five, harem, call them what you wish they were five attractive young women with pleasant personalities. How come they haven't got hitched? It was a question he didn't need to answer.

As far as he was concerned, they were nice company to be with once a week in the Roa Boat and he hoped it would go on for some time. But seriously, why were these girls not courting? Certainly, there were no eligible bachelors living on Roa apart from George who had his card marked as far as these girls were concerned. They did tend to go out on Friday nights either together or on a date and for whatever reason Friday nights in this part of the world seemed to be *thee* night!

Sunday nights were popular too but they always decided to keep Saturdays for their weekly committee meetings here in the Roa Boat. Nights out during the rest of the week were almost totally non-existent. True, they did swap notes about potential dates on Saturdays but Justin usually turned himself off to such conversation and drifted into light insomnia until one of them dug him in the chest with an elbow or sometimes in a more heavenly way, with a breast or two.

Talking of breasts or two, Sheila drew his attention in that way before asking him about the concert in the Roxy.

"Did you and Lyn enjoy the concert last night?"

"Yes, we did, thanks."

And then, just like Annie Isherwood had, she questioned the wisdom of being seen with Lyn too often.

"Oh, Sheila don't you harp on about that as well. We have only been to two concerts spread over two months and there aren't any more until September."

"Who else has been harping on about it then?"

"Annie Isherwood."

"She treats you like the son she wishes she had had."

"She's a very nice lady."

One final visit to the bar brought Justin face to face with Emma busy pulling pints as usual.

"Watcha Justin, how's your sex life?"

It was a question that rapidly turned the heads of four of his drinking friends and the other just blushed.

"Emma, you have a real way with words."

"It's not just words, my dear but you're too young for me to go into any detail."

Justin who had just raised his pint to his mouth to take a drink burst into laughter spraying Emma with best bitter in the process. He rapidly made his way back to the laughing troupe in the corner of the room whilst listening to the slanderous comments wafting its way from the bar.

Not been a bad night out, he thought as he ambled back to number eleven.

The first early potatoes were ready and Justin removed them from their rows and placed them on the ground for an hour before putting them in baskets for storage in his shed until they would be required for cooking.

It was quite a decent crop, more than he could personally use. He decided to put some of the baskets near the fence that surrounded his plot and place a notice on the fence letting his neighbours know that they could help themselves to what they wanted.

"Morning, Justin. You've got quite a good crop of spuds there. Well done, lad."

"I'm quite pleased with it especially since it's my first go."

"You'll be off to the Isle-of-Man soon."

"A fortnight tomorrow and it can't come soon enough," replied Justin.

It began to rain and both men headed indoors. There would be no more work on the plots today.

Amy, out of the admin office, was only too happy to share a table with Justin in the works canteen and the tea and toast helped to make it that bit more enjoyable. The canteen was kept spotless by Brenda and Gladys and they put on some cheap but tasty meals at lunchtime.

They could both be feisty and if anyone left any litter about the place, they would be onto them like a ton of bricks. Mid-morning tea break was a chance for a breather and a catch up on what was happening in the world and Amy was something of a reporter on matters close to Roa.

"Eileen's having a tough time at present."

"Why, what's happening?" asked Justin.

"She's having bouts of morning sickness now and she's been late for work a few times and her boss is not too pleased."

"That must be a bit tough for her."

"It is. She can't afford to lose that job. She and Fred are struggling to keep up the payments on their mortgage."

"I assume that Rupert is not helping out?"

"No, he isn't and from what I've been told he's disputing that it's his child."

"How's Fred taking that?"

"Fred's raving mad about it and if it goes on much longer, I think there will be a hell of a bust up between him and Rupert. He thinks Rupert is saying that Eileen goes with lots of other men."

"Could that be true?"

Amy looked very sternly at Justin before telling him, "Eileen isn't like that. She was besotted with that womaniser Rupert Isherwood but it was a one off. She fell for his so-called charms and she wouldn't be the first or the last. Your Jean almost did too but at least she did see-through the scoundrel before it went too far."

That was not something that Justin wanted to hear and tea break began to lose its attraction.

"And I will tell you something else. That bugger has been seen with a young woman half is own age recently."

Justin's ears were pricked.

"You know that Mr Edwards has a daughter, don't you?"

"I do, she's called Irene."

"Well, she's the one and it's like adding salt to the wound for Eileen."

Tea break ended and much to the relief of Justin everyone headed back to their respective work places. Justin wondered what this Irene girl would turn out to be like when he met her in just over a week's time.

"This is going to be the last dance before you fly off to the Isle-of-Man," said Sheila as she appeared to cosy up to Justin.

"I need a break, Sheila. I'm not really bothered where I go, any change of scenery would be welcome."

Sheila sensed an undertone of something more serious and decided to explore his thoughts further.

"What do you think the future holds for you, Justin?"

"I am less sure of the future now than I was six months ago. I'm starting to think that maybe I should move on to somewhere else and start afresh."

Sheila wasn't altogether surprised but she was certainly disappointed to hear this. The fact that Jean wasn't here was tending to put a nail in the Roa coffin as far as Justin was concerned.

"That would be a shame, Justin. All your colleagues would be sorry to lose you and our sessions in the Roa Boat wouldn't be the same either."

"I haven't made my mind up yet. I'm only just beginning to think about it. Perhaps, after a break I might feel differently."

'Well, if he doesn't make a move to get reunited with Jean, I might consider making a serious pull for him myself,' thought Sheila and just then, one of her more regular suitors asked her for a dance.

The evening at Rampside Village Hall was pleasant enough but it was never going to be completely self-fulfilling without a certain somebody being present and as Joanne dragged Justin around the dance floor, she could tell.

"You know the saxophone player in the band, Justin?"

"I don't know him but go on."

"He's called Ivor Ball."

"I know."

"Well, he lives in Rampside and we are going out together."

"I'm really pleased for you, Joanne. Does this mean that we won't see you on Saturday nights in the Roa Boat from now on?"

"No. Ivor plays in a dance band in Barrow on Saturday nights so it's not going to stop me from joining all my friends."

"I'm glad to hear it, I would hate to lose you."

Before the last dance of the evening, Sheila made a point of getting Justin up and she intentionally used her body to make Justin aware that she was very much a female and she succeeded since he had to ask her to wait a little before going back to where they were seated to allow a part of his anatomy to subside.

Justin had thought that he was probably going to leave the dance tonight feeling a little empty but after his exotic experience with Sheila, he was feeling far different, perhaps even randy and he felt that he was wasting an empty seat in his car. Like always, he didn't do anything about it but there would come a time, and he knew it.

Sunday was turning out to be a grand day weather wise and Justin walked to his plot in a good mood. He recalled in his mind the almost erotic dance he had

had with Sheila the night before and his forthcoming holiday in the Isle-of-Man. Things were looking up. The rows of plants needed watering and there was hoeing to do as well and he got on with both under the rays of a powerful sun. The first crop of peas were ready to harvest and the baskets in his shed came in handy again.

He took some into his kitchen and washed them before placing them in a large bowl to dry. Nellie made her Sunday appearance during the course of the day and work stopped to enjoy the tea and cake she had made for Arthur and himself. Justin treasured his neighbours from number twelve. They were good to him and whenever Nellie did some baking she never forgot him. It was good to take a break and enjoy the view on a superb day like this.

Justin began day-dreaming and pictured days in the past when a railway engine of the Furness Railway Company would steam across the causeway from Rampside with half a dozen passenger carrying carriage's bound for the Fleetwood Ferry. He could hear the sound of the engine's whistle just before it entered Roa Railway Station and disembarking all those local folk looking forward to a trip across Morcambe Bay to Fleetwood.

A crowd of people would make their way the short distance from the Station to the Jetty where the steamer awaited them and once aboard it would cast off with a stream of folk lining its side waving and cheering to no-one in particular but it added to the excitement of the day. The steamer would head south past Piel Island and on toward Fleetwood sounding its ships horn as it set out.

Later in the day, the steamer would return but its passengers were short on energy and made their way to the station in a much quieter manner than they had earlier, after a good day out. It was a lovely scene to depict in one's mind's eye and it was perhaps just as well that Nellie had tapped him on the shoulder to ask if he would like more tea otherwise he may start dreaming all over again.

It was time for Justin to provide his Managing Director with an update on how things were moving along getting a new production section set up in the factory.

"How are things progressing, Justin?" asked Mr Isherwood.

"Slowly but surely. I took all the necessary dimensions of the room and created a scale drawing."

Justin gave the drawing to William before proceeding.

"I then had to make identical drawings one forty-eighth the size of the original which I could use to build a cardboard model of the room."

The additional drawings and the model were then presented to the MD for his perusal.

"I then had to do exactly the same with all the machinery and furniture that are going to go in the room and so far I have made models of a half of those."

The models were given to William and he studied them carefully.

"I suppose you are going to complete the rest and, as you told me last time, decide the best place for each one."

"That's right and I intend to have completed that by the end of July."

"Good man, Justin. That should fit in nicely with the delivery of all the new machinery."

And with that, the meeting was terminated until the next one in another month's time.

Annie Isherwood was waiting for Justin in his office complete with canteen coffee and cake when he arrived to do some paperwork.

"Hello Justin, are you ready for your holiday?"

"Yes, I am. Just two more days here in the factory and the shutdown starts."

"Are you going to the Isle-of-Man on Saturday?"

"No. It will be Monday when I go."

"Monday, why Monday?"

"Paul is taking his daughter over on Monday and he wants me to go with her so that he doesn't have to make an additional flight."

"I suppose that's sensible but it means you will lose two days of your holidays."

"True but I'm not bothered about that."

"Did I tell you that William and I think that Rupert has got himself a new job."

"No, you didn't, what's he doing?"

"He hasn't started yet and we aren't sure what he's doing but whatever it is, he starts next week."

The rest of this week's conversation was mundane in comparison to previous weeks and didn't amount to much.

Annie left Justin's office wishing him a good holiday and then as she was about to leave she said, "Nicola and our grandchildren are coming up from Plymouth tomorrow for the summer, do pop in and see them."

"I will, I promise, Mrs Isherwood."

"It's Annie to you and don't forget."

It was strange walking into the Roa Boat and not finding any of his drinking friends present and it was left to Emma behind the bar to offer Justin a greeting.

"I thought all the factory staff were on holiday today?"

"They are, Emma but I'm not going away until Monday."

"You're going to have a quite night then."

"It looks like it, doesn't it!"

"If I were you, I would pick a seat over there," said Emma pointing to where she was talking about.

"There's a rowdy lot from the sailing club coming in later. Anyway, how's your love life coming on?"

'What or who is she talking about?' thought Justin, is it Lyn or Sheila or Jean? In the case, of all of them there is no love life, worse luck.

"I'm not having a love life."

"You could be next week."

"With who?"

"That lass of Paul Edwards. You know who I'm talking about, Irene."

"I have never met her."

A large group of thirsty men from the sailing club then appeared and Emma became fully engaged in pulling pints and her conversation with Justin got no further. Soon after, he drank up and went back to number eleven.

Revealing Truths

Everything was packed and ready for his flight to the Isle-of-Man tomorrow and so there was time to spend an hour or two on the plot. A little hoeing and weeding together with some watering would suffice until his return and Justin engrossed himself in the gardening work. Something like an hour had passed when he spotted two young children looking over his fence, one boy and one girl.

"Hello. Are you looking at anything you like?" enquired Justin.

It was the little girl that answered.

"Are those potatoes that you are growing?"

"Yes, they are. Would you like to see one that as finished growing?"

"Yes, please. My grandad grows potatoes."

Justin lifted up one of his baskets full of potatoes that he had left for his neighbours to help themselves.

"Take one and feel it."

It was then the turn of the little boy to ask something.

"What else are you growing?"

Justin pointed to his broad beans, carrots, radishes, parsnips, peas and turnips.

"That's a lot of different things."

Both children were very inquisitive but where were their parents. No sooner had he asked himself that question when he saw a young lady approaching and he recognised her instantaneously. He was temporarily stumped as to how he should greet her but she beat him to it.

"Hello Justin, how are you?"

"I'm fine Jean and what a nice surprise to see you. Are these two children yours?"

Jean laughed out loud and that was lovely to see. Her face lit up when she laughed.

"No, they are not my children. This young lady is Simone."

Simone chipped in with the information that she was seven years old and of course it was important to get this kind of detail correct especially when you are seven. The boy wasn't going to miss out and volunteered the information that he was five and that was no less important than being seven.

"And this young five year old man is Ian. They are Nicola Isherwood's children."

"Auntie Jean as taken us on that boat to Piel Island," said Simone pointing toward the boat tied up at the nearby jetty.

"And we also went round the castle," volunteered Ian.

"Nicola has come to stay with her parents whilst she sorts out stuff in her house and she asked me if I could have these two for the day and they wanted to see Piel Island, so here we are."

"Auntie Jean, I need a poo," exclaimed Simone.

"Let's go into my house and you can go to the toilet and I can make you some tea," said Justin.

Jean seemed uneasy at this suggestion but she couldn't think of an alternative solution to Simone's impending poo and so she condescended and they all trooped into his house. When inside Justin told Jean to take Simone upstairs to the bathroom whilst he, with the help of Ian would make some tea.

"We can't stay long," remarked Jean before ascending the stairs.

'That's a pity,' thought Justin but he put the kettle on and got some cake from his small pantry.

"Have you got something fizzy to drink, mister?" asked Ian.

"I'll take a look Ian and you can call me Justin."

Everything was placed on the table waiting for the two other's to appear.

"You shouldn't have gone to such trouble," remarked Jean.

"Auntie Jean, there is a photograph of you here."

Justin looked at Jean and for a moment they seemed to be taken back to happier times but neither made any comment and from that moment on there was something of a strained atmosphere between them. With drinks drunk and cake eaten, Jean stood up and announced it was time to go and within minutes they were departing through the front door of number eleven.

"Can we come to visit you again Justin?" asked Ian and Simone chipped in with a 'Yes, please'.

Something was clearly holding back Jean from adding anything and Justin thought it prudent not to make life difficult for her and simply replied, "All of you are welcome to call at my house anytime," and he pointedly looked at Jean at the same time.

"Thanks Justin for being so kind to us."

They were the only words spoken by Jean and the trio of visitors walked away from Marine Terrace to wherever her car was parked.

Monday finally arrived and Justin's holiday could begin. He drove through Barrow to reach Walney Airfield and found a place to park his car. The airfield was used by the RAF during the war but nowadays it was far less busy simply accommodating flights bringing engineers and top men in the ship building industry to Barrow.

On the other side of the airfield hangars, there was a small flying club which had a ramshackle club house. Justin grabbed the small amount of luggage he had brought and headed for it. He thought it was the most likely place to meet Paul. On arrival, a chap behind a scruffy looking bar asked if he could be of help and Justin explained that he was here to be picked up and flown to the Isle-of-Man.

"Ah, yes sir, you will be Paul's other passenger. Do make yourself comfortable, he will be landing any time soon."

Looking around the place Justin saw a stunning looking young woman sat down on the far side of the room and guessed that she was Paul's daughter, Irene. She looked across at him but did not acknowledge his presence. So this was the young woman Rupert Isherwood was knocking off. *'God, she's a lot younger than Rupert,'* he thought.

The barman or office guy, it was hard to tell which he was, announced that Paul was just landing. Soon after this announcement Paul came into the clubroom. He asked for a cup of coffee and shouted hello to his daughter before welcoming Justin to the Walney Aeroclub.

"I suppose you have met my daughter Irene," and he pulled her forward as he said it.

"No, I'm afraid not."

'Par for the course,' whispered Paul to himself. Irene nodded in Justin's direction but didn't utter a word.

"Right! Well I'm going to drink this coffee and you two can go and get in the aircraft. Tommy behind the bar here will give you a hand and the three of them walked out to the Cessna 172 aircraft parked on the apron."

"You two can get in and fasten your seat belts whilst I put your luggage in the back," said Tommy.

The door on the right hand side of the aircraft was open and Irene marched up to it and stopped. She then turned round to look at Justin and told him that he could sit on the back seat. Both passengers got in the aircraft and fastened their seat belts but no words were shared between them. It was something of a relief when Paul climbed into the pilot's seat, checked if everyone was OK and then started the engine. The aircraft taxied out to the end of a westerly heading runway and with clearance from the tower began its take-off.

Once in the air, the aircraft continued on a westerly heading over the Irish Sea and the next 40 minutes passed comfortably watching the Cumberland coastline drift into the background whilst the Manx coastline came ever nearer. Ronaldsway Airport on the southern tip of the Isle-of-Man came into view and Paul made a straight in approach to touch down on the airfields main runway.

Like Walney, this airfield had been used by the military during the war but this airfield had been home to the Royal Navy and was named HMS Urley. The touchdown was smooth and in no time the Cessna 172 had taxied to the east side of the airfield where the local flying club had its facilities. The aircraft was parked and everyone got out. Paul had left one of his cars here and they travelled in it to Peel where Paul had his second home. Justin began to appreciate the degree of wealth his colleague possessed.

The Edwards Peel residence was a fairly large house situated behind the northern end of Marine Parade and as Paul drove up to the front entrance of the house his wife was stood on the front step waiting to greet everyone.

"Hello Justin, welcome to Peel. Paul has told me so much about you; Oh, by the way I'm Evelyn."

She even hugged Justin and he took to her straight away.

"Hi Mum," was all that Evelyn got out of her daughter who ran into the house and straight upstairs.

Paul joined his wife and took Justin through to a large lounge at the rear of the house where, looking out of the window they could point to what they had called a chalet at the bottom of a long garden partly shielded by trees. It looked more like a small cottage than a chalet thought Justin who couldn't wait to take a look inside it. It had been a busy day for Paul and he made himself comfortable in a lounge chair whilst Evelyn escorted Justin to his holiday home.

The cottage was whitewashed on the outside and through the front door he stepped into a beautifully furnished small living room. A small bedroom, bathroom and kitchen made up the rest of the property which had been tastefully furnished throughout. The biggest surprise however came when Evelyn took him into the kitchen. She opened cupboard doors to reveal enough food supplies to keep him going for a week.

"Just help yourself to whatever you need Justin, it's all yours. By the way you won't see much of Paul or myself this evening, we are going to visit some friends but it's not far to the centre of Peel if you fancy a walk and there are some nice pubs in the town." Just as she was about to leave she turned to Justin and told him that he was unlikely to see much of Irene who was going through a phase of impolite indifference so best to ignore her, and then she left him to acclimatise.

After he had had something to eat, Justin strolled down to the Marine Parade and walked along it in the evening sunshine to the town itself and he noted that it had taken him no more than ten minutes.

He spotted a pub called 'The Central Peel' in Castle Street which looked inviting and he decided that this would be his haven for the evening. The pub wasn't full but there were enough people in it to make it feel good at least that was his initial thought until he saw Irene snogging a chap in the far corner of the place whilst surrounded by a group of other young women.

He deftly moved along the bar so that he was less conspicuous. He was not going to move to another pub, the beer tasted good and some of the locals were already saying hello. This, he decided, would be his drinking hole for the week.

"Good morning, Justin. Did you sleep well?"

"Yes I did thank you."

"Where did you get to last night?"

"I found a pub in Castle Street and had a few drinks in there. It was quite nice."

"Did Irene give you a lift?"

"No but I don't mind."

"I don't know what's happening to that daughter of ours."

Justin didn't know how much Irene's mother knew about what she was up to and he decided not to get to involved in any conversation on these lines.

"What are your plans for today then Justin?"

"I thought I would get a bus into Douglas and have a look round."

"I think I put a bus timetable in one of those drawers" remarked Evelyn who opened one and retrieved it. "There you are, that may be helpful."

The journey by bus didn't take long and Justin spent his day in Douglas having a good look round. He started with the railway station and ferry terminal at the south end of Douglas and steadily walked all the way along the promenade to Onchan at the northern end with stops in-between for pie and chips and some ice-cream. The return journey was made by horse tram. Being bang in the middle of the holiday season the place was teeming with good natured holiday makers. The bus back to Peel was something of a relief.

After making himself some tea, he headed back to the pub in Castle Street and got talking with a local chap called Albert. They talked about nothing of any importance but the beer made it sound interesting.

Albert said he was free on Thursday and Friday if he would like a ride somewhere and Justin thanked him saying he would let him know the following night. Irene was in the pub again with her friends but there was no sign of the bloke he had seen her snogging with the night before. Her friends kept looking across at Justin and it appeared that he had their approval whilst Irene was indifferent.

On Wednesday, Justin decided that he would spend the day exploring Peel which had a nice feel to it. The view along Marine Parade was splendid and he walked along the jetty well beyond the RNLI lifeboat station where he called to view the many rescues the local crew had been called out on. Up on the hill behind the lifeboat station were the ruins of Peel Castle and from which Northern Ireland could be seen, particularly the Mountains of Mourne.

Several RAF Canberra aircraft made low flypast's to the west of Peel and they no doubt had been using the air weapons range on the west side of the Isle-of-Man with its headquarters at RAF Jurby Head just up the road. It was good to just laze around and eat and watch the girls go by especially those heading for the beach who in some cases were wearing expensive skimpy beach wear and they looked good in them. And so went Justin's Peel excursion.

The evening was hot and steamy none more so than in the pub on Castle Street. Whirring fans were attempting to cool things down but in reality all they did was to ensure every corner and crevice in the place got an equitable share of the nicotine laden air. Years of wall staining were getting a touch up along with a couple of dozen human lungs but no-one seemed bothered and beer was King even if there was a Queen on the throne. Albert was present and acceded to a request from Justin to take him to St Patrick's Church in Jurby tomorrow but he seriously wondered if the beer had been an influence.

Irene and her friends were busy gassing in their usual place and periodically one of them would perform a recce to check out what members of the male population had wandered into the pub tonight. Some got the thumbs down whilst others were given the opportunity to buy them all a round, something which Albert and Justin avoided demonstrating how experience can be an advantage. Where exactly Irene featured in all this was hard to tell but that was no surprise considering that the mist in here was now like a fog.

Albert rolled up to the front of the Edwards house in a clapped out Jowet Javelin car and at first sight Justin wondered how far it would get them. Nevertheless he got in and off the two of them drove in the direction of Jurby.

"What's so special about this church you want to see?" enquired Albert.

"I want to take a look at RAF Jurby first, if you don't mind."

RAF Jurby, was situated in the north-west area of the island. The airfield had been used by a number of flying training units since 1939 and now it was the home of the Officer Cadet Training Unit which had moved here from Millom in September 1953. The airfield looked devoid of aircraft save for a single Avro Anson and two Chipmunks.

Having taken a quick look at the place Justin asked Albert to drive him to St Patrick's Church which was a short distance to the west of the airfield and virtually on the edge of the Irish Sea. The church is located on slightly raised ground with views across the Irish Sea to both Ireland and Scotland. The present day St Patrick's Church was completed in 1829. There are several Viking carved crosses and gravestones within the church grounds.

What Justin had really come to see were the war graves. There were 43 war graves of servicemen from Britain, Canada, Australia and Poland varying in age from 19 to 53 all of whom had died whilst training at nearby RAF Jurby. They varied in rank from an AC2 to Flt.Lt and a First Officer from the ATA. The first burial dated back to 1940 and the last internments were in 1946.

An additional grave marked the final resting place of RAF Jurby's Station Commander Group Captain Francis Richard Worthington who had been the pilot of an Avro Anson aircraft flying from Millom to Jurby in September 1953. The aircraft had crashed on Snaefell mountain near Laxey killing all four persons on board. Justin dwelt on the fate of all these men and their sacrifice. He was moved by the scene before him and he paid homage in his own way. Albert was a witness to all this and respectfully left Justin to his thoughts favouring a fag behind the church.

It was less sombre in the pub at the end of the day and apart from deciding where he wanted Albert to take him tomorrow there was nothing else for it but to ogle at the girls and drink beer and Albert got through a few fags to add pub flavour to the evening.

The following day Albert's trusty Jowet Javelin chugged along on its journey to Port Erin in the south-west of the island. This small seaside resort had a railway station and folks could travel to Douglas on a single line journey through picturesque country and coastline in small carriages pulled by steam engines.

The whole day was spent walking from one end of the small promenade to the other and back again several times with breaks for pie and chips or ice-cream, at least that's how it seemed. The novelty of walking up and down the promenade wore off and the two men chugged back again to Peel in a car which gave distinct clues as to its general condition, it was definitely in need of some TLC.

The pub in Castle Street really had its attractions for Justin, less so for Albert. When all said and done if you booze in the place 365 nights of the year, there is a tendency to develop an immunity to a place but Justin hadn't reached that point yet. Irene was present this evening and she was wearing a rather daring low cut dress and she stood out amongst her friends and a couple of other places to.

She had ignored Justin for the last five days and no doubt she would continue to do so. She seemed to get irritated when her friends kept drawing her attention to him and they looked as if they were egging her on to go and chat him up but she clearly declined and applied her attributes to other possible unsuspecting conquests but it was enjoyable to watch.

A knock on the cottage door made Justin jump. He had been having a snooze in the living room when the door knocker sounded. It was Evelyn come to check how he was coping and to thank him for the beautiful flowers he had bought for her and Paul.

"We have left you to your own devices all week and wondered how you were?"

"I'm fine, Evelyn. All the food you provided has been more than ample."

"Have you enjoyed your time here?"

"Yes I have. I've seen part of the island and I have enjoyed the evenings in that pub in Castle Street. All in all it's been a relaxing few days."

"I'm glad to hear it. Irene tells me that you have made friends with our local joiner."

"You mean Albert. I didn't know he was a joiner but he has been good company."

"Albert has his own joinery business. What plans have you got for today?"

"I'm just going to have a lazy day today and I'm going to hang around the cottage until this evening and then I'll have a couple of final drinks with Albert before turning in."

"Paul is going to fly Irene and yourself back to Walney tomorrow isn't he?"

"That's right."

Evelyn left Justin to carry on doing nothing but he did make a point of placing some money inside a thank you card which he would leave behind for her as a token of gratitude.

The last night in the pub was just as good as all the others and shock of all shocks Irene wandered over to him.

"We fly back tomorrow," were the first words that she had said to Justin in all the time they had been here.

"Do you know Albert?" was Justin's reply.

"I don't associate with joiners."

Albert coughed in his beer and burst out laughing which did nothing for Irene's superior image and she returned to her group of female fans without saying another word. Shortly afterwards she left the pub.

"Strange girl, that one," remarked Albert and they both drank to it.

Justin made his way back to the Edwards cottage earlier than on previous nights. He had in mind the flight back home tomorrow. As he approached the whitewashed cottage he noticed a light on but he couldn't remember leaving one on before he had gone to the pub.

He went in and shouted, "Anyone here?"

"In here."

The voice came from his bedroom. On opening the door, Irene stood there stark naked. His initial surprise gave way to an admiration of her very female body. Of course, it was the bits you didn't normally see that grabbed his attention; two fabulously shaped tits and a mound of black pubic hair. His second reaction was to look around the room to see who was having his way with this wayward beauty but he espied no-one.

"Come on, fuck me." Irene was very conservative with words when it came to Justin.

Part of him was ready for action which Irene could clearly see but something stopped Justin from leaping into action.

"You ignore me all week, you act as if I am beneath you and now you want to be beneath me. Irene what gives?"

"You know, you want to fuck me, I can tell. Come on, get going."

God, he was sorely tempted. *'To have a good-looking woman throw herself at you like this is any man's dream so why can't I just get on with it,'* thought Justin. For the next few seconds, a myriad of thoughts flashed through his mind, if she's this easy with me who else is she easy with and he could guess the answer to that question. His next thought turned to a friend of his from the days he lived in Bolton. This friend was lured into a similar situation and once he had seduced his taunting partner he was accused of getting her in the family way and he had to marry her whilst she carried someone else's baby.

"Irene, I think you better get dressed and leave."

Irene went into a rage and began shouting at him.

"You are an idiot. I'm the best woman you will ever get an offer from. You stupid man you still fancy your chances with that girl Jean Baxter. You'll never get that girl. As long as Rupert Isherwood wants her, you have no chance. You are too stupid to see that she wants you to think that she is protecting you from him but that's just to put you off the scent. Right now, Rupert is pursuing his goal and it is only a matter of time before he gets her."

"Get out now, get out and stay out," was Justin's response.

He watched as she put her knickers back on and her bra. It was erotic watching her do this but he knew he had made the right decision. Once she had put her dress on, she left and he locked the door behind her.

How much of all that she had said to him was true? He didn't know and he wished he had never heard it. It was going to play on his mind all night.

Evelyn hugged Justin before he got in the car to join Irene and Paul for the drive to Ronaldsway Airport. He liked Evelyn and was a little sorry that he hadn't taken the time to get to know her better. She was a good partner for Paul. No-one spoke on the journey to the airport. On arrival, it was a similar process getting into the Cessna 172 as it had been at Walney. Just as Justin was about to climb aboard the aircraft he was able to take a good look at Irene.

She was swollen around the eyes and looked pale and drawn. It looked as if she had been crying and he wondered if she had had a row with her parents. She looked at him in a meekly fashion and his inert empathy forced him into giving her a slight smile perhaps in forgiveness for rejecting her the night before. Next, Paul clambered aboard and soon the aircraft's engine was spluttering into life.

The take-off was smooth and the flight to Walney lasted about 45 minutes during which time Justin wondered why Irene had behaved the way she had the night before. It certainly wasn't simply lust, it was deeper than that. Had Rupert dumped her and let her know whilst she was in the Isle-of-Man? It could explain things but there was no way he was going to ask her, certainly not now.

The aircraft made a smooth landing at Walney and each of them went their own way. Paul was flying back to collect his wife later in the day before flying to Walney once more in preparation for the start of another working week at Isherwood's. Irene would be going in her car to the family's home in Barrow whilst Justin would be heading for Roa Island.

On his first Monday evening back at home, Justin toyed with two ideas, first and most important, he wanted to call on Jean and try and get to the bottom of the issue with Rupert Isherwood but he would need to find out where she was living. Second, since he had decided that he had too much time on his hands he wanted to cancel the arrangements he had in place for washing his clothes. The latter he could sort out by going around to number three where Marion Quinn and her husband lived.

It was Marion's husband Roger that answered the door and he beckoned Justin in.

"Hello, Justin. Is everything alright?" asked Marion.

"Yes, it is Marion thanks. I'm calling on you to tell you that I want you to stop doing my washing and ironing."

"Oh. Is it not up to standard?" said Marion looking a bit perplexed.

Justin realised that he could have put it a bit more delicately.

"I'm sorry for being so blunt, Marion. I didn't want you to think that you weren't doing a good job for me because you really are. It's not that. I have too much time on my hands and when I have nothing to do it drives me nuts and so I thought that if I did my own it would help keep me occupied."

"I understand pet. Don't you worry about it. I suppose you're thinking too much about that young lass of yours."

Justin blushed and the cat was out of the bag.

"You can't hide anything from Marion," said Roger who had been following the conversation quietly.

"I might ask you to do it all again for me though if you wouldn't mind."

Marion looked at Justin with a puzzled expression on her face.

"I'm thinking of joining the TA and if I do then I won't have any time to do my washing and ironing. Would you consider doing it for me again if I do join?"

"Of course, I will. Don't go bothering yourself."

"The TA in Barrow meet on Tuesday and Thursday nights, don't you work on them nights?" asked Roger.

"You're right. I would have to change my nights at Isherwood's but since I work on my own I can't see that being a problem."

With the arrangements cancelled, it was time to check out the washing machine and dryer and put washing powder on his shopping list. Finally, he rooted out his iron and ironing board and a clothes maiden. He was now ready for some very boring domestic work but if it kept him busy it would have served its purpose.

"How did you enjoy your holiday in the Isle-of-Man?" asked Annie.

These visits by the bosses wife were now a regular feature of Justin's employment at Isherwood's and he was beginning to find them in a way reassuring.

"I found the change enjoyable. The cottage that Paul and his wife Evelyn let me stay in was lovely and they even went to the trouble of providing me with all the food that I needed."

"They are a generous and warm-hearted couple. What about Irene? Did you spend any time with her?"

This was obviously the main thing that Annie was interested in but how much should he tell her and how much does she already know about Irene and Rupert!

"She ignored me all week and then on the final night she came to see me but the exchange of words we had was not pleasant."

Annie could see that she had touched on a delicate issue and carefully navigated a different route to where she wanted to get.

"Rupert started a new job last week."

"Oh! So where is he working now?"

"A friend of his from his Navy day's has given him a job in a tyre distribution centre. It's a bit of a let-down after his job here but at least he now has a wage coming in."

"Is he working locally?"

"That's the bad news. The firm is located close by that pharmaceutical company that Jean works for in Ulverston and it's not far from where she is living. I just hope that he's not going to make her life difficult."

This news got Justin's alarm bells ringing. Maybe there was something in what Irene had told him.

Annie continued, "Rupert has been a big disappointment to William and I. His marriage break-up was bad enough and the damage he has done to the Atherton family makes it even worse. He caused the break-up between you and Jean and now he is seeing Paul's daughter who is so much younger than he is. It really is awful."

A tear came to Annie's eye's and Justin couldn't help but feel for her. Annie was a strong woman and she didn't allow this display of feelings to last for long.

"Both Paul and Evelyn have sat down with William and I to discuss things and we have concluded that there is nothing we can do to stop these goings on. We can only watch and advise but it's impossible not to be judgemental and that gets in the way."

"I'm sorry to add to your torment but Irene told me that Rupert is trying hard to strike up a relationship with Jean again. I got the impression that he has stopped seeing Irene now."

"I am unaware of that but what do you propose doing about it?"

"I must get to see Jean and talk things through but I don't have her address."

Annie got a notebook out of her handbag and read out Jean's address to him—"number six, Kennedy Street, Ulverston and I wouldn't leave it too long, if I were you."

"I saw Jean on the Sunday before I flew to the Isle-of-Man. She had Nicola's children with her."

"Yes they told me about that and they like you. Did she mention anything about Rupert to you?"

"No, she didn't but I felt she was under a bit of strain which may have been holding her back from being herself."

"Go and see her as soon as you can, Justin."

"I will and I did promise Nicola's children that I would come and visit them at your house."

"Anytime Justin, anytime. Just ring first to check that they are in."

Friday night couldn't come soon enough and as soon as he was done at Isherwood's Justin climbed into his car and drove to Ulverston. He wasn't sure exactly what he was going to say to Jean but if she was under threat from lover boy Rupert he was going to do something about it.

It took a little time to get to Ulverston on the coast road from Rampside and normally he would enjoy the view but right now he was oblivious to it. He reached the first important road junction in Ulverston and took a right hand turning, then it was first right onto the road that heads for the big pharmaceutical company Jean worked for and Kennedy Street where she lived. This was the road that led to the Ulverston Canal Lock he remembered.

Justin slowed down so that he could pick out the street he was looking for which should be on his left. Eventually he saw some plots and they backed on to a row of terraced houses. Kennedy Street then hove into view. It turned out to be a street with terraced houses on both sides There were perhaps ten houses on each side and beyond the end of the street was the Ulverston Canal. It didn't look as if there were any flats in this street but he parked up outside the front door of number six. A knock on the door brought a middle aged looking lady to answer it.

"What do you want?"

Not a very cheery beginning thought Justin.

"I'm sorry to trouble you but I'm looking for Jean Baxter."

"You're not the only one. Who are you?"

"My name is Justin Ebberson and I have been told that Jean lives here."

"At least, you're not that horrible bugger as works across the road that keeps mithering her. She told me your name. You best come in."

The lady took Justin into the front room and sat him down.

"Now, what is it that you want from this young lass?"

"Does Jean live here. Have I got the right address?"

"Yes, she does. She rents upstairs but we don't have a separate entrance to it and any visitors have to knock on our front door."

"Is she in?"

"Are you the fella she was courting with last year?"

"Yes, I am."

"She's gone to stay with a friend in Cornwall for a couple of weeks to get away from a bloke that keeps calling on her. She's pretty fed up with it."

"Is that bloke called Rupert Isherwood?"

The lady looked at Justin in surprise.

"You know him then?"

"Yes, I do."

"Well, you want to sort him out. He's getting that girl down and he won't take no for an answer. Do you know my husband as had to get the police in twice just to get rid of him."

"I'm sorry to hear that Mrs…"

"Mrs Jones. I'm Ivy Jones."

"When she comes back, will you tell her I called and I would like to speak to her?"

"I will. Does she know how to reach you?"

"Yes, she does."

With that, Justin left but before heading back to Roa, he made a point of looking for the tyre company Rupert was working for and he found it just down the road and only five-minutes-walk from Kennedy Street.

All the talk in the Roa Boat was about the holidays which in a sense was a relief thought Justin after the last two weeks that he had experienced. It was great to know that all of 'Team Five' had enjoyed themselves. Sheila and Nadine discussed the virtues of Blackpool or at least the men in Blackpool whereas Lyn and Amy claimed that Scarborough was superior both as a place and for male talent.

Joanne was keeping quiet about her experience but the others taunted her wanting to know if her saxophonist friend was a bit of sexophonist but she wasn't being drawn. There did seem to be more than a keen interest in what Justin had done in the Isle-of-Man and his description of the places he had been to and his favourite drinking hole did not satisfy them.

Irene ought to be figuring in this conversation but it wasn't and that was a disappointment to all. Irene's nakedness presented itself in Justin's mind but he had no intentions of sharing that with these five girls and that was a shame since it would have ended up as the highlight of the evening, or would it?

There seemed like a lot of work to do on the plot having been absent from it for two weeks. Hoeing, weeding, watering and putting some mulch down was just the start. It was time to watch out for blight disease on potatoes and to spray them on both sides of their foliage whether it had appeared on them or not. Having completed the spraying Justin washed all the utensils he had used immediately.

"Hello, Justin. Not seen you here for a couple of weeks. I bet there was a bit to do today?"

"Hello, Arthur. Yes, you're right but I'm back on top of things again now."

"Some of your stuff should be ready for taking out next week."

"I think you're right, Arthur."

"Nellie's none too good today. We shan't be having tea and cakes until the old girl is up and running again, I'm afraid."

"It's nothing serious, I hope?"

"No, no. She's got a migraine. She has 'em now and again."

On walkabouts at work, Justin met security man David Smith doing his rounds. The two men had not spoken before and this was an opportunity to exchange pleasantries. David was married and had two children and lives in Barrow. An ex-Army man David was well-suited to his role at Isherwood's. During his Army service, he had served in the Korean War and also in Malaya fighting the Mau Mau.

Isherwood's employed four security men and Justin had always been mystified as to how four men could provide 24 hour coverage 365 days a year for the firm. David was able to describe how the system worked. The four men employed by Isherwood's only covered Monday through to Friday and each day was split into three eight hour shifts with one man on each. Each of the three men did five shifts a week which meant that they worked a forty hour week. The fourth man would have a week off. A four week rotation operated.

"What about weekends and holidays?" asked Justin.

"The company has an agreement with the MOD police in Barrow. They provide cover at weekends and during holiday periods."

"I'm sure I met Albert Clitheroe whilst he was on duty one Saturday."

"You may have. We are offered the opportunity of doing an overtime shift at weekends if we want to."

After a full year working at Isherwood's Justin now knew how the security cover worked.

Wednesday night had been set aside to visit the TA unit in Barrow and Justin made his way there after work. *'He was not sure if this was something he really wanted to do but a preliminary interview couldn't do any harm,'* he thought.

The Royal Corps of Signals, Alpha Squadron Headquarters was based in Holker Street, and Justin presented himself at the reception desk. He had an interview arranged with the 2IC who turned out to be Captain Ernest White who began by describing what the Corps did.

"The Royal Corps of Signals provide the Army wherever they operate in the world the full telecommunications infrastructure. The Corps has its own engineers, logistic experts and systems operators to run radio and area networks in the field."

After a rather drawn out description of what the Corps was involved in doing, the Captain turned to Justin and asked him about his military experience. Two years National Service in the Royal Air Force didn't seem like a lot to talk about but when Justin described what he had ended up doing at RAF Sealand he seemed suitably impressed.

"I understand you were a commissioned officer in the Air Force?"

"Yes I was. I was a Flying Officer."

"In the Army that equates to a Lieutenant. We do have a vacancy for a Lt. In 'B' Troop if you are interested."

"I'm just weighing things up at present," replied Justin.

The interview then moved on to what making a commitment to the TA involved but Justin had already read all about this. Things then moved on to Justin's civil life, in other words, where he lived, his marital status, type of employment and finally, hobbies. The Captain thought that Justin would be an excellent candidate for the TA and moved on to 'what to do next' if he was seriously interested in becoming a part-time soldier.

There was a form to complete which would have to be submitted along with a list of documents which included his birth certificate. If he was accepted, then he would be called forward for a medical and then be sworn in. Once all this had taken place he would have to attend a fortnights basic training course for Royal Signals Corps Officers at Catterick Garrison in Yorkshire.

On his way back to Roa, Justin began thinking about his current employment and the probation period he had agreed to in his contract of employment. The contract would come to an end on September 30th and he would have to sign a new one to continue his employment with the company.

Given everything that had happened in the last six months, he had to ask himself if he wanted to continue living and working on Roa. At the moment, he didn't know and consequently he felt it would be unwise to make any commitment to the TA until he knew what he wanted to do.

Sheila leant over to share a private moment with Justin whilst the rest of Team Five got on with their girly talk, it was a typical Saturday night in the Roa Boat!

"I hear you went to see Jean in Ulverston last week?"

"How the devil do you know that?"

"Justin, I am an old friend of Jean's and I have been to see her in Kennedy Street more than once."

"Oh, I forgot that. Anyway, I didn't see her. Mrs Jones, the landlady told me she had gone to Cornwall for a couple of weeks."

"I suppose, you know that Rupert has been chasing after her again?"

"That's what I had gone to see her about."

"I wouldn't worry too much about that, Justin. Mr Isherwood and Mr Edwards have both confronted Rupert about his inappropriate behaviour and warned him of the consequences of his actions."

"I didn't realise that Mr Edwards was aware of all this."

"Come on Justin, you must know that Rupert has been knocking about with Irene Edwards."

A moment of caution was needed thought Justin before saying anything else.

"You did know, didn't you, Justin?"

"Irene told me when I was in the Isle-of-Man." He left out the bit that Rupert had dumped Irene whilst he made a bid for Jean but Justin needn't have bothered.

"He dumped her for Jean and when she went to Cornwall, he hitched up with Irene again. The man's a total louse."

The conversation that Sheila and Justin were having was being eavesdropped by their fellow drinkers who had decided that what they had overheard was far more interesting than the shoe and bra sizes they had been discussing but were given short shrift when discovered and shoe, and bra sizes came back into vogue.

Although the weather was a little indifferent, it didn't prevent Justin from working on his plot, a pastime which he felt was boring but therapeutic at the same time. There were more potatoes to lift out of some of the rows which he had planted earlier in the year and he dried them before storing them in baskets in his shed. He planted turnips, beet and carrots for winter using rows previously planted with peas. Being a bit more ambitious he planted celery, cabbage, sprouts and broccoli.

"By gum, Justin! Your taking this gardening lark seriously."

"I might as well give it a go, Arthur."

Nellie came out to join them and she brought tea and home-made cake on a tray.

"Nice to see you, Nellie. Are you feeling well?"

"I've seen better days Justin but I'm OK now. You just have to carry on don't you?"

"That's just so but it's good to see you."

"Good to see the tea and cake, more like," interjected Arthur.

The three Roa residents sat and chatted for a good hour and when they had put the world to rights they packed up and went indoors.

"Have there been many applications for the MD position?" enquired Justin as he sat down with Paul in the works canteen.

"We had eight. Six were chaps retiring from the military, one from Vickers in Barrow and one from a bloke in Kendal whose business is about to fold."

"Why would someone unsuccessful in business want to apply for a job here? Are you going to interview him?"

"As a matter of fact we are. There's more to the story than meets the eye. He has his own business, which does similar work to what we do, and he is established in a rented property. He has been given notice to quit it in a matter of months and he has been unable to find anywhere that would be suitable to relocate to and he has decided that it would be best to pack the business in."

"Oh! That puts a different complexion on matters. What about the others?"

"All the military guys have the right background but what concerns me is whether they have the ability to relate to an all civilian workforce."

"What about the chap from Vickers?"

"He looks like a strong candidate for the job and I have decided to interview him."

"Are you going to interview all of the candidates?"

"No. Only four of them. I have already highlighted two of them and as far as the other two are concerned, one will be from the Royal Navy, someone that knows William and the other is someone that I believe you have met, a Captain Ernest White from the Royal Corps of Signals."

"He interviewed me recently for a post in the TA."

"I didn't know that you were thinking about becoming a part-time soldier."

"I have been thinking about it but I haven't made my mind up yet. When are you holding the interviews?"

"The third week in August."

The conversation then moved on to more personal matters.

"Justin, take my advice and keep away from Rupert. If you have a confrontation with him, it may go badly. Believe me I know how you must feel about that young lass you fell for. I'm in a similar position with regards to my daughter Irene. Both William and myself have threatened Rupert that if he carries on as he has done, then we will ensure that his womanising reputation will be spread across all the newspapers in the country. I think you will find that he will amend his behaviour or better still move to another part of the country."

"I will bear in mind what you have said, Paul."

"Good morning, Justin."

"Good morning, Mr Isherwood."

"Now, how are things moving with the new section?"

"Well, you know, that the room we are using to accommodate it is ready and I can now show you exactly where all the new equipment and furniture will go."

Justin placed in front of William the model he had made which had laid out inside it everything that the new section needed. William peered inside the model and asked a number of questions as he pointed to each item included in it.

"You know, presumably, that all the equipment and furniture will be arriving over the next two months."

"Yes I do and the order in which they arrive has been fixed to enable me to install and test everything virtually as it arrives."

"Thank you Justin. It looks as if it is going according to plan."

It was the hottest night of the year and Rampside Village Hall was full of hot and sweaty dancers all attempting to get the best performance out of their partners. The atmosphere may have been sultry and smokey but it wasn't preventing tonight's participants from having a good time. Fresh partners took Team Five's members on to the floor for nearly every dance and for once Justin took to the floor with an unknown girl.

"Justin, you did it!" exclaimed Joanne.

"Girls, we are all going to be redundant if Justin carries on like this."

Everyone seemed to be in good spirits, even Justin and that was in spite of the fact that Jean was not in attendance.

Sheila made a point of dancing several times with Justin and did so in an intimate fashion. When all the other four girls had been enticed onto the dance floor by eager young men, Sheila took advantage by talking to Justin.

"I thought you might be disappointed by Jean not being here."

"I had hoped she would be," he replied.

"She doesn't get back from Cornwall until tonight. She sent me a letter Justin and asked me to tell you that she didn't want you to get involved with this Rupert business."

That felt like another blow. Why was he bothering himself over this girl!

"You're not going to get back with her, Justin. If there was any chance of that, she would have let you know by now."

Sheila was probably right but he wasn't going to say so.

"Why don't you give me a try?" asked Sheila.

"You Sheila, you told me that you already had several men in your life."

"I'm sure I could fit you in somewhere." As she said this she dragged him up to dance and the night continued on in an energetic fashion until throwing out time.

A Month of Routine

Roa Island baked in a weekend of good weather and in spite of a late lie in bed after Saturday night's dance in Rampside Justin was ready for a bit more work on his plot. Has he walked the few steps from his front door he was distracted by a low flying seagull and has he turned his head to follow its flight path his attention was drawn to a huge ship under construction in Barrow shipyard. Ever since he arrived on Roa the ship had been there and it was getting steadily larger. He made a mental note to ask Arthur if he knew anything about it.

The view south from the front of Marine Terrace was splendid. Any heat haze had not yet materialised. In the immediate foreground was Piel Island with its prominent castle perched on top of a hill. Beyond Piel was Walney Island and Fleetwood on the other side of Morcambe Bay and he could just make out Blackpool Tower in the far distance.

Looking to his left, the view was restricted by the lifeboat station and its walkway mounted high above the water level by sturdy steel columns. A ramp allowed the lifeboat to slide down into the estuary when launched and it was spectacular to watch it splash into the water with its crew aboard when called out. The sailing club was busy today judging by the number of yachts bobbing about on the water in the slight breeze that was blowing. All that apart however, it was time to get something done.

The joyous part of gardening today was that it was going to be a day of harvesting. The last of the first crop of potatoes could be lifted out of their rows, dried and stored. Providing his broad beans were not infested with fly he pulled them out of the ground whole and hung them on a makeshift line that he had erected. It passed the time nicely on such a beautiful day.

"Are you ready for a drink, Justin?" asked Nellie over the fence.

"You're just in time, Nellie!" shouted Justin and he joined her and her husband Arthur on the park style wooden seat behind his garden shed.

On a day like today, this was a good sun bathing spot but tea and cake was far more important than turning skin brown thought Justin as he took his first bite into Nellie's home-made cake.

"Did you enjoy the dance last night?" asked Nellie.

"It was packed in the village hall last night and everyone had a great time."

"I think the girls from numbers one and two must have had a good night. They're still in bed yet. Their bedroom curtains are still closed," remarked Nellie.

"They've probably got a man in with them."

"Now, you watch your tongue Arthur. They might hear you."

"Arthur, I was looking at that large ship under construction in Barrow and wondered if you knew anything about it"?

"Oh, that's the SS Oriano. She's due for launching in November. She's the last of the 'Orient Steam Navigation Company's' ocean liners. The company began planning to replace the SS Orontes and RMS Orion in 1954 and decided that one ship would do. They are going to use her on the United Kingdom to Australia route. The vessel was ordered in 1956 and laid down in September 1957. She's going to cost £12.5 million pounds."

"How many passengers and crew will be onboard her when she sails?"

"The crew will be 980 strong and she can take 638 first class and 1,496 tourist class passengers."

"That's impressive, Arthur."

"It certainly is."

Taking a walk outside the factory to get a breath of fresh air Justin bumped into another member of the firms security team Leonard Grogan who was doing his rounds. This was the first time Justin had met him and they paused for a few minutes to introduce themselves. Leonard, like his colleagues Richard and David Smith, was ex-Army, unlike his colleague Albert Clitheroe who was ex-Navy.

Leonard however had never been a regular soldier he had been in the Army whilst doing his National Service. Security was not something he had been involved with in the Army. He had served with the Army Catering Corps and hated every minute of it. His association with security began with the British Railways Police Service which he gained employment with after he had completed his National Service. He worked a shift pattern that didn't fit in very well with married life and that had been his reason for joining Isherwood's.

Leonard had been married to a girl called Jenny whilst he worked on the railways and although he didn't like his shift system she did and so did the various boyfriends that she had acquired when he was not there. Coming home unexpectedly early from a shift had been Jenny's downfall and her two male bed partners had had to leave in a hurry but not before collecting a few bruises on the way out. Jenny's reputation flourished around the pubs in Ulverston, their home town, but the marriage didn't and Leonard was now a divorced man.

Fortunately, no children had been involved. He still lived in Ulverston but not in the house he had shared with Jenny he shared it with the local council. Talking about sex, Leonard could tell a tale or two about what he had witnessed on trains. Locked lavatories had been popular brothels on some lines and on others overhead luggage racks had served sexual purposes but not without a degree of trepidation.

One thing that Leonard liked about his current job was that it allowed him time to socialise and he was now a stalwart member of his local pubs darts team. He got on well with the other three members of Isherwood's security team although he rarely bumped into them all at one go, more usually it was just a handover to one or other of them at the end or a start of a shift.

"Have this cup of tea, Justin and sit down for five minutes," said Annie Isherwood who had already made herself comfortable in Justin's office as she always did when she was visiting her husband William in the factory.

"How are you, Mrs Isherwood?"

"Justin, when are you going to call me Annie?"

"I'm afraid old habits never die."

Annie went on to describe how worried she was getting about William. He shouldn't be spending so much time in the factory as he is and finding a replacement for his son Rupert was a source of anxiety.

"The Personnel Officer Mr Edwards seems to have that in hand. I believe that a short list of applicants will be interviewed later this month."

"Paul is doing a splendid job which is great relief but that's only half of the story. Getting the extra staff for the new production section is also playing on Williams mind."

"Annie, you must try to get your husband to accept that everything is in hand and will be taken care of in good time."

"You called me Annie! Well, that's an unexpected breakthrough and since we are now on the subject of you do you know what you are going to do at the end of September when your probationary period ends?"

"I'm afraid, I don't know at the moment but as soon as I have made a decision I will let the boss know."

"It's another thing that has been worrying William. I suppose that if everything had gone OK with Jean we wouldn't be having this conversation."

Justin didn't respond to this last comment and he changed the subject.

"How are you all coping with having Nicola and the grandchildren with you?"

"We are loving it. It's a pity that Nicola has to spend so much time looking at all her belongings in her house at Newbiggin."

"What is she doing with everything?"

"For the moment, we are storing her stuff in our garage until she finds a place in Plymouth?"

"And what about you and Mr Isherwood, when are you going to move?"

"Certainly not before Christmas. We will have to sell our place in Rampside and find a place down south. There's just so much to do at present."

"I understand. It is all stressful at present but this time next year you will be sorted out."

"None of this would have happened if our stupid son Rupert had kept his dick in his trousers!"

Justin was quite surprised to hear such an expression coming out of the mouth of Annie Isherwood but he realised that being the wife of a senior Royal Navy officer for many years she was a woman of the world.

"At least, he has his flat in Ulverston to live in and a job, and he has the house in Newbiggin up for sale. Hopefully, he is not pursuing Jean or going out with Irene Edwards any more. That just leaves his responsibilities to his child with Eileen Atherton to be sorted out."

"As Rupert accepted that the child is his?"

"Not yet. Justin. I hope you haven't written that girl Jean off yet. I firmly believe that she has and is trying to protect you from my son. I'm sure you two will get together again."

"Annie, it's over six months since I had anything to do with Jean. I do still care for her but I am a man and like any other man I want some female company, perhaps even more than just company."

"I understand that but I would ask you to be patient for a little longer. As you pointed out to me, this time, next year everything will be sorted out."

"It wouldn't be fair of me to promise anything in matters of the heart but I will remember what you have said to me."

"Well, that brings me to the subject of visiting. Nicola's children keep pestering me to ask when you are going to call and see them?"

"Would next Sunday be OK?"

"Splendid and you called me Annie twice today. Things are on the up."

This had been a pretty routine week thought Justin and it was nice to finish it with a routine weekly visit to his routine watering place with his—er well, drinking partners. Team Five were in excellent spirits and there were some nice sun tans on show after an extraordinary week of good weather.

Loose-fitting cotton dresses were the order of the day, Justin excluded, and Team Fives corner of the pub was gaining extra interest amongst the sailing club members that had drifted in to the Roa Boat to swap sea waves for friendly girl waves. Justin was beginning to think that he was in the way and spoiling some potential fun but his team was having none of it, he was to be their source of protection.

Tonight's conversation highlighted the fact that some of these team members were already in the mating game. Joanne was still seeing her sexophonist, as the others would call him, when he wasn't playing saxophone in some dance band. Amy was making inroads with a joiner from Barrow who was having a rest from a heavy petting session. Nadine had gone upmarket and found herself a junior doctor who was on shift in Barrow Infirmary.

And finally, Lyn. To everyone's dismay Lyn was giving George, Emma the Landlady's son another go, but she didn't know where he was tonight. That left Sheila but she wasn't saying anything, she just periodically slipped her arm over Justin's shoulder pressing her left breast in his shoulder at the same time. God this sun has got to me thought Justin as he blissfully drank his beer! If all routine weeks are like this, bring them on, I like routine!

There would be no gardening on this Sunday, Justin was heading to his bosses house in Rampside to visit his two grandchildren, Simone and Ian. Once he was across the causeway he turned right as if he was driving to Rampside village hall and the house he was looking for was directly opposite to it. As he turned into the drive he spotted the house name 'Indomitable'.

That was the name of a Royal Navy aircraft carrier and Justin assumed it was a ship that his boss William had sailed on. Before he could get out of the car, two very happy looking youngsters came bounding down the drive to greet him and their mother was not far behind.

"Hi, Justin. You have come to see us!" shouted seven year old Simone excitedly and Justin knew immediately that his visit was the right thing to do.

"Of course, I have. I had to come. I made you a promise, didn't I?"

Both Simone and her five year old brother gave Justin a big hug which was most pleasing.

"Thank you for calling, Justin. Have you been to my in-laws house before"?

"No, this is the first time."

"In that case, let me show you around."

"Are your in-laws around?"

"No, they have gone to look at something in Barrow but they may be back soon."

The house was quite large. Downstairs featured a huge kitchen, a living room and lounge plus a study whilst upstairs had two bathrooms four bedrooms and a box-room. The whole house was very tastefully decorated throughout and beautifully furnished. A number of nautically related memorabilia could be found almost everywhere which was not surprising given the fact that William Isherwood, had been a Captain in the Navy.

Both of Nicola's children were anxious to drag Justin outside to show him the extensive ground that the property was situated in. The rear of the house faced Morcambe Bay and the back garden extended a considerable distance until it reached the shoreline.

Flower beds, vegetable plots, trees, children's swings, a sand pit and a very large well cut lawn all featured in this idyllic place. *'Annie and William Isherwood clearly had good taste and surely,'* thought Justin, *'it would be a great wrench to leave this place.'*

Justin sat on a garden chair looking out at Morcambe Bay and Simone and Ian gathered around him to talk and they did so with great gusto! They told Justin how much fun it was living in Plymouth with Nana and Grandad Sinclair.

They described how big their bedrooms were and then went on to tell him about their new school and teachers, and of course, their new school friends. Justin gained the impression that these two lovely children were coping with their parents separation pretty well.

"Right, children, now let's give Justin a break. Go and do whatever you were doing before he arrived. Come on, Justin, I will make you a coffee."

"How are you coping, Nicola, with all this upheaval?"

"I don't get the chance to think an awful lot about it really. There seems to be so much to take care of. You know that our house in Newbiggin is up for sale?"

"Yes, I know that."

"Did you ever see the house that Rupert and I and the children lived in?"

"No, I didn't."

"Well, if you take the road from Rampside to Ulverston when you get to Newbiggin there is an 'S' bend in the road and when you get to the second bend our house was immediately on the left."

"Ah! I know the one you are talking about. It's a nice house."

"Yes, it is and I'm sorry to be losing it but I need my share of the money it may bring in so that I can get myself a place in Plymouth."

"So, you definitely don't intend living up here in the north."

"No. My roots are in Plymouth and so are my childhood friends. My parents are being marvellous about everything but I want my own place now and I want to stay in the neighbourhood of my parents and the kids new school. I don't want them to have to change school again. My parents will look after the children whilst I am out at work."

"Have you got a job in Plymouth Nicola?"

"Yes. I don't start until September. That's why I am here now getting all the furniture together that I am taking back with me."

"What kind of work do you do?"

"I'm lucky really. Before I married Rupert in 1950, I was a bank cashier and that same bank has taken me back after all these years."

"What kind of a house will you be looking for?"?

"Something very modest in comparison with our place in Newbiggin. My dad will help me out along with Rupert's parents who have been very generous as well but I must cut my costs accordingly. At least, I might have all the furniture that I might need. Rupert hasn't quibbled about the house contents, he's told me to take whatever I want."

"Are you storing it somewhere?"

"Everything is going into my in-laws garage and when I have got a place that I want I will get it moved to Plymouth."

"Is your dad going to store it for you?"

"Well, I hope that I can find my own place first and move all the stuff straight there. My dad will store it for me if I need him to."

"Are you a Plymouth girl originally?"

"Yes. Both my parents were born and bred in Plymouth. My dad had his own cabinet making business before he retired and my mother was a teacher."

"Are you the only girl?"

"I don't have any brothers but I have a sister called Sally. She's married and has two children and she lives in Taunton where her husband comes from."

Justin paused at this point not wishing to say anything about the relationship between Nicola and Rupert in case he was going to open up a wound but looking at her right now gave him the impression that talking about him might bring her some relief.

"I hope you won't mind me asking but how do you feel about Rupert now?"

"I don't mind you asking and sometimes it helps to talk about it. Rupert has been cheating on me for years and whilst I may have suspected something was going on awhile back I couldn't accept it. I know that I could never live with a man that I couldn't trust and that's the case with Rupert. He has been a louse. I don't want to live close to another woman that has had his child whilst he was married to me and living with me."

"In spite of saying that I feel sorry for the plight that Eileen Atherton and her husband Fred are finding themselves in. What adds to the pain is finding out that his advances on Jean in the admin office, the girl you fell for, had led her to leave the factory to get away from him and then he tries it on with the Personnel Officers daughter, Irene. My father-in-law William is furious about his behaviour especially since his Personnel Officer, Paul, is such a close friend."

"How has Simone and Ian reacted to Dad not being with them?"

"On more than one occasion, they have got into bed with me and cried. The worst question they have asked is why does Daddy not want us anymore?"

Tears appeared in Nicola's eyes and this was the right point at which to change the subject and fate, in a way, stepped in.

A car arriving in the drive announced the arrival of Nicola's parents-in-law. Annie hugged Justin and announced how pleased she was to see him, and his boss, William, gave him a hearty welcome. Justin remained in the 'Indomitable' much longer than he had expected to but the remainder of the time was enjoyed by all and it was clearly an excellent respite from the current family tribulations.

Amy Jones had a habit of revealing snippets of gossip that were very significant and today in the works canteen was no different.

"Justin, have you heard that Rupert Isherwood is seeing Irene Edwards again?"

Justin almost allowed the biscuit he was dipping into his hot tea to melt away leaving him with nothing but a crumb between his fingers to lift to his mouth.

"What!"

"You know Janice Jones in the works office?"

"Not really."

"Well anyway, she lives in 'Dragley Beck' in Ulverston, the same street that Justin lives in in his flat. She tells me that she has seen Irene's car parked next to his, a couple of times this week. She doesn't stay over but she is visiting him."

Justin was careful about what he would say to Amy in case it got any further. If Irene's father, Paul, got wind of this or the boss, William, there would be hell to play. Paul and his wife had been hoping that if they could keep Irene away from Rupert until the end of September when she would return to university in Manchester then the liaison would fizzle out. This information would be most unwelcome.

"This is news to me," replied Justin and the subject was not pursued any further.

A knock on the back door made Justin stop ironing his shirt and he went to see who it was.

"Hi, Sheila, what brings you here on a Wednesday evening?"

"These two bottles of red wine so let me in and grab two glasses."

The ironing was put on hold, the ironing board was put away and two glasses found pronto. You don't keep an offer like this waiting for too long.

"Where's your house-mate, Nadine, tonight?"

"She's gone for a practice wrestling match with a fella."

Sheila was always good company and Justin was pleased to see her.

"Well, how's your love life Justin?"

This seemed to be a pretty standard question put to him these days.

"I don't have one. I keep telling you that."

"A couple of glasses of this and it could all change," said Sheila as she cheekily snuggled up to him. She placed one of her hands on one of his knees which brought a response from Justin.

"Turn it up, Sheila."

She wasn't sure what he meant by that so she turned her hand around leaving her palm facing upwards.

"There, is that what you ordered, sir? I am your obedient servant."

Sheila arched her shoulders back and her breasts became more prominent. Her blouse developed a slight opening between two buttons revealing her white bra underneath. Justin was fully aware of Sheila's sexuality and was enjoying it. Why should he resist, he thought!

I don't have any obligations to anyone and he proceeded to begin unfastening the buttons on Sheila's blouse and she wasn't objecting. When a sufficient number of buttons had been unfastened, he slid his hand under her blouse and wrested it over the top of her right breast. She was a real handful and Justin was warming to the experience. If he got any hotter, he would have to take something off and so would Sheila.

A loud knock on the back door interrupted what was turning out to be an erotic moment and neither Justin nor Sheila were very happy to intoxicating sex being so abruptly interfered with. Justin jumped up and went to the back door to see who had made this inconvenient call whilst Sheila busied herself fastening up the buttons on her blouse.

"Hello Nellie, what do you want?"

"You're not usually so offish," remarked Nellie as she stepped past him holding a large earth-ware bowl filled with a good smelling potato pie.

"Hello, Sheila love. I didn't know you were here. Wine as well eh. Just what you two want with this lovely pie for a bit of supper. Right, I can see I'm in the way, so I'll see myself out," and as she reached the back door she turned to face Sheila and said, "you missed a button" before leaving.

Both Sheila and Justin burst out laughing at each other and decided to exchange sex for wine and hot pot and whilst the rest of the evening was less adventurous they still enjoyed each other's company.

Nadine was missing in the Roa Boat this Saturday and enquiries amongst the drinking group revealed that her junior doctor friend was operating on her tonight which they found amusing and a number of saucy suggestions outlined what the junior doctor may try to cure Nadine of a bad bout of expectations.

Amy was interrogated about her ongoing friendship with a joiner from Barrow but whilst she wasn't to forthcoming she did inform her friends that they were enjoying each other and that prompted a few smart suggestions about the meaning of enjoying each other. Attention then moved on to Lyn which the group were a little concerned about but needn't have been.

"George, that great oaf. I don't want to see him again. You know last week when we were having a drink in here he was out with a till girl from Woolworth's in Ulverston."

"How do you know that, Lyn?"

"She's a friend of mine and she told me he was the randiest big handed bloke she had ever been out with and she should know what she's talking about, she's been out with loads of blokes. She said he had his hands all over her and she kicked him into touch."

Everyone were losing touch at this point about what this had to do with Lyn going out with George again and so they persisted.

"What's this got to do with you going out with George again?"

"Oh. I forgot about that. Well, he tried it on again with both of them big hands of his. He got em up my skirt and I wasn't having it, so I gave him the biggest kick I could and he went home with a bruised crotch."

It was some time before the laughing died down and Lyn continued again.

"Anyway, his mother Emma was telling me that he came home walking bow legged and she had the job of treating him cos he was in such pain. When she had finished, she gave him a small bottle of diluted sulphuric acid and told him to rub it into his balls twice a day."

Talk about hysterical laughter! The Roa Boat echoed with it for several minutes. The remaining two girls, Joanne and Sheila were suspiciously quite along with Justin but Emma behind the bar thought she detected vibes between two in the group.

Justin had not expected to be at Walney Airfield on the third Sunday in August but he was certainly not objecting to the pleasure flight he was about to embark on care of Isherwood's Personnel Officer, Paul Edwards. Before walking out to the Cessna 172 aircraft that they were about to fly in, Justin asked about the airfields history.

"The airfield only reopened this year. It was formerly an RAF Station but they finished here in 1955. Vickers bought it earlier this year."

"What did the RAF do here?" asked Justin.

"They trained air gunners. Number10 Air Gunnery School was here from 1941 until 1946 and then moved to Mona on the Isle-of-Anglesey."

"What kind of aircraft did they fly?"

"Lysander's, Defiant's, Anson's, Wellington's, Hurricane's and Spitfire's. Lots of iconic aircraft. By the way, an RAF Mountain Rescue Unit arrived in 1945 from Cark but I don't know what happened to them."

"What happened after 1946?"

"Well, in 1947, number 188 Gliding School arrived here from Cark to fly cadets from the Air Training Corps and they remained here until 1955 when the airfield closed."

They both got in the Cessna aircraft, Paul taking the left hand seat and Justin the right hand one. To get the engine started Paul primed the engine before pressing the starter button. Once the engine had started and the propeller was turning a number of instruments were looked at to check that everything was OK; oil temperature, oil pressure, fuel tank contents, magneto's functioning.

Satisfied that everything was in order a radio call was made to the tower and the aircraft was taxied to the end of the runway in use. Soon the Cessna was powering down the runway and took off to begin a climb to the height required for the first part of the route.

There were a lot more instruments on the flight deck compared with Justin's car and Paul pointed some of them out to him; airspeed indicator, altimeter and a tachometer which showed how many revs the engine was doing and that was set by the throttle control. That was enough to be going with for it was now time to concentrate on where they were flying to.

Paul had the flight path marked on a chart which was resting on his knee and he had planned a flight that he thought Justin would really enjoy. From Walney, they flew east to pass over Piel and Roa Islands which gave Justin his first view from the air of Marine Terrace, Isherwood's factory and the Roa Boat pub. They then followed the causeway to Rampside and circled over the village hall and Isherwood's family home but there was no-one there to give them a wave.

Next came, Newbiggin and Rupert's place followed by Ulverston. Paul deliberately circled over Ulverston so that Justin could see Johnson's Pharmaceutical Plant where Jean currently worked and nearby Kennedy Street where she lived. He also got to see the Roxy Cinema and Coronation Hall.

Heading east again Paul pointed out a housing estate arranged in a half-moon shape pattern that was named Ravenstown. The place had been built by Vickers to house workers at a proposed new airship station during the First World War. The proposed new site was meant to be built on a site which is now a disused airfield called Cark. Some 250 houses had been built in 1917 but the airship station was never started, They now began circling the old airfield whilst Paul related its past history.

"This was another war time airfield in the south of the Lakes. It only had a short life span being opened in 1941 and closed in 1945. A Staff Pilot Training Unit operated from here with Anson, Martinet, Spitfire and Tiger Moth aircraft. In 1944, gliders belonging to the Lakes Gliding Club were requisitioned and used to form 188 Gliding School and as I told you before they operated from here until 1947 when it moved to Walney."

The history lesson was then put on hold as Paul headed north to reach Lake Windermere. The aircraft throttle was pushed forward to increase the engine revs and the Cessna climbed to a safe height to clear the hills they had to fly over to reach it.

"Right Justin, it's your turn to do the flying, so do everything that I tell you to do."

He started off with the control column which Justin rapidly found out lowered and raised the aircraft nose as he pushed it forward or pulled it towards him. Next he moved the column to the left and the aircraft banked to the left and the opposite occurred when he moved it to the right.

An instrument called an attitude indicator gave an indication of whether the aircraft's nose was above or below the horizontal and whether the wings were level or tilted to the left or right. Finally, Justin was introduced to the rudder pedals which if pressed to the left swung the nose to the left and when pushed to the right swung the nose in that direction.

Lake Windermere came into view and the flying lesson came to a stop whilst Paul flew the aircraft the full length of the lake passing White Cross Bay in the process. The bay was on the east side of the lake, north of Bowness. Between 1942 and 1945 a factory existed here and was operated by Short Bros and they produced some 35 Sunderland flying boats for the RAF.

On reaching the northern end of Lake Windermere, Paul swung the aircraft onto a south-westerly heading to head for Lake Coniston and indicated to Justin how he was using the aircraft compass to get him on a heading that would take him towards Barrow. They flew down the whole length of Coniston and continued on the same heading until Millom could be seen on their right hand side at which point Paul detoured the flight to let Justin see the former RAF airfield located there.

Flying from Millom had started in 1941 and ceased in 1946 It had been the home of number 2 Air Observer School during this time using Botha, Blenheim, Battle and Anson aircraft. The station was reopened in 1953 for a year when it was the home to number one Officer Cadet Training Unit which Justin had previously heard about in the Isle-of-Man where it had relocated on leaving Millom.

The day's flying was all but over and the Cessna headed back the short distance to Walney. Paul demonstrated the use of the aircraft's flaps which allowed the aircraft to fly at a lower speed whilst landing and at the same time prevented it from stalling and head diving into the ground.

Once they had landed, Paul mentioned to Justin that there were only two other instruments in the aircraft that he had not mentioned during the flight, a rate of climb indicator and a turn and slip indicator both of which he would tell him about on another flight. Justin, however, was over the moon by the flight he had just enjoyed. It had not just been a sightseeing flight but also a history lesson in an aeronautical sense and a flying lesson. What more could anyone ask for!

Interviews for a new Managing Director had been held today at Isherwood's and Justin was anxious to learn how things had gone. The interviews had been conducted by the Personnel Officer, Paul Edwards, the Company Secretary, Joshua Turner and the Company Treasurer, Ronald Bright.

William Isherwood, the current Managing Director did not engage in the process at this stage since he was of the opinion that he would not be working on a day to day basis with whoever was selected but he would play an advisory role after the interviews to ensure that the best candidate was chosen.

An opportunity occurred during mid-afternoon tea break for Justin to get some idea as to how things had gone from Ron Bright.

"I'm relieved that the interviews are over," remarked a weary looking Ron.

"Have you chosen anyone for the job," enquired Justin?

"Oh no, not yet. We found out a lot about each candidate but I think we will be mulling over who would be best suited to the job for a few weeks. We don't want to make a bad decision."

"Have you got a favourite?"

"No but I would rule out one of the candidates."

"Are you at liberty to tell me who that was?"

"Yes. It was Captain Ernest White of the Royal Corps of Signals. He was knowledgeable about communication systems but horribly boring. Furthermore, he could work to the book but he wasn't much good when it came to improvisation and he wasn't flexible enough to take on someone else's role when the need arose. He won't get the job."

Justin couldn't help wonder if this would have any impact upon his application to join the TA.

"What about the others?"

"There was a Lieutenant Commander currently serving in the Royal Navy due to be demobbed in March next year. He was a good candidate. Very knowledgeable in our field of work, a good team player, lots of useful contacts and he came across as being very personable. He would fit in with our workforce very well. The obvious drawback is his demob date plus the fact that he currently lives with his wife in Devonport and she doesn't want to come north. He says that he would commute staying in Roa Monday to Friday each week. He knows William from the past."

"That's a pity."

"So it is but we don't want to write him off yet."

"And the other two?"

"Gordon Blears from Barrow was an interesting guy. He currently works for Vickers in Barrow. He was a joiner by trade but seems to be a bit of a rising star in the Vickers organisation. They have him involved in the planning department where he brings together everything and everybody required to develop and produce specialist equipment as the need arises. He has limited experience in the electronics field but his planning skills more than make up for that and he lives in Barrow."

"Is he married?"

"No, he's quite young and I believe he is seeing one of our girls at present."

That must be Amy thought Justin but he kept it to himself.

"Who was the last candidate?"

"That was a chap from Kendal, goes by the name of Andrew Marr and he lives in Kendal. He currently has a business of his own doing similar work to ours but for the railways. The lease on his factory comes to an end at the end of November and he's given up hope of relocating and all the expense that would involve. He seems very sorry for his workforce. We think he would be well liked here and his experience would be valuable. He's married and has two sons both of whom are married and have left home."

"How would he get here?"

"If he got the job, he would try and buy a property closer to Roa but in the meantime he would try and rent a place Monday to Friday."

"Well, at least, things are moving on then. When do you all intend making a decision?"

"In a few weeks' time. We are going to sit down with William and thrash out who we will appoint."

Annie Isherwood didn't seem to be her usual self when she popped in to Justin's office for a friendly chat. Indeed, she wasn't very friendly at all and Justin was left guessing what had gone wrong.

Had she heard about his erotic encounter with Sheila? But if that was the case how did she know? Would Nellie have told her? On Roa nothing could be kept secret, that much was true. On the other hand, it may be something completely different that had affected Annie and maybe she would tell him what it was.

"Rupert has managed to find a buyer for the house in Newbiggin."

'Is this what as upset Annie,' thought Justin.

"It will take a couple of months for everything to go through but at least it may be one hurdle out of the way."

"Has Nicola managed to get everything she wants out of the property?"

"Yes, she has. The house is empty now and she will be going back to Plymouth next week with the grandchildren. I just hope that Rupert gives Nicola her share of the sale money so that she can find herself a home. He is in a position to do that. He owns the flat he is living in in Ulverston, he has his car and he has a job."

"Do you think he will offer any help to Eileen?"

"The mother of his illegitimate child-to-be! I haven't the faintest idea but I think he should."

With that, Annie left Justin's office and he was no wiser as to why she had been so frosty with him.

The full complement of 'Team Five' were not present in the Roa Boat for its weekly catch-up drinking session and this appeared to be the beginning of a new era. Joanne was absent and no-one could say why although it had been noticed that she had been rather secretive recently. Everyone's love affairs were temporarily pushed to the back of tonight's agenda and top of the list, for now, was the flight Justin had with the Personnel Officer Mr Edwards.

Justin would have liked to describe it in great detail but the girls were adamant that he stuck to a brief resume. Questions then turned to the interviews held earlier in the week for a new Managing Director and the name Gordon Blears was mentioned, revealing at the same time, Amy's current male acquaintance.

"You kept that quiet," remarked Lyn.

"Well, if you get the landlady to erect a bulletin board, I'll keep you all updated in future," replied Amy and this brought a few chuckles and the odd titter.

It was surprising how much the girls seemed to know about the four candidates but Justin continued to be discrete and added nothing extra to what they apparently already knew.

Nadine was probed about her junior doctor friend.

"Was he any good on the operating settee?" enquired Amy in an attempt to get her own back.

"I'd say, he was fairly accomplished," she replied and this encouraged a degree of Ooh's and Aah's.

Lyn had nothing to report, sadly, but she promised she would work on it or him.

Justin went to the bar to get a round of drinks and Emma, the landlady, leant over toward him to deliver one of her clandestine bits of gossip.

"George is out with Joanne."

The message was short but perplexing. Not another word was spoken and Justin went back to his drinking partners taking his perplexed face with him which was picked up on instantaneously.

"Well!"

No other prompt was needed.

"Joanne is out with George."

A muted silence descended on the group until someone else could think of an alternative topic of conversation.

Justin turned to Sheila and told her about the frosty reception he had got from Annie when she had come to see him.

"Do you think she knows about you and me?"

"What you and me? We only had a bit of fun. There was nothing in it."

In a way, Justin was disappointed that Sheila had said this but felt she had missed the point.

"Someone seeing us may have got the wrong impression."

"The only person who saw us, and she didn't see anything, was Nellie. You better ask her."

It looked as if Justin had annoyed Sheila which is not what he had intended.

"Your probation period ends at the end of September. Have you decided yet what you are doing?"

This seemed like a pointed question given what had just gone before and Justin answered no.

"Hi, Justin. It seems like some time since I last saw you on your plot. I thought you might have packed it all in," commented Arthur over the dividing fence.

"No, I'm not packing it in, Arthur. I just had some other things to do this last couple of Sundays."

"What are you doing today then?"

"I thought I would clear away all the spent crops and then I'm going to dig the ground over. I'm not going to use it again for a little while."

"Ah well, you're keeping on top of it."

"Arthur, does your Nellie chat at all with Annie Isherwood?"

"Our Nellie chats with anyone she gets the chance to but I wouldn't think Annie Isherwood is a lady she bumps into too often. Why do you ask?"

"No reason really, Arthur."

Justin returned to his work at this point leaving Arthur a little baffled.

Justin gave his monthly report on the preparation of the new production section in the factory and his boss Mr Isherwood sat patiently, listening carefully to what he was being told.

"About a third of the equipment and furniture has now arrived and are in the room that I prepared for them. Everything that needed testing has been tested and I have found everything in working order."

"That's good news, Justin but what about the rest of the equipment that we need, when will it arrive?"

"There has been a delay with some of the equipment but I fully expect that everything will have arrived by the end of October."

"Will that stop us from getting the new products online in January?"

"No, we are still on course for that deadline."

"Good man, Justin. Keep me in touch with any problems that might occur?"

"I will, Mr Isherwood."

Amy seemed eager to give Justin the latest news doing the rounds on the shop floor when she sat down with him in the works canteen.

"Eileen has had to pack her job in."

"Why? As anything happened to her?"

"The birth of her child is only a few weeks away and she's found it difficult carrying this one. She's had terrible morning sickness."

"I'm sorry to hear that but hopefully it will all be over fairly soon for her."

"I don't know about that. She's worried sick about how her family will cope with the loss of her wage. They were only just surviving as it was but now they are going to reach breaking point."

"What do you mean?"

"They can't go on paying their mortgage. The mortgage company will acquire the house and they will have to go to the local council to see if they can house them."

"Have her and her husband Fred got any relatives that could help them?"

"I don't know. I've never heard Eileen mention anyone."

"What about Rupert? Has he come forward with any offer of help? When all said and done, Eileen is carrying his child."

"Fred and Eileen have approached Rupert and asked him to pay towards his child's upbringing but he has not committed himself to doing anything."

"They must be devastated by all this."

"They are and Eileen feels terrible about what she is putting Fred and their children through."

It was a glum tea break and Justin was glad when it was time to get back to work.

The monthly dance at Rampside was losing none of its popularity judging by the number of people present and the mediocre band was having no detrimental impact. All of 'Team Five' were present including Joanne. She was of course the focus of her friends attention at the start of the evening.

"Go on then, tell us how you went on with handyman George," asked Lyn, the last of the girls that any one of them would have thought would ask her.

"He's tame compared with my sexy saxophone player," replied Joanne to everyone's surprise.

"Are you still going out with the saxophone player?"

"Course, I am. Why wouldn't I? He's loveable and he kisses well."

There were a few looks between the girls before anyone responded.

"What about George? Are you going to carry on seeing him?"

"No. He's not up to my standard. Anyway, he's knocking about with a landlady's daughter from up Barrow way."

It was around about this time that Justin saw Jean on the other side of the hall. She was sat with some female companions. Their eyes met and both smiled at each other. Justin's preoccupation with Jean had begun to subside. Time had this impact on people. It was the result of a built in desire to survive but he had been damaged by Jean's rejection and couldn't bring himself to approach her through a combination of fear and pride.

'Team Five' were in great dancing demand throughout the evening but they all found time to share a dance with Justin. It was also evident that Jean was in great demand too but not by Justin.

"What's holding you back, Justin? Go and ask the girl for a dance." It was almost a command that Sheila gave him.

"You two have been gazing at each other for half the night."

No matter what Sheila said to him, he was not going to make the first move, that had to come from Jean, of that there could be no doubt.

Sheila seemed to have a special follower this evening judging by the number of times, he asked her to dance and like everything else, man related, amongst Justin's female friends, they wanted to know who he was and whether she fancied him.

"I can't tell you anything about him. I only met him tonight," was all they could get out of Sheila.

The night was drawing to a close and Justin was questioning himself as to why he shouldn't ask Jean for the last dance of the evening. He had to admit to himself that he was always drawn by her presence. He loved the way she looked and had been heartened by the smiles they had exchanged as the evening had progressed.

He finally plucked up enough courage to go and ask her to dance and as he got up out of his chair, someone beat him to it. For a moment, she looked at him as her partner took her onto the dance floor and she appeared to be full of regret. The evening ended a bit flat for Justin and he drove home with fond memories rekindled haunting him.

Moving on

It was pouring down on the first Sunday in September and there was no chance of doing anything on his plot and Justin settled for washing some of his clothes. The problem with that was that when everything was in the washing machine there was time to kill waiting for the machine to complete what it was doing. He strolled into his front room and from the front window he could see a large ship leaving Barrow via the Piel Estuary and heading into Morcambe Bay and the Irish Sea.

The ship was virtually on his door step and was spectacular to see. This wasn't the first time that Justin had seen a ship arriving or leaving Barrow dockyard it occurred fairly frequently but usually whilst he was at work and was hence unobserved. Ships were not the only vessels that past by Justin's front window, sometimes it was submarines.

A knock on the back door brought Justin's ship spotting to a temporary stop as he walked back into his living room to reach the back door. His neighbour from next door was stood in the rain waiting for the door to open.

"About time, too. I was getting soaked on your back doorstep," said a slightly bedraggled Nellie.

"You can't grow veg in this weather so come and have a cup of tea with Arthur and me. I've baked an apple pie to go with a cuppa so come and join us."

'Perhaps these neighbours of mine are getting a bit lonely,' thought Justin. They have married children but they don't call very often.

"That apple pie sounds good, Nellie. I'll just put my coat on and I'll come and join you both."

Nellie and Arthur were a grand couple and they kept their house looking neat and tidy. Apart from a twice weekly shop Nellie never left Roa. A small bus ran daily from Roa to Ulverston but you could change at Rampside for another that went to Barrow. The service was a lifeline for Nellie and a small number of other Roa residents who didn't own a car. The majority of folk on Roa didn't have a car. Affluence was slow in reaching the Furness Islands, Arthur never left the island at all.

His work at the sailing club provided him with all he needed in life. He kept up to date with what was happening in the world via newspapers, the radio and a recently purchased television set which was currently a huge draw for Nellie and himself. It seemed to bring the two of them much closer to the rest of the world. Reading was Arthur's real passion and the fortnightly visit by Barrow Library Service mobile library provided him with access to a vast number of potentially interesting books.

"Did you see the ship leaving Barrow this morning, Arthur?"

"I did, lad and a grand sight it was, too."

"How long have the docks existed in Barrow, Arthur?"

"In the 1860s, there were a number of highly productive iron and steel works in Barrow and they built the dock system so that they could ship the stuff out to other places at home and around the world. In 1871, the Barrow Shipbuilding Company was created and they brought in experienced ship builders from Scotland to build ships using iron and steel from local firms."

"What was the first ship launched in Barrow?"

"That was the steam yacht *Aries* in May 1873 and in June of the same year the passenger cargo vessel *Duke of Devonshire* was launched. The ship was named after its main financier. It was owned by the Eastern Steamship Company and it was used to make voyages to Asia."

Nellie arrived with tea and home-made apple pie and all interest in Barrow's ship building history came to an end and it was well worth it.

'An opportunity to grab a cup of tea would be most welcome,' thought Justin as the day's work had been taxing to say the least with one minor equipment breakdown after another and he rushed to his office to take off his dust coat for five minutes.

He arrived at the same time as Annie Isherwood who looked glum to say the least. She joined him in his office but not before asking Gladys in the canteen to bring some tea. Looking glum was not something that Annie did as a rule, she was probably the most positive person Justin had ever met, alongside her husband. What was making her feel this way?

"You look down in the dumps, Mrs Isherwood."

"I see you're back to calling me Mrs Isherwood again."

"I had the feeling that I was in your bad boots after our last meeting and so I thought, I better be a bit more respectful."

"It's nothing to do with respect but I will put that to one side for a moment. William has just put the 'Indomitable' up for sale."

"The Indomitable! You mean the house."

"Of course. I mean the house. It's been our home and joy for the last thirteen years. William bought it when he left the Navy in 1946 and since then we have done lots of things to it to meet our needs and suit our interests. Its location is a dream and we have spent many hours in the garden watching out to sea. Our grandchildren loved it too. It's so sad to be losing it."

"I take it that you have committed to moving then."

Annie sat for a moment stirring her cup of tea contemplating what had passed and what was to come.

"Yes, we have committed to moving. We want to share the joy of our daughter-in-law and grandchildren in our final years and moving is a must. There's no point in remaining here and watching someone else run the business that you had set up or being so close to a son who is dedicated to making a fool of himself."

Annie, Mrs Isherwood, it mattered not what Justin called her was entitled to some comfort but he couldn't fully share her burden just yet.

"Did you buy the house off someone local?" It was a stupid question really and more of an attempt to act as an ice breaker after a fairly long silence.

"The people who lived in it were London financiers with a number of interests in the Barrow area. They rarely stayed in it only using it when business meetings had to be made. I think they were called Bowens, Mr and Mrs Bowens. Yes that was it. I can't remember meeting them they never seemed to have any time to talk."

This tea break had gone into extra time and Justin felt that he had no alternative but to get back to work. After his experience earlier in the day, something else was likely to break down and he began to make a move.

"Before you go, Justin, I wanted to have a word with you about something else."

Maybe I'm going to find out how I have upset her thought Justin.

"I was disappointed to learn that you have a new woman in your life. I was hoping that you could give Jean a little more time. She does love you but she has to be sure that her love for you doesn't bring with it all sorts of complications."

Justin blushed. He hadn't thought that his trial lesson with Sheila could cause all this fuss. The truth of the matter was though that it was getting on for nine months since Jean had given him the elbow and she had never made any attempt during this period to tell him that she felt any different about having a relationship with him. He couldn't be expected to put his life on hold whilst Jean made her mind up about what she wanted to do and anyway he didn't have another woman in his life but he had to concede that he just might do.

"Annie, I really don't have another woman at present. Yes, I have kissed a girl that I like but I'm not in love with her, at least I don't think so. Jean has her own life to live just like I do and neither of us owe each other any explanation as to who we like or dislike."

'Perhaps, he had been to finalistic with his last comment,' he thought.

"Ah, so we are back with you calling me Annie again! That's an improvement. I understand what you are saying but just pay heed to the fact a certain young lady does love you very much but is not in any position to do anything about it right now but will do when the time is right."

Amy was always guaranteed to keep Justin up to date with all the latest comings and goings and she was not going to let him down during this tea break.

"I suppose, you have heard about Lyn's latest heart throb," enquired Amy.

"No. Who is he, anyone I know?"

"In a way you do. You know the new clarinet player in the village band?"

"I don't know him but I did see him last Saturday. Why?"

"He's Lyn's latest."

"But how can he be Lyn's latest? He only played in the band for the first time last week."

"Well, Lyn claims she's in love with him and he'll come round to loving her by the time she's finished with him."

They both laughed before moving on with more details.

"After the dance ended last Saturday, she hung around until everyone bar the band had gone home and they chatted and he agreed to take her out. They had a snog in the car park before going their separate ways."

"Most romantic! But what does she know about him? Is he married? Where does he live? What's his job?"

"Blimey Justin, your inquisitive."

"Musicians have a bit of a reputation. They play away a lot in more ways than one. They are surrounded by pretty girls all over the place."

Nobody had thought about asking what his name was and it was too late now since tea break was at an end.

Lyn's new flame was again the talking point in the Roa Boat but she wasn't there to be cross examined by her friends but there was general agreement, without any evidence, that the clarinet player from Rampside Village Hall Dance Band was most likely to be a better bet than randy George the landlady Emma's offspring. Come to think about it, they all thought, where is George tonight, or, more importantly, who was he getting his hands on tonight?

Sheila, Nadine, Amy and Joanne seemed to prattle on about nothing for ages tonight thought Justin and his inability to say much led to him drinking more than he usually did making him slightly tipsy. Sheila eyed an opportunity to have fun and nestled her shapely self into his right side. Justin was most susceptible to any close encounter with Sheila's body but this was too public a place to respond in the way he was currently imagining.

By the time it was time to go home, he was in no fit state to take any advantage of anyone since he had fallen asleep. He awoke in the arms of the landlady who was uttering the words 'up, up, up' evidently trying to convince Justin that his right hand needed to be raised in that direction to successfully grope her right tit.

All the other girls had gone home so there was no-one present to witness this scene. It wasn't long however before Emma realised she was wasting her grope and slung Justin out apologising at the same time that she didn't have a compass to help him with the navigation.

Gardening was rained off for the second Sunday on the trot and Justin found himself in his next door neighbours house once more. This could become a habit. Whilst he liked his neighbours, Nellie and Arthur, he also enjoyed his privacy and felt that he should be on his guard against this becoming a regular thing but for the moment there was no point in not enjoying the pleasure of sampling Nellie's baking or, for that matter, another history lesson by Arthur who was certainly very knowledgeable about Barrow and the Furness Islands.

Suitably lubricated with tea, Arthur began relating the history of ship building in Barrow.

"I think, we ended the story last week in 1871. In the first ten years of its existence, the shipyard got orders for passenger liners, sailing ships, paddle steamers and dredgers and in 1881 they launched the 'City of Rome' which at the time was the largest vessel in the world."

"I never associated ship building on this scale with Barrow," remarked Justin.

"They built their first submarine here in 1886," Arthur continued.

"As far back as that! That's amazing."

"They started producing ships guns here in 1886 as well and the company was renamed the Naval Construction & Armaments company. They launched a battleship named HMS Vengeance in 1899 having also built and fitted its engines and armament. Achieving all that in one place made Barrow a very attractive place to invest in. Vickers Sons and Company, a Sheffield based steel-making firm, formed a new company with an American-born inventor Sir Hiram Maxim and took over the shipyard in 1887."

"That's enough, Arthur. You'll be boring this young chap to death," said Nellie bringing the lesson to an abrupt end and Justin returned to his home next door to embark on another clothes washing session.

Tea break at Isherwood's & Sons, Etching Specialists was looked forward to by everyone in the firm. Fifteen minutes of a break to chat and drink was just the therapy needed to cope with the daily routine of work. Coming twice a day was a bonus and throwing in an hours break for dinner was truly a good way of keeping everyone happy.

Tea break was also an excellent opportunity to share news and the firm had one or two astounding reporters who in different circumstances may have been classified as gossips. Amy was probably the most prominent one and she sat down with Justin, who was something of a regular listener.

"Have you heard the latest on Eileen?"

"No. What is the latest, Amy, I'm sure you will know?"

"Don't be like that, Justin. I thought you would like to know."

"My apologies, Amy. I do want to know."

"She's had her baby."

"And is she OK?"

"Both she and the baby are fine."

"Well come on, tell me what's she had?"

"She's got a beautiful baby girl."

"How does she feel now that the baby is born?"

"Eileen is greatly relieved that all her morning sickness is over and that her little girl is fine. She is worried about how Fred will react although up to now he has been good to her and the baby."

"And what about Eileen's two children, how have they reacted to the new arrival?"

"She has a son called Wilfred and he's six years old. He's puzzled by it all but he likes the baby. Her daughter, Emma, is eight and she's just glad that Mum is fine."

"Has Eileen and Fred decided on a name for the baby?"

"Yes. They are going to call her Susan."

"Susan Atherton! That sounds good. Has there been any reaction from Rupert?"

"Not a thing. Not even a card wishing them both well. That man's a real bastard. Excuse me for the language Justin but that's just how I feel."

The new arrival must create a huge strain on Eileen's family's finances and with no-one to turn to something was going to happen thought Justin but this was not the time nor the place to dwell on that and so the subject was not raised.

"Are they both at home now?" asked Justin.

"At present, they are in Ulverston Maternity Home but they will be discharged in a few days."

"Has Eileen got everything she needs at home for the baby?"

"She's short of a pram and she could do with some more baby clothes."

"Perhaps, we could organise a whip-round and buy something for them."

"Justin, that's an excellent idea."

Annie Isherwood always called into the factory on Mondays to check that her husband William, the Managing Director, was coping OK. She also popped in on one other day each week but it was not always the same one.

This week it happened to be Thursday and she particularly wanted to break some news to Justin. *'She arrived in his office having first arranged for some tea with the canteen girls who were always so obliging,'* she thought. It was nearly three and she knew that Justin would be here any moment and he was.

"Hello Annie. I wasn't expecting you."

"You never are but considering your calling me by my first name, I'll forget it."

"And tea as well. You obviously have some influence around here," retorted Justin.

"Less of the cheek if you don't mind. I have some rather interesting news."

Justin's attention was well and truly grabbed by this statement and he listened intently.

"My son Rupert has just had, or should I say, Paul's daughter Irene, has just had an almighty row with him. Neither William and I or Paul and his wife had any idea that the two of them were still seeing each other especially after the threats that William and Paul had issued to Rupert. Nevertheless, they have been seeing each other."

"Do you know what the row was about?"

"I'm just coming to that! The row was about Jean. Jean Baxter. I think you know her!"

Justin didn't know at this stage whether he wanted to know any more but more was what he was going to get as Annie was now in full flow.

"Evidently, Irene was aware that whilst Rupert was seeing her he was trying to induce Jean into becoming his partner."

That was a stunning revelation and Justin was very saddened to hear of it. Annie went on.

"Rupert made the mistake of denying it to Irene who then went ballistic and attacked him in his flat. His neighbours called the police and they came and separated the two of them and then cautioned them."

"How did Irene know it was true?"

"She had suspected something was going on behind her back and decided to stalk out Jean's place in Kennedy Street. She saw Rupert arrive after work had finished one evening and she watched him trying to gain access to Jean's rooms in number six but Ivy Jones, the house owner wouldn't let him in."

"Rupert pushed Ivy to one side and he got in but her husband Ernest confronted him and a scuffle started. She saw Jean come downstairs from her room and she called the police. When they arrived, they arrested Rupert and Irene clearly heard Jean shouting at Rupert telling him that she had never been interested in him and never would be interested in him and he should leave her alone."

"Phew! So where is Rupert now and what's happened to Irene?"

"Rupert has been given a warning by the police and that's the end of it for now, stupid boy! As far as Irene is concerned, she broke down whilst telling her parents what she had been doing behind their backs and promised she was going nowhere near Rupert again. The good thing is that it will only be another couple of weeks and she will be back at university in Manchester and that will be a relief to her parents."

"Are Paul and William going to carry out the threat they had made to Rupert?"

"No. They both hope that the situation as resolved itself."

"The owners of number six Kennedy Street are not too happy being caught up in all this and they have warned Jean that if they face this situation again, she will have to go and she might find it difficult to get another place without a recommendation from her old landlord."

"A pretty bleak picture," commented Justin who was beginning to wise up on Jean's predicament.

A night in the Roa Boat was most welcome after a week of momentous events and the full Team Five were all there much to Justin's delight. These five girls had been the plaster between the bricks for Justin and had helped him keep his feet on the ground and he would always love them for it. Tonight's major topic was very much the same as it had been for the last several weeks, namely; dating.

A roll call was held and Nadine kicked off by telling her friends that she was still enjoying her junior doctor who was engaging her in the subject of anatomy and he was exploring her with great vigour much to everyone's amusement. Amy reported next with the news that she and Gordon Blears, the joiner, were enjoying seeing each other but not with a fantastic amount of enthusiasm since he was turning out to be more groove than tongue but no-one really understood what all that meant.

Joanne was still seeing her saxophonist on a regular basis which she was pleased about. Lyn spoke next and suddenly, interest levels increased, her intentions regarding a certain clarinet player having been made clear on a previous occasion.

"Well, go on, Lyn, we're all ears," remarked Amy.

"I haven't got much to tell. That lousy clarinet player called Cecil Smith was already married. I met a friend who lives in Furness where Cecil lives and she told me that he lived in Furness with his wife, three children and four clarinets."

"Did you get to date him before you found out?" asked Joanne.

"Yeah. I arranged to meet him in a park in Barrow."

"Go on then. What happened?"

"He turned up with his three kids and a note from his wife asking me to take him off her hands along with the three kids and four clarinets."

It took some time for the laughter to die down and then Lyn proclaimed she was back in the market for another man. All eyes now fell on Sheila.

"Girls, I have to disappoint you. There's little movement in my love life at present but I'm considering giving George a go."

Booing was not something you heard the girls do as a rule but when the name George was mentioned they did it with gusto and gained the attention of Emma the Landlady who joined in enthusiastically.

Attention now focussed on Justin but he was turning out to be rather boring in the love affair compartment that was currently under the microscope. What he was able to tell them about was the row that had taken place between Irene and Rupert over Jean and that satisfied their curiosities no end. Amy followed this up with the details of Eileen giving birth to a baby girl she was naming Susan and how they were organising a whip round at Isherwoods to get her something.

Coming near to the end of the evening Lyn sat next to Justin and asked if there was a Brass Band concert tomorrow night at the Roxy in Ulvertson. He knew what this meant and made it easier for her by telling her that there was and it was Fodens Motor Works Band that would be playing and if she would like to come with him she would be more than welcome.

Justin had never been strangled but he now knew what it must feel like as Lyn got him in a tight embrace and kissed him to everyone else's delight, and his, if truth be known, and they all clapped for more, with Emma joining in as well.

A dry Sunday at last thought Justin has he peered out from his front bedroom window. Maybe he could get some cleaning up done on his plot. It was time to clear out all the rows of vegetables that he had planted earlier in the year. For a novice, he had done well and he could be pleased with what he had achieved. But, first things first, he needed to get dressed, get downstairs and get some breakfast. Justin was no cook and everything that he made for himself was pretty basic. Breakfast was either toast or a cereal. The best meal of the day was at dinner time in Isherwood's works canteen.

The two canteen ladies, Brenda and Gladys, made some good meals. Liver, chips and peas was one of his favourites. Justin couldn't remember when the last time was that he had been in a restaurant and had something special like a steak. Later today he would make himself a nice salad using some of the things he had grown on his plot together with some cheese.

With breakfast over, it was time to get on with a few more domestic chores before venturing out to the plot. Clothes needed putting in the washing machine, socks needed darning and some buttons needed sowing on a couple of shirts. Darning and sewing were two skills he had picked up when he was doing his National Service in the Royal Air Force. Prior to then his mother had done all these things for him. He had a vivid memory of an occasion when he was serving in the RAF and he had gone on parade with a hole in one of his socks.

He had hoped that it would not be noticed but no sharp eyed Corporal would miss something like that and he had got bawled out about it in front of his fellow servicemen. He spent the whole of the next three evenings learning and practising how to darn socks and he never forgot how. In a bedroom drawer, Justin had a collection of darned socks, many of them being darned with a colour of wool that didn't match that of the sock but with no sharp eyed Corporals about who cares!

The plot was going to look bare when all the crops were removed. Potatoes, broad beans, carrots and parsnips were the first to be cleared and then placed in baskets for storage. Next would come the turnips, beet, the early celery, cabbage, sprouts and broccoli.

There was no sign of Arthur or Nellie which was a shame thought Justin who had become accustomed to having a drink with the couple and he would especially miss her home-made cake. Perhaps they were visiting some of their family. He was going to have to make his own cup of tea today and eat some of the fig biscuits he had in his kitchen cupboard.

With all the gardening, washing of clothes, sowing and darning out of the way, it was nice to be driving to Ulverston with Lyn for comfort. They chatted about everyday things until they arrived at the Roxy. Tonight's concert was being given by a famous Brass Band from the north-west of England, Foden's Motor Works Band.

The band came from Sandbach in Cheshire and got its name from a truck manufacturer called Fodens. The origin of the band went back to 1900 when it was formed as a village band to feature in the celebrations marking the relief of Mafeking in the Boer War. After a couple of years, the band wound up but was reformed by the industrialist Edwin Foden as Fodens Motor Works Band.

Conductor Fred Mortimer (1880—1953) led Fodens for 27 years from 1927 until his death in 1953. During this time, the band won the National Championship eight times and made over 250 radio broadcasts.

"Justin what have Fodens achieved recently?"

"They won the National Championship in 1958 and they are in it again next month."

"Who is conducting Fodens tonight?"

"Rex Mortimer who comes from a famous family of musicians. His father Fred Mortimer was once the band's conductor and Rex and his other two brothers played under him, Alex on euphonium, Harry on cornet and Rex also on euphonium."

"They sound like quite an accomplished musical family."

"You're right, Lyn, they are."

Once the band started to play, Lyn was spellbound. The rich sound of the band was captivating and the programme of music was splendid. Justin enjoyed the enthusiasm that Lyn displayed and it was obvious that she was becoming a fan of this genre of music and the traditional way that Brass Bands conduct their concerts.

On the drive back to Roa, Justin took the opportunity of asking Lyn about the musical background of clarinet player Cecil Smith that she had recently kicked into touch.

"Cecil was professionally trained but I don't know where. Doing National Service interrupted his musical career but he was able to get work with a few local ensembles when he was demobbed and when he got married what money he earned didn't matter since he married into money."

"Good job you didn't get hitched with him then."

"You can say that again!"

Once back at Marine Terrace Lyn, in spite of being slightly on the plump side, gave Justin her special kind of thanks leaping on him with both of her arms around his neck and both legs wrapped around his waist whilst she planted a huge kiss on his cheek. How the devil does she do that thought Justin but he liked it. It was a good way to end a Sunday and is washing was done as well.

Company Secretary Joshua Turner was taking Justin to the Roa Boat for lunch which Justin knew meant an extended lunch break and a lot of drink but given how much of his time was devoted to work he wasn't going to complain about it.

Josh seemed to love going on a bender periodically and this lunch time might just turn out to be one for he seemed to smell of port when he arrived in Justin's office. They walked the short distance to the Roa Boat past the on-duty works Security Officer Albert Clitheroe who gave Justin a knowing nod.

Emma was delighted to see the two men from Isherwood's although clearly happier to see Josh.

A light meal was chosen from Emma's limited menu and suitably large drinks to go with it. Justin wasn't sure if he possessed the stamina or not to endure a session with Josh but he was determined to give it a go.

"Well, Justin! We have got our man!"

"That was a good start to matters thought Justin but what on earth is he talking about?"

"We have a new Managing Director starting the last week in December."

"So you all reached a decision then."

"So, we did Justin, so we did."

"How did you come to a conclusion?"

"Good question, Justin, good question."

The alcohol was playing its part and drama was creeping in.

"Well, it was like this. Lieutenant Commander Archie Whales RN."

There was a pause whilst Josh chuckled to himself.

"Fancy being in the Navy with a name like Whales."

This was followed by a bout of chuckling by both men plus Emma who was tuning in from the bar.

"Now where was I. Ah yes, Lt Cdr Archie Whales RN, he was a fine candidate but his wife let him down."

"What do you mean his wife let him down?"

"You see, she was not prepared to come up north from Devonport with him and the three of us on the interviewing panel plus William all felt that after a time the Lt Cdr would want to be reunited with his wife on a more permanent basis and therefore wasn't likely to stay with us for very long."

"So he hasn't got the job then."

"Absolutely, bang on old chap!"

Josh ate some of the meal that Emma had brought him and drank a lot of the alcohol she had also brought and his face was beginning to go slightly red but mostly around his nose. His appreciation of Emma was multiplying exponentially as he drank more.

"Fine woman, that landlady is!"

Justin passively agreed but wanted to move on to finding out who was going to get the post of new MD before he sank into a state of oblivion. He recognised that it wasn't far away.

"That young joiner fella from Vickers! What was his name? Ah yes, Gordon Blears. A real star blazer that one, or was it star gazer? Anyway, whatever! We decided that there was simply not enough rungs left on the Isherwood ladder for him to climb up."

What a good way of saying that he couldn't get any higher in status at our place thought Justin.

"Well, come on, Josh, who have you given the job to?"

"I would have thought you would have worked that one out by now. You need a drink, now try this new port Emma has got in for me."

So Emma is getting port in specially for Josh. These two must have an understanding.

"Do you remember Andrew Marr?"

"No. I never met him."

"He was the chap who has his own business in Kendal."

"I remember him now."

"Do catch up old boy!. Well he's got it, the post I mean. And he is the best man for us."

"But he lives in Kendal. Is he going to commute every day from Kendal?"

"He's going to try and find a place for him and his wife to live nearer the factory and he's interested in William's place."

"The Indomitable?"

"Yes, the Indomitable."

"What's he going to do in the meantime?"

"If he has to, he will stay here during the week."

"You mean, in the Roa Boat."

"Precisely, old boy. You are catching on now."

With the important part of the conversation over, both men indulged further until they were incapable of indulging any more. Emma had the delight of escorting Josh to her spare room whilst Josh had the delight of leaning on her. In Justin's case, he had to spend the rest of the afternoon leaning on a pub seat until Isherwood's finished for the day and Sheila, escorted by Nadine could come and provide him with an escort home.

During the short journey to number eleven Marine Terrace, he had the pleasure of leaning on two delightful young ladies. He passed out before experiencing the thrill of being undressed and tucked in bed which he couldn't regret until the following morning when he had a hangover to remind him. Still it was better than Joshua Turner who wasn't found until the end of the week and no-one would reveal the secret of where.

Walking into the Roa Boat for his Saturday evening drinking session with 'Team Five' was usually looked forward to by Justin but this evening he was arriving with a feeling of trepidation. At least, two of the team had seen more of him than anyone since his mother and he knew that he was going to get some stick but face them he must and in he went. The first thing he noticed as he stepped into the pub was the additional young woman, a young woman by the name of Jean Baxter.

The rowdy reception that he had expected didn't happen instead there was almost complete silence and it was as if his friends were anticipating both his and Jean's reaction to his entrance. *'His friends were protecting his reputation in order to facilitate some kind of reunion between Jean and himself, at least that's what it might be,'* Justin thought. Those thoughts rapidly evaporated as he got nearer to the group and Nadine provided a pointed comment that aroused everyone's interest including Jean who had already been brought up to speed regarding the fun the group intended to have at Justin's expense.

"Well, big boy, how are you today?"

Justin responded in a less than confident voice, "Fine thanks."

Jean looked across at him with a wide grin on her face and Justin melted just seeing it.

Conversation didn't linger on Justin's encounter with the Company Secretary Joshua Turner as no-one had a desire to impair any chances of these two lovers in their midst getting together again, instead the talk was directed onto the new Managing Director that would be joining Isherwood's in the last week of December.

Sitting opposite Jean, separated by a large table, did not allow any intimate conversation between the two of them which was perhaps just as well since neither of them had the slightest idea how to make a start. The first half of the evening was spent taking nervous glances at each other and nervously smiling when their eyes met.

Most of the groups' conversation passed over both their heads but that didn't matter as far as Justin was concerned as it was just great that Jean was here right now looking as lovely as she was the first time he had laid eyes on her and the smiles she sent in his direction looked warm and special.

When it came to Justin's turn to go to the bar, it would normally be an opportunity for Emma to have some fun with him and tonight, after his recent drinking session with Josh, he waited for her to get started has she was getting the round of drinks together but it didn't happen. Jean came up from behind and leant on the bar next to him. The proximity of her body was exhilarating but he tried not to make it obvious that was so.

"Justin, I'm so pleased to see you."

"I'm glad to see you to."

"It seems like ages since I last spoke to you."

"It is Jean. You were with Nicola's children, if I remember."

"That was at the start of July."

"Yes, it was."

The two of them were finding conversation awkward almost child-like but it was progress, it was an interchange of words that could lead anywhere and both seemed desperate for it to continue. One or two more pleasantries were exchanged before they joined their friends who had been taking a great interest in their rendezvous at the bar. Emma gave a thumbs up behind their backs as they took the round of drinks back to their table and 'Team Five' were very pleased.

Just as the evening was about to end Jean made a point of taking Justin to one side and asking him if he was going to the dance in Rampside next Saturday and when he said yes she looked very happy and then she went on her way. Whatever had happened tonight and in reality that hadn't been much. It felt like a dam was being breached in Justin's heart but he warned himself not to get ahead of himself. Nevertheless he couldn't help looking forward to next week's dance.

Although this morning was overcast, it couldn't dampen Justin's spirits. After last night's drink in the Roa Boat, he had felt something of an uplift. Even a dull breakfast of half-burnt toast and a mug of tea tasted better, but what didn't raise his expectations of a brilliant day ahead was another round of washing and more work on his plot. He certainly felt that he needed to reflect on what he intended to do at the end of the month, was he going to stay at Isherwood's in the new year or not.

He seemed to be arriving at a cross roads and all this was due to seeing Jean the night before. If he left Isherwood's and Roa Island, he would probably never see the girl he had fallen for again, on the other hand there was no guarantee that they would get together again. For the moment, it was best to put all this to one side and do something on the plot.

Most of the plot was now empty and Justin hoed and weeded nearly all the rows in preparation for whatever he decided to try and grow next. Talking of growing next a host of spring cabbage plants that he had acquired from Arthur could be planted now in some of the vacant rows and he got on with it.

"Morning, Justin."

"Good morning, Arthur. I missed you last week."

"Happen you did. I always takes Nellie to the cemetery in Ulverston at this time of the year to look at her parents grave."

"How is Nellie?"

And just as Justin said this she came out to the plot with tea and cake on a tray smiling as she did so.

Justin called into the Company Personnel Officer's office to see Paul Edwards regarding the recruitment of new staff for the extra production section that was to open in the new year. He need not have worried for Paul was a very meticulous person and he had already created advertisements for two workers to mount components on the new circuit boards coming on stream in the new year plus an extra inspector who would be involved in checking the final products.

The advertisements had already been placed in local newspapers. Feeling reassured that everything was in hand Justin went back to his own work. He had been tempted to enquire about Irene, Paul's daughter, but thought it prudent not to at this point in time and he left Paul's office with an image of Irene's pubic hair and tits in his mind. One or two of Isherwood's employees looked enquiringly at the smile on Justin's face as he walked through the factory to his own office.

Annie Isherwood was sat waiting for Justin in his office.

"Hello, Justin."

"Hello, Annie. How are you?"

"Justin, I'm OK and I hope you are, too. I have some interesting news for you."

Annie always had interesting news thought Justin.

"Nicola has filed for a divorce from Rupert."

"I suppose she has grounds for that."

"Of course, she has." Annie had replied in an agitated manner but continued, "She is divorcing him on the grounds of adultery."

"Well, things are moving on, Annie. By the way, I meant to ask you the last time that I saw you about your own family in Barrow. If you move to Plymouth, won't you miss them?"

"My family, the Taylor's, have been used to my absence many times in the past. I travelled the world with William when he was in the Navy. My family are quite used to me not being around and anyway William will want to come back here now and again to see how the factory is doing and I'll come with him and I can visit them then."

"A little bird tells me that you and Jean have seen each other." Annie said this with a twinkle in her eye.

"Well, she came to join a group of her friends in the Roa Boat, so, yes, we did see each other."

"And!"

"It was a bit like two people meeting for the first time and realising that they liked each other but didn't know what they should do about it."

"Just like children, you mean."

Justin didn't reply to this but knew she was right.

"You know, Justin you are going to have to decide very soon whether you are going to stay on at Isherwood's after the new year. Your decision will affect any relationship you may want to enter into."

Annie Isherwood was a wily old bird thought Justin but he loved her for it for in some ways she was his surrogate mother.

Rampside Village Hall dance was full to the gills with local folk, young and old, all with the intention of enjoying themselves. Some danced, some drank the alcohol served from a couple of trestle tables, some did both and everyone ate the locally made pie or cake or both. The music provided by Alison Pringle's five piece ensemble was bearable as it beat out a rhythm that helped would be dancers to navigate the floor with a minimum of mishaps.

Some danced with passion, some danced to be passionate and others just danced because everyone else was doing it. Either way, Justin and his five female friends were there to join in. The presence of Jean Baxter with some friends was a huge bonus for Justin but he was frustrated by the fact that Jean had chosen to sit with her friends on the opposite side of the hall rather than with him and his five colleagues.

Sheila noticed Justin's disappointment but kept it to herself. All the single girls in the place were popular partners for the men although some were popular partners for each other but no-one minded. Lyn, Nadine, Joanne, Amy, Sheila, you name them, they were all partners for Justin during the evening but there was one important name missing from tonight's list.

With the evening getting closer to its end, a certain Jean Baxter made her way over to where Justin was sat and in a gentle voice asked him, "Can I have this next dance please?" At that moment that was the nicest question Justin Ebberson had ever been asked and he gladly escorted his charming new partner onto the floor hoping at the same time that he wouldn't tread on her feet.

A dancing embrace can take a number of forms and in the case of Justin and Jean it began rather formerly and as they became more comfortable with each other it became tighter and when their cheeks met the embrace developed into pure passion so much so that at the end they had difficulty disentangling themselves from each other.

With a simple thank you and without any kiss, the two quavering dancers returned to their respective chairs to try and recover from the wonderful experience. The end of the evening soon came and both partners went their separate ways with a polite 'goodnight' and both of them thinking—there has to be more than this—surely! Sheila and the rest of Justin's friends left equally baffled by what they had seen but whatever it was that they had witnessed it was certainly passionate.

There was not going to be any work done on the plot today decided Justin as a result of the fact that he felt distinctly unwell. He had been sick, several times during the night and this morning, he felt shattered. The rain outside helped to convince him that the best place for him was in bed. At least, he could listen to a couple of his favourite radio programmes namely, *The Navy Lark* and *The Goon Show* and hopefully by tea time he would be feeling better.

Wednesday was Annie Isherwood's usual calling day and hence it was no surprise when Justin arrived in his office at around 3:00pm and found her waiting. She always brought news and took an interest in his well-being.

"Justin, I am pleased to tell you that William has found a new house for us in Plymouth."

"That's good news. Is it near to where Nicola and the grandchildren are living?"

"Yes, it is although Nicola will be moving from her parents' house when she finds a place of her own and we hope that will not be too far away."

"Whereabouts in Plymouth is the house you have found?"

"It's on the outskirts of Devonport and it's where the Isherwood family come from."

"Everything seems to be coming together now, Annie."

"William is very tired and I can't wait to get him somewhere away from here. This place has been a big strain on him since Rupert left the scene."

For once, Justin was glad to see Annie leave, he didn't want to get into any conversation about Rupert.

On Friday, Justin was called into his bosses office to provide another update on the progress he was making in preparation for the new circuit boards being constructed in the new year.

"How are things going, Justin?"

"We are pretty much on target at present. About a half of the new equipment has been delivered, installed and tested and I expect everything will be in place by the end of October and we should be in a position then to call in Her Majesties Inspectorate to certify that we are ready to go."

"Excellent. I understand that you have had a problem installing one bit of kit?"

"Yes, that's true. I have followed the installation instructions correctly but I still keep running into problems with it. I have been in touch with the manufacturers, Thomson, in Carlisle and I'm going to have to make a visit to their place so that they can show me what to do."

"Is that the solder bath you are talking about?"

"Yes, it is."

"Thomson's factory is sited on the airfield at Crosby-on-Eden. Get Paul Edwards to fly you there, it would save a lot of time."

"Fine, I'll do that."

"Now, what about the extra staff we are going to need?"

"Paul has sent out adverts and I expect he's waiting for applications right now."

"Good. And what about you Justin! Today your probation date with the firm ends. I know that you have agreed to stay on with us until Christmas to get everything sorted for our new project but what about after that? You do appreciate that if you are going to leave we must have enough notice to find a replacement, so what have you decided?"

"I have decided that I want to stay with Isherwood's."

"Excellent. Let's get Paul in and we will have a drink to that. By the way, on the subject of drink, don't let Josh lead you astray. Ever since his divorce, he has been very lonely and sometimes, he hits the bottle a little hard."

At that point, in walked Paul and William greeted him with the news that Justin was staying on with the firm and then he poured three glasses of port.

"I suppose, that young lass Jean Baxter has something to do with this," remarked Paul and William intervened saying, "I understand one of our young ladies in the office is pregnant and will be leaving at Christmas. Why not ask your Jean to apply for the job? If she worked here, you could marry her and she could live at number eleven with you. There you are, Justin, all done and dusted, what do you say?"

That was getting too far ahead but Justin liked the sound of it.

"Come on, William, you can't expect Justin to respond to that," said Paul slapping Justin on the back at the same time.

Another couple of glasses of port followed before the congenial meeting ended.

'Team Five' was down to three on Saturday night in the Roa Boat. Nadine was subjecting herself to another operation with her junior doctor boyfriend whilst Amy was out with her rising star, Gordon. The big disappointment for Justin however was the absence of Jean.

He had been intending to take their new born affection for each other onto the next step up the charm ladder and for the moment the wind had gone clean out of his sails.

Sheila turned to Justin and whispered in his ears, "You need to get a move on with that girl or you will lose her to someone else," and that thought stuck in his head for the rest of the night.

The evening was pleasant but uninspiring and Justin was eventually happy to get back home.

Is This the End of the Beginning?

It was the first Sunday in October and being autumn there should be lots of leaves on the ground but not on Roa Island. There were no trees on Roa and some of autumns traditional scenery was not to be seen here. Just half a mile away via the causeway leaves were in abundance around Rampside.

There may not have been leaves on Roa but there was always an abundance of sea weed. Step outside Justin's front door, walk just beyond his plot to the shore line and you would find the stuff mingling with the beach pebbles and lots of detritus swept ashore by the ships sailing back and forth to Barrow.

An all-year-round tradition on Sundays had been fostered by Justin, weather permitting, and that was working on his plot. Gardening was a bit of a misnomer considering that he grew no flowers nor had he a lawn to cut. He really wasn't that interested in gardening, it had simply developed as a time filler but it did have its compensations.

First, it was in the fresh air and the location of Marine Terrace ensured that it couldn't get any fresher. It could be cold here even when it was hot. Second, the views were really great. Looking south was the nicest direction to look in; Blackpool, Fleetwood, Knot End, Piel Island were all visible on a clear day and the list could go on. Looking west the view was more industrialised. Ship building cranes standing between buildings on Barrows dock side and the very prominent new liner the SS Orion which was waiting to be launched could be seen.

Third, it had been an opportunity to socialise with his neighbours from number twelve, Nellie and Arthur who between them had widened Justin's knowledge of the area including ship building in Barrow. Fourth it had turned out to be an opportunity to sample some really good home cooking thanks to Nellie.

The tasks for today on the plot were purely menial with a continuation of hoeing and weeding but with one novelty thrown in to add to the variety and that was digging into the ground some lime. It wasn't long into this work that Justin started to wonder if he hadn't already hoed and weeded certain rows more than once but he turned a blind eye to it and hoed and weeded on.

Around half way through today's labour of love Arthur's head appeared above the fence that divided the two plots and he called out, "Hello Justin."

Justin's reply was equally brief, "Hi Arthur."

"Did you hear that Barrow Council want to ban plots on Roa?"

Justin was totally unaware of any discussions that had been taking place regarding the plots on Roa which only amounted to two anyway, his and Arthur's.

"No, I didn't hear that."

"They reckon they spoil the look of the island and they are considering banning them next year."

"That would be a shame," replied Justin but he had mixed feelings about the possibility of losing it thinking that there were perhaps more interesting things to do with his time, maybe joining the TA!

It was Tuesday before Justin could call and see Paul Edwards in his office to discuss flying up to Carlisle or Crosby-on-Eden to be more precise. Paul was in the middle of putting the final touches to an advertisement for five cleaners to join the payroll. Cleaning of the factory was currently being carried out by the existing work force but with new regulations coming into force the firm had to meet new conditions in order to produce new merchandise in the New Year.

The adverts created by Paul described what the cleaners had to do and what training they would be given along with the working hours and pay. Apart from placing these adds in the local press, posters had been printed and would be put on display in suitable places in both Roa and in Rampside. Paul's hope was that some local folk would jump at the opportunity the jobs provided especially for people with limited transport means.

Since the work that Isherwood's was involved in was classified; the cleaning staff would have to be security cleared and Paul had already made arrangements for that to happen. Once Paul had put his work on cleaning staff to one side he gave his attention to the idea of flying Justin up to Carlisle. He could spare the time to do it, his aircraft was both serviceable and available and a quick check on the weather revealed that Thursday would be a good day to go.

The Company Treasurer Ron Bright confirmed that Isherwood's would pay the costs involved with using Paul's private aircraft and some expenses would be provided for a meal. That only left a phone call to Thomson's in Carlisle to confirm that it was convenient to fly there and it was all set up. Justin would drive in his own car to Walney Airfield to meet Paul on Thursday and flying they would go.

Amy looked in good form when Justin caught up with her in the works canteen during one of the firms tea breaks. The conversation between the two of them was largely much to do about nothing but the shared company made it passable and to an extent enjoyable but not informative until Amy determined it was time to get on with something more serious.

"Eileen and her husband Fred and her children have lost their house."

Justin wasn't quite prepared for this news and he looked at Amy as if he was astonished.

She went on, "They had been struggling financially since Eileen had to give her job up and when she did they couldn't keep making mortgage payments. They have had to give their family home up."

"So, where are they living now?"

"Ulverston Council have found them a three bedroomed flat."

"I suppose, they could furnish the flat with what they had in the house that they were buying?"

"Fred has a pal who has a large van and between the two of them they managed to shift all their belongings to their new place."

"What about the kids' school? Have they had to move?" asked Justin.

"Luckily, the flat they have been given is not far from the school the kids go to so there hasn't been any upheaval on that score."

"It's a great shame that all this has happened and I hope that Fred and Eileen will cope OK. It might be something of a relief having no mortgage to pay." Commented Justin who went on to ask.

"They will be paying rent though, won't they?"

"Yes but it's nowhere near as much as their mortgage was."

When the tea break was over, Justin strolled back to his office thinking to himself how much trouble an affair can cause and how much more responsibility Rupert Isherwood should be taking about the situation and the baby that was his as well as Eileen's.

To get away from Roa and Isherwood's factory for a day was just what the doctor ordered thought Justin as he drove to Walney Airfield to meet Paul Edwards, Isherwood's Personnel Officer. The weather was good, just a few cumulus clouds drifting across the sky on a light westerly wind nothing to prevent the flight to Carlisle. Paul was waiting in the Walney Flying Club headquarters and informed Justin that they would be getting airborne shortly but he had to make a phone call before they left.

Evidently, their destination which was Crosby-on-Eden airfield was, technically disused. Thomson, the company they were going to visit, flew aircraft into Crosby periodically and kept part of the wartime main runway swept along with a short section of taxiway that led to their factory on the north side of the airfield. There was no air traffic control system in operation at Crosby and hence the need for the telephone call in advance of departing. There was a windsock at the airfield to indicate the direction the wind was blowing in and that was about all.

Paul's Cessna 172 looked pristine and it felt much better climbing into the front right hand seat rather than sitting in the back as he had done when he last flew in the aircraft to the Isle-of-Man with Irene, Paul's daughter. Having completed his outside checks Paul clambered onboard and having fastened his seat belt and donned his headphones started up the aircraft's engine. The fuel gauges indicated that there was enough fuel to get them to Crosby and back with a good margin of reserve in case any diversion became necessary.

A few more checks, a radio call to the tower and the Cessna was soon taxying to the end of the runway in use. The aircraft was brought to a stop at the runway threshold for some final checks and then they were off. Straight onto the runway, turn into wind, open up the throttle and accelerate down the centre line, it was all routine to Paul Edwards with his RAF background but to Justin Ebberson this was a thrilling treat.

Once airborne, they were heading west over the Irish Sea but a steeply banked turn to the right brought them on to heading that would take them along the Cumbria coastline in a northerly direction. They flew at about 3,000 feet following the Cumbria coast passing Whitehaven, Workington and Maryport on their right hand side. Next came Silloth and Paul made a radio call to the RAF Station there.

They could clearly see the airfield but other than a few Anson aircraft there was little else to see. RAF Silloth was in the process of closing down. The station had been the home of No.22 Maintenance Unit for many years but was no longer required. During the Second World War, many pilots had been trained here with No.1 Operational Training Unit using the American Lockheed Hudson aircraft many of which had crashed in the waters near here which is known as the Solway Firth and because of its notoriety amongst the aircrew undergoing training it became known as Hudson Bay.

A second airfield followed which had originally been RNAS Anthorn. They continued following the coastline and their heading gradually changed from a northerly to an easterly heading and they began flying inland. The former Navy airfield at Anthorn had been known in the Navy as HMS Nuthatch and had served a similar function to Silloth maintaining naval aircraft. Now disused Anthorn had until 1957 been the home of an Aircraft Receipt and Dispatch Unit.

Heading inland the Cessna passed over a main road that ran from England to Scotland and running parallel with it was a railway line. Gretna Green, just over the Scottish Border was on their left and Carlisle on the right. They were skirting the north of Carlisle to reach the airfield at Crosby-on-Eden that lay to the east of the city.

Flying over Crosby which Carlisle City Council were currently considering reopening as a permanent airfield, the windsock could be seen indicating that it was still a westerly wind blowing and Paul flew on past the airfield to do an about turn and come in from the east which meant he would be landing into a head wind. The touchdown was smooth and the aircraft departed the runway to head along a strip of useable taxi way to Thomson's factory.

Thomsons were most helpful and took Justin through the full installation and testing process of the equipment Isherwood's had bought from them. They organised a full hands on simulation of the job and amended the instruction manual they had previously issued. Justin was perfectly happy that he would know what to do when he got back and thanked his Thomson host before rejoining Paul for a mid-afternoon flight back to Walney following the same route they had used getting there.

All five of Justin's female colleagues were present in the Roa Boat when Justin came in and his disappointment was plainly obvious. Where was Jean? It was now two weeks since he had last seen her and on that occasion he had felt that something was being rekindled between them. Sheila recognised how Justin had been affected by Jean's non-appearance and made a point of nestling up to him.

Sheila's motives were a mixture of empathy and desire. When all said and done, she was a woman with her own desires and for some time she had felt as if she was on a journey through a world lacking in desirable men and she had no intention of letting it go on. She might just try her desires out on Justin since he was likely to continue to be unattached for some time but this was not the place.

Chit chat went back and forth between the girls whilst Justin was unresponsive until he felt a hand under the table stroking his right leg and it was progressing toward a sensitive part of his anatomy. He looked at Sheila and she smiled at him as she moved her left hand to its final destination. Justin just hoped that he wouldn't have to go to the bar right now for a round of drinks for it would be far too embarrassing, he had a grand 'hard on' and Sheila knew it.

This couldn't continue or he might just make a public mess of his trousers. He took another look at Sheila in-between a bout of heavy breathing and whispered 'later' in the hope that she would desist but made no attempt to remove her hand. It was hard to tell which of the two of them were enjoying the moment the most and it was all enhanced by the presence of the other four young women.

Justin's earlier disappointment was parked up for the night and replaced by a forceful feeling of true lust but what was he going to do about it. Was he going to take Sheila back to his place or what? He needn't have bothered thinking about it for Sheila whispered to him 'not tonight Justin but I will be round on Wednesday'. It was the second time he had been disappointed tonight but it saved any embarrassment when he had to get up to go to the bar.

A final touch to the end of the evening came when everyone were leaving. Sheila, in the shadows just outside the pub doors kissed Justin on the lips and in a low voice told him she would look forward to seeing him in his place on the following Wednesday. He didn't answer, he couldn't get the words out, she was holding him in a sensitive place again.

The morning after his lustful night in the Roa Boat it was raining and Justin couldn't help reflecting on what had happened. Sheila was an attractive young woman and Justin liked her a lot but he knew that he didn't love her. Maybe he just loved her body? He was grateful to Sheila for the support she had given him over the last nine months but whether that was a good enough reason for him to satisfy her sexual desires was another matter. There was a question of respect involved here. Justin knew that if he had intercourse with Sheila and then dumped her it would be a damaging experience and he did not want to inflict that on her.

The trouble was, his lust kept coming to the forefront and he wanted to see her naked, he wanted to explore her more intimate parts and kiss every part of her. As luck would have it a loud knock on his back door snapped him out of his erotic fantasising. Good old Nellie was demanding his presence next door where ample supplies of home baked cake and tea awaited him. He couldn't help giggling at the relief Nellie had unknowingly brought him and he grabbed her around her buxom waist, kissed her on her cheek and called her an angel. Nellie responded by telling him to stop being soft and threw in a 'gerr off' for good measure.

Arthur was glad to see Justin and even more pleased when he was asked to talk more about the history of Barrows shipyard.

"Where did we get to before?" asked Arthur.

"You got as far as 1899," responded Justin.

"The shipyard owners Vickers Sons & Maxim Limited increased the productivity of the shipyard in the early 1900s and they obtained many overseas orders. They got orders for military vessels from Peru, Russia, Brazil, Mexico, China, Turkey and Japan. In 1900, the Mikasa was launched and she became a flagship in the Japanese Navy."

"The Royal Navy chose Barrow shipyard to build their first submarine in 1901 and it was called Holland 1 and Barrow was at the forefront of developing submarines into effective fighting machines. In 1908, Barrow was chosen by the Royal Navy to pioneer new technology by placing the first order for the design and construction of Airship No.1."

"Arthur, that's impressive. Submarines and airships! Barrow was on the map! Remarked Justin."

"That it was, and during the First World War the workforce was over 30,000. The yard not only constructed ships and submarines but armaments as well. The production of airships also proceeded aided by a young engineer and designer by the name of Barnes Wallis and I'm sure you will recognise that name Justin?"

"Yes, I do," he replied.

Today's history lesson was brought to an end as Nellie required his nibs, Arthur, to perform some engineering in the kitchen which he knew meant washing up.

Paul Edwards had been busy once more with staff recruitment and was able to inform Justin that he had over a dozen applications for the three new posts coming up in the new section. Most of the applicants had good credentials and Paul intended inviting those that he had selected as possibles for interview the first week in November. Things were progressing fairly fast and Justin realised that he better have his side of things completed soon but he was confident that he could do it.

Annie Isherwood popped in to see Justin as she usually did on Wednesday afternoon and the news she brought with her was not the best.

"The pot has finally come to the boil," she said.

"What's happened Annie?" asked a perplexed Justin.

"Rupert has been confronted by Eileen's husband Fred!"

"I bet that didn't go down well."

"No it didn't but Rupert should have seen it coming."

"So what happened?"

"Fred made it very clear that he was not happy at losing his home and having to go and live in a council house. He's also not happy about the fact that he would find it very difficult to get another mortgage in the future having defaulted on the one he had."

It was pretty obvious looking at Annie that the worse bit was to come and she went on, "Fred demanded that Rupert should make a regular financial contribution to the welfare of his daughter Susan."

"What was Rupert's reaction to that?"

"He made the fatal mistake of laughing at Fred and told him to go away. That really set the cat among the pigeons. Fred was apparently incandescent with anger and he and Rupert got into a fight."

"Bloody hell!"

They hurt each other a lot and an ambulance had to be called to take both of them to hospital. They both had stitches but Rupert came off worse than Fred and he has been kept in hospital. Fred was allowed home.

"Have the police been involved?"

"The hospital called them and they have made notes but unless Rupert or Fred accuse each other no offence has been committed. So far, neither men have made any accusation."

"This must be worrying for you, Annie?"

"Rupert has got what was coming to him. He has to face the consequences. It's not fair to that little baby of his not to be helping in whatever way he can."

Annie was about to leave but raised one final subject before she left, "Justin I know that you are going to have a visitor tonight, an amorous one I am led to believe. Please be cautious. I know that you haven't seen Jean for the last couple of weeks but I can tell you that she still loves you. She lacks the courage to tell you that after what she has put you through and needs a bit of understanding. By the way, she will be in the Roa Boat on Saturday. I'll say no more but please bear in mind what I have just told you."

After work on Wednesday, Justin walked home wondering what he should do about Sheila and Jean for that matter. He was clear about how he felt about Jean and he would have to let Sheila down carefully but how? On a whim almost he got home wrote a short note and pushed it through the letter box of number twelve and began making his tea.

Once tea was over and the dishes washed, it was time to smarten up his appearance and then find that bottle of wine he had left over from Christmas. A knock on the front door announced the arrival of Sheila looking as attractive as she always did and it was that knock that made Justin check that he had unlocked his back door. Sheila made herself comfortable on the settee in the back room and Justin joined her having poured two glasses of wine first.

There was no doubt that this girl was quite something and it was going to be fairly difficult to exercise full control if the evening progressed as Sheila intended it to do. It wasn't long before Justin was embraced and drawn into a snog and he began to lose his grip on things, swapping it instead to Sheila's ample breasts. He glanced at his watch before beginning to undo the buttons on Sheila's blouse.

After another glance, he began to sweat a little but lust was taking over and with Sheila's help, he removed her blouse to reveal a bra filled with two breasts not that that was novel in any way, just plain sexy. When he glanced at his watch again, Sheila noticed but said nothing as he deftly removed her white bra at which point he was intoxicated by lust and desire but mostly lust.

He was just about to have a test run on Sheila's right nipple when the back door burst open and in stepped Nellie with a pot full of hot stew shouting 'come and get it' which he was doing until she arrived on the scene.

Sheila jumped off the settee grabbed her blouse and covered her breasts with it before almost running into the apparent safety of the front room revealing her nakedness to Nellie as she went out shouting at the same time, "Do your neighbours always choose moments like this to call on you?"

Nellie laughed evilly whilst holding a finger up against her mouth. She put the pot of stew down and slipped out the way she had come in shouting at the same time, "I know when I'm not wanted."

When Nellie had gone, Sheila reappeared with her blouse on, she took a swig of wine from her glass, bid Justin farewell and left in a bit of a humph.

An hour later, there was a knock on Justin's door.

"Can I have my bra back please?"

Sheila was invited back in and they both laughed, leaving sexual encounters for another time.

There she was and Justin was delighted to see her. Just as Annie said she would be Jean Baxter was sat in the same seat in the Roa Boat as she had when Justin had first set eyes on her and just as then he felt a flutter in his heart. *'Get a grip man,'* Justin thought to himself. He was becoming afflicted by love and lust and he was at a loss for a cure. Whilst Jean sat opposite to him on the other side of the pub table Sheila was by his side.

This could turn out to be tricky he thought but he needn't worry, Sheila saw Justin's face as he looked at Jean, she had witnessed this before and knew in a sense that the game was up. She wasn't terribly upset since the most she had wanted was sex with a decent looking bloke who wouldn't use it as something to brag about with his pals. Justin, she knew was not that kind of a man and there would be no loss of respect between them. She didn't know about the plan Justin had made with Nellie.

Smiles were exchanged between the two lovers but not a lot more and Sheila had to nudge Justin and tell him, "Don't leave it too late or you will regret it."

It gave Justin the push he needed and he got up to go to the bar and he asked Jean if she would join him. As they stood together waiting for Emma to serve them they had the first conversation that could be called normal for a long time and they became more relaxed with each other as they talked.

It was all small talk, nothing too heavy, just work things and home things. There came a point when they thought that they ought to go and join the others and as they did Justin brought up the details of tomorrow night's Brass Band concert at the Roxy in Ulverston.

"I'm sorry Justin but I can't make that, I have other commitments," said Jean.

"Oh that's a pity. By the way, Lyn loves Brass Band music and she has been coming with me to listen to the band's. She will probably ask me if she can come with me again. Would you be OK with that?"

"Of course, I would, Justin but if I may I would like to make one condition."

Justin was all ears.

"If you are going to the next dance at Rampside, would you please ask me to dance with you?"

Justin was choked by this request and he held Jean's hands in his but he still couldn't bring himself to kissing her but it would come, he knew it.

"Of course, I will."

Not long having sat down, Lyn shouted across the table, "Justin, how am I fixed for tomorrow night at the Roxy?"

She got several glares from her friends but Jean chuckled to herself and Justin just rolled with it saying, "Meet you same time as usual and in the same place," for which he got a double thumbs up and she got a kick under the table.

Sundays were coming around ever faster thought Justin as he stretched his arms behind his head and looked out of his front bedroom window. Whilst it was overcast he would be able to get some work done on his plot.

He felt happier today than he had done for some time. There was plenty of time to reflect on last night but that could wait he needed some breakfast and feeling as he did he thought he would be extravagant and he broke open a box of weetabix.

With breakfast over and one or two other small chores completed, Justin strolled out of his front door and walked to his plot. Since he had taken the decision to stay on Roa for the foreseeable future there was good reason to keep this plot going, at least until Barrow Council announced that it had to be removed thought Justin, That apart it was time to do some planting and several of the plots rows were ready for that purpose.

Lots of cabbage and rhubarb were planted in the next few hours and it was something of a relief when Nellie appeared with a tray of tea and home-made cake. She truly was a star thought Justin who thanked her for being so kind. Arthur seemed to appear from nowhere to join them for a relaxing drink and chinwag. Naturally, Nellie was itching to get into the subject of Sheila's visit last Wednesday.

"Well, Mr Ebberson, you were having your wicked way with Sheila when I last saw you."

Arthur's eyebrows lifted as his wife said this, she had never shared this titbit with him before.

"It was lucky you came when you did, Nellie."

"I could see that lad. She was already naked by the time I arrived."

Poor old Arthur nearly had a heart attack and spluttered tea all over the place.

"Nellie, you should have come earlier. I was getting worried that you wouldn't."

"If I had come any earlier, I might have seen the two of you shagging each other."

Arthur dropped his cup of tea and swore at the same time.

"I hadn't got that far but I might have if you hadn't arrived when you did."

This was the most bizarre conversation Arthur had ever heard in his life and he was forced to take out a handkerchief from his pocket and use it to wipe his brow.

"At least, we won't expect another increase in the world population," remarked Nellie.

Justin was not sure how all this information would change Arthur's opinion of him especially after the reaction he had just witnessed.

"Did Sheila come back for her bra?"

"Bloody hell! What have you two been up to?" Asked Arthur who seemed totally confused.

"She did and we both had a good laugh together about the whole experience but I have not told her about our plan," replied Justin.

Arthur looked at Nellie waiting for an explanation.

"Don't you look at me like that Arthur. I'll fill you in with all the details later," and with that she went back in doors.

Arthur lifted his flat cap off his head and looked at Justin in amazement.

"By gum lad, I never realised that Marine Terrace was the place for sex. Where do I go to get some?"

Lyn was raring to go when Justin called for her to take her to Ulverston for the latest Brass Band concert. They both got into Justin's car and drove over the causeway that connected Roa with Rampside and proceeded along the coast road to their destination. Lyn wanted to know as much as Justin could tell her about the band being featured at the Roxy tonight.

Carlton Main Frickley Colliery Band was not one that Justin could tell her much about. It was certainly one of the best bands in the country and was based in West Yorkshire. The band had its origins in South Elmsall Village which formed a village band in 1884. The band was adopted by the local Frickley Colliery in 1905 and adopted its present name in 1923.

"I can tell you one thing about tonight's band Lyn, they are on top form."

"What makes you say that?"

"Earlier in the year, they came second in the Yorkshire Area Championship and as a result they qualified for the National Championships in the Albert Hall, London next Saturday and on top of that they came second last month in the British Open Championship."

Lyn was suitably impressed and in double quick time they were seated in a full house waiting for the band to make its entrance on stage. Neither Lyn nor Justin were disappointed with the concert. The programme was excellent and so was the playing and during the interval Lyn got talking to another Brass Band music follower.

"Who was that, Lyn?"

"His name is Bernard and he's from Rampside."

"I can't remember ever seeing him at any of the dances in the village hall," said Justin.

"He's been attending university in Liverpool but his family live in Rampside."

"You should get to know him."

"I will. I've arranged to see him on Wednesday."

Blimey! That was fast working thought Justin but good luck to her.

The drive back to Roa was not like the other's that Justin had made with Lyn, she had little to say. Perhaps she was thinking about the new man that had just sprung into her life, Bernard. Again, unlike previous occasions, Lyn thanked Justin for taking her to the concert by kissing him on his cheek and then dashing into the house she shared with Amy. She had been far more passionate before.

Isherwood's Personnel Officer Paul Edwards was glad to catch up with Justin and let him know that he had received applicants for the cleaner jobs that he had advertised. He was disappointed that only five local women had applied, two from Roa and three from Rampside. He had made arrangements to interview all five during the first week in November which meant that he was going to have a very busy time in the very near future.

Paul seemed relieved that his wayward daughter Irene was settling back into university life in Manchester and well away from Rupert Isherwood who he had learned was now out of hospital.

"That man seems to have made a shambles of his life," said Paul.

"I'm pleased to hear that Irene is away from him. Do you know if any charges have been made by the police regarding the fight?"

"No, they don't appear to be doing anything so I assume neither he nor Fred have made any accusations."

Walking back to his office Justin bumped into Amy who asked if she could have a quick word with him.

"I had a coffee with Jean the other day and she wanted me to tell you that she won't be able to get to the Roa Boat this Saturday."

"Did she say why?"

"Something to do with work she said but I'm not sure."

"That's a pity, I was going to ask her to come with me to a play at the Roxy. It's the last of the year."

"It is a shame but Jean also told me to tell you that she will be attending the dance at Rampside a week this Saturday and she will be holding you to a promise when she's there."

Some consolation thought Justin. He had hoped that things would be a little less stressful. He decided on the spot that he would still go and see the play.

Justin had an empty feeling as he made the drive to Ulverston to see the final play of the year being performed at the Roxy. It was only a week since he had seen Jean but it felt more like a month. Patience was not one of his virtues at present and he hoped that he would get beyond this current disposition of his.

The play being staged tonight would hopefully take his mind off things. Arriving in Ulverston Justin headed for the car park that he always used and was soon walking past Coronation Hall to reach the Roxy and he was encouraged by the number of people outside the venue when he arrived. The play was at least popular.

Tonight's play was called 'In at the deep end' and it told the amusing story of a highly moral Mr Potter who ran a health farm. Mr Potter was proud of the high standards he lived and worked by. A client called Gerald Corby arrived in search of peace and tranquillity and he was followed by a trio of ladies in his life and a sex mad window-cleaner.

A number of misunderstandings and mix-ups subsequently occurred which proved to be a headache for the hapless Mr Potter as he strove to maintain the moral integrity of his health farm. Justin found it highly hilarious and his drive back to Roa found him in much better spirits.

Another wet Sunday would leave time on Justin's hands and for once he didn't expect to have an invitation to tea and cake next door. Arthur may not be looking upon Justin in a favourable light having got to know how he had involved

Nellie in a plot, a plot very different to the one he normally cultivated. How mistaken he was, a loud knock on his back door announced the arrival of Nellie and within minutes Justin was sat down with Arthur and the tea and cake never tasted better.

"Come to organise another surprise visit by our Nellie have you?" enquired Arthur who was trying to bring a laugh under control at the same time.

"No, Arthur, I'm not plotting anything else."

"I bet you have a collection of bras hung up somewhere in your place," said Arthur laughing out loud at the same time.

"Arthur, you just watch your tongue," said Nellie.

"Why don't you tell Justin a bit more about the shipyard?"

"Happen, I will, Nellie. Now where did we get to last time?" enquired Arthur.

"I think you got as far as the end of the First World War."

"After the war, orders for ships decreased and the workforce was reduced. The shipyard got some orders for liners from the Orient Line but a financial crises in 1927 forced an amalgamation between the yard and one of its rivals Vickers Armstrong Limited who were based on the River Tyne in the north-east of England. Vickers shared the orders it got between its two shipyards. There was a rise in orders in the 1930s for passenger liners and cargo vessels and when another war was seen as inevitable, what would become World War II, orders were received as part of a rearmament programme."

"The majority of British submarines that were used in the Second World War were built in Barrow as well as some well-known vessels such as HMS Ajax and the aircraft carrier HMS Illustrious. During the war the workforce grew again but after peace was declared in 1945 orders reduced again and so did the workforce. By the 1950s, the worldwide demand for oil increased and the shipyard began constructing oil tankers and some more passenger liners."

"Fascinating, Arthur. Thanks for telling me all about this."

"Don't mention it lad but it wasn't half as interesting as that plot you did with our Nellie! If you ask her nicely she might give you one of her old bra's for your collection."

"Arthur Elwell, you are going to get the sharp end of my tongue if you're not careful!" shouted Nellie.

When Annie popped into Justin's office, she was bubbling with excitement. This was most unusual since Annie was one of those ladies who seemed very adept at keeping their emotions well under control. On reflection, Justin decided that wasn't really true. He had witnessed many different emotions during a number of visits that Annie had made to his office over the year.

Perhaps, he was in the privileged position of seeing the real Annie Isherwood and not the formal business person version. He liked Annie and admired her as he did her husband. Both of them had been extremely good to him and he wouldn't forget it.

"Annie, you look so excited. You must have some good news?"

"Indomitable has been relaunched," was Annie's reply.

This was typical of Annie. She always gives answers to questions which demand another question and Justin dutifully did just that.

"What on earth do you mean?"

"William has found a buyer for our house, the Indomitable."

"That's good news. I bet it's a relief too?"

"Yes, it is. It's good news since we had already started buying a place in Plymouth and this will ensure that there will be no financial difficulties."

"Will it take long for the sale to be finalised?"

"We don't think so. I think William said that he expects the sale to be finalised by the end of next month."

"You're not moving out at the end of November are you Annie?"

"No, no! We expect to move just before Christmas so that we can spend it with Nicola and the grandchildren."

"And how are they all down there in Plymouth?"

"They are doing OK. Nicola gets a little depressed now and again. She needs to involve herself in a social life. It doesn't help either when the children miss their father."

"Annie, who bought your house in Rampside? I hope you won't mind me asking?"

"Not at all, Justin. Your new Managing Director has bought it."

"You mean Andrew Marr from Kendal?"

"Yes I do, and he loves it. I'm not sure that he likes the name but I think he's going to keep it."

It was time for Annie to leave but she enquired as to whether Justin was going to the dance in the village hall on Saturday before she left.

"Yes, I am."

"Good. I know Jean is going to be there and I would love to see you two together again before William and I leave this place,"

"Come in Justin and sit down. I know that a lot of work has been going on behind the scenes to ensure that the factory is ready for its new challenge in 1960 and I would like you to bring me right up to date please?"

William Isherwood the owner and Managing Director of Isherwood & Son, Etching Specialists was an extremely polite man but if anyone made the mistake of thinking he was a soft touch they would be rudely awakened. You don't get to be a Captain in the Royal Navy without being able to assert authority and authority was certainly exercised by William.

In a civilian setting, authority had been achieved through respect and a combination of control and empathy and Justin hoped that he could follow his bosses example in the years to come but for now he better settle for bringing him up to date.

"All the equipment and furniture that we ordered for the new factory section have been delivered and installed. Everything has been tested and is working fine. The section is ready for work."

"Excellent news, Justin. When are the inspectorate going to take a look at everything? We can't begin production until they are satisfied and provide us with certification."

"That's all in hand. The inspectorate will visit the factory in the second week of November."

"Good. Now, what about the new staff we need, where are we with regards to that?"

"During the first week in November we are interviewing all the potential staff we need including cleaners and that means that when the inspectorate arrive we will be able to tell them that we are ready to go."

"That's good too but it sounds a bit risky working on the notion that you can guarantee having all the staff you need after one interview week."

"Mr Edwards has done a brilliant job narrowing down the applicants and he is fairly confident that we will recruit everybody we need."

"Well, let's hope so. We have our new Managing Director, Andrew Marr, and he will be available to attend our training week just before Christmas and that will free me from this desk at last."

"I believe, he is buying your house in Rampside?"

"Yes, he is and that's a load off my shoulders. I'm also greatly satisfied Justin that you are staying with the firm."

"Thanks, Mr Isherwood."

"Justin, I think we can drop the Mr Isherwood business. We know each other well enough now. It's William to you."

"Thanks, William."

"That's better. Now, a final question and that's about the December training week, where have things got to on that front?"

"The weeks programme is almost finished and Paul and I will be putting the finishing touches to it next month."

"Good work, Justin, now join me in a glass of port."

This Saturday night at Rampside Village Hall would, hopefully, mark a turning point in the relationship between Jean Baxter and Justin Ebberson but in order for that to happen they both needed to be there and they were. Initially Justin sat with his five female colleagues from Isherwood's.

Nadine's steady boyfriend, a junior doctor in Barrow was working, Joanne's boyfriend was playing the saxophone in the band whilst Amy's, a joiner called Gordon Blears was due later. That left Lyn and Sheila but both of them were destined to spend most of the night dancing with the same partners all through the evening.

Justin recognised the bloke Lyn was dancing with, he was the one she had spent a lot of time talking to at the Roxy recently. On the other hand, no-one recognised the burly chap that Sheila was clinging to. Enquiries revealed that he was a butcher from Barrow but no-one knew his name.

Jean had arrived with some friends and sat with them on the opposite side of the hall to Justin but that wasn't going to last. Early on in the evening Justin built up the courage to tell himself that this was what he really wanted to do and just as the band began to play a waltz he made his way across to Jean making sure that no-one beat him to it and asked her if he could have the next dance with her.

Jean looked delighted that he had asked her and immediately accepted. As the couple found a space to slot into on the crowded dance floor they looked at each other intently and it only took a couple of slow circuits before they were embracing each other cheek to cheek. The way she felt, the smell of her, everything about her felt superb and Justin didn't want to let go. He had endured ten months without Jean and it had not changed his feelings for her one iota.

When the dance ended Justin asked Jean to come and sit with him and his friends. There was so much he wanted to talk about and he felt ready to do so. The invitation was accepted and she was part of the group in no time. Looking around it was obvious that one or two males in the hall were disappointed that such an attractive dance partner as Jean had been taken off the market. Jean and Justin were extremely happy to be conversing with each other and in such an easy way.

They both caught up on work and home but had to be a little discrete when talking about the current love lives of the other five girls. The conversation was not confined to that between Jean and Justin for the others were also eager to welcome Jean back into her old Isherwood's fold. This was like old times thought Justin and he had not been so happy for a long time.

The evening came to an end far too soon and everyone began to leave. Justin still had a hang up about moving too fast, he couldn't completely remove the memory of the New Year just gone and he needed to be sure that Jean wanted him before he became so involved again. When it came time to say goodnight, he kissed Jean on the cheek and told her how much he had enjoyed her company.

He then went on to ask her if she would come and join him at the Roa Boat next Saturday. Jean assured him that she would love to join him. She was a little disappointed that the evening couldn't have ended in a slightly more passionate way but she understood why and went on her way.

Final Preparations

It was a cold and misty Sunday morning and one which Justin wouldn't mind giving a miss. Opening his bedroom curtains revealed a world cloaked with vapour and he had to wipe some condensation off his window pane to view an uninviting scene. Perhaps another half hour in bed wouldn't do any harm and he could take himself back to last night's dance. The prospect of holding, of kissing, of making love, to that delectable female called Jean were images that he found tantalising.

This girl had an incredible hold on him and the thought of seeing more of her in the future delighted him. He took his thoughts back to last New Year's Eve and the celebration ball he had planned to take Jean to and the necklace with a ruby that he had intended to give her at midnight. Maybe the past could be finally put to rest if he planned to do the same thing this New Year's Eve. He still had the beautiful necklace, it was in a drawer by the side of the bed and he took it out to enjoy its splendour. Jean would love this and it would be grand to see her wear it.

Time to end the day dreams, there were domestic chores to carry out and Justin was hungry. A cup of tea and a couple of slices of toast wouldn't go amiss. Once again Justin had difficulty getting the settings on his toaster correct and two slices of black coloured bread shot out and he just managed to catch them before they landed on the kitchen floor. After that, it was a toast salvage job, he scraped the black cinders away to reveal pale coloured bread which he then buttered and ate. He really ought to sort this toaster out but this was something, like so many others, he had planned on doing ages ago.

With breakfast over, it was time to put a load of shirts into the washing machine adding some Persil washing powder at the same time. Washing, drying and ironing clothes was a real bind and Justin began thinking about the Territorial Army. Was he going to sign up or not? If he was going to sign up then he could call on his neighbour at number three, Marion Quinn and ask her if she would take the task on again for him.

With domestic chores done, Justin wandered out to his plot. The mist had lifted by this time but everywhere had been left damp which did not engender any enthusiasm for gardening.

"Good morning Justin"

Nothing would stop Arthur Elwell from getting something done.

"Morning Arthur. I don't fancy doing much on the plot today."

"I know the feeling. When it's like this, I tend to do repair work on the fence around the plot and my shed."

"I hadn't thought about that but now you mention it I think I should take a look at mine."

Justin walked around the outside of his plot and inspected his fence and gate and spotted several bits that could do with replacing and the whole lot would benefit from a coating of creosote.

It was a nice break when Nellie popped out with a steaming cup of tea and some cake which was most welcome on such a dismal day.

"Are you going to the bonfire on Wednesday Justin?" asked Nellie.

"I forgot all about it Nellie. Whose organising it?"

"I think, it's the members of the sailing club."

"I could ask Jean to come."

Nellie looked at Justin and although she hid it she felt pleased that maybe her neighbour would be getting back with that lovely lass he was going out with last year. Arthur just wondered to himself how many young women Justin had on the go but rather than ask he just got on with the serious business of drinking tea and eating home-made cake.

"By gum Nellie, you can make a lovely cake."

Amy was exceptionally chatty when Justin joined her in the works canteen for a tea break. She couldn't wait to tell Justin about the new men on the scene.

"Lyn is dating a man now. Oops! I should have said that a man is dating Lyn. I think you met him?"

"Oh you mean that chap from Rampside called Bernard?"

"You know already," exclaimed Amy.

"No. Not really. I know she met him at the Brass Band concert at the Roxy."

"That's right she did, anyhow, she's quite smitten with him and he's taken a shine to her. They are seeing a lot of each other."

An image of Sheila almost naked shot through Justin's mind but he was sure that was not the picture that Amy was painting.

"Do you know what Bernard's last name is?"

"Yes, it's Ball. He's Ivor Ball's brother. You know who I mean, it's Ivor the saxophone player in the dance band."

"Isn't that strange, Lyn is going out with Bernard Ball and his brother Ivor is going out with Joanne."

"Isn't it?"

"What does Bernard do for a living?"

"Lyn tells me he got an engineering degree studying at Liverpool University and he has a job at Vickers in Barrow."

"Good for Lyn then. I hope it works out for them."

"You will never guess who else has started dating?" asked Amy.

"Go on, don't keep me guessing."

"Sheila."

"Really!"

"She's going out with a butcher called George Belshaw."

"I've heard of Belshaw's. It's quite a big butcher firm in Barrow."

"It is and George is quite big too."

So all the members of 'Team Five' now have boyfriends thought Justin. It won't be long before Saturday night sessions in the Roa Boat will come to an end and that would be a pity.

"What about you Amy? How are things between you and your boyfriend?"

"Gordon's fine. We get on well together but I don't have any plans to take things any further at the moment, I'm happy with the way things are."

"Amy, I forgot that there is a bonfire here on Roa tomorrow night and I thought I would ask Jean to come along to it but I can't get in touch with her at such short notice. Will you be seeing her tonight?"

"No, I won't. Sorry, Justin."

"Not to worry. I might give it a miss."

"Before I forget Justin. We had a whip round in the factory, as you know, and we got a pram and some clothes for Irene's baby."

"That's brilliant. Have you given them to her yet?"

"Yes and she was overjoyed by what everyone had done for her. She cried."

"I'm very pleased for her," replied Justin.

It had been a very busy week for Paul Edwards. Interviews had occupied the first four days but now they were over and Isherwood's was going to have eight new people on its payroll in the new year.

Justin had been present as applicants for the two fitter positions along with the one for an inspector were being carried out and so he was well aware of who they were but he was not present at the interviews for five cleaners.

"Did you appoint any cleaners Paul?"

"I appointed all five that I interviewed. They were all satisfactory and you may know a couple of them."

"Who were they Paul?"

"Margaret Green who lives with her husband at number seven Marine Terrace and her neighbour from number eight, Joyce Fry."

"I know them both. What about the other three?"

"They were all from Rampside, Ingrid Jones, Samantha Prior and Elizabeth Battersby. Do you know any of them?"

"No, none of them."

Paul went on to talk about the three new appointees for the new section in the factory when it opened in the new year.

"We got two good fitters from Vickers, don't you agree Justin?"

"Yes, I agree. We must let the Company Treasurer and Secretary know about all these new appointees. What was the names again of these two?"

"Malcolm Brown and Alistair Burgess."

"I thought the new woman we selected for the role of inspector was pretty impressive," added Paul.

"Myra Farrimond, yes she was good. I suppose working for a big firm like Vickers a lot of these people are just part of the furniture and when they get the chance to work for a small firm like Isherwood's they are more identifiable," commented Justin.

This represented another milestone in the firm's development bringing the total number of employees to 39.

Given the fact that all 'Team Five' members now had boyfriends it was surprising that they were all gathered together, as they had been so many times before for a Saturday night drinking session. It was more of a social gathering than a heavy drinking bout and judging by tonight's conversation all five were working on the possibility of getting their partners to join them here in the future and this was a goal that they set themselves and landlady Emma was only too pleased to hear it.

There was one couple however that was beating them all to it and that was Jean Baxter and Justin Ebberson. Jean had joined the gathering that she herself had been a part of last year and she looked as if she was renewing her membership. Justin was happy to see how much more relaxed Jean looked back amongst her friends and, hopefully, back with him to. Wearing just a touch of lipstick and a faint touch of make-up she looked exquisite in Justin's eyes but he made a point of not constantly looking at her.

Much of this evenings talk surrounded the men the girls were currently enjoying. Joanne gave a descriptive account of her saxophone playing partner Ivor which should have caused a few blushes but it didn't. Amy bored everyone with Gordon's joinery work whilst Nadine finally revealed her junior doctor's name, Theodore Grant. She refused to go into any details about the operations that Theodore had performed on her but she was saved by the interrogation of Lyn that everybody else was anxious to move onto.

Bernard Ball, brother of Ivor and a university man; it sounded good but was he any good? Lyn made the mistake of telling her friends that he had lovely hands which they all capitalised on much to her embarrassment. Then it was Sheila in the firing line but everyone trod more carefully than they had with Lyn. Burly butcher boy George Belshaw was not a man to toy with but Sheila didn't toy with boys she ate them if the desire was strong enough, at least that's what her friends assumed. Justin new that Sheila was a lot more tender than that but he wasn't going to say, especially since Jean was present. Surprisingly Sheila was not forthcoming about the new man in her life.

The night moved on and new topics to talk about came and went. Purchasing a pram and clothes for Eileen brought some sympathy whilst news about eight new employees was met with mild interest. Roa's bonfire to celebrate November 5th hardly drew any interest at all. For Justin, maximum interest was reserved for the girl sat opposite, Jean. Conversation may have been confined to the week's events but she was there and just seeing her was enough a fact picked up on by Emma behind the bar.

"You two look happy just to be in the same room together."

"I think you hit the nail on the head Emma," replied Justin.

Outside the pub it was time to say goodnight to everyone and Jean was saved until last and a parting hug and kiss ended a pleasant evening. It was obvious that parting in this way was not providing the fulfilment that they both were searching for and soon they would both have to decide how they should change this.

Over Sunday breakfast Justin turned his mind to his relationship with Jean. Simply seeing her on Saturday nights and sharing her company with his Isherwood's colleagues was not enough, he wanted more but did Jean? He still felt damaged by last New Year's experience. He knew that the escapades endured by Jean at the hands of Rupert Isherwood were responsible for what she had done but the scar it left had made him cautious.

No-one else could see that, they, that is to say, all his close friends and especially Rupert's mother Annie, were of the opinion that both he and Jean should now be carrying on as if nothing had happened, but it had, and he couldn't do that. In spite of all this, he did not want to lose her for a second time. It was all a question of time. After several cups of tea, he decided that he would not push things any further until the end of the month.

In December, he would ask her to stay over on Saturday nights after a drink in the Roa Boat and see what her reaction would be. He felt a bit hamstrung at present due to the extra time he had been putting in at the factory preparing for the opening of the new section but that would be out of the way by Christmas and he would have a lot more time on his hands. Christmas was something he hadn't given much thought to and then it struck him. If Jean was happy to stay overnight after a drink in the Roa Boat on a Saturday, then maybe she might consider staying with him over Christmas. She lived on her own, she had no family and the same went for him, so why not?

Enough contemplation, there was stuff Justin could get on with outside on the plot and out he went. The fence work hadn't been finished and he carried on with that before turning to the plot gate. The hinges and latch needed attention and there was more creosoting to do. He hadn't seen Arthur so far but eventually he popped up from behind his shed where he had been doing some work inside.

"Morning, Justin."

"Morning, Arthur."

"Doing a bit more maintenance eh?"

"That's it, Arthur."

"If you intend to get anything planted for next spring, you'll have to do it in the next two weeks."

"It's a good job you told me, Arthur. I'll get that sorted out for next Sunday."

"They launch the SS Oriano in Barrow next week. Do you think you might get to see it?"

"I doubt it, Arthur. We are getting to a crucial stage at Isherwood's setting things up for the new year."

Nellie came out to the two men carrying a welcome tray of refreshments which, given how cold it was, was most welcome.

"What are you doing for Christmas, Justin?" asked Nellie.

"I haven't made any plans yet."

"Are you not going to invite Jean?"

Arthur looked at them both thinking to himself, *'Who is he knocking about with'* but didn't think it worth asking.

"We'll see," replied Justin.

This was a crucial week at Isherwood's. Her Majesties Inspectorate were visiting to ensure that the factory met all its requirements before issuing a licence for the firm to produce a new version of electronic circuit boards that would be used on a raft of Royal Navy vessels. Justin Ebberson's reputation was on the line and he hoped that he had made all the necessary arrangements. The inspectorate were extremely thorough and began their inspection in the stores section, manned by Lyn Gore.

Everything used in the production process arrived here and continuous production relied on the availability of every single item. The inspectorate were well satisfied and moved on to the cutting section where Bert Farington cut circuit boards to the size required. No problems were found and the inspectorate moved on to the circuit tracing section. Here Bob Burns and John Smith traced out the circuits on both single and double sided copper plated boards in preparation for etching. It was problem free, and Justin could heave a sigh of relief that the first day of inspection had gone well.

The following day, Tuesday, the inspectorate were back and continued their work by going to the etching section were Nadine Dorris, using acid baths, etched away surplus copper from the boards leaving behind the tracks that electrical currents would flow along. The inspectorate were well pleased with what they saw. Next it was on to the drilling section in which Amy Fisher and Stuart Naylor drilled holes in boards in which components would be inserted.

Full marks once more and then it was the turn of the new section where components would be soldered on to the boards. This section was ready for action but not currently being used. The two staff that would work in here

Malcolm Brown and Alistair Burgess had not yet started work with the company but at this stage it was not considered as an impediment to the inspection and it got a thumbs up. The last section to be visited today was where the edge connectors were fitted manned by Sandy Fredericks and Johnny Davies.

Wiring looms with plugs on each end were used to plug into edge connectors mounted on the circuit boards so that boards could be connected to each other. It was not Isherwood's responsibility to produce the wiring looms but they did fit edge connectors to the boards and they did it well and the inspectorate were impressed.

Two days of the process finished and just two more to go. Justin would be glad when all this was over.

Wednesday and day three. Everything had gone well so far and fingers crossed it would continue to do so. First section visited today was the inspection section. Currently Sheila Dobson did all the inspections of completed circuit boards but she would share the work in the new year with Myra Farrimond, a future new employee. Another thumbs up and it was on to the packing section, home to expert packer Alan Tinker.

Here, all the completed and inspected circuit boards were carefully packed for onward dispatch. With everything found satisfactory, the inspectorate moved on to the final section, dispatch where Joanne Cooper ensured that everything was sent to where it was supposed to go. No problems here and another thumbs up.

Having inspected the whole of the production facilities, the inspectorate turned next to the maintenance department where Bill and Ben Stone showed all the maintenance schedules they worked to and the manuals and spares held for all the equipment in the factory along with any special tooling. The whole inspection had gone well and Justin thought that it was all over but it wasn't. The inspectorate would be back again tomorrow and that was a surprise.

Thursday morning dawned with an air of anxious expectancy around Isherwood's and when the inspectorate arrived all the employees became apprehensive, 'what on earth do they want to see now'?

It was a great surprise when the works canteen received a visit but Brenda Smith and Gladys Aspinall ran a tight ship and hygiene was top of the bill. Plenished with tea and cake the happy inspectors asked to visit the company office where they met Manager Martha Appleton and her four staff, Eunice Critchley, Joyce Turnbull, Janice Jones and Marion Holmes. Martha did a marvellous job of describing all the work that went on in her department and the inspectorate were satisfied The final subject of inspection was a real matter of concern, keeping the factory clean.

Fortunately, Justin had already prepared the cleaning routine sheets for staff to work to and he was able to inform the inspectorate that he had a team of five ladies doing the work but since they worked in the evenings they were not available to meet them. He did however have to produce a list of their names which he did; Margaret Green, Joyce Fry, Ingrid Jones, Samantha Prior and Elizabeth Battersby.

Justin made no mention of the fact that the present cleanliness of the place was down to all the current shop floor workers. The inspectorate were satisfied with everything they had seen and congratulated Justin. The licence that Isherwood's needed was issued and everyone could celebrate.

"I believe congratulations are in order," said Paul Edwards as he met Justin in his office.

"Thanks Paul. I must confess that I'm relieved that it's all over."

"I know what you have been through. I have experienced inspections in the past and I know they can be mentally draining. Anyway we have our licence. I must say you got away with the factory cleaning issue very nimbly."

"I was really lucky to get away with that but I'm not going to fret over it."

Paul then turned to the subject of getting security clearance for the eight new personnel about to start work.

"It has been hard work getting all the new employees to complete the lengthy forms and bring me all the documents required for me to apply for clearance. Fortunately I got everything required and the whole lot is now in the post."

"It's cutting it a bit fine isn't it Paul? The training week is in five weeks' time."

"That's true. We will just have to keep our fingers crossed that the authorities don't come across anything."

What a relief to get to Saturday night and push Isherwood's business into the background and even better having Jean in the foreground thought Justin as he sat down next to her in the Roa Boat. He had no intention of letting her sit opposite him on the other side of a pub table anymore and she had no objections. The visit by Her Majesties Inspectorate was the main topic of conversation until a certain man called Bernard Ball made an appearance.

As he did so Lyn got up out of her seat and rushed across to meet him. An embrace and a kiss encouraged an applause from the rest of 'Team Five', all present and correct, plus Jean and Justin. Whilst Bernard was nervous at first he soon settled in with the group and became the centre of attraction as everyone wanted to know as much as possible about him.

Jean and Justin were able to talk more intimately as everybody else were focussing on Bernard. Inevitably the subject reverted back to the week Justin had just been through and then moved on to Jean's work in Ulverston at Johnson's Pharmaceutical Plant. Working for a big company on the admin side of things meant working in a large office with nine other women.

Everything was done in a strictly regimented fashion. Tea breaks and lunch time in the large works canteen was the only opportunity each day to meet fellow workers. Being such a large company Johnson's had its own social club and its own sports facilities and Jean had taken advantage of these from time to time. Tomorrow there was another Brass Band concert at the Roxy and Justin dearly wanted Jean to go and enjoy it with him and he asked her.

"Will you not be taking Lyn with you?"

Before Justin could answer, Lyn piped up.

"You can have him. Jean. I've got someone better now."

Jean looked at Justin and smiled at him.

"Stop worrying. I know there was nothing between you two."

Arrangements were then made for the two to meet up outside the Roxy. Neither of them talked about which band would be performing.

The rest of the evening passed quickly, too quickly and it was time to head for home. Justin didn't want the evening to end at all especially after the two had shared an extremely passionate embrace and had kissed each other and not on the cheeks this time. They almost moulded together on the pub doorstep but Emma helped them on their way with a slight push and a little advice.

"You two need a night in bed with each other." But it was not going to be tonight.

This could be the last opportunity to plant stuff for next spring and Justin made a special effort to brave the cold outside and get on with the job. Well-wrapped up, he went across to his plot and got a garden fork out of his shed. Some of the ground he intended planting things in was infested with pests and hence his first task was to turn the soil over and then fumigate it with a pesticide.

This took a little time but when it was done he could get on with planting broad beans and horse radish.

Not exactly exciting stuff to grow but they were all he had and, more importantly, he hadn't taken the trouble of studying the gardening books his uncle Dick had left behind. Even if he had Justin doubted that he would have done much more, when all said and done, he knew he was a lazy half-hearted gardener. The best part of working on his plot was sitting down with Arthur from next door and having a chat whilst enjoying the refreshments supplied by Arthur's wife Nellie and this Sunday morning was going to be no different.

"Good morning, Justin."

Arthur was making his usual entrance on the scene which meant that tea break was imminent and true to form Nellie made an appearance with mugs of steaming hot tea and some home baked cake to help it go down.

"Eee I am pleased that you are taking up again with that lovely lass Jean."

Roa Island has the most efficient communication system in the world thought Justin.

"We are taking gentle steps forward Nellie."

"It would be nice to see her around," Nellie went on.

"Give the lad a break, Nellie. He'll have to get rid of all his other women first," said Albert.

"Now, let's not have any more of that talk Arthur, if you please," said Nellie getting slightly annoyed.

This was always a signal for Arthur to change the subject.

"I heard you got a licence for the factory last week."

"Yes, that's true and I must confess that I'm relieved that we have got it. I'm looking forward to ending all the extra work that I've had to put in to get everything set up."

"What's left to do then Justin?"

"The programme for our training week needs finalising and then we can run it."

"Can you do that before Christmas?"

"I hope so."

Things then moved on to Brass Band concerts at the Roxy.

"Are you going to the concert tonight at the Roxy?" Asked Arthur.

"I wouldn't miss it for anything. I've been to every single one this year and next month will be the last this year."

"Which band is playing tonight?"

"It's the 'Cory Band'."

"That's a Championship Section band from South Wales isn't it?"

"Yes it is and we are very lucky that they are visiting Ulverston."

"That's a band with a fine reputation Justin. Should be a good concert."

Later that same day Justin rushed down his evening meal and got ready to meet Jean outside the Roxy Cinema in Ulverston. It was important to make an effort to look smart, he wanted to make a good impression. He shaved carefully in order to avoid nicking his skin. A touch of aftershave on his cheeks, a quick gargle with some mouth wash and a little Brylcreem on his hair would add a nice touch. Next, check that his clean shirt was nicely ironed and in the cuff's he would fit his favourite cuff-links.

Choose a good tie and wear it with a Windsor knot. Suit trousers well pressed and brushed along with the jacket. Now a clean handkerchief. It was all done to the standard he had been taught when he did his National Service in the RAF. A final look in the mirror to ensure his tie was lying in the correct position and then he combed his hair. It was a cold night and Justin finished his preparation by choosing a nice scarf to wear underneath his overcoat to keep the cold out from around his neck.

The drive to Ulverston seemed to take ages but in reality it was only as long as all the other journeys he had made in the past. It was the anticipation of seeing Jean that was making it seem so long. Justin parked his car close to Ulverston's Coronation Hall, a venue he intended taking Jean to on New Year's Eve. He then walked the short distance to the Roxy where, on arrival, he saw the girl that had captured his heart.

Standing tall, wearing a dark coloured coat she looked wonderful. Her shapely legs had always been an attraction for Justin and they looked exquisite and her tall heeled shoes enhanced them further. When Jean saw Justin walking towards her, she smiled and that smile almost overpowered him and he couldn't help asking himself why such a good-looking girl would want to be seen on a date with a man like him?

As he got nearer, that thought went out of the window, he was going to enjoy her company as much as possible. When they came together, they kissed lightly on the lips, there was no point spoiling the light touch of her lipstick, that could come later. The sheer joy of meeting each other was obvious to anyone that cared to notice but most didn't, they were here to get inside the Roxy and listen to one of the world's finest Brass Bands.

Having taken their seats, Justin and Jean looked on at the stage which was set out in readiness for the band making their entrance. Music stands were in position along with seats for the twenty-five players and a rostrum for the conductor. Brass instruments had been placed either on seats or on the floor in front of them. Behind the far set of seats all the kit used by the percussion section had been set up and was ready for use. All that was needed now was the band.

In the few minutes left before the concert started, Jean wanted to know something about tonight's band and Justin told her what he knew.

"The band was formed in 1884 in the Rhonda Valley in Wales. It was originally called 'Ton Temperance' as it was associated with the South Wales Temperance movement. In 1895, Sir Clifford Cory, Chairman of Cory Brothers provided financial support for the band and as a result in 1920 the band changed its name to Cory. Since then the band has gone on to win many awards."

"How do you know all that?" Asked Jean.

"It's all written down in the concert programme," answered Justin and the two of them laughed.

The players made their entrance on to the stage as the audience clapped. When seated, the band looked splendid wearing their red blazers. As Conductor Tom Powell walked on all the players immediately stood up until he had bowed to the audience. He then turned to face the players, raised both arms whilst holding a baton in his right hand and signalled the start of the concert with a rousing march. This was followed by an excellent choice of 'arrangements for brass' of a number of classical compositions. The whole concert was well received and the end was marked with a thunderous applause. Ulverston had been done proud by this Welsh Band.

"Did you enjoy the concert Jean?"

"Of course, I did. Thank you for inviting me."

Parting from Jean when things had come to an end was not what Justin or Jean wanted to do and Justin took a chance and told Jean that he hoped she would come to the Roa Boat next Saturday as he wanted to talk about seeing more of her, if she agreed. Jean looked into Justin's eyes, this was something she had been hoping he would say to her. The business with Rupert Isherwood had got in the way of everything and she desperately wanted to put it all behind her.

"I would love to talk about that Justin and I will see you next Saturday."

A loving embrace marked the end of the evening and both of the happy music lovers went their separate ways.

Walking back home after work, Justin decided to walk past the front of all the houses in Marine Terrace and as he did so he suddenly became aware that the huge liner, the SS Oriana had been moved. It was just visible in the fading light and it was docked in a different position within Barrow dockside area. It must have been launched! As he got to the last two houses in the terraced row he saw Arthur standing on his front doorstep.

"Hello, Arthur. I see the SS Oriana has been launched."

"Aye, it has. It was launched a fortnight ago. I got the date wrong."

"When did it get launched then?"

"It was on the third of November. The Queen's cousin Princess Alexandra performed the launch and when it was over it was moved to its 'fitting out berth' where you can see it now."

"How long will it be there?"

"They reckon it will take about twelve months and next year Queen Elizabeth II will get a tour of it when she comes to Barrow to name the nuclear submarine HMS Dreadnought."

The Saturday night group of regular drinkers at the Roa Boat was getting bigger, much to the delight of landlady Emma Barton. 'Team Five' was now, with the addition of Jean Baxter, 'Team Six'. The expansion of the group was down to the amorous pursuits of its members. Lyn's boyfriend, Bernard Ball, was no newcomer, he had made his debut last Saturday but new on the block this week was Gordon Blears who was dating Amy.

The odds were evening up now with three men and six ladies and they were accommodated by bringing two large pub tables together occupying the whole of one quarter of the main room. There was a great deal of speculation regarding future attendance by the partners of Sheila and Nadine but they would not be drawn on the subject. In the case of Joanne, it was assumed that her boyfriend, saxophone player Ivor Ball, was never likely to join them but she vowed to work on him or his blasted saxophone.

When the opportunity presented itself, Justin nervously approached Jean with what he had had in his mind for some time. *'He was genuinely worried about how she would react but here goes,'* he thought.

"Jean, I hope you will come to Rampside Village dance next Saturday?"

Jean was really hoping that there would be a bit more to talk about than this and sheepishly replied.

"Of course, I will, Justin."

"Well, I have been thinking."

"Go on."

"Well, after the dance, I wondered if you would come and stay the night at my place. It's much nearer than yours in Ulverston?"

No matter how low people kept their voices in the Roa Boat, other folk seemed to be able to listen in and the silence around the table became acutely apparent. Not only Justin was waiting for the answer.

"I would love to, Justin. I have been longing to have you to myself."

This was the highlight of the evening and everyone clapped and shouted out loud all kinds of things but the most memorable was 'about time' to which they all raised a glass to toast two blushing companions.

Emma Barton got caught up with the excitement and treated the whole group with a free round of drinks. Secretly, if Emma could ever do secret, she was very happy for both Justin and Jean.

The night had ended well and what was one week in a lifetime thought Justin as he walked back to number eleven.

November was certainly turning out to be a cold month and the time to feel it most was when working on his plot. For the first time, this winter Justin had been forced to wear gloves but being made of wool he soon created holes around the finger tips and by the end of this gardening session they would be fit for nothing.

On days like this, it was only fit for general maintenance work and the fence, gate and shed ended up on today's 'to do' list. Finishing creosoting everything was a most time consuming job but by the end of the daylight hours it was done and it all looked good. Nellie made an appearance with some refreshments for Arthur and himself but, feeling the cold, she soon went back indoors.

For some reason, Arthur didn't have much to say, he seemed content to warm his hands around his mug of hot tea and enjoy the view of Piel Island and beyond. When he did speak it was only to acknowledge how cold it was. Justin was in no way put out by Arthur's lack of conversation he could see that Arthur looked contented and he left him to his own thoughts.

At precisely 3:00pm on Wednesday, Annie Isherwood, arrived at Justin's office followed by Brenda, one of the works canteen ladies, with a tray of tea and cake. Justin arrived almost immediately afterwards.

"Hello, Annie, lovely to see you."

"And you Justin. We won't be meeting like this after Christmas will we?"

"No, I don't suppose that we will. I'm going to miss the tea and cakes that you bring."

Annie knew that Justin was just winding her up.

"Is that all you are going to miss?"

"No, not at all. I'm going to miss you. I'm going to miss how you mother me."

"Do you miss your real mother, Justin?"

"Yes I do, and my father. They gave a lot up for me. Mum and Dad both worked hard to fund me when I attended university in Manchester."

"I'm sure they would both be proud of you."

Justin could sense that Annie was itching to tell him something and she did.

"Rupert has at last done something decent."

"Really, and what was that?"

"The sale of the family house in Newbiggin brought a tidy sum of money and he has given a half of it to Nicola."

"That is good news."

"Well, now she can get a place of her own in Plymouth which is a good thing. She likes her independence and whilst her parents have been really good with her and the children it's not what she wants on a permanent basis."

Annie shuffled in her seat for a moment or two and then continued.

"The biggest surprise is that Rupert has given a sizeable amount of the money he received to Eileen for the welfare of his daughter, Susan."

"That is a surprise and I'm sure it will be a great relief to the Atherton family. Fred and Eileen have been struggling financially for some time."

"That's true. It may not get them their own home but at least they can be comfortable where they are and provide for the three children they now have."

"I know I shouldn't ask this but is Rupert OK financially?"

"Oh yes. He already owns the flat he is living in in Ulverston and he has considerable savings. He will still be left with a lot of money from his house sale after paying out to Nicola and Eileen. I almost forgot, he still has his favourite car, that maroon-coloured Alvis of his."

Annie seemed to be cherishing every minute with Justin in his office. She was going to miss him greatly when she and William left to go and live in Plymouth. Justin was the son she had hoped Rupert would have been.

"Justin, I am really happy that you and Jean are getting back together. Cherish her as much as you can. Living on her own and with no family around can be incredibly lonely, you know."

Justin knew that, he was experiencing the same thing and cherishing Jean Baxter was something he fully intended to do. He told Annie of his intentions and she hugged him before leaving.

William welcomed Justin into his office. It was time to receive the monthly update on Isherwood's preparations for the new product they had got a contract to produce starting in January 1960.

"I know that a lot has happened in the last month, Justin and you must have been very busy. Tell me where we are at."

"The most important thing of all is that Her Majesties Inspectorate have issued us with a licence to go ahead which means that they are satisfied that the factory meets all their requirements."

"That's absolutely excellent news, Justin. Well done."

The other good news is that we have now recruited two component fitters to work in the new section and one additional product inspector.

"So, we are fully equipped for the new work and we have the new staff. What about training the staff, is everything in place to train them?"

"The third week in December as been set aside as a training week for all our current staff as well as the new employees. Paul Edwards and myself have been putting the details together for the training programme and it will be completed in the next fortnight."

"Excellent. Now what about the raw materials that we will require to make these new products?"

"Everything has been ordered and it should all arrive over the course of the next three weeks."

"That's cutting it a bit tight Justin?"

"I'm afraid it's the best that the suppliers we use could do. If we used other suppliers, we could have had earlier shipments to us but at rather exorbitant prices. I am confident that everything will arrive on time."

"Did we manage to get some cleaning staff?"

"Yes we did. We got five local ladies and they will attend our training week."

"Good, that will make them feel part of the team and I'm very pleased that they are all local ladies. There isn't a lot of work in the immediate vicinity and I like the idea of local families benefitting from our enterprise. Well done Justin. Is there anything else that I need to know?"

"We are still waiting for security clearance for our eight new employees. Applications have been sent to the appropriate authority but they do take their time. I have my fingers crossed that they are all cleared to do the work and we get notification in the next three weeks."

"A bit of a nail biter then," commented William.

"Boss there is something I would like to ask you."

"Go ahead Justin."

"I would like to take a couple of days off to get some stuff together for Christmas. Working six days a week doesn't allow me any time to get anything."

"Do you really need to come into work on any more Saturday's?"

"I could cope without doing that. I have four more evenings to work before our training week and I could finish off everything that needs doing then."

"Well that's settled then. Take those two Saturday's off and I'll arrange you don't lose any pay."

"Thanks William."

"Now before you go let's have a drink together and tell me how you and Jean Baxter are getting on?"

Once Justin had got in from work around tea time on Saturday he made a point of leaving the gates open at the back of his house so that Jean could drive her car into his backyard. The yard wasn't very big but it could accommodate two small cars and there would be enough room for Jean's as well as Justin's. Just after tea Jean arrived and it was a thrill to welcome her into his home.

She had brought a small overnight bag with her which she took upstairs and placed in the back bedroom. She wasn't sure about the sleeping arrangements and was too shy to ask. They travelled together to Rampside Village Hall to join their friends for the monthly dance. Tonight's surprise was Sheila's new boyfriend, George Belshaw, joining them. The group was getting larger every week, six young ladies and four young men, Gordon and Bernard had joined them along with Justin.

Joanne's man, Ivor, was busy making music on the stage which only left Nadine's junior doctor friend to make himself known to everyone but that wasn't going to happen tonight. The night passed quickly as everyone talked, danced, ate and drank and had a lot of fun. Justin, in spite of enjoying the dance was looking forward to what would follow and he suspected that Jean did too. The end did eventually come and once the Royal Anthem had been played by Mrs Pringle's ensemble everyone ambled out into the cold air.

Good nights were exchanged and a variety of small cars conveyed the retiring dancers to wherever they were going which in the case of Jean Baxter and Justin Ebberson was number eleven, Marine Terrace, Roa Island.

Sharing coffee Justin and Jean sat together on the settee in the back room and talked.

"What do you do during the week, Jean?"

"Not a lot really. I do my own cooking, I do my own shopping, washing and drying clothes and keep my place clean. After work, that doesn't leave a lot of time for anything else."

"But you do have some friends, don't you?"

"Yes I do. They are all girls that work at Johnson's. We meet up once or twice a week, mostly at Johnson's social club. We go to the pictures in Ulverston now and again."

"Is the social club any good?"

"It's OK. Nothing special but I started going there because I knew Rupert couldn't get access."

That was the first time that name had cropped up all evening.

"Talking of Rupert, I have wanted to explain to you for a long time why I did what I did last New Year's Eve, Justin."

"Jean, you don't have to tell me right now and I don't want anything to spoil this first night together."

Justin took Jean by the hand and led her upstairs to his bedroom. Trembling a little, she excused herself and went to retrieve her overnight bag. In her absence, Justin put his pyjamas on and got into bed. When Jean entered the bedroom, she too had put some pyjamas on.

Justin pulled back some sheets and she nervously sat on the bed before taking the plunge and swung her legs under the bed sheets to join him. The two apprentice lovers embraced each other tightly and the kissing began. Things initially moved slowly as they fumbled for each other's sensuous parts.

The newness of this wonderful night did not proceed as far as intercourse or even to being naked. It would take time for these two to be free of their inhibitions but the journey into this universe of pleasure would be an exciting experience. If it had been a bit warmer, it might have helped.

The Final Coming Together

Waking up on Sunday morning lying next to the girl you are so passionately in love with must be a dream, but it wasn't. Justin had slept embracing his greatest desire. It was something that he had thought not too long ago would never happen but here she was and he felt incredibly happy. Without waking Jean he got out of bed and went downstairs to make some tea.

He momentarily toyed with the idea of making some toast but then remembered that he had still not mastered the damn settings on the thing and he didn't think that double sided semi-black toast would create a good impression. Jean was awake when Justin arrived with the tea and they both enjoyed their first hot drink together in bed.

As Jean got out of bed and went to the bathroom, Justin followed her every movement. She looked quaint in her pyjamas. When she came back into the bedroom, she was wearing her knickers and bra. It was the first time that Justin had ever seen Jean so naked and he couldn't take his eyes off her. He felt a strong urge to drag her back into bed but he resisted. *'Why rush everything,'* he thought, *'just enjoy the journey.'*

Jean was acutely aware that Justin was looking at her and she hoped he would be pleased with how she looked. She wasn't thin just nicely proportioned. She didn't stand on ceremony as Justin gazed at her longingly, she just got on with putting her dress on. This morning moment of bliss had to come to an end for it was already mid-morning and life's demands still had to be attended to.

As the day went on, Justin decided to show Jean the plot outside his front door that he had been cultivating. Being the start of December the weather was not to good. A cold breeze was sweeping across the open space in front of Marine Terrace. Even the seagulls were taking shelter. It wouldn't be long before some rain would be heading in and so it didn't pay to remain outside too long. They didn't get back inside before Nellie spotted them.

"Eee lass, you don't know how nice it is to see you again. Two young lovers and living next door to us as well!"

The two, so-called lovers, blushed but felt happy knowing that Nellie was feeling for the two of them. Unmarried couples living together, which they were not, not yet, were often frowned upon and sometimes shunned but not by Nellie, bless her.

Arthur came on the scene and peered at the couple over Nellie's shoulder. He scratched his head and couldn't help thinking what a lucky blighter this Justin bloke was with women but he was pleased to see Jean, he liked her. With pleasantries exchanged, it was time to get out of the cold and indoors again.

"Justin, I better get home. I've got quite a few things to do to get ready for work on Monday but I would like to call and see you after work on Wednesday if that's OK?"

"Of course, it is, Jean. I'll look forward to it. Before I forget, next Saturday I'm planning to go into Barrow to do some Christmas shopping and I wondered if you would like to come?"

"I'm sorry, Justin I can't. I'm taking my car to have a job done on it next Saturday and I made a commitment to some of the girls at work to do some shopping in Ulverston. I hope you don't mind?"

"No, no, that's fine. I'll see you on Wednesday."

Lyn called in to see Justin and told him that a load of stuff had arrived for him and she had put it all on display for him in the factory store. When he arrived, he could see what Lyn's stuff amounted to. There were fire extinguishers, first aid kits and wall safety posters. These were all items that Her Majesties Inspectorate said that either Isherwood's needed or needed replacing.

Now, it was a case of placing all these things where they needed to be. Justin made several trips around the whole factory fitting them in place. He got rid of the bulkiest things first namely the fire extinguishers and then followed on with the first aid kits. The wall posters were left until last and the old stuff was placed outside for collection along with other rubbish. The exception to this were the old fire extinguishers which had to be removed by a specialist firm because of their contents.

"Justin this place looks even more professional with all this stuff around the place," remarked Lyn.

"Well, we have to be prepared. We need the right equipment to cover any potential accidents and the posters are there to educate and inform everyone about safety. It really is important."

"Do we have any designated first aiders in the factory, Justin?"

Blimey, that was something he had not sorted out and it needed to be. It was not just a case of designating someone, they would have to be qualified and notice's created telling the workforce who the designated first aiders were.

"Lyn, you have just reminded me of what I need to do," and with that Justin left.

Paul Edwards was in his office when Justin called and was only too happy to listen to what he was concerned about. After discussing things Paul informed Justin that he would let all the employees know that Isherwood's were looking for a number of volunteers to act as designated first aiders. He would also look at the courses that the 'Red Cross Society' and 'St John's Ambulance Brigade' ran to train people to perform this function.

"I will have a word with the Company Treasurer, Ron Bright to see if we can make a financial payment to those that we designate and to cover the costs of the courses they will need to attend to get qualified."

Thank goodness I got that sorted thought Justin. He had clean forgotten about it.

Jean arrived soon after tea on Wednesday evening and Justin was very happy to see her. As soon as she came into number eleven she seemed at home. They sat down together and Jean began the conversation.

"Justin, I really want you to know what really happened between Rupert Isherwood and me. It's not what some people would like you to believe."

"You don't have to tell me. I'm just happy that you have chosen to be with me now."

"I know but I don't want any stories reaching your ears that may get you thinking twice about me."

Jean then went on to describe how Rupert had constantly made approaches to her in the last half of 1958 so much so that she couldn't put up with it anymore and she decided to get a job somewhere else, away from Isherwood's.

She found a job at Johnson's in Ulverston but soon realised that it was a long drive to work each day and she was spending a lot of money on petrol and that's why she left Nadine and Sheila's place where she had been living and found a flat in Kennedy Street, Ulverston.

Rupert continued trying to date her even though he was seeing Eileen Atherton. She did go on a date with him twice but her plan had been to convince him that she wasn't interested in him. She never kissed him or did anything else with him and she certainly never moved into his flat as some people may have said.

"Over a long period of time this year, Rupert has tried to make me go out with him but I have never given in to his desires. I hate that man and want nothing to do to with him."

By this time, Jean was shaking a little and tears began to appear in her eyes. Justin embraced her and assured her that she had nothing to worry about, she had him and that was all that mattered. It was a little strange after this outpouring. A slightly strained atmosphere existed as each of them came to terms with what had just been said.

"Jean, will you come to the Roa Boat on Saturday night and stay with me again afterwards?"

"Are you sure you still want me, Justin?"

"More than ever."

What a change it was not to have to go into work on a Saturday thought Justin. It was almost a year since he had a free Saturday except for holidays. He didn't waste too much time getting off into Barrow to do some shopping, there were lots of things to buy. First, he bought Christmas cards, he bought one for each of the employees at Isherwood's and some for all his neighbours on Marine Terrace, then there was one for Emma Barton at the Roa Boat and one for the lady in his life, Jean Baxter.

Second, he bought some Christmas presents, nothing special, he couldn't afford it but he wanted to give the five girls from work something especially for the way they had supported him in this dark year. He also wanted to get a present for his neighbours at number twelve, Nellie and Arthur.

The list seemed to be getting longer, he couldn't leave out Paul Edwards and his wife or Annie and William Isherwood, they were all special people that were playing a special part in Justin's life. He decided he must make a big effort to get something really nice for Jean. He planned on doing that next Saturday when he could devote all of his attention to that one special thing.

Once back from Christmas shopping, Justin set about making his house as warm as possible before Jean arrived. He built up the coal fires in both of his downstairs rooms. He rarely lit a fire in his front room and at this time of year it felt like the inside of a fridge. He filled two hot water bottles with boiling water and placed them both in his bed.

When Jean arrived, she brought with her some crumbly Lancashire cheese and some sausages. She baked the cheese in Justin's oven and served it hot with grilled sausage and it tasted delicious and soon after they joined their friends in the Roa Boat.

Tonight the group of drinkers was swollen to eleven, the new addition being one junior doctor by the name of Theodore Grant and he was proudly presented by Nadine as her medical advisor. Theodore was tonight's central attraction and the poor doctor was bombarded by medical queries not all of which had a sound medical basis and some were clearly sexually orientated.

Theodore had heard it all before and took it all in good part and everyone loved him for it. Little attention was paid to Justin and Jean, it was as if they had been together for years, just another part of the furniture and they felt all the better for it.

Back at Justin's place no time was wasted going to bed. Although the fires had kept going in their absence, they had died down and in the battle between warmth and cold, cold was winning. Best to be between the sheets at times like this and Justin was delighted when Jean aimed straight for his bedroom, unlike the previous week. The two hot water bottles had done their stuff and the bed sheets were lovely and warm. The two of them, once in bed, tightly embraced and kissed each other and then got on with the more interesting part of 'getting to know you'.

Hands wandered freely inside and outside of pyjamas and Jean's firm breasts and proud nipples became the focus of Justin's lust. He had to see them and without any struggle, two pyjama tops were discarded and flung out of the bed. Skin-against-skin can be so intoxicating and both enjoyed their own orgy until the cold, freely supplied by nature, began to get a stronger grip than their own hands had. It was time to stop all this sex stuff, don pyjama tops, tightly embrace again and let the self-generated heat induce some sleep and it did.

A hot drink in bed had never tasted better. The presence of Jean was making everything taste sweeter. Justin watched Jean go to the bathroom in pyjamas and return in her knickers and bra. As she was about to put on her dress he asked her to take off her bra for him and she obliged. Looking at half naked, well almost naked, Jean was an immensely pleasurable experience. Her tall slim figure, almost hour glass curves, and her firm breasts together with her attractive face made her incredibly desirable. Nevertheless Jean got on with dressing herself once she had satisfied Justin's ogling.

Once downstairs and with breakfast out of the way Jean revealed the contents of the second bag she had brought with her, Christmas decorations. The rest of the day was spent putting up the decorations in both Justin's living room and front room and his house was transformed, it felt like Christmas was just around the corner. Only a Christmas Tree was missing and Justin promised he would do something about it.

Thoughts turned to what they should do over the Christmas Festive Season and after a little discussion they agreed that come next Saturday they would talk to their friends about celebrating Christmas Eve in the Roa Boat and if they agreed they would ask Emma Barton if she would put some food on for them all. Then they agreed that they would both keep Christmas Day for themselves and Jean would stay at Justin's place.

"Justin, could we organise a party in your house on Boxing Day? I could help to pay for all the food and drink and prepare everything?"

How could he refuse. Justin wanted this Christmas to be the best ever with the most wonderful girl in the whole wide world.

Soon after making plans for Christmas Jean had to head off back to Ulverston but she promised to stay longer next Sunday and to attend the last Brass Band concert of the year at the Roxy with Justin.

"Are you calling on Wednesday night?" asked Justin.

"Yes I will."

And then Jean drove home to Ulverston.

Paul Edwards was looking particularly down in the dumps when Justin walked into Isherwood's canteen for some lunch. Respecting Paul in the way he did Justin couldn't ignore him by sitting at another table and so he joined him.

"Mind if I sit here, Paul?"

"No. Go ahead Justin."

"You don't look in good form today?"

Paul looked up at Justin and his jaw was set firm and he had a distinctly hostile look about him.

"That stupid daughter of mine has got herself pregnant."

This piece of news stumped Justin. He hadn't seen this coming and he felt too embarrassed to ask who the father was but he didn't need to.

"That bloody sex maniac Rupert Isherwood has got her in the family way."

"But I thought she was at university in Manchester and out of his way?"

"So did we as well. The deceiving bugger was going back to his flat whenever she could and never told anyone and that bastard took full advantage of a young woman in a cruel way. He's much older than Irene and should have known better."

"What are you going to do?"

"Justin, what can I do? Irene has made her choice and she'll have to live with it. I suppose my wife and I will have to pick up the pieces when it all goes wrong."

There was no consoling Paul, it was just a sad episode in his life and probably worse in the long run for his daughter Irene.

Jean arrived on Wednesday evening just after tea and immediately began putting up more Christmas decorations. At this rate, the house would resemble Santa's Grotto thought Justin. Eventually they got sat down together and Justin broke the news about Irene's pregnancy.

"Rupert Isherwood is an evil man. What's her dad got to say about it?"

"He's deeply disappointed with Irene and very annoyed with Rupert but there is nothing he can do about it. He and his wife have talked to Irene and advised her to stay away from Rupert but she has chosen to ignore their advice."

"I think she will regret it," commented Jean.

"Jean, I have decided that I am not going to join the Territorial Army."

"I'm not sure that I knew you had been thinking about it."

"I started thinking about it when I thought I had too much time on my hands and I would spend it all just dwelling on things."

Jean put her arm across Justin's shoulder and her cheek to his. She kissed him before saying, "You have no need to dwell on things anymore and I'm sorry I put you through all that torment. I was going through it too but now we can both put that behind us."

"Well, anyway, I was also thinking about asking one of my neighbours to do my washing again. I hate doing it, especially the ironing. If I don't join the TA and the extra work I have been doing for Isherwood's comes to an end, then I'm going to have plenty time on my hands to see you."

"But you will lose some pay from Isherwood's, won't you?"

"Yes that's true. Maybe, I will just keep doing my own washing and ironing."

"Now, you are being sensible."

On his second Saturday off, Justin headed back to Barrow. He had deliberately not asked Jean to accompany him this time for he wanted to keep something secret from her. He bought her a jacket that he knew she would like, but the real reason for not bringing her was that he was going to search for an engagement ring. He visited several jewellers in the town before he finally settled on a single diamond solitaire ring.

Justin intended proposing to Jean before they set out to Ulverston's Coronation Hall on New Year's Eve where he would give her the necklace that he had intended giving her last New Year's Eve. *'Everything would then be where it should be,'* he thought to himself. On his way back from Barrow, he called at a farm that advertised Christmas Trees for sale and chose one that was far too big to bring home in his car. Fortunately the farmer had engaged the services of a delivery firm and within an hour of him arriving home the tree arrived.

In the Roa Boat, Joanne was cock a hoop that Ivor, her saxophone playing, boyfriend had got a night off to join her and her friends. Six men and six women! It was a sizeable group and a most welcome one as far as the landlady, Emma Barton, was concerned. Ivor Ball got a lot of stick from all the ladies present. It was an adopted enrolment ceremony but he passed OK.

Ivor was a nice bloke but a bit odd. Most folk put it down to the amount of time he spent blowing his brains out but Joanne didn't mind at all, in fact, she thought it improved his kissing technique and it did something for his finger work to but she wouldn't say in what way.

The most talked about subject tonight was Irene Edward's pregnancy and that predator Rupert Isherwood. Questions focussed on how she would be able to continue with her studies at university, would she live with Rupert and how will her mother and father cope with the news. Throughout all this Jean just hoped that she wouldn't feature in the discussion, he wasn't someone she wanted to recall. Her friends were diplomatic and did not draw Jean into the conversation.

Matters now turned to Christmas and everyone thought it would be a brilliant idea to meet up here in the Roa Boat for a Christmas Eve knees-up but they would have to run it past Emma.

"You mean you want me to put up with you lot on Christmas Eve and feed you an all?"

Emma agreed and a price was worked out that everyone could afford. Next it was Jean and Justin's turn to invite everyone to their Christmas party on Boxing Day but they were sadly disappointed. Only Joanne who was from a Roa Island family would be able to make it. She would be able to bring Ivor with her but they would be the only ones from amongst the group that would be there, all the others were going home to visit their own families over the festive period.

Sheila tried to move things on by asking the disappointed duo if they were going to the Brass Band concert at the Roxy tomorrow night and shortly afterwards everyone headed for home. Jean and Justin returned to number eleven slightly deflated and they both wondered how they could overcome running a party with only two other people. Justin suggested that they ask all their neighbours in Marine Terrace and Jean agreed and that was something they would talk about tomorrow.

"It's really cold in your house, Justin."

"I didn't get the chance to light two fires and I forgot to shore up the one in the living room."

He had also forgot to put any hot water bottles in bed and he had to fill two before Jean and himself headed upstairs to bed. The cold made them both embrace tightly and it also dampened their ardour. It was purely a case of keeping each other warm on this December night. No prolonged body exploration was going to be indulged in which was just as well since Jean was on her monthly period. It was a lot nicer sharing a bed than being on your own thought Justin.

Justin leapt out of bed on a freezing cold Sunday morning and rushed to get dressed. He left Jean who was still sleeping and went downstairs to get a good fire going in both of his two downstairs rooms. He cleaned out the ash from both fireplaces before filling them with newspaper on top of which he placed pieces of firewood and some firelighters. He lit the newspaper with matches and when the wood and firelighters began to show flames he put a small shovel of coal on each one. It didn't take long to get the two fires going but it would take some time before the two rooms started to get warm.

Then he took an enormous risk by attempting to make several burn free slices of toast in his temperamental toaster whilst boiling water at the same time to make some mugs of tea. The risk paid off and using a tray he took the fruits of his cooking skills up to the bedroom he was sharing with Jean. The hot tea was enjoyed by both as they sat up in bed with dressing gowns wrapped around their shoulders. Fed and watered the two of them ventured downstairs into a warmer place which Jean greatly appreciated.

The day really began by putting the Christmas Tree up that Justin had bought and hanging tinsel, and coloured balls on it and topping it off with a silver winged angel. Matters then turned to the Christmas party they wanted to hold here in number eleven. Both agreed that it would be festive to extend some goodwill to all their neighbours and they would call at each house on Marine Terrace and invite them.

There was no need to call at numbers one since Nadine and Sheila lived there or number two where Lynn and Amy lived and so they started at number three where Marion and Roger Quinn lived. They were both delighted to be invited and accepted the invitation as did Flora and Angus Campbell at number five and it was a relief to them that they could also bring their two daughters.

Then it was on to number four, the home of one of Isherwood's canteen ladies, Brenda Smith plus her husband and son. Brenda was really pleased to be asked to attend the party and immediately volunteered to help with the food preparation and suggested that if her workmate, Gladys Aspinall who lived at number ten was invited then she too could also help with the food.

Brenda even offered to make a list of everything that would be needed if she knew how many people would be going to the party and if anything perishable was left in Isherwood's canteen on shutdown for the Christmas break she would bring it to Justin's place. Number ten was the last port of call for today and they made Gladys and her husband and daughter very happy by inviting them and of course she would help out. At each house that Justin and Jean had called on a long conversation had ensued and the day soon passed by.

"What about the others at number six, seven, eight, nine and twelve?" asked Jean.

"If you call at my place on Wednesday, we can call on them all then."

Whitburn Band from West Lothian in Scotland was due to perform at the Roxy in Ulverston on Sunday night and both Jean and Justin intended to be there. They drove in separate cars to Ulverston since at the end of the concert they would be going their separate ways. This was the final Brass Band concert of the year and looking back the venue had brought some of the best bands in the world to entertain the many local fans and tonight Whitburn would continue the tradition.

Once inside the Roxy, Justin and Jean had the opportunity of learning something about the band from the concert programme. Whitburn Band was formed in the heart of the coal mining area of West Lothian in 1870. The band performed in local parades and gala days. It was many years before the band had any significant competition wins, the first coming in 1954 when they won the Third Section National title in London.

Wearing red blazers the band came on to the stage and got a warm welcome. Tonight's Conductor Mr Harry Holwill followed and the music soon began. The Brass Band concert tradition of starting with a rousing march followed. Whitburn delivered in excellent style a varied and entertaining programme of music with a Scottish flavour. Some of the numbers played had been composed for brass, others were arrangements of existing pieces of music originally composed for other kinds of musical ensembles but they were all good.

When the concert was over, Justin watched Jean drive off home before he got into his own car to drive back to Roa. As he was driving back he couldn't help feeling comfortable knowing that Jean would be back at it his place on Wednesday.

This week at Isherwood's was going to be different, it had been designated as a training week and it was going to be extremely busy for both Justin and Paul Edwards. The firm had a large south facing room that had been unused for some time and Justin and Paul had turned it into a training centre. On a south facing wall, they had fitted a blackboard and screen onto which they could project images using a slide projector. They could also project images onto the same screen using an epidiascope.

The problem with using an epidiascope was that the room had to be totally blacked out when using it and in order to do that they had fitted thick curtains to cover the large windows on the south side of the room. Lots of posters had been placed on the walls and lots of different kit was available to use in practical demonstrations. Chairs and tables to accommodate all 39 staff were in place.

The training programme covered first aid, using visiting specialists from the Red Cross Society, fire-fighting, again using specialists but from Barrow Fire Service. It then moved on to cover all the new production processes that would come in to operation in January and this was the main focus of the whole programme which would end on Thursday.

During the first four days of the training course security clearances arrived for Isherwood's eight new workers which was a great relief. A further source of relief was the fact that all the raw materials that would be required for the new production run had also arrived. Good news all round.

When Jean arrived at Justin's place on Wednesday evening, she was clearly distressed about something and broke into tears as Justin embraced her.

"Whatever is the problem?" asked Justin.

"It's Rupert again. He's been waiting for me coming out of work."

"What's he done to you Jean," said an enraged Justin.

"Nothing. He keeps asking me to go out with him and I keep telling him no but it doesn't deter him."

"I'm going to sort that guy out once and for all."

"No Justin. Don't try and do that. You wouldn't be a match for him, the big brute. He will get fed up trying, I'm sure."

Justin had to admit that he probably wasn't a match in any fight with Rupert but he must do something.

"Jean on Friday night Isherwood's are holding a Christmas party for all their employees and their families. Come along as my guest and stay over at my place until Sunday."

"Thanks Justin that's nice of you."

"Are you working next week?"

"Yes Johnson's work all week until mid-day on Friday, Christmas Eve and then they stay shut down until Monday, January 2nd."

"When you finish on Christmas Eve come and stay with me until New Year's Day."

"I'd love that."

"Good. Maybe it's time to consider finding another job nearer to Roa so that you could move in with me permanently. What do you think?"

"Justin you are so good to me. Yes I will."

They were supposed to have called on some other neighbours this evening to invite them to number eleven on Boxing Day but under the circumstances that would have to wait. The rest of the evening was spent consoling Jean and talking about Rupert Isherwood and Irene Edwards. Where did Irene figure in this latest chapter in the sex maniacs saga. It was a sorry story and if Paul got to hear about it then fists could really fly.

Jean left for Ulverston feeling a little better but anxiety still nagged away at the back of her mind.

Isherwood's training course ended mid-afternoon on Thursday and all the employees gathered around the Managing Director, William Isherwood who had been in attendance for most of the week alongside the new Managing Director Andrew Marr. William's wife Annie arrived in time to see the presentation of an engraved silver clock to her husband as a token of gratitude from his devoted staff.

Annie received a bunch of flowers and both she and her husband received a framed photograph of Isherward's factory on Roa Island and a framed painting of their house in Rampside titled 'Indomitable'. There were tears in both Annie's and William's eyes and several of the employees. A photographer from the local press was there to record the proceedings which would shortly feature in Barrow's local paper.

With the presentation done, there was one final event to finish off. A professional photographer had been hired and several photographs were taken. The first featured William and the whole of his work force. The second featured Andrew Marr and all the work force that he would shortly be responsible for and thirdly one of William congratulating Andrew on his take over with, once more, all of the work force in the background.

Annie wasn't left out, she featured prominently in each. A call was then made for volunteers to help clean and prepare the training room tomorrow for Isherwood's Christmas party. The original plan had been to hold the Christmas Party at the Roa Boat but on reflection it had been agreed that the pub was not big enough. Fortunately, Emma had not been approached to make a booking.

Justin and most of the work force got to work on Friday morning and in no time what was once a training centre was now a mini ballroom with tables and chairs around the edge and a small stage for a band. A piano and drum set arrived in a van and were manhandled on to the stage. The works canteen was specially prepared by Brenda and Gladys and tables were laid with food and drink. William Isherwood had ordered that no expense was to be spared. The scene was set.

Justin got home mid-afternoon and Jean arrived soon after. She hadn't had any further contact with Rupert which was good news. They both got dressed up for the party and Justin was delighted at how Jean sparkled in her simple but elegant looking dress. Isherwood's was teeming with folk on Friday night, all eager to eat, dance and drink.

The place hummed as everyone enjoyed chatting. Annie waved to Justin to come over to where she was sitting with William and Andrew Marr and his wife. They pulled up two chairs and sat and talked to Annie and William for quite some time and it was touching how Annie held Jean's hands and looked at her so affectionately.

"This is the right man for you Jean. He will love you and care for you."

Jean blushed and tensed a little and then whispered, "I know."

Annie then turned to Justin.

"And you young man better care for this young woman or I will want to know why not"

They all laughed a little and then Annie announced that she and Willian would be leaving for Plymouth on Thursday but she would make one final call on Wednesday to see Justin.

Annie never mentioned anything about Rupert's latest attempt to woo Jean. Perhaps she didn't know. Paul and his wife seemed also to be in good spirits suggesting that they didn't know either' At this point Alison Pringle and her ensemble began chucking out crotchets and quavers that masqueraded as music but no-one minded since it at least had rhythm and the floor was soon full of happy but not so good dancers.

When the dance was over Justin and Jean walked the short distance from Isherwood's factory down the front of Marine Terrace to number eleven. They spent little time getting into bed and embracing each other and were soon sound asleep.

The following morning Justin decided that he better get round to next door to invite Nellie and Arthur to his Christmas party on Boxing Day. He didn't stay long but they were delighted to be asked and they accepted and then enquired as to where he had been keeping himself lately.

Next port of call was to Brenda's at number four where they could chew over what food and drink he needed to buy in. Brenda, armed with the number of people coming compiled a list and gave it to him before saying that there would be stuff she could bring from Isherwood's that would only perish otherwise. She would nip to the factory with Gladys on Boxing Day morning and bring it round and they could help with preparing everything as well. All that was left to do now was to go into Barrow and buy everything that was on the list and the rest of Saturday was spent doing just that with Jean.

In the Roa Boat, it was fairly quiet. Justin was the only male member of the group present for one reason or another but his jibe that all the other guys had seen sense and had left them brought a round of good hearted boos and one or two well developed raspberries. Conversation covered, amongst other things, Next week's dance in Rampside Village Hall.

Next Saturday was Christmas Eve and the dance had to be rearranged due to Mrs Pringle and her ensemble not being available and no other band could be found in time but it had been rescheduled for Friday, December 23rd. Next, matters moved on to the idea of the group meeting up between Christmas and New Year for one more time to see the year out together and it was agreed that they would do so on Friday, December 30th right here in the Roa Boat. With conversation waning it was time to go home and everyone left.

It didn't take long before Justin and Jean were in bed and in spite of the cold they both felt a desire to take their love making a little further than they had before. They kissed passionately and Justin pushed his hand under Jeans pyjama top to fondle her breasts and she responded by arching her back. Pyjama tops were soon discarded and Justin moved his hand inside her knickers to feel her pubic hair.

Jean was clearly excited by this and removed both her pyjama bottoms and knickers at one go. The couple were steadily losing their inhibitions and were enjoying themselves. Justin's finger began exploring her erogenous region as she held is erect penis. His pyjama bottoms were discarded as his climax was imminent and the two climaxed together ending this moment of bliss.

Work on his plot seemed to have come to a halt and he must do something about it thought Justin but it would have to wait until the Christmas holiday. Waking up with Jean by his side was special and he was treasuring the experience. Having arisen Justin got to work on lighting the house fires whilst Jean made breakfast.

Both of them thought that this was much better than living on your own. With breakfast out of the way, they turned their heads to what still needed doing to complete the organising of the Christmas party they were putting on on Boxing Day.

"We can't leave out your other neighbours on Marine Terrace" suggested Jean.

"Well, let's call on them."

They called on number six first where Richard Smith and his wife and two children lived. Richard was one of Isherwood's security team. Justin and Jean were given a nice greeting and invited in. The Smith family were delighted to have been asked to come to the party but had to decline since they would not be at home on Boxing Day, they would be with their own families celebrating. Next call was to number seven, home to Margaret Green and her husband.

Margaret was one of the new cleaner's that would be starting work at Isherwood's in the New Year. The Green's would be staying with one of their daughters over Christmas and had to decline the invitation. The same applied to Joyce Fry and her husband at number eight and that left number nine, home to Alan Tinker and his wife.

Alan worked in the packing section at Isherwood's. Once again Justin and Jean were invited in and thanked for their invitation but as with all the other houses they had called on today they got another no. The Tinker's as with the other families were using Christmas to get together with other family members.

The house calls brought home to Justin and Jean just how much they both missed their own parents at this time of the year but no-one can alter the march of time and they had each other now which was a wonderful consolation. At least now they could count those that had said they would come and it added up to 18 including themselves.

"Do you think we have enough food and drink?" asked Jean.

"Brenda and Gladys tell me we have. They will be bringing some food from the freezers in Isherwood's so we should be fine."

"What about chairs. We can't expect people to stand all night."

"Again Brenda and Gladys are going to bring some from the works canteen."

Before Jean left to make the journey back to Ulverston, she told Justin that she wouldn't come back to his place until the following Friday afternoon. She had a lot to take care of especially if she was going to stay with Justin for a prolonged period.

"Are you sure you will be safe doing that?" asked Justin.

"Don't worry, it's only five nights. I'm not worried."

"If that guy Rupert starts making a nuisance of himself ring the Roa Boat, The landlady, Emma, will bring me any messages, she's good that way. Perhaps I might think about getting a telephone installed in the New Year."

Having placed her bags in her car Jean set off toward the causeway and gave Justin a wave as she did, leaving Justin a little concerned about her safety.

The final week at Isherwood's before the Christmas break was used to do a stock take and to check that all the factory production equipment was fully up to scratch. The Company Personnel Officer Paul Edwards made an announcement during the week that four designated first aiders had been appointed and they were; Sheila Dobson from inspection, Eunice Critchley, office staff, Johnny Davies, edge connector and Bob Burns, circuit tracer.

Paul went on to make it known that he would inform the new designated first aiders when and where training courses were being held to enable them to get a qualification that would enable them to take on these posts.

Annie Isherwood made her final visit to Justin's office on Wednesday at 3:00pm on the dot and for once Justin was waiting for her.

"Nicola has got a place in Plymouth for her and our two grandchildren. The money Rupert gave her from the sale of the family home came just at the right time."

"That must be a relief for William and yourself."

"It is. Once we have got settled into our new place we can help Nicola get settled into hers and, hopefully, life will settle down and take on a more sedate pace, I hope so for William's sake. By the way Justin, I do know that my son Rupert has got Irene Edward's in the family way. He's an absolute fool. That silly girl should not have encouraged him. She's going to pay the price!"

Justin wondered if Annie knew that Rupert had been making advances on Jean recently but he wasn't going to raise the subject unless she did.

"One good thing about William and I going to Plymouth for good tomorrow is that there can't be any embarrassment with Paul's current close proximity with William."

"Forgive me for asking but has the situation caused any fall-out between the two of them?"

"Not at all. Paul Edwards and my husband are both level-headed men and wouldn't allow it to come between them."

"So, you are away then tomorrow, no more tea and cake on a Wednesday afternoon from now on."

"I'm going to miss you, Justin but before I go I want a firm commitment from you that you will love and cherish that girl Jean Baxter for as long as you both shall live?"

"You sound as if you are marrying us off?"

"I would, if I could."

Annie embraced Justin and wished him a happy Christmas and hoped he would have a prosperous New Year.

When Annie had left, Justin felt that he had lost someone very special and it was going to leave something of hole in his life for some time.

Jean arrived at Justin's place around mid-afternoon on Friday, Johnson's having broken up at lunch time for the Christmas break. Justin arrived just five minutes later and seeing her sat in her car in his back yard he made a note to get a house key cut for her. Once inside Jean got unpacked before helping to make something for tea and then getting changed for the dance tonight.

The two of them drove in Justin's car to Rampside Village Hall to join their friends for this month's dance. Everyone found it a little strange being present on a Friday rather than a Saturday but it wasn't going to stop anyone enjoying themselves. There were mince pies galore on the refreshments table and dozens of bottles of brown ale. No-one would go short on food or drink tonight.

Alison Pringle's ensemble didn't sound any better than normal but having developed a degree of immunity to the sounds it produced, dancing was as popular as ever. Tonight the only member of Justin's group not accompanied was poor old Joanne whose partner was busy blowing his brains out with a saxophone in Pringle's ensemble. Spirits were high and jollity was in abundance. Jean and Justin danced together with a smile on their faces and the night was going well.

Justin took the opportunity to get some mince pies and drinks for Jean and himself whilst the band was taking a rest between numbers. There was a queue of people waiting to get refreshments and the band began to play again before Justin had got as far as the food and drinks table. During this time, a certain Rupert Isherwood made his way to where Jean was sitting and as the band began to play he asked her to dance with him. When she refused, he asked again and again and she was beginning to get upset by the attention he was giving her.

Sheila's partner, George Belshaw, caught Justin's elbow and told him about the discomfort Rupert was causing and Justin left the queue immediately to confront Rupert and make him go away. How on earth had this guy got into the village hall without anyone of the group recognising him thought Justin as he went back to the table where he had left Jean sitting amongst their friends.

"Why don't you leave the lady alone?" said Justin, looking straight at Rupert.

"Shove off, Ebberson. The girl needs a man not a boy," came back the reply.

Justin's temper flared and without much thought he threw a right handed punch at Rupert's jaw and it glanced off. Rupert responded with several rapid blows to Justin's face from which it was difficult for him to recover. Justin aimed a good blow in the direction of a blur he could make out in front of him and he heard a thud as he made contact with Rupert's chest which knocked him away. Before any more blows could be exchanged, several of Justin's male friend's, George, Theodore, Gordon and Bernard had intervened and held Rupert by his arms.

"You better bugger off or you will have us to answer to," said George.

Rupert was a pretty well-built chap and whilst in the Navy had done quite a lot of boxing. He would be more than a match for Justin and whilst he was restrained he glowered at him and then looked in the direction of Jean.

"Why are you wasting your time on this drip, Ebberson? You would be much better off with me."

Before he could get any more words out, the four men restraining him took a leg and an arm each and marched to the village hall front entrance to a round of cheers from the crowd within and two kindly gentlemen opened the doors. Through the open doors they went and with a 'hey ho' they jointly threw him as far as they could. It was no Olympic quality throw but Rupert had a heavy landing ensuring that it was not just his pride that was hurt.

"Now bugger off home and don't come back," added George as he and his three companions watched Rupert struggle into his maroon-coloured Alvis and drive off in the direction of Ulverston.

Inside the hall, a keen interest was being taken in Justin's welfare and after a short inspection, he together with Jean were ushered into a side room. A kindly member of the audience who was first aid trained took a look at Justin to ascertain what damage had been done. His face would have a few bruises showing by the morning and one black eye but no bones had been broken. The village hall caretaker came in to the room with a small bucket of ice and a couple of tea towels which he gave to Jean.

For the next twenty minutes, she held some small ice blocks wrapped in one of the towels to his face to ease any discomfort. Justin couldn't put up with this any longer and told Jean that he wanted to get back inside the dance hall. His arrival was met with cheers and a few stares. His newly acquired bruises were gaining attraction.

He danced a few times but became aware of discomfort from several different parts of his body but he had no intention of surrendering to it, he had Jean in his arms and that was enough. Nevertheless the whole incident had affected them both and, sadly, they were glad when the dance came to an end. Jean insisted that she would drive Justin's car to get them back on Roa and as she helped him in she could tell that he was stiffening up.

Getting in bed was not so comfortable but having Jean by his side made up for that even though he couldn't make love to her in the way he wanted to. The bond between these two was getting more powerful by the hour. The persistent pain continued until Justin finally succumbed to sleep and Jean gladly followed his example.

The following day the bruises on Justin's face were obvious to see and he found himself feeling stiff when he first sat down or walked. Fortunately there was little to do today and both he and Jean took it easy before they finally got ready to go to the Roa Boat. They had to remind themselves that it was Christmas Eve. Neither of them referred to what had happened the night before but it wasn't going to go away.

As Jean and Justin walked into the Roa Boat, Emma gasped when she saw the state of Justin.

"What the hell happened to you?"

Jean filled Emma in with the details and then they joined their friends around a table that was full of Christmas food prepared by Emma. It was a joy to see it all and everyone thanked Emma for the trouble she had taken. Emma was pleased with the gratitude she was being shown, she was even more grateful for the payment she got.

Justin's war wounds were the talk of the table but he took it all in good part. There was a lot of conjecture regarding Rupert Isherwood and his reputation sank to depths unknown. Jeans long-time friends managed to elicit the fact from her that Rupert had been making advances for a while and given that he had got Irene pregnant they were all disgusted by his antics.

The Christmas Eve gathering did eventually get jolly but broke up relatively early since most of them were departing to their parents homes to spend Christmas and Justin with the aid of Jean more or less limped back home.

Justin apologised to Jean, this was not how he had intended Christmas Eve to be but Jean was having nothing of it. In her view, they had each other and that was the most important thing in the world as far as she was concerned. They both had a glass of wine before heading upstairs. Justin felt frustrated that he couldn't embrace Jean as he had been doing. He was feeling a little sore and dam it that's not what he thought he should be feeling as the end of a difficult year approached and it was only one week away, but he would make up for it, yes he would!

On Christmas Day morning, Justin got out of bed, limped downstairs and made breakfast for Jean and himself. It was nothing fancy, his culinary skills were primitive to say the least. Bowls of cornflakes and mugs of tea would have to do, Christmas or no Christmas. He took his tray of breakfasts back to the bedroom where Jean, sat up in bed, was waiting for him and she had a beaming smile when she saw him enter the room.

"Merry Christmas Jean."

"Merry Christmas Justin."

They exchanged a kiss before getting on with the business of eating.

Once breakfast was over, both of them donned dressing gowns and went downstairs to discover what Father Christmas had brought them both. Jean loved the new jacket that Justin had bought for her and Justin was pleased with his two new shirts and matching socks that Jean had got for him.

"I'm really pleased about the socks Jean, I was getting fed up having to darn the holes in those I already have."

They stood under some mistletoe that they had hung from the ceiling in the front room and kissed each other. This was already a very special Christmas. But there were things to do and they both got washed and dressed before turning their hands to what was needed. Justin lit two fires that would heat the house whilst Jean started preparing the Christmas meal that they would eat later.

Justin had managed to get a small turkey which would be a real seasonal treat. When the initial chores were completed, they sat down and talked about the lives they had lived before they knew each other. Justin talked about how he was brought up in Bolton by his late mother and father, Glenda and John Ebberson. He was an only child and they had worked hard to support him when he had been an undergraduate at Manchester University. He went on to describe how he got his first job at Salmesbury and left home to live in Mellor before making his last move to Roa.

Jean had heard all this before but it made a good topic for conversation. Jean did her share of reminiscing and described how she had been brought up in Barrow-in-Furness by her late parents, Susan and George Baxter. She also was an only child. Leaving school at 18 she had got a job with 'Vickers' in Barrow before moving to 'Isherwood & Son Etching Specialists' and left home to live on Roa with Nadine and Sheila.

They ate an excellent Christmas dinner and then took a walk around the island to work off some of the excesses of eating. It was a nice day and they were not the only islanders out for a stroll. They lost count of the number of 'Merry Christmas' greetings that they exchanged and it made the day feel euphoric.

Back in number eleven Justin proposed that Jean consider finding a new job in Barrow and moving in to number eleven permanently. It was a much shorter distance to drive to Barrow than to Ulverston. Jean replied that she had been thinking about that for some time and said that she would do that.

The subject of Rupert was not brought up but it was clearly in both their minds. Justin didn't want Jean to live or work in Ulverston any longer than was necessary with that crazy man around. If it came to it, Jean could pack her job in at Johnson's and move in with him immediately and then look for a job in Barrow but he knew that Jean was independent and would probably not want to feel that she had been forced to move so things were left as they were.

They had a light meal later in the day and Justin began to wonder when he should make his most daunting move. He had planned to do what he was now contemplating on New Year's Eve but after his recent encounter with Rupert he had decided to bring it forward. Nerves were getting the better of him and he didn't want Jean to notice.

At least, he had no father-in-law to face but that didn't take away the enormity of what he was about to do. He was going to change the course of his life and that of someone else. After an undue amount of time pontificating, he got a grip of himself.

He turned and faced his beloved Jean, got onto one knee and said, "Jean, will you do the honour of marrying me?"

Jean looked intently into Justin's eyes and tears rolled down her cheeks as she replied in a quiet voice.

"Yes, yes, yes. Justin, I don't deserve you but I do want to marry you."

Justin held out to her the diamond solitaire engagement ring in its presentation box and he took out the ring and slipped it on to her finger. Jean was slightly overwhelmed with happiness and they spent the rest of Christmas Day feeling extremely happy that they had made this commitment to each other and Justin had completely forgotten about his bruises and stiffness but the latter came back to bite him once he was back in bed.

Brenda and Gladys were around at number eleven just after breakfast on Boxing Day to help prepare the food for tonight's party. Justin and Jean were glad for the help.

"Bloody hell, Justin, what have you been up to? Got on the wrong side of Jean did you?" asked Brenda.

Justin obliged by explaining what he had really got himself into.

"Bleeding maniac that Isherwood fellah is," remarked Gladys and Brenda chirped in again.

"He wants his balls chopping off."

It wasn't often that you would hear women speak in this way and it tickled Jean to hear it but Justin wasn't sure that he should show support for the suggestion or ignore it; he ignored it.

A little later, a knock on the front door announced the arrival of Brenda's husband Frank and Ernest who was married to Gladys.

"Hello Justin, we have come to give a lift with the chairs you need. Bloody hell, you look as if you have been in a fight."

Brenda rushed to the front door and saved Justin having to explain again what happened to him. In fact, Brenda took control of what was going to happen next and three women and three men headed to Isherwood's to collect food and chairs. The security man on the gate at Isherwood's had no problems letting them all in but was a bit anxious when he saw all the stuff going out. Even Brenda had a bit of a problem convincing him that everything was legitimate but a bit of arm bending solved the issue.

Within a short time, all the food that had been set aside in Isherwood's canteen fridges were in Justin's kitchen and the chairs brought over were placed around his two downstairs rooms and Frank and Ernest disappeared. Most of the afternoon was taken up with the three ladies sorting out the food whilst Justin arranged the furniture. Brenda and Gladys went home once the food prep was done leaving Justin and Jean to take a breather and then get ready for the party.

First to arrive for the party was Brenda and Frank and their eight year old son Jeffrey followed by Marion and Roger Quinn. A short interval passed before the next party-goers came knocking on the door and Jean and Justin greeted Flora and Angus Campbell with their daughters Peggy aged seven and Jill aged five together with Joanne and saxophone player Ivor Ball. Nellie and Arthur drifted in via the back door almost unnoticed and finally Gladys and Ernest together with their nine year old daughter Kathleen arrived to join everyone.

Number eleven was full of folks all too pleased to have the chance to relax and chat and the huge supply of food and drink helped to oil the human machinery that was busy sorting out the world and laughing at each other's short comings, the latter particularly poignant in the case of Justin who spent half the evening explaining how one could acquire bruises for free.

For those who had not already noted Justin called for everyone to stop talking or kissing whilst he made an announcement and when he called Jean to his side most had guessed at what was coming next.

"Jean and I would like you all to know that we are glad that you have come along to our Boxing Day party."

"Come on, lad, get on with it," said Arthur.

"Now, you just behave yourself, Arthur Elwell, you've had enough already," said Nellie.

When the laughter had died down, Justin continued.

"Jean and I want you to know that on Christmas Day, we got engaged."

The room erupted with cheers that could probably have been heard by the King and Queen on Piel Island and a great deal of hand shaking and kissing followed. Jean's diamond solitaire engagement ring fostered a lot of attention and of course the big question of when are you both going to 'tie the knot' did its rounds.

Jean did a lot of crying, the emotion associated with the occasion was all a bit too much for her. She had never been as happy in her life before and Justin was a happy witness.

The evening soon seemed to come to an end with folk drifting off home allowing in a blast of cold sea air as they left via the front door. Brenda held Jean's hand before she and her family left and told her that she and Gladys would be around in the morning to help clear up and their husbands would get the chairs back to Isherwood's. A very tired happy couple then retired to bed and both fell into a deep sleep.

True to their word Brenda and Gladys arrived at number eleven mid-morning to help get Justin's place looking ship-shape once more and with Jean's help they got it done double quick. Husbands Frank and Ernest with help from Justin returned all Isherwood's chairs to their rightful place placating a certain security officer in the process.

For Jean and Justin, calm descended and they spent the rest of the day relaxing. The day was somewhat enhanced however when they got a wonderful view through the front room window of a huge cargo ship sailing straight towards them in the deep water channel leading from Morcambe Bay to Barrow. The ship got ever closer and then turned to port to follow the channel into Barrow docks.

As the ship turned it's true length could be appreciated and the height of its superstructure was impressive. Justin had seen ships come and go using the deep water channel which was regularly dredged but not too often because of the time he spent in work. Jean was probably more familiar with this sight than he was but it was still spectacular.

It was Wednesday already, time was flying by and Justin decided that he ought to check his plot over. It seemed like ages since he had attended to it and whilst he got on with some digging to aerate the soil Jean got some clothes washed. It was inevitable that Arthur would pop up at some time and he did.

"Good morning, Justin."

"Good morning, Arthur."

"It was a grand do at your place on Boxing Day."

"I'm glad that you and Nellie enjoyed it."

"She's made up now that your back with that pretty lass Jean. What are you going to do with all the others?"

True to form, Nellie appeared on the scene and immediately scolded her rascal husband.

"Take no notice of him Justin. Eh them bruises are not fading much. Come inside and let me tend to them."

Justin dutifully followed Nellie into number twelve where she took a bottle of something from a cupboard and using cotton wool she wiped over his bruises delicately with some of the bottles contents.

"What have you used Nellie."

That's witch hazel and it will help to get rid of the bruises faster, but it will still take some time.

"Thanks, Nellie."

"Why not come round for some tea with Jean? It'll save her some work and I've baked a steak pie and a gooseberry pie for afters?"

"Thanks, Nellie, that's very kind of you. We would love to join you."

Jean was grateful that she need not make any tea and they both enjoyed a meal with Nellie and Arthur. Steak pie, chips and peas went down a treat and the gooseberry pie with cream over it was delicious.

The day had gone nicely and the newly engaged couple retired to bed. Justin was feeling particularly amorous and Jean was responding to him in an intimate way. It wasn't long before both of them had removed their pyjamas and were relying on their physical motions to ward off the cold. It had to happen, it had been going to happen and now it was happening!

Justin was thrusting his penis into Jean's vagina and she was rising and falling in unison with his movements. The two of them were getting carried away with the sublime feeling that they were experiencing but they were also aware of the consequences should they climax together in this position. Whilst they continued with their sexual pleasure-making, neither of them wished to bring a child into the world just yet and when the climax was imminent. Justin withdrew and his sperm was deposited on Jean's stomach.

"Justin, that was close. Do you think you should get something before we do it again?"

He wasn't sure what to say. He had always been embarrassed by the idea of asking for a Durex especially if the person behind the counter in the chemist's shop was a lady. But he did want to do it again. He was no longer a virgin and neither was Jean.

"I'll try."

Thursday was a quiet day. Justin did some more digging on his plot and Jean occupied her time with some ironing. What time was left was spent walking and talking. The highlight of the day was hearing the lifeboat siren blaring out which brought the pair of them to the front room window.

After what seemed like an inordinate time, the lifeboat house doors opened and a manned lifeboat emerged sliding down it's steep ramp and splashing into Piel Estuary to begin a rapid journey via the deep water channel into Morcambe Bay and onwards to the Irish Sea to the scene of some unfolding crisis.

The final gathering of 'Team Five' plus one was set to happen on Friday night in the Roa Boat. For some reason or another, only the five regular girl members of the original Justin's harem turned up. Nadine, Sheila, Amy, Lynn and Joanne joined Jean and Justin for a final drink together and when they did they were delighted by the news that they had got engaged and wanted to know when the wedding would be and if they would be invited. All in all they made a great fuss of Jean and were joined in doing so by the landlady Emma.

"Justin, your bruises have begun fading," remarked Sheila who looked a little down this evening. Talking of bruises there was no doubt that at least five of those present had a desire to find out more about the current whereabouts of Rupert Isherwood and Irene Edwards. Nothing had been heard of Rupert since Christmas Eve and it was even longer in the case of Irene. Fortunately, diplomacy prevailed. No-one intended taking the limelight away from the newly engaged couple.

The week was passing by fast and after tonight Jean would only be spending one more night with Justin before she had to head back to Ulverston.

News Year Eve approached and Justin made sure that he had the tickets for the ball being held in Ulverston's Coronation Hall in a safe place to take with him. He took the ruby necklace from the drawer he had hid it in and placed it in the glove compartment of his car.

Both Jean and himself spent some time getting ready for the ball, they wanted to look their very best. Justin was anxious to get back to this time last year when he should have gone to the ball and presented Jean with the lovely necklace now in his car's glove compartment, he just hoped that he had not left it too late.

They drove to Ulverston in Justin's Ford Popular car and parked in the Theatre Car Park just off Benson Street. They both stepped out of his car and made their way into Benson Street from where they would walk the short distance to Coronation Hall. They crossed the street and had only walked a short distance when Justin realised that he had not got the necklace in his coat pocket, he must have left it in the car. He asked Jean to wait for him whilst he dashed back for something he had forgotten.

She thought it was the tickets for the ball. Reaching his car, he unlocked it and opened the glove compartment, took out the necklace and put it in his coat pocket and then locked the car again whilst growling at himself. He hurriedly made his way back to Benson Street and could see Jean across the street.

He started to cross the road when a maroon-coloured Alvis car with two occupants, one a woman, came speeding down Benson Street from his right. Jean shouted out a warning but before he could respond, he felt a huge thump on his right side and the world went suddenly black, very black.